BOARDING
HOUSE
REACH

PETER CRAWLEY

Matador
9 Priory Business Park
Kibworth Beauchamp
Leicestershire LE8 0RX, UK
Tel: (+44) 116 279 2299
Fax: (+44) 116 279 2277
Email: books@troubador.co.uk
Web: www.troubador.co.uk/matador

ISBN 978 1783063 390

British Library Cataloguing in Publication Data.
A catalogue record for this book is available from the British Library.

Typeset in Centaur MT by Troubador Publishing Ltd
Printed and bound in the UK by TJ International, Padstow, Cornwall

Matador is an imprint of Troubador Publishing Ltd

For Charlotte
of whom I've heard it said,
"She lives the dream."
Though the mountains can be unforgiving,
they are worthy of respect.
Those who work upon them are surely
worthy of the same.

By the same author:

———— ⟆⟆⟆ ————

Mazzeri

———— ⟆⟆⟆ ————

Foreword

I must confess! Like every writer, I like to think of my work as my own; original in both conception and construction, and, most importantly, bearing no resemblance to the work of any previous author. But is it? Can any author really claim to be the originator of his work? Surely, the primary tasks of a writer are to observe and to question, and, in due course, to record. And in this way our material stems not wholly from within, rather it stems in the greater part from those we observe and question. So, I ask again, can our material ever be described as original? Characterisation is generally defined as the description of characteristics and it is these characteristics we observe which we assemble and order into each of our individual characters. Some writers are prone to sit more comfortably in the belief that the invention of a character comes from deep within their imagination; their psyche. I am not so inclined, preferring to believe that the characters we create stem initially from those individuals we observe and question, for it is they who provide the handfuls of clay which we mould into the souls who stalk our pages. In *Boarding House Reach*, I cannot claim to know or to have met any of the characters, and neither are they based on my perception of any one singular person. The characters in this novel are entirely fictitious and bear no relation or comparison to any person either living or gone before. And yet, I feel sure I must have met them, or some part of them, at one time or another; perhaps it was last week, perhaps last month, or was it perhaps long ago?

And as the brilliant scientists of the modern era come to understand more about the complexities of our genetic construction, so are we beginning to understand more about how nature and nurture combine to provide us with our individual characteristics. If nature instils in us the will to survive, then surely nurture educates us as to how best to. Coming to terms with the two, particularly when life is neither straightforward nor smooth, is not easy, and on occasion the two work against each other, inclining us to act against our better judgement; the body intent on taking one course, while the mind insists upon another. It is amidst this confusion that we strive to maintain our balance; a balance which is neither innate nor easily acquired.

Like any author, I could not have written *Boarding House Reach* without the help of many others who have all given freely of their time and knowledge. Tony O'Brien provided useful insights into the running of a guesthouse, Ronnie Puttock introduced me to football, the Canaries and the Carrow Road ground, Emma Brooks corrected my view of Norfolk, and Daisy Crawley introduced me to college life in Cambridge.

Tom Westcott and his fellow fire-fighters at the Retained Duty System Fire Station in Gomshall welcomed me into their exclusive fold and answered what must have seemed a host of very naïve questions. They are the brave souls who we depend on in times of emergency; their dedication and skill is paramount. They have my admiration.

Emma Brooks, Gill Buckland, June Deeker and Sally Duhig read and reread the initial drafts of this novel, and helped focus the direction and detail in my work. If there are mistakes, they are without doubt mine and mine alone.

To the marvellous team at Troubador Publishing, I must say a very considerable 'thank you': Jeremy Thompson, Amy Statham, Amy Cooke, Jane Rowland, Sarah Chetwyn, Lauren Lewis, Rachel Gregory,

Rosie Grindrod and Terence Compton are all professionals in their own right. Where others fail, they succeed.

Sue Woods, of Mintsource-uk.com, was instrumental in organising the launch of *Mazzeri*, my first novel; her generosity and experience proved invaluable and contributed much to making the event a success. Peter Matthews' contribution was also fundamental, his choice of questions astute and his ability to create a relaxed empathy with the audience undeniable.

Pam Masco, a sublime artist and friend, designed and painted the artwork for the covers of *Boarding House Reach*. Pam is unselfish with her gifts; they are manifold and she deserves a wider recognition.

And, finally, I must thank my wife, Carol, for her support, her belief and her encouragement; for when my hand is uncertain, it is Carol who steadies it.

PART I

THURSDAY

I

⚊⚊⚌⚌⚊⚊

Hacker

Somehow, it always came down to just the one card.

And it never seemed to matter how many columns there were left open to him or how many suits he'd stacked away-

An enormous container lorry thundered past, throwing up a vast, opaque curtain of water which hung for a split-second before falling with a startling, fat slap against his windscreen.

No, it didn't matter which way he looked at it: in the end it was always down to just the one card. And, even when it was perfectly obvious to him that the game was lost, he still couldn't help from playing it.

Hacker glanced at the bright, fluorescent-green lights of a petrol forecourt.

"Green?" he muttered. "How can selling fossil fuels be green?" He peered at the prices.

"How much?" He rubbed his face. "Hacker, me old mate, they need to sort out your mileage allowance, otherwise it's going to cost you more to get to work than they're paying you to do the work when you get there."

He shifted in his seat; the dull pain in his right knee nagged at him.

A trail of freight lorries stood in a lay-by like elephants waiting their cue to enter the Big Top. A sodden Union Jack hung straight down the pole above a white caravan dubbed TEA-N-BURGERS, and a couple of drivers taking their mandatory break huddled beneath the fragile awning, clutching polystyrene cups, smoking, staring.

Hacker lifted his right hand off the steering wheel and drew back his shirt cuff. The cuff, the colour of carnations left too long in a vase, was frayed. But, the delicate hands and creamy-white face of his gold rimmed watch brought a warm comfort to him. Of course there was a digital clock on the dashboard, and of course it would have been safer not to move his hand from the steering wheel, but he was fond of the watch. He liked to believe it lessened the discomfort in his legs the way a brass bracelet is supposed to reduce the pain of rheumatism.

Hacker wasn't fond of much, but the watch? That was different.

Normally he would've stopped for a bite to eat; a bit of a chat and a chance to stretch the pain out of his knee. But once, halfway up the A1, he'd been recognised by a couple of truckers. "You'd have been in my team any day, Hacker," one of them had piped up. But Hacker didn't stop there again. Recognised or not, he didn't need to be reminded that he'd really only nearly made it.

"Nearly, Hacker, you sad bastard! Only nearly!"

Then a bright and breezier tune on the radio broke the rhythm of his downbeat mood and he realised that if he'd been recognised by some trucker in a lay-by off the A1, then, by most people's reckoning, he had made it. That logic and the cheery music lifted his spirits for a while.

He was lucky, really. Even though he'd not made the transition to the Premiership, seven years of Divisional football had had its benefits. Of course he'd like to have played on for long enough to have run out for what was now called a Championship game; after all, Championship did sound a little more exclusive than First Division. And, by anybody's standards, the wages in the Championship were now far higher than anything he'd earned in the dizzy heights of the Football League. At least, and he supposed it was at the very least, they'd had that good run in the FA Cup.

But then with a name like Hacker, he was always going to be a target: Hacker by name – Hacker by nature, Hacked by Hacker and Hacker the Hatchet. He'd been an editor's dream.

But, above all the headlines, his personal favourite was scrawled on the wall of the urinal in the Borough Arms:

HACKER IS HARD

Hacker and Hard, Jennings and Jesus, Clapton and God; he'd joined the immortals, nearly.

But, ultimately, Hack'd Off had read his rather fitting epitaph, penned as it had been on the third from back page the day after that animal from Senegal had clattered him. So maybe the coach had been right; maybe it was mean of him to nutmeg the fellow and make him look a dipstick in front of his home fans in an FA Cup semi-final. And, maybe they had been four goals down and Hacker didn't know when he was beaten. But, he remembered saying to the bastard: Welcome to the club!

Then the bloke blindsided and flattened him and left his foot in for good measure. Still, Hacker consoled himself; he'd finished the game, the other fella'd hadn't.

But after that tackle, his right knee had begun to moan. It was only a slight, niggling twinge at first; a message that advised him he couldn't rely on it to turn or twist when he needed it to. But when the physio poked, prodded and pulled his right leg in ten different directions, he discovered a pool of molten lava lying beneath his kneecap. It hurt so much he often had to wait until the other players left the medical room before he could stand up without screaming. A few weeks later, he heard himself lying to the physio just to get a place on the bench.

And when he finally got to go on, his knee lasted all of fifteen minutes: One tackle. Bang! Excruciating pain!

Still, he'd been more fortunate than most. If that bloke Beasely hadn't collared him, he might never've'ad a job to fall straight into. It wasn't as though there weren't enough ex-pros propping up wine bars, giving some goggle-eyed jailbait the 'more I drink, the better I was' routine. But that wasn't for him.

"Don't know when to stop, do you?" Beasely shouted in his ear as they sat in the Director's Box watching the boys struggle to avoid relegation. "You could've left that big bastard alone. What the hell are you going to do now?" he asked, only to follow his question with the answer, "Sales, that's where it's at. Think it over."

"It makes sense." Beasely paused and breathed hard. "You are, as they say, a face. People know you. You'll always be able to get your foot in someone's door. And you're not the sort to get taken for a mug. Crikey, I've seen what happens to players when they try to put one over on you. Why not pool all that experience and come and work for me?"

What with watching the game, thinking he'd have gone left and not right, and only catching half the conversation due to the mindless ranting of the pillock sat next to him, Hacker rather stupidly replied, "What, work for you, Beasely?"

Beasely, breath heavy with beer and eyes beady and calculating behind thin, wire-framed spectacles, sucked on his teeth and shook his head, "No, not me, you idiot, ME. M-E! Marchman Engineering."

Hacker didn't bother to stay for the post-match piss-up.

After that it was the customary testimonial, a kind of authorised begging: coins tossed into a blanket, a fawning farewell dinner, and several indigestible rounds of flesh-pressing and windy flattery. And, right at the last minute, the club bean counter grabbed him and whispered, "Don't forget to drop your car back by the end of the week."

Hacker had earned the right to wear the watch that graced his right wrist. Earned it! And that's where it was bloody well going to stay.

A few days later, he found himself sitting on the end of his bed with no particular place to go, so he sold his soul, dodgy right knee and his reputation for flooring chippy forwards to Marchman Engineering.

The urgent, blaring horn of a pantechnicon and yet another wall of water fell on his windscreen, puncturing his daydream.

Hacker turned off the radio and checked his mobile; he hadn't missed any calls. His mouth was dry and he noticed he was out of Sprite and smokes.

Hacker was nervous and nervous the way he used to be before a big game. Only this weekend, it wasn't a game of soccer he was off to play.

2

Stella

"Before we start, I'd like to note that Ms Anworthy has waived her prerogative of attending this meeting with a representative from her accountants. I am Selina Doyle representing HMRC and also present is Robert Barnes."

"Is that how this is going to be?" Stella asked.

The woman peered over her glasses, "Is that how what is going to be, Ms Anworthy?"

"Well, you know, writing everything down? You know, recording everything? Only I'm not a very fast writer. I don't do shorthand and I'll never remember everything for later on."

The woman smiled a thin, sly smile. Before her on the desk sat Stella's last three years' accounts; shiny, blue lever-arch files bulging with poorly punched papers tagged with tiny, coloured markers, "Ms Anworthy, this is an informal meeting; merely a chat to discuss your accounts. Do you understand what I mean when I say it is not a formal interview?"

"Then why the note just now that I haven't got a representative from my accountants with me? You know Harry's not well. I'm sure he would've come if he'd been well enough."

That wasn't strictly true, of course. There was nothing wrong with Harry apart from forty fags and a bottle of Scotch a day. But, Stella had told him to go sick if the Revenue asked; she didn't need him.

"That's fine," replied the woman, Doyle, "as I said, this is merely a discussion so that we may better understand how you manage your accounts." Her colleague, Barnes, a middle-aged man in a black suit, said nothing.

Stella feigned a slight unease, "But I don't, manage them. Harry does."

"Yes, Ms Anworthy," was all she said.

Stella pulled her old, faded leather jacket open. The top buttons of her blouse were undone just far enough that both the man and the woman across the table could not escape the promise of her cleavage. Granted, her hair did look nice; all neat and tightly curled, and her make-up was fresh, but not too heavy.

"And you are, for the record, Ms Stella Anworthy, proprietor and owner of The Reach Guesthouse, 162 The Promenade in Strand-next-the-Sea?"

"Do you really want me to answer that? I mean I'd hardly be here, would I?"

The Revenue Offices were across the Wensum from Norwich station, opposite the Compleat Angler. A mattress shop and a Premier Inn fronted the Prince of Wales Road; the offices were out the back.

"Yes, alright, I am."

Doyle wrote on her notepad and then looked back up, "How long have you been at The Reach, Ms Anworthy?"

"Five years. You know that."

"And how long have Tanners & Co been your auditors?"

"'Bout the same. And you know that, too."

"Happy with them?" Doyle: early thirties, perhaps a couple of years younger; slim and straight, dark hair tied up, piggy eyes and a nose fit to locate a stash of truffles a mile away.

"Yes. Harry's alright. Smokes too much, which is why he's always catching a cold."

9

"I meant are you happy with the way he prepares your audit, Ms Anworthy?"

"Oh, I see. Yes, thank you. I mean he's the one with letters after his name. Why? Does he not do them properly?"

"Yes, to a point." Doyle continued to write down Stella's replies to her questions.

"Well, as I said, he's the one with letters after his name. If you're not happy with the accounts he submits, then you'd better speak to him about it. I pay his bill. I'd like to think I'm getting what I pay for. Isn't there some ombudsman or something I can appeal to if he isn't sorting my accounts correctly?"

Doyle shifted in her seat. "Mr Tanner would appear to be lodging correctly audited accounts. We're more concerned with the information you supply than his audit. He can, after all, only audit from the accounts that you provide."

"I'm not with you."

Doyle lowered her head and examined Stella; school marm with dim pupil, "What I mean is, Ms Anworthy, do you supply Tanners & Co with a comprehensive set of accounts or are there items that you pay for, invoices that you issue, that you don't include for one reason or another?"

"Why would I do that?"

Doyle glanced at the man next to her, but he didn't acknowledge her aside. "Well, that's one of the things we're here to sort out."

But, before Stella had a chance to get in another question, the inquisitor moved right along. "Ms Anworthy, there are a few things I'd like you to confirm for me, if you don't mind? I note that your register is made up of a ring-binder file with loose sheets. How long have you used such a format?"

"Long as I can remember? But-"

"You don't use a computer?"

"Not for accounts. Never have. Don't trust them, but-"

"And your paper invoices are issued in two forms; one for the room hire and the other for sundry items."

"Yes, but-"

"But, Ms Anworthy, none of these invoices are numbered. There's no chronology to them. The only identification they carry is the room number and the guest's name. And often there's only an amount identified as sundry items or services. There is little information as to exactly what your guests have paid for."

Stella frowned and pursed her lips. "Forgive me," she said, "I'm just not with you." But there were no clues coming back the other way, only silent expectation. "You're not suggesting there's anything fishy about the services I provide, are you?"

She allowed just sufficient time for Doyle to open her mouth before she continued, "I hope you're not implying that any of the services I provide are... inappropriate!"

"No, not at all, Ms Anworthy, I merely-"

"I can't believe my ears," Stella said, "I thought you'd asked me in here to talk about my VAT, not to accuse me of running a house of ill-repute. God, what would my neighbours say? What about the B&B Association?" Stella began to hyperventilate.

The man in the black suit rose from his chair, but Doyle motioned him to sit back down.

"No, Ms Anworthy, I am not suggesting anything of the sort."

"Oh," said Stella, panting. "Thank goodness for that. I'm sorry, I... Could I have a cup of water, please?"

Doyle nodded. The man got up and fetched Stella a cup of water from the dispenser.

"Thank you. I'm sorry. I don't know what came over me."

"Please," Doyle said, "Take your time. I wasn't suggesting or implying any impropriety. My point was that I fail to see how you can justify some of these invoices to your guests and, further, how you manage to account for some of the goods or services you actually supply."

"Well," replied Stella between sips, "I don't need to, that's why. I know what they've had and they usually know what they've had, too."

"And just what do they have, Ms Anworthy? Indulge me. Explain to me what it is that your guests do demand over and above clean sheets, a hot shower and full English breakfast."

"Not much really. I don't have a liquor licence, so mostly it's just bottled water, cups of tea, the odd sandwich if they come in late. I don't have satellite television, so-"

"Ah, yes," said Doyle, rifling through her notes. "How many rooms do you let?"

"Four. You know that, too."

"I see that last year you purchased four new televisions as part of your refurbishments."

"Yes. That's correct. Needed them for the digital switchover, didn't I?"

"One for each room?"

"That would be so, yes."

"Didn't fancy one for yourself?" Doyle's pen hovered over her pad.

"No," she said, "don't watch a lot of television. Can't be doing with all that crash, reality television! There's more than enough reality wandering along the front in Strand, not that I'm one of those net curtain twitchers, or whatever it is that Alan Bennett fellow calls them. Do you know, the other day-?"

"And what about computers, Ms Anworthy," Doyle interrupted. "Do any of your rooms have work stations?"

"Work stations? Like PCs, do you mean?"

"Yes. Like PCs."

"No."

"But you have Wi-Fi, I notice."

"Yes."

"You don't use it?" Doyle's tone assumed a slight air of surprise.

"Of course. I have a small computer, just for the bookings I get on the internet and stuff. But mostly the WI-Fi's for my guests; they often have laptops and things. Amazing what you can get these days."

"Are you aware of the regulations setting out how your invoicing should be ordered and numbered?"

Stella frowned.

Doyle pushed a small booklet across the table at her.

"Mmm! Thank you," Stella said, stretching for it.

"Ms Anworthy, I must ask you how up-to-date you keep them. How often do you sit down and collate them?"

"Ooh!" she replied. She leaned on the palm of her right hand, elbow resting on the table. "I dunno. Well, I do the bills for the guests whenever they're about to leave, of course. But in terms of the rest? Once a fortnight; maybe three weeks. Depends how busy I am, I suppose."

"Petty cash?"

"What about it?"

"How often do you reckon up your petty cash?"

They batted her petty cash back and forth for a while: Doyle didn't like the way she cashed large cheques to supplement her float.

"How much money do you normally carry, Ms Anworthy?" Doyle asked.

"What, like every day in my purse?"

"Yes."

"Depends," said Stella.

"On what?"

"On what I need it for," she replied, with measured incredulity, "I mean it depends on what I need the money for when I go out."

Doyle lowered her head slightly, "Well, let's imagine a day like today."

"Good point, Ms Doyle. You've just reminded me, I've got to get a couple of light bulbs on my way back." She lifted her voluminous handbag onto the table and began to unload the contents, "But if you mean what have I got on me right this minute; I'd have to look."

"There's no need to..." Doyle began.

Stella continued unpacking, "No, no. It's a good point. I should know."

Eventually, she came to her purse. She opened it and turned it upside down. A couple of notes and a few coins fell out. She made to grab them as they rolled across the table, "Fourteen pounds sixty-five! There you are. That car park downstairs is not cheap, is it?"

"Now, about some of your recovering VAT on certain items..."

They argued the toss regarding the split between her business and house phone expenses, but to Stella it was all too obvious they could have sent a young ferret out to do that.

Doyle moved the papers to one side and opened one of the audited accounts files. She had long slim fingers and they worked through the file like a tall spider walking through long grass, "Now we come to your recent refurbishment."

"Yes," Stella said. "I guessed you would."

Her reply stopped the woman, Doyle, in her tracks. "What makes you say that, Ms Anworthy? Why should you guess so?"

"Well, I suppose it's because I've claimed for all the expenses relating to the refurbishment and you are going to suggest that what I've achieved is a... Oh, what did Harry say it was; a capital improvement? But it's not, is it? It was just work that I'd ignored over the years; work I could not afford to pay for. It had to be done, you know. The place would've been a ruin if I'd left it any longer."

"Yes, Ms Anworthy. I'm sure it would." Doyle's piggy little eyes lit up. "Double glazing, plastic pipes, steel for beams, dry rot treatment, replacement tiling... etcetera, the list is endless. But all these things, as you so rightly point out, are allowable. You can offset the costs of all of these against the business." She twirled her pen around her index finger as though it was a baton. "And, as your accounts show, Mr Tanner has correctly offset these items against any tax that you might have been liable to pay." Doyle twirled her pen for a couple more seconds, then put it down and sat perfectly still, silently waiting for her quarry to speak.

Stella, none the wiser, said, "The problem is then?"

"The problem, Ms Anworthy," Doyle paused. "The problem is that we don't understand how you managed to pay for all of these improvements, especially when one considers you haven't lodged accounts showing a profit for the previous three years? Further, when you do eventually show a profit, why is it that the profit rather coincidentally matches your improvement costs? And, finally, and considering the breadth of the refurbishments you have made, how you have managed to pay such a paltry sum for such comprehensive work?"

An ambulance wailed its way down the Prince of Wales Road and a helicopter hovered low somewhere over the city.

Neither woman blinked. And neither spoke until Doyle's patience exhausted, "Do you have any other bank accounts?"

"Other bank accounts? I'm not sure what you mean. Sorry. Do you mean ISAs, stuff like that?"

"Yes, exactly that. But also any other bank accounts from which you either derive an income or could have used to pay for the work you've had done?"

Stella looked out of the window. The sky was darkening; rain was on its way.

"Well, besides the business account and my personal account, no. I've got three ISAs, but they're from a few years ago, before I came up here, when I was married..."

Her husband Vernon had sorted those out.

Vernon: He hadn't been a bad sort; a bit too intelligent for her; a bit by the book; liked a certain way of doing things, but not altogether such a bad lot. He'd been on a work placement in a local pharmaceutical company in Brighton when they first met. Then she bumped into him a few weeks later at King's and then again a while after that at the Shades. He was not as leary as some; never seemed to have enough money for being leary, did her Vernon. And besides, he made such a change from the usual lads who wanted sex without conversation. But Vernon hadn't been like them and that was what had singled him out.

Then the pharmaceutical company offered to train him up as a researcher and he got all serious and business-like. A year later, they promoted him head of department.

Stella got a job in the new supermarket up at Hollingbury and they bought a bungalow in Hangleton above Hove. There were a few hick-ups; Vernon always liked his dinner on the table when he got home, but the supermarket was open late and she had weekend shifts.

Then he got another promotion and wondered whether they could afford to try for a child.

It was the most wonderful thing he'd ever said to her; better even than hearing him tell her he loved her on their wedding day. At that moment she knew she loved him, every inch of him, and loved him all over. But he worked hard and got home late, and Stella only saw him for about as long as it took to get pregnant.

The only trouble was Stella miscarried and miscarried every time she fell pregnant.

Stella looked up at Doyle very slowly and said, "It's not easy, you know. I know I might have been doing this for five years, but it's still not easy. The public can be very fickle when it comes to choosing their holidays. Norfolk's hardly St Tropez, is it?" She blew her nose noisily. "The first year I think I was lucky. Maybe I benefited from the previous proprietors good management. They were nice people, the Watermans. And that was before the bloody bankers mucked it all up for us, don't you think?" She looked across the table and waited for a reply.

The woman, Doyle, smiled a thin, uncompromising smile. "Yes," she said, "strangely enough, I do think. But that doesn't explain where you got the money for the refurbishment. As far as your books show, the number of residents at The Reach increased disproportionately last year and, strangely, some of them according to your records would appear to have occupied the same room at the same time. Can you explain how that might have come to be?"

Stella pouted and rubbed her chin with the tips of her fingers. "Er, no. Not unless they were a couple of… well, you know… an unmarried couple who signed the register and wanted separate bills."

Doyle opened the file at a yellow-tagged page: "Mr John Smith and a Mr David Jones, same room numbers, November 2009, separate invoices, differing amounts?"

"Well, I don't discriminate, Ms Doyle." Stella assumed a most disapproving expression; one bordering, but only bordering, on distaste, "Especially after the palaver in Blackpool with that gentleman couple."

"Separate invoices? Different amounts?"

Stella threw the woman a look that suggested she ought to know better. "If they ask me to divide the bill up, I do. Sometimes," she winked, "one of them can be a bit more male than the other, if you know what I mean?"

"I'm not sure that I do, actually," Doyle replied, fidgeting. The man next to her looked at the floor and coughed.

"Anyway, as long as the bills total the correct amount and that is the amount that gets paid, I don't see the problem."

The woman turned through the pages to another yellow tag: "October 25th 2010, Parkinson family, Room 2. This receipt is unusually comprehensive. It notes jelly and ice cream as an extra; value £50.00?"

"The Parkinson family? Oh, yes, I remember. Boy and a girl. Lovely."

"Aged?"

"Seven and eight, I think. It's so difficult to tell these days. They grow up so fast."

"Twin bedded room, Room 2?"

"I have a couple of collapsible cots for those family occasions."

"Thorpe family. Same thing. Two children."

"Would've been."

"More ice cream?"

"If that's what it says."

"Similar age?"

"I don't recall. Why?"

"Because, Ms Anworthy…" Doyle indulged in yet another pregnant pause, "the paperwork informs me that both the Parkinson and the Thorpe families stayed in Room 2, with all of their children sharing. And, according to this receipt, it appears they enjoyed what I can only describe as a consuming passion for ice cream — in October. And, what's even more surprising is that their stay took place during term time, not during the holidays."

"Clerical error," said Stella, "I must have written down the wrong room number. The Thorpe family must have been in Room 4."

"Room 4 was occupied by a…" she examined a separate sheet, "Ms Smith." Doyle fingered a third sheet, "Room 1 a Mr Ralph: a Mr Ralph who, it doesn't say. And Room 3, a longer-term resident it would seem, a Mr Margetz."

Stella blinked.

3

Philip

Philip took the earlier train into town. He didn't have the energy to stand in a crowded carriage and so rather than miss out on a seat, and with the added benefit of being able to avoid Fiona, he was down at Barnes Bridge station well before seven.

Once on the train, he sat and stared out the window, oblivious to Putney and Wandsworth flashing by. He was too absorbed with the previous evening's events and trying his damnedest to work out at which point tragedy had descended into farce.

For certain, allowing Maja to get hold of his phone in the restaurant two evenings before had been his most critical folly. It was only natural that Fiona should resent a late night call from a strange woman on his phone. He could hardly blame her for losing the plot over that.

But last evening, Fiona had gone to bed leaving him to stare at the Jackson Pollock Rice Masterpiece plastered across the kitchen wall. He'd cleaned it up as best he could and poured himself a whisky. The sofa hadn't been comfortable, but at least it didn't wriggle and smoulder.

During the morning, Philip found concentrating on work difficult. At the back of his mind was not the thorny issue of how he was going to get through the coming evening at home, rather it was where he was going to get hold of the colossal sum of money he needed.

He couldn't extend his mortgage; the housing market was pretty flat and the bankers still had their hands thrust deep in their pockets. Other loans were available but only at exorbitant rates of interest and his credit cards were so flattened by overuse the numbers were almost illegible.

At lunchtime, his secretary told him he looked so awful he ought to call it a day. She informed him that the enormous bouquet of flowers he'd ordered had arrived and suggested he'd look a right Charlie struggling home with them on the train. Should she order him a taxi?

Philip groaned. He couldn't go home early, he'd promised... "Oh, no," he sighed.

Then his phone rang and his secretary said: "A lady for you; says her name is Archie; says you'll know her?"

4

Phoebe

Somehow the light from the opalescent bowl seemed a shade dimmer this time, almost as if the lamp, like her, was subdued. And the dust motes, which usually reminded her of eagles gliding on airy thermals, now seemed more like vultures circling in a heavy atmosphere.

The Dean of the College was present. He was a heavy set man with a large bald dome for a head. He wore his official robes and the grey light of autumn framed his ample profile.

This time, they did not sit by the fire — it was not lit — and there was no exchange beyond Dame Clarissa, her Director of Studies, introducing the Dean.

Phoebe was ushered to the naughty chair and in doing so fought to stifle a chuckle. She couldn't understand why she should find their stiff countenance and furrowed brows remotely comical. The Dean's presence alone suggested her situation was grave and Phoebe saw herself, the prisoner before the camp elder.

This time, Dame Clarissa didn't try to put Phoebe at ease; she got right to the point.

"Phoebe, it gives me no pleasure at all to tell you that this is a disciplinary meeting, which is why the Dean is present, but one that for the moment we are going to afford you the latitude of keeping informal. Your conduct has deteriorated to such a level that we can no longer tolerate your presence in the college. You are to go home for the rest of the Michaelmas term and not return here until Lent." Her delivery lacked even the slightest trace of sentiment.

Phoebe reeled under the assault. For a few seconds, she lost her bearings as waves of anger and resentment washed over her. She had been selected; her future at college was now out of her hands.

"There is no need for any further hearing," Dame Clarissa was saying. "There is no point in producing witnesses at this stage. If you feel harshly treated, then you have the right to request a more formal hearing. But, I put it to you, Phoebe, that your tutors are all too aware of your continued plagiarism, about which you have already been warned. And your abuse of alcohol and very probably other substances has overwhelmed you to a degree which, if it is allowed to continue, will seriously injure your health. For that reason alone, we cannot permit you to remain here. Is that clear?"

Phoebe looked up. Without realising it, she had been looking at the floor whilst listening to her sentence. Her eyes watered and whereas before her expression had trumpeted a fleeting defiance, now all she could manage was abject surrender.

She felt a tear splash against the back of her hand.

"That will be all for the moment," Dame Clarissa was saying to the Dean. "Thank you."

The Dean left. He'd not spoken and he showed no recognition of Phoebe as he passed her, as though, for now, she no longer existed.

"Phoebe," Dame Clarissa said softly, leaning forward, offering a tissue, "Phoebe, what we are most definitely *not* saying is that your life at college here in Cambridge has come to an end. That would, on my part, be an admission of failure and that is not what we are about. What we are saying or, more accurately, what I am saying is that it is time for you to find the means by which to get yourself back on track."

With the exit of the Dean, Dame Clarissa invested herself with an almost motherly instinct.

Phoebe looked up briefly, "I suppose it reflects badly on you if I fuck up in a big way, doesn't it?" Her response was not worthy of her DOS's regard. "I'm sorry," she said, "I wish I knew why I felt so... so very different about... well, about everything." The room felt cold and the light from the window lent her only the palest promise of a future.

"Phoebe," Dame Clarissa said, but then she hesitated and held out another tissue, "you have a nose bleed. Here, take this." She paused until Phoebe had attended to her nose. "Now, there may be many reasons why you have, or your thinking has, changed. Some of these reasons may be to do with whatever substance it is that you are taking. If it is this wretched Mephedrone that would appear to be flooding our halls, then you need to quit taking it before it destroys your aspirations beyond any hope of reclamation. There are already moves afoot to have Mephedrone classified, but the legislation is a few months away. In the meantime, you and others who use it will have to convince yourselves of the dangers it carries. We can educate you to those risks, but we cannot prevent you from indulging in them."

Like any addict committed to her poison, Phoebe began to object, but her DOS held up her hand to silence her.

"I am also led to believe that all is not well at home. And before you go upbraiding any of your friends for abusing your confidence, you may like to stop for a moment and reason that without them, or perhaps I should say some of them, you might have finished up a good deal worse off. That, though, is for you to work out."

Dame Clarissa retreated, consumed by the shadows cast by her high-backed chair, "I know from your absences that your mother is not well, but if you had informed me of the severity of her illness, there is a good chance I might have reacted differently to your sudden rash of plagiarism. I am far from happy with myself that I did not take the time to better understand your situation. For that, Phoebe, I apologise."

"Thank you, Dame Clarissa, but you've no cause to apologise," Phoebe sniffed and dabbed at her nose. She looked up at her senior tutor, "I'm afraid I was altogether rather too proficient at disguising it. I —"

"And it's why you sought to disguise it that intrigues me, Phoebe. I perfectly appreciate that your mother's illness is a worry and therefore a distraction for you. But, in the great scheme of things, and especially when I take into account your very developed intellect, it doesn't explain this pilgrimage of self-destruction upon which you are so hell bent."

She waited for a reply. When none came, Dame Clarissa tried again, "Let me put this another way, Phoebe: I'm not sure from where, but I get the feeling this chaos of plagiarism and its inherent dishonesty is either a distress signal for some more compelling unpleasantness that has infected your psyche, or perhaps it is a metaphor for some appalling emotional disruption you are suffering. Which is it?"

Dame Clarissa Hale was watching her closely now; watching her the way a fisherman scans a pool of water for the slightest ripple in the surface.

Again, Phoebe did not respond. Her head thumped, her face ached and she perceived a chilling, sepulchral tranquility to the room. And, though she felt a drip of blood about to drop from her nose, she remained completely still and looked back expressionless at her inquisitor.

The silence endured for a full minute.

"Very well," Dame Clarissa conceded, "I don't know what it is that has prompted such a radical metamorphosis in the young lady we all know as Phoebe Wallace, and it would seem that I am unable to provoke any reasoned response through a logical progression of my rather dilatory thought processes. So, let me put it to you this way, Phoebe, you need to go away and learn that there are some roads better left untravelled."

5

Stella

"In fact, Ms Anworthy, all your rooms were occupied on October 25th 2010, but Room 2 was occupied by two couples with, supposedly, four children. How is that?" Doyle sat back from her papers. Her expression demanded not only an answer, but also a capitulation. The man next to her, the dark-haired man who had so far not said a word, sat back too.

Stella decided she must have been watching the television when she wrote those two invoices.

Of course, the television hadn't helped; over time she'd become a bit of a slave to it. The doctor had told her she needed to rest up if there was any chance of her hanging on to her pregnancy and that was when she took to watching daytime television.

Vernon, bless his heart, took out a subscription to Sky, saying he liked the sport at weekends too.

Then she lost that third pregnancy and it was three strikes and she was out.

Stella couldn't remember who'd been the one to suggest they separate. She liked to think it was Vernon, but the truth was she'd mentioned it to him first one day when the guilt began to weigh too heavily. Being in bed with him had seemed like little more than a prelude to miscarriage. She didn't resent him for it. It wasn't his fault.

Then her Mum passed away just after the divorce came through, and her skinny, dark-eyed sister suggested it was Stella's divorce that had done for her mother and therefore she wasn't entitled to her share of the house. That was when Stella realised her life anywhere near Brighton was over.

At least Vernon had left her the bungalow up in Hangleton.

Stella remembered it was a Monday morning and she was sitting in the front room watching a program on families relocating to Australia. She envied them their courage, their enthusiasm. And after that she watched a holiday programme from the Norfolk Broads. She'd never been there; it looked a calm place – serene was the word the presenter used and it stuck in her mind.

At lunchtime Stella surfed the web and came across The Reach.

By teatime, her bungalow was on the market.

With the money her Mum had left her and the sale proceeds from the bungalow, Stella had not needed to borrow from the bank. That had made the transition to Norfolk so simple.

She went on a cruise in the Caribbean over Christmas and moved in at the beginning of 2005; January 7th, grey, wet and windy, and Norfolk oh so flat after living near the downs. But she liked to be near the sea. And that had been the date, January 7th.

"I suppose I must have put down the wrong date," Stella said, as if talking from a dream, "Could it have been a week earlier or later, half-term? Did they pay by credit card? I can't remember without checking."

Doyle looked hard across the table. The look suggested the revenue inspector was no longer prepared to treat her as the guile-less naïf she was pretending to be. "Now we come to the matter of the extent of the refurbishment. The bills here note that you have had work carried out on a grand scale: new roof tiles, pointing, flashing, guttering, etcetera…"

Stella nodded, "All necessary work, I can assure you."

"Well, I'm not a qualified surveyor, Ms Anworthy, but even I can equate cost to work carried out. The invoice for this work would barely cover the costs of the materials, let alone any labour." At this Doyle took off her glasses and rubbed her nose as though she had a headache.

"My builder... William," she said. "Nice lad. He's very reasonable, quite diligent. And I could only pay the bill he gave me, couldn't I?"

"You paid Mr William Martin in cash, I see."

"He prefers it that way. There is a receipt."

"Of sorts," said Doyle, examining a sheet in the file. "And what about the exterior wall painting, the barge boards, the window boxes, the wrought iron gate..."

William had been the first person to be genuinely polite to Stella.

Most of the people she'd met when she first arrived in Strand had given her the cold shoulder, or if not frigid then rather frosty. But she hadn't really expected to fit in right away anyway, especially what with Stella being in her thirties and the other dumplings having one foot in the grave and the other on a bar of soap.

Fortunately, William was not like the rest of them.

The previous owners had left The Reach in a pretty ordinary state, but it wasn't until a couple of years after she'd taken over that the list of things giving up the ghost started to grow. Minor electrical items and a bit of filler here and there she could manage, but when the roof started to leak and the drains backed up, she knew she would need help.

In the newsagent's window, she saw a card for a handyman. She phoned him out of desperation when the toilet in Number 4 backed up for good.

He turned up pretty quick; no overalls, jeans and well-worn sneakers. But he arrived with a bag of tools and said he'd an idea what the problem would be. He even popped down the plumbers' merchants for a new gismo and had the whole thing fixed inside an hour.

Stella offered him a cup of tea before he left. She was short of cash and wondered if he wanted to hang about while she nipped down the bank?

Will accepted the cuppa, but said the money could wait.

He was short and wiry and had a nice smile. His black hair might not've seen a brush for a few days, nor his chin a razor, but his eyes were bright.

Stella considered him a bit of a dish and, even though she had a few years on him, she flirted with him while they sat.

A couple of weeks went by and the loo worked better than before. Then the cold water tap in Number 2 began to drip and dribble all the time. She tried to replace the washer, but however hard she tried, she couldn't undo the nut.

William fixed it without even having to go to the plumbers' merchant and he refused to charge her. They drank more tea.

He lived in a caravan park just beyond the town, had done for a few years. William, Will, didn't spend much of his spare time in Strand, he preferred to drive into Norwich; it was a bit more vibrant, had a bit more to offer. After all, Strand could get a bit quiet.

It turned out he did odd jobs for many of the other B&B owners, and if the assignment proved too large for him alone or required more professional talents, then he knew where to source the craftsmen and the materials. He preferred cash, though he always knew someone who could handle a cheque.

"You don't like to be tied," Stella said to him one day.

He didn't answer that.

Once he came round to mend a broken light fitting, and afterwards they walked over the promenade and sat on the beach watching the seagulls wheel and drift on the wind. She noticed he was wearing a heavy aftershave and he called her Doll, not Stella, and she'd liked him for it. They drank a bottle of wine, and later she fetched over a plate of pâté and biscuits, and they warmed with the sun at their back. She tried to place him, tried to press him for some information about his background, but he brushed off her questions, pointing out a ketch he said was usually moored up near Cromer. No matter how hard she probed, Stella couldn't draw him out and so came to the conclusion that his biography was not for others to read.

"This Mr William Martin?" Doyle asked.

"Yes? What about him?"

"Does all your work?"

"Pretty much."

"And you pay him cash?"

"It's what he asks for. Not up to me how he likes to be paid, is it? As long as the work is good, I'm happy to pay him in the way he asks. No problem with that, is there?"

"Not as long as he issues you with the correct paperwork and you pay a satisfactory rate." Doyle sat up straight, composing herself. Then, she leant forward, "Ms Anworthy, when it appears to us that a business is benefitting from maintenance supplied at what we would reckon to be below the market rate, we naturally have our concerns that payment is being made in a manner that conceals the true value of the work, thus allowing the maintenance provider the facility of avoiding tax that is due. It is not only the maintenance provider who is breaking the law in that case; it is also the business or person who contracts the work." Doyle paused to allow the weight of her allegation to sink in.

"In many of these circumstances," Doyle continued, "we take into consideration how cooperative the subject of our investigation has been." She paused again.

"Mr William Martin, who it seems is also known as Tom Martin, and, as far as we have been able to ascertain, John Melville, undertakes work for a considerable number of businesses up and down the Norfolk coast, including some of your neighbours. Is there anything you might want to tell us with regard to those others of your neighbours who have benefitted from similar work undertaken by the man you know as William Martin?"

"What on earth do you mean?"

"I mean, Ms Anworthy, are you aware that it appears Mr William Martin, Tom or John Melville undercharges some of the other B&B businesses in the same way that it would appear he's undercharged you?"

"I... No. Absolutely not!" Now it was her turn to pause for effect. "What William charges other people is no concern of mine." She was certain she'd heard him called Tom in that club they went to.

Stella wasn't sure what had held her back from asking Will to stay the night after they'd drunk all that wine on the beach. However, she did hold back and in the morning she was a shade more relieved than disappointed; she hadn't been to bed with a man since she'd parted with Vernon. Even though the wine had corralled most of the what-ifs running around in her head, she hadn't drunk near enough of it to want to get naked with him.

A couple of weeks later, Will rang and asked her if she fancied a night out in Norwich. Usually she couldn't have left the place, but that night the two couples who were booked in had cancelled, so there had been no reason not to.

She squeezed into a shortish black skirt and a white silk blouse, and wore heels and her hair up because she'd recently seen a make-over program that suggested wearing it that way made her look taller.

Will drove; he had a small Ford. It smelt of grease and freshly sawn timber, and he drove like a man who ought to be on the bus. They went to the Castle off Ketts Hill. They sat in the beer garden and everyone got talking about how warm the summer of 2006 was turning out to be, and, later, they walked arm-in-arm down by the river.

They went to a club, which, Stella realised, was just round the corner from where she was sitting. The music wasn't to her taste, but Stella reminded herself it was a good while since she'd been out to a club. And, after a couple of those blue cocktails, she really started to relax, so she left Will at the bar and danced with some girls who didn't mind strutting their stuff with a bit of attitude.

As Will was steering her out of the place, she overheard one of the doormen say, "Goodnight Tom. Mind how you go." Goodnight Tom, that was exactly what the doorman had said.

"What William charges other people is up to him. And furthermore," Stella leaned forwards so that although she wasn't right in Doyle's face, there would not be the slightest chance the woman might mistake what she was about to say, "if you are trying to suggest that there is some kind of improper relationship between me and Mr William Martin, then I can only reply that we have been enjoying a proper relationship for some time and therefore some of the maintenance he undertakes for me, he undertakes out of love and not in order to avoid paying whatever it is that you think he ought to be paying." Stella sat back from the table. "And would you mind writing that down as well," she added with a glare.

The man beside Doyle glanced up at the ceiling and wiped his handkerchief across his face.

Doyle winced. "It was not my intention, Ms Anworthy, to question your relationship, or more particularly your personal relationship with Mr William Martin, whatever that may be. I was merely-"

"I know what you were asking," Stella said, "And I know what you were implying."

"And what would that be, Ms Anworthy? What am I implying?" Doyle wasn't done yet, but she was looking distinctly uncomfortable.

"You're suggesting that my William is sweet on the other B&B owners and he's doing work in return for favours from them; favours of a dubious nature." There, she said it. Stella sat back again. The sun came out and trumpets blew. She still had to appear affronted, outraged and injured, but inside she was all Green and Blacks and sweet Martini.

"That is absolutely and categorically not what I am asking, Ms Anworthy," replied Doyle. And this time she was horrified; horrified and clearly worried. She looked nervously at the man Barnes, who ignored her and blew his nose.

"That is most certainly not what I am trying to find out. And if Mr William Martin does work for you because he is in a relationship with you, then that is perfectly and completely acceptable. Please rest assured that I in no way meant to suggest or imply that your relationship with Mr William Martin was in any way problematic or in question." Doyle paused again, this time to adjust her jacket and check her hair was still in place. She smiled and the corners of her mouth softened. "I am sure your relationship is perfectly normal."

Stella smiled back. Her relationship with Will was normal; as normal as any relationship could be between a straight woman and a gay man.

Doyle took her time to rearrange some of the papers on the table before her. Judging by the way she snapped and grappled with the ring-binder file, she was more than a little brassed off and was growing increasingly frustrated at not being able to locate some of her paperwork.

Stella struggled to suppress a snigger, "Are we nearly finished, Ms Doyle? Only I've got a guest arriving sometime this afternoon and I can't remember how much time I've got left in the car park. I wouldn't want a parking ticket because I've had to come in here and answer all these silly questions."

The woman's eyes widened and she exhaled very slowly, "Oh yes! Here we are." She picked a mauve file up from the floor.

Doyle read it and, when she got to the bottom of the page, said, "I have been asked," she looked up over the rim of her glasses, "to ask you, again strictly on an informal basis, what you recall of one of your longer-term tenants from last year: a Mr Margetz?"

Stella blinked again.

6

Philip

She was already at the restaurant in Holborn when he arrived.

"Thank you for coming, Philip. I'm afraid I haven't got long," she said.

Maureen Davy, or Archie as she was known, wore a white two-piece and pearls, and her dark-brown hair was tied up and back. Her nose didn't seem to dominate her face as much as he remembered and she looked broader in her cheeks. But her face had lost none of its imperious countenance and she still wore the same pencilled eyebrows that looked ready to arch in displeasure at the slightest opportunity.

The waitress appeared and waited for him to choose.

Philip wasn't hungry and neither did he like being rushed, but it was evident that his mother-in-law had already ordered, "A Caesar salad, please, and a bottle of Pellegrino."

"I've seen you look better, Philip," she stated. "A little grey around the gills, if I may say."

"You may," he replied. His suit may have been fresh from the dry cleaners, but as to the contents... "By the way, I haven't told Fiona I'm meeting you, but I'm sure she'd want me to pass on her love. I-"

As if on cue, Archie raised her right eyebrow, "No? I didn't tell her I was meeting you either."

"You've spoken to her this morning?"

"You may be surprised to find out, Philip, that since the birth of my grandchildren, Fiona and I have spoken often. She may possess her fair share of motherly instincts, but let me tell you, as one who knows, however competent Fiona may perceive herself to be, there is nothing like a quick dose of grandmother's wisdom and reassurance every now and then. And especially when her confidence has deserted her," she sipped her wine, "or when her husband has gone on the missing list."

"I knew you two spoke, but I didn't realise Fiona had a hotline to Hanger Holt."

"Very droll," she said, looking away from him.

He knew it would be difficult to plead his case without criticising Fiona and in spite of the previous evening's injustice, he was unwilling to take that line with her mother. "Yes," he replied, looking very directly at her, "it was. But as you know, Archie, timing is everything."

The waitress appeared with his Pellegrino and a small basket of bread rolls.

"And my timing," he said, once the waitress had gone, "has been a touch off the mark this past twenty-four hours."

But, before Archie could reply, he held up his hand to stop her, "And I'm very aware that over the last few weeks both my domestic and familial duties have suffered from too great a focus at work, but I will change that. I haven't as yet got a clue how, but my guess is it will have to change if the situation at home is to improve."

He paused, but as there was nothing forthcoming from his mother-in-law, he went on, "I also appreciate, and if I'm way out of line here I'm sure you'll tell me, that Fiona is frightened I'm behaving in a manner that reminds her of her father. And," he lifted his head and looked at her, not in defiance as Fiona had done the evening before, rather more in acceptance of the verdict he was expecting her to pronounce, "she may have some cause to feel that way."

Archie looked at him and laughed. She leaned back and laughed so loud the tables either side of them turned to see what it was that had caused such amusement.

"Oh, Philip," she chuckled, "you're such a boy; nearly thirty years old and still such a boy."

He hadn't expected her to react so and his expression must have betrayed his thoughts, as it provoked a fit of almost childish giggling from her.

When Archie regained her composure, she reached down for her handbag and withdrew a handkerchief with which she dabbed at the corner of her eyes.

"Oh, Philip," she said again, "may God forgive you the enthusiasms of your youth? I'm sorry. I'm not laughing at you, though in a curious way I suppose I am, but not in a bad way. There's nothing risible in your sentiments. It's just that I've never met anyone who's so eloquent at expressing them. You're so quick to nail your colours to the mast; so willing. I really should be grateful that Fiona has found someone like you." She paused and dabbed at her eyes again. "If only we were better able to appreciate what we have before we go and squander it." She beamed a warm and very affectionate smile at him.

When she realised he was not going to react to her compliment, she sat back and was quiet too.

Fortunately, the waitress appeared with their food.

They ate in silence for a few minutes and he began to feel slightly less awkward.

"I'm not inclined to believe you share any of my late husband's more dismal traits," she said. "You may be as tempted to stray as any man, but you and Bob Davy are worlds apart." She chuckled at the literal accuracy of her statement. "No, you're quite his reverse. You're success may encourage you to desire its attendant trappings and most of those trappings will be material, but there's only, I think, a slim chance they will turn out to be of the lascivious variety. If the latter is the case; well, as long as Fiona and I don't see it, then we won't have to grieve over it, will we."

"Oh! Don't look so surprised," she said. "A relationship changes when a child is introduced into it. And it's not only a woman's body that changes either, I'm sure I don't have to tell you that. A mother's focus is rightly concentrated on her child, which means you will have to put up with being bored in the back seat for the next stage of your journey. If you can't get used to that in the short term, then find some other way of putting up with it. But don't go confusing your need for greater love and affection from Fiona with a spurious desire to seek it in a temporary satisfaction of the flesh."

Archie organised her salad, methodically and meticulously separating the individual lettuce leaves and folding them carefully with her knife and fork so that she could eat them elegantly.

"But, if you can manage to keep yourself from scratching any seven-year-itch," she went on, "you'll give yourself a better chance of getting through it. Jimmy Carson thinks there is a more spiritual side to you; not any kind of religious spirit, but more a spirit that is essential to your mettle, your backbone. I'm inclined to agree with him. If you remember, it's what I suggested you would need if you were to make a go of it with Fiona."

Again, Philip felt the colour of offence flood into his cheeks. "What makes you think my intentions have changed?"

"I don't think your intentions are any different now from when you asked Fiona to marry you," she said. "The terrain's altered a little, I'll grant you that, but that's all. You've come out of the cosy little forest you've been living in since you got married; the forest where nothing and nobody can find you because you've been so lost in each other. And now, having children has brought you out onto the Purple Plain where there is nowhere to hide. It's a much harsher environment in which to live."

"If that isn't the truth," he said.

They ordered coffee.

Philip related the saga of the previous day's events and was surprised his mother—in—law showed no reaction when he mentioned Howard Marberg's offer of becoming a partner in Mason Marberg Associates.

"Oh! But of course!" he said. "You already know: Jimmy Carson." And for the third time in as many minutes, he was offended. But, realising he would only invite a typically withering reply regarding the fact that he now knew what it was like to hear news which, by rights, should only have come from the horse's mouth, he swallowed his offence and decided against recounting how completely deflating the previous evening had turned out.

"How much do they want you to put in?"

"A considerable amount."

"Come, come, Philip. There's no need to be coy," she countered. "Jimmy Carson didn't know. And for that matter, Fiona doesn't need to know either. But if I am to assist you in buying your membership to the higher echelons of Mason Marberg Associates, which I would most certainly advise is a step in the right direction; then you will have to tell me. Unless, that is, you have access to the funds."

Philip got the feeling he was being played.

"I do wish you'd stop expecting skeletons to leap out of the cupboard, Philip," she said, a hint of impatience creeping into her tone. "Just because I have the chance to do you a good turn doesn't imply I'm doing so out of some sinister motive. I may possess a touch of the Medicis," she raised an eyebrow, wanting him to know Fiona had told her that that was one of the ways in which he perceived her, "but I am certainly not Machiavelli. What's good for you is good for Fiona and Harry and Hattie. Any fool would understand that."

Boxed into the corner as he was, Philip said, "£150,000."

"Mmm!" She weighed the amount in her mind and glanced down

at the table cloth as though she expected a genie to swell up out of it, "I thought it might be more. Do you have it?"

"No, I don't."

"Do you have any means by which to obtain it?"

"I'm working on it," he replied with all the wan dejection of a miner swinging a pick.

She was studying the table cloth again; her eyes darting this way and that as though checking a balance sheet, "How soon do you need it?"

Philip fought back a smile. Archie had a plan; he was intrigued, "In due time, was all Geoffrey Mason said. I got the feeling he would be patient, but wouldn't necessarily buy a promise."

"Good." She smiled, "Mason is the money man. He's a bit of a cold fish, but he holds the purse strings. Go and see him tomorrow. Tell him you're good for the money, but that you will need a few days to bring it off deposit otherwise you will lose a chunk of interest; a bonus, something like that, but don't make it too fanciful. He'll understand that; he won't like to think someone outside the company will be earning from his offering you a partnership. But make sure your offer to take it off deposit is unequivocal. Once he's got that on board, ask him if you can pay the money in instalments, say £25,000 a month; that way you'll be clear within six months. Offer fifty. He won't take it." She sat back again and drank her coffee.

"How will they know I'm good for it? As you've probably guessed, poker isn't my game."

"You won't be bluffing, Philip," she said. "Jimmy Carson will tell them you're good for it."

He looked across the table at her and, even though he understood where the money was going to come from, he also understood she was going to wait until he asked her for it before she would talk again, "So why should I be good for £150,000?"

"The money is available, Philip." She looked more serious now, her eyes goading him into asking the question she so obviously wanted to hear.

"You're making the money available to me? Just like that; £150,000?" He delivered his questions with a liberal and, he considered, appropriate dose of surprise.

"Yes."

"What about terms?" He knew she would want to hear him ask that, too.

"Terms? There are no specific terms, Philip. Outside of paying me back as and when you can, which I would imagine with your increased salary and the odd bonus and dividend should be within five years, we'll not indulge in any interest or terms of arrangement. Let's just call it an agreement between ourselves. The world doesn't necessarily need to know about it."

A flock of queries flew through his mind.

"It's all above board, Philip," she said, looking round for the waitress. "As far as the revenue is concerned, this will be a personal loan without formal terms for repayment."

The waitress appeared. His mother-in-law looked to him.

As he counted out the notes, he began to grasp the fact that he could not refuse her offer. For a start, he had no other avenues to explore and to refuse it would not only be ungrateful; it would be plain, bloody stupid. His only concern was that she'd asked for no formal terms for repayment; the loan was open-ended and he would have preferred to know exactly where he stood in his mother-in-law's great scheme of things.

"I'm staggered; staggered and extremely grateful," he said. "In fact, extremely grateful doesn't really suggest how grateful I am. I'm not sure how I can thank you. . . adequately."

The elegant lady dressed in white, who had just offered Philip a leg-up onto the next rung of life's tall ladder, rose from her chair, "Don't worry, Philip. Strangely enough, I'm sure you'll think of a way.

And thank you for buying me lunch. Let me know what Geoffrey Mason says and I'll transfer the funds as and when you need them."

"Archie?" Philip said, moving to stand in front of her.

She'd been checking something in her handbag and when she lifted her head to look at him, she looked a little bothered, "Yes, Philip?"

"Archie, I really am very, very grateful for this opportunity; not only for me, but for Fiona and the children as well. It's really fantastic. You won't regret it."

"Yes, Philip. I'm sure you are." She held out her hand for him to shake.

Instead, Philip leaned forward and kissed her on her cheek; something he'd only done once, the day he'd married her daughter.

She did not shrink from his familiarity, but still she sought out his hand with hers and shook it softly.

"Oh, Philip," she said, "I'd like to have the children this weekend. Why don't you bring them up tomorrow morning? I'm sure the business can do without you for a day, especially now that the Crawford's deal has been signed off. There's a nice B&B in Strand-next-the-Sea on the Norfolk coast. Fiona's father and I used to stay there. It may not boast sufficient glitz for your crowd, but it's a nice place; quiet, you'll like it. Do you two good to get away. I'll book the room for you; text you the address. Bye."

7

Stella

"Margetz?" she said, rubbing the hard patch of bone behind her ear. "Margetz? Well, he died, didn't he? I don't like to think about it. First time it had ever happened to me; someone passing away on the premises. And the last, I hope. Awful, just awful it was!" Stella looked down at her hands as though somehow they'd been responsible for Margetz' death. "What do you want to know?"

"Simply whatever it is that you recall about this Mr Margetz." Doyle and the man Barnes glanced at each other. "Let's start with when he first came to The Reach."

Whether it had been late October or early November was probably the only detail she couldn't bring to mind. Whenever it was, the weather had been foul; the rain lashing the windows like a whip flailing a penitent's back.

When she opened the front door and saw him silhouetted against the outside light, she almost screamed. He was wearing a wide-brimmed hat – a Fedora, not a trilby; it looked more American than British.

"I have booked," he stated. "You have a room for me?"

He wasn't English, or British for that matter. His delivery was faltering as though he was unsure of his choice of words, and his accent was soft and rounded one minute, then slightly harsh the next.

She couldn't see his face, not just because of the light behind him, but more because he tilted his head forwards slightly, as if he was searching for a spot on the floor in front of him — or was, perhaps, a little hard of hearing.

"Of course, come in," she said. "It's not as though you don't know the place."

He stood in the hallway, dripping; his hat turned black by the rain, his raincoat sodden and lank. He held the same old suitcase in his left hand; an old-fashioned, hard-sided, rectangular frame suitcase sporting an eclectic collection of resort stickers: Cancun, Ko Samui, Rio, St Petersburg.

"The usual room, Mr Margetz?"

"Margetz," he said, slowly. "It would be, like always, I am grateful to you, Madame. Would you like payment now?"

"I'd like a swipe of your credit card please, Mr Margetz. Not that I imagine you'll be doing a bunk in this weather. You know where your room is." She wondered, truly, whether it was necessary to take a swipe of his card. After all, he'd been coming to The Reach longer than she'd been in residence. Margetz was her most regular customer: every year, one week late autumn, paid properly, always tipped her generously.

"Margetz," he said again. "Only Margetz, please." He handed over his credit card.

Stella slipped his card into the terminal on the counter, waited for the cue and then stood back, "Your pin, please?"

He stepped forward and tapped out his code.

"Thank you," Stella said, trying hard not to study him too closely.

"No, thank you," he replied, nodding his head once as though he wanted her to know how grateful he was that she should provide him with shelter on such a rotten evening.

"That's alright, Margetz. Will you be going out for something to eat?" She noticed his fingers were long and slender, and his palm felt hard and firm as she placed his room key in it. "Will you be going out for something to eat?" she repeated.

He clearly didn't understand the question. He said nothing. He just stood staring at her.

"If you're going out, Margetz, I need to give you a front door key."

"Oh, I understand," he said. He shook his head once. "No, thank you. I have eaten this evening."

"Breakfast from eight o'clock, unless you need it earlier. It's not a problem if you do.

"That is good. I see you then." Margetz went upstairs.

Stella watched Doyle across the table. The man, Barnes, sitting to her left, was now paying more attention. Whichever department it was that wanted to know about Margetz, he worked for it.

"He was German, I think," she said. "Had a bit of a stoop. I suppose he was late fifties, maybe older; I'm not much of a one with guessing people's age. Didn't say much, polite though; seemed a bit of a lost soul, if you ask me."

"Yes," said Doyle, "we are asking. Please go on. When did you next see him?"

Margetz came down to breakfast the next morning. He was courteous towards her and ate everything she put in front of him.

"That was excellent. Thank you," he said, in between wiping his mouth on the napkin. "I apologise for last night. I was tired, Ms Anworthy."

Whenever he used the letter W, it came across almost as a V, she noticed.

"I think, Margetz, it's about time you started addressing me by my given name, Stella."

"Thank you, Stella." He held out his hand for her to shake; he was a bit formal that way.

Stella said to the man, Barnes; he was the one taking notes now,

"I gave him a front door key. Didn't see him much after that. He came and went pretty much the same way other guests do."

Barnes asked, "Did you ask him why he was in Strand-next-the-Sea?"

Stella frowned, "Good gracious, no. I don't ask and they don't offer. Least said the better. Hear only the things you should hear. How many other sayings from the book of Good B&B Keeping would you like, Mr Barnes?"

Doyle twitched, but Barnes leant back and smiled so that his colleague would not notice.

Of course she'd asked Margetz what he was doing in Strand in the depths of a winter. Apart from the trading estate out on the old airfield, there was only the amusement arcade on the front or the walk along the coast into Cromer, and he didn't seem to have a car. He just ate breakfast and then went out and came back about teatime, or later.

However, this time he stayed on after his first week.

Then one morning he asked her, "It is a nice walk, this walk on the coast... to Cromer? You walk sometimes to Cromer? There is something to see?"

"I'm surprised you've not walked over that way before, Margetz. Mind you, this time of year it can get a bit chilly walking along the coast," she replied, "but there's the pier and the Prospect in Cromer, the gardens on the cliff-top; it's a pretty town. The crabs are famous, if you can catch them."

Margetz stared back at her, unmoved.

"The beach is very lovely," she carried on. "They have a carnival every year, but that's in August. The carnival is a big hit with the tourists; bonny baby, glamorous grannies, treasure hunts, even the Red Arrows once. It's quite a do."

"Thank you, Stella. Thank you, I will go there."

And the next day he did.

He came down to breakfast wearing a pair of heavier shoes and a Guernsey-style sweater that hung over the top of his corduroys. He set his heavy raincoat on the chair and draped a scarf over the back.

"Can I get you something in Cromer?" he asked.

"No thank you, Margetz. You might like to try the Old Rock Shop if you've got a sweet tooth. It's in the middle of town."

Margetz ran his long hands through his curly mop and grinned. For a fellow with a rather stern and unapproachable bearing, he could seem quite boyish at times.

The sky was a bright blue and the wind biting from offshore, and he cut a solitary figure striding off northwards along the front.

Naturally, when he'd so obviously avoided her enquiry as to what he was doing in Strand, she began to wonder about him all the more. Most of her guests were a pretty open book to an experienced B&B keeper, even the couple of lovebirds who had recently occupied Room 4 and who so keenly wanted her to think they were actually married. But, she found Margetz increasingly mysterious and she began to fantasise about what he might be up to or whether he might be hiding from someone.

Later, when Stella embarked on her round of housekeeping, she left Margetz' room until last. If he was going to come back it would surely be sooner than later, so she gave him enough time to make it most of the way into Cromer.

His bed was, as ever, quite tidy; he wasn't a busy sleeper like some, and his room never required more than a quick hoover and a wipe-round. On the bedside table stood, leaning up against the lamp, a photograph of a young woman sitting on a breakwater, her hair tousled by the wind. His jacket hung from the back of the door, a well-thumbed, red, leather bound book and reading glasses lay on the bedside table and his old suitcase stood handle up beside the chest.

Stella stared at it for a while. The stickers were rather bright and gaudy, but further than their exotic titles they also suggested there was far more to Margetz than met the eye.

"Ms Anworthy," Ms Doyle said, smiling and warming to her task once more, "I'd like to ask you again what you think Mr Margetz was up to in Strand-next-the-Sea?"

"Yes. Please," the man, Barnes, asked. He had a Midland's accent — a bit flat, rather tired. "Why don't you indulge us, Ms Anworthy? I am sure that staying with you for as long as he did, you must have been able to form some opinion as to the purpose of Mr Margetz' visit. Please feel free to share your opinion with us."

It was time to tread very carefully now that the man, Barnes, had entered the fray.

"No, not really. I don't really have one. I mean I know he was with me for, what was it? Nearly two months in all. That was unusual. He'd never stayed that long before." She sat up and pretended to try and read the notes in front of Doyle, suggesting she couldn't remember how long he'd stayed. "But I tend not to form opinions of my guests. In the early days I used to; before I knew better. But, you see, one grows rather prone to becoming judgemental when you form opinions. I mean you form an opinion about someone and then you start to reflect your opinion in your everyday attitude towards them. It's not healthy, is it?"

Stella glanced at Doyle and Barnes, but all she could think about was Margetz' suitcase.

She'd gone downstairs and found a heavy paperclip in the penholder on her desk; one of those longer, thicker ones she used for sorting the food bills. Stella had a quick look outside to make sure that no one was about to ring the bell and then grabbed a pair of pliers from the utensil drawer in the kitchen and went back up to the room.

In keeping with the age of the case, the locks were old single tumbler locks. Stella opened the paperclip out and bent one end using the pliers until she'd formed an L-shape. Careful not to scratch the lock, she inserted the bent clip and wiggled it slowly around the inside of the lock until she felt the pressure of the lock-pin. She pressed the release button beside the lock and held it down and wiggled the clip around a bit more.

The latch snapped up open.

Quickly Stella moved to the second lock, but then she heard a noise from the front door.

Hurriedly she removed her clip, shut the open lock and pushed the suitcase back beside the chest. She stood up and smoothed down her apron. Her heart beat so fast it felt as though it was going to explode out of her bosom and her head thumped to the beat of her blood pulsing through it.

Trying her best to look as calm as possible, Stella left the room, closed the door and padded down the stairs. She knew the open paperclip stuck out of her apron pocket, but she couldn't leave it in the room.

When she reached the bottom of the stairs, she saw the cause of the interruption; a pile of mail lay at the foot of the front door.

Stella went into the kitchen, slipped the extended clip into the cutlery drawer and put the pliers away. She made herself a cup of tea.

When she'd calmed sufficiently, she took the tools of her trespass back upstairs and pulled out the case.

There was nothing out of the ordinary: a few dirty garments, a prescription-like bottle of pills, two more books, both red and leather bound similar to the one by the bed, a hand-painted tin box of something called Läckerli which smelt of ginger and cinnamon, a black pocket telephone-address book and a large manila envelope.

The books were old and the jackets almost worn through in places. The authors' names illegible.

The envelope was thick and heavy, but not sealed.

"Bloody hell!" she swore in astonishment. The envelope contained two bundles of banknotes.

Stella had a quick count up. Both bundles of Euros were tied with blue elastic bands, "Well, I never...?"

She put them back in the envelope, replaced the envelopes in the suitcase and closed it carefully. She stood it back exactly where the metal studs on the bottom had made little indents in the carpet.

There was nothing strange about the contents of the case, except perhaps the money.

Stella finished cleaning the room and went back downstairs. She switched on her computer and, when it had eventually come to life, logged on to Google and typed in Euros to Pounds. She found a currency conversion site, located the currency from the drop-down boxes and typed in 20,000 Euros.

Bang! Up it came: 20,000 Euros was over £18,000.

Stella sat back and felt hot all over.

£18,000 upstairs in an envelope and Margetz gone out for a stroll!

"So no, not really," she said to Barnes. "I didn't really know enough about him to form an opinion. He seemed pretty normal. As I said, a bit quiet, a bit of a loner, but nothing out of the ordinary."

"He was at The Reach for two months?" asked Barnes.

"Overall probably."

"I suppose you would be inclined to remember how long he'd stayed, Ms Anworthy. A very unfortunate way to remember Christmas; not very nice, I shouldn't think." Barnes sounded almost concerned, almost consoling. "And there were just the two of you staying at The Reach during that time, you and the unfortunate Mr Margetz?"

If Barnes was the copper she thought him to be, he'd know bloody well there was only one person entered in the register as staying at the time. And he'd also know from the police and the hospital report that Margetz was that person.

Only Stella didn't so much mind that Barnes's sympathy was disingenuous, for in a way she was lying too.

Margetz had left a week or so before Christmas, but he was only gone for a few days; said he wanted to go to London, to look for a friend. He gave her £1,000 in cash – new notes, flat and shiny – and said he'd be back in a few days.

Stella didn't think she'd see him again. Then, he just reappeared out of the blue. The doorbell went and there he was, late Monday afternoon, freezing bloody cold; and her looking down the barrel of a snowy Christmas all on her own. She was so pleased to see him, she could've kissed him.

Later that week, she did.

She asked him if he'd had anything to eat. Margetz said he did not like the look of the sandwich they showed him on the train, which sort of did and didn't answer her question.

So Stella nipped out to the supermarket and returned with the closest thing to a German feast: rye bread, a selection of cold ham, a jar of gherkins and a few cans of beer which read as though they might be German. She knew the Germans liked pork too, so for a main course she cooked him pork mince meatballs in gravy with mushrooms and onions.

"I have brought a present," Margetz proclaimed in a rather grand fashion. From his suitcase, he produced a bottle; a rich amber-coloured bottle with a white label overwritten in black.

"Looks like the kind of bottle one ought to avoid," she said, examining it, "but thank you, Margetz. Thank you very much. I suppose we should try it?"

Margetz grinned, pointed at the plate of meats and said, "You are a clever lady, Stella, to find this food for me. You have some small glasses?"

She didn't have any brandy glasses, but she had a pair of tumblers.

He filled them and handed one to Stella. "Santé!" he said.

"Bottoms up," Stella replied.

The Asbach was piercing and pungent. She swallowed it down

and a slow, glowing fire ignited in her stomach, "Wow! That's good. That's great."

"You like it?"

"Like it?" Stella replied, smiling, "I love it. That's incredible. Makes you feel like walking in the snow without your clothes on." Quickly realising that she did not mean her observation in a way that he might misconstrue it, she added, "I suppose that's why you drink it, isn't it? Rolling around in the snow after the sauna and beating each other with birch twigs as you do. Not my scene, that."

Margetz studied her, "We don't do this beating with the wood. It is not a favourite of mine. But a sauna is good for the muscles."

They chased the brandy down with some of the Läckerli biscuits he'd brought down from his room; they were heavily spiced and not much to her liking.

They drank some more brandy and the second time round she let the raw alcohol roll round her mouth. It was a shade too fiery for her taste, so the third and the fourth she threw straight back and soon they were talking and laughing and laughing and talking.

By the time she left the table to start washing up, Stella knew for certain that when the morning came she would wish she'd avoided the brandy.

She was not wrong. She woke up in her bed without a clue as to how she'd got there. She wasn't wearing the sweater and jeans or shoes she'd been wearing the evening before, but thankfully her underclothes were exactly where they should have been.

It wasn't that she didn't fancy him. True, he was a fair bit older than her, although, surprisingly, she didn't mind the idea of that. And it wasn't that she fancied him either. It was just that Margetz wasn't the kind of guy she would ever have put herself with — grey-haired and foreign as he was.

There was no one else staying at The Reach, so Stella invited him into the kitchen for breakfast.

He asked her to join him. She hesitated, but then decided to accept his invitation. True, she'd entertained him with dinner the night before, but allowing him into the kitchen in the morning with the washing-up from the previous evening still not done was almost like letting him see her without her clothes on. Then she remembered that was pretty much how he must have seen her when he'd put her to bed the previous evening.

Three nights later, Stella did sleep with him. At the end of the evening, she asked him to stay with her rather than go upstairs alone. It wasn't simply because it was Christmas Eve; he'd brought her a present.

The finely wrapped box alone would have been sufficient to breach the redoubt Stella had long ago hidden her delicate emotions behind, but the beautiful silver choker within it comprehensively reduced her redoubt to a pile of smouldering rubble.

He didn't want to sleep with her to begin with. He shook his head that way he did; shaking it only the once. "No, I cannot do this," he said. "It is not right for me." He looked away as he spoke.

She told him everything would be alright, that there was nothing he should worry about and that she would expect nothing from him as long as he expected nothing from her.

Margetz appeared to understand this, perhaps even associated a little with what she was saying.

He was far gentler than she thought a man with long fingers and broad palms would be, and, when he was on top of her, he sought not to bear down on her; rather he rested up on his elbows so that he would not crush her.

But Stella did not want him at a distance. She reached for him and showed him just where she wanted him to be. She needed to feel every inch of him against her skin, every fibre, and every slight adjustment to his slow rhythm. So she pulled him down and listened to his breathing and felt his quickening pulse.

Very soon afterwards, they both slept.

Stella wasn't exhausted the way she used to be after sex with Vernon on a Sunday night. Now, she simply drifted away on the warm tide of satisfaction that welled up gently from between her hips.

Before dawn, Stella woke. She could hear a dreadful noise like a train rushing through the house.

Margetz was snoring.

Stella lay and watched him for the few minutes it took her to realise that she would not be able to sleep whilst he made such an extraordinary sound.

She woke him gently and tenderly, stroking his shoulders and his chest until he stirred. And, once he was half awake, Stella left him in no doubt that she wanted his full attention and that she was not going to leave him alone until he responded to her demands.

They talked a little afterward; a few soft words recognising the pleasure each had given the other; phrases of appreciation about sensations neither had met for far too long.

She got up and made them hot chocolate.

Stella giggled at the strange irony of his snoring; it'd been so long since she'd had a man in her bed and wouldn't she just have to pick one who snored?

A conversation with one of the other B&B owners at an Association meeting came to mind as she waited for the milk to heat up. Betty Laws it was who had a guest snoring so loudly he kept the whole house from sleeping. One of the other ladies suggested she make the man cocoa and slip some Nightnurse into the cup. Apparently, that usually stopped the men from snoring. They laughed all the more when at the following meeting Betty Laws told them how it had worked a treat.

So Stella went to the medicine cabinet, retrieved a bottle of Nightnurse and poured a measure into Margetz' mug; not much so that he would taste it, but just sufficient that she hoped it might muffle his musical accompaniment.

Margetz didn't taste it or if he did, he was sufficiently taken with her body that he failed to notice.

Much to Stella's surprise, Margetz, once rested and refreshed, wanted to make love again.

This third time, though, he was not so tender; he was more wanting and shade too physical for her liking.

Stella didn't mind, though. How could she mind a man who paid her such compliments?

They slept after that; quickly and soundly.

And in the morning, Margetz was still lying next to her.

So, what had gone on between them had not been the wishful fulfilment of some pre-menopausal fantasy, as Stella had feared it might be. She leant up on her elbow and yawned. She watched him for a while and began to worry that her morning breath was a little stale.

"Oh God!" Margetz wasn't breathing.

8

Audrey

The postman used to come to her house at eight thirty, but of late the timing of his arrival had been erratic. She didn't think him muddled or lazy; she just supposed the local office had decided to even up the round so that everyone received their post sometimes late, sometimes early. After all, it was fairer that way.

And when it wasn't bucketing down with rain, Audrey liked to dawdle by the gate. She was aware she must have looked to all intents and purposes like the dowager waiting for news from abroad, but she liked to watch Mr Stimson push his bicycle up the hill and she liked to smile at him; he was a nice man.

"Small parcel for you, Mrs Poulter," he said, puffing a little as he handed her a yellow A3 Jiffy bag, "and a couple of circulars; estate agents, pizza delivery..."

"No thank you, Mr Stimson. I've got a binfull already!" It was one of the things that made him such a nice man; taking all that unwanted mail away with him.

"Very well," he sighed.

"See you tomorrow, Mr Stimson. Thank you. Goodbye," Audrey waved after him and went indoors.

There was, she realised after she'd broken a nail, no way to open the jiffy bag easily, so she took a small cheese knife from the cutlery drawer, but even that proved ineffective.

"I suppose," she grumbled to herself, "it'll be one of those mailshots from some new estate agents. Well, I've no intention of selling, thank you very much. And I don't care how much its value has increased recently; I'm quite happy where I am."

Eventually, Audrey lost patience, tore open the jiffy bag and tipped the contents out onto the kitchen table.

A bundle of envelopes bound with an elastic band and an accompanying sheet from an estate agent tipped out.

The letter explained that they had been appointed agents to sell her old flat in Fulham. It went on to state that whilst cleaning the premises they had come across the enclosed letters and, as they had handled the sale of the flat some years before, they noted from their records that Audrey had been a previous owner. The most recent owner had very kindly furnished them with Audrey's current address and as a result they were very pleased to be able to pass on the enclosed letters, which, it seemed, had hitherto remained undelivered.

Audrey felt faint and had to rest her hands on the kitchen table to remain upright. She would not sit down. She absolutely could not sit down now that she was reminded of that wretched woman. She was simply too angry.

Audrey placed the letter from the agent very carefully on the table and stared at the pack of envelopes; a dozen of them, perhaps more.

Audrey recognised the handwriting instantly.

"Oh, no," she whispered.

Then she noticed that some of the letters had been opened.

The kitchen clock quieted and the world stood still. Down below the village, the Evenlode ceased to flow and the train from Paddington rested in the station. Across the road from the house, the bells in the Norman tower of St Mary's church,

Charlbury, silenced and not one car passed either up or down Park Street.

"So she knew!" she whispered. "The bloody woman knew! And if she knew, then Richard knew. Damn you!" she shouted at the cold, vacant house. "Damn you both to hell!"

9

Stella

Stella reached across and touched Margetz' forehead. She pulled her hand back quickly.

She prodded his cheek. His flesh was limp and cold; not cold like ice, but cold like the floor of her kitchen in winter.

"Oh, for Christ's sake," she moaned and leapt out of bed. She was naked and the room too was cold, but that wasn't why Margetz was cold. "Oh no," she whispered. "Margetz," she said, hoping she was wrong and that he would wake up, "Oh Margetz! Wake up, man. For pity's sake, wake up."

Stella knelt on the bed and put her hand over his mouth, hoping that that would make him gag or cough or splutter or something. Nothing happened. She felt for his pulse, knowing that she could never locate her own when she tried.

"Oh Margetz, please, please, please wake up. Come on, please."

Stella felt legs go numb and her head weigh like lead. She grabbed her dressing gown off the bathroom door and stumbled into the kitchen.

She'd heard of residents dying in B&Bs before, but it was something that happened to other people — not her. And it was certainly not what should have happened to her the very first and only time she'd slept with one.

She didn't have the first clue as to what to do. Absolutely, Stella did not know what to do. She'd ask Betty Laws. Betty would know.

But she couldn't ask Betty because the woman was a gossip, and if she found out that Margetz had died in her bed, Stella would be laughed out of Norfolk — never mind Strand. And besides, it was Christmas Day. How could she ring Betty Laws and say "Happy Christmas Betty. Can you tell me what I should do with the dead German in my bed?"

The proper course was to ring for an ambulance straightaway. And she should ring for the police, too; they would know what the procedure was for this kind of thing.

But she couldn't ring the police while Margetz was still in her bed. Somehow she'd have to get him back upstairs into his room.

"Think woman! Think!" she shouted at the fridge.

She reached for the bottle of brandy and took an enormous slug. In her shivering, unsteady state, she did not swallow the sharp liquid properly and some of it found its way down into her windpipe, which made her cough uncontrollably.

When, eventually, the coughing subsided, she wiped her eyes and rang Will.

"What time do you call this, Doll?"

She glanced at the oven clock: half past six. "Oh God, Will. I'm so sorry."

"You do know what day it is, don't you?"

"Yes I do, Will, I do. Only my Christmas isn't very happy right now." Stella couldn't think of what to say next, "Will... I..."

"Doll, what's wrong?"

She couldn't reply. The words disappeared before they got to her mouth. Ever so slowly, Stella began to cry, "I... It's that man... the one I told you about... the one with the money, he-"

"Doll?" Will asked, a little angry now. "Have you been drinking? I know Christmas is a difficult time for you, darling, but it's a difficult time for a lot of people."

"I know, Will. I know," she whispered between deep, staggered breaths. "No, I haven't been drinking. I... haven't... honestly."

"Doll? Are you alright?"

Stella still couldn't reply. Every time she began to think of Margetz lying in her bed, she plain lost it and held the phone away from her so that he wouldn't hear her crying.

The pause was too much for him.

"Ten minutes, Doll. I'll be there in ten minutes. Can you get to the front door? Can you let me in?"

Will was surprisingly calm when she told him what had happened. Perhaps it was her distress that made him appear so calm, but he sat her down and put the kettle on.

She told him she knew she would have to call for an ambulance, but, "They can't find him in my room. They simply can't. It's not right."

"Doll," he said, "get your act together. Come on! We have to move him before he gets too cold."

Visions of Margetz' limbs breaking off as she pulled on them jumped into view, "God, Will, I'm sorry."

"Time for sorry later. Not now. Come on."

"I don't know how I'll ever be able to repay you."

The bedroom was chilled like a butcher's cold store and when they pulled the sheets back, they saw that with his final heartbeat Margetz had emptied his bladder on her sheets.

"I'll burn the bed. I'll never sleep in it again. How can I?" she asked.

The corpse called Margetz no longer resembled the warm, enveloping, insatiable, and surprisingly agile lover he had been the night before. Now the corpse called Margetz was nothing but a cold, exposed, limp and unresponsive lump.

They wrapped the bottom sheet of the bed around him and dragged him off the bed, with Will pulling and Stella trying to help by lifting what she could.

Getting him to the bottom of the stairs was the easy part, but getting him through the fire door and up the stairs was another matter entirely. She hauled and shoved and strained with every sinew to encourage the lifeless bulk upwards. She cried and moaned, and moaned in a completely different manner from the way in which she'd moaned a few hours earlier.

Once up in the room, they stripped the bottom sheet off the bed and got the body into it. Stella remade the bed about him, made it so that it was tidy, and then went back downstairs for his clothes.

When they'd finished, Stella began to shake so much that Will had to put his arms around her to stop her from falling over.

"Doll," he said, "this is not easy. It has no right to be and you shouldn't expect it to be. It's natural that it should affect you like this. It's the shock of it. Sit down and I'll make us another cup of tea."

Stella sat and reached across the table for the bottle of Asbach, but Will grabbed it.

"That won't help any," he said. "You'll have to call the doctor and the police – oh, and the undertakers too. It won't help if you reek of alcohol."

She rubbed her hands roughly over her face to try to bring herself round and got up and lifted the phone off its cradle.

"Doll," said Will, "put that down."

But Stella was already dialling.

Will grabbed the handset from her and jammed it very forcefully back in the cradle, "Come on, Doll. You've got to think. I can't help you if you don't think about this."

He was right; she had to think things through. She couldn't have the police turning up with last night's make-up smudged all over her face.

"Sorry, Will," she mumbled. "You're right. I just, I mean I've never..."

Will put his arms around her again and tried to calm her, "I know," he said. "I know."

He poured the tea. "Now, what about a bit of thought and a plan? How does that sound?"

Stella nodded and blew her nose. She glanced at the oven clock, expecting it to tell her that morning was almost through. "Seven fifteen?" she said, as though the clock must be wrong. "Oh God! I can't call the doctor until ten. I mean if he didn't come down to breakfast, I probably wouldn't bother him until ten when I did my rounds. I'd hardly wake him up on Christmas Day, would I?"

So, between them, they hatched a plan.

Will helped Stella tidy up her room, see to the washing up and they had another cup of tea while he worked out what she was going to say to the police and the doctor; it was best to keep the story as near to the truth as possible. The only change to the pattern of events, the only lie, being that Margetz had not slept in her bed.

"What about his bill?" Will asked.

"Well," Stella stared into her cup, "he settled most of it in cash before he went off to London, but not since he came back."

"In cash? He settled in cash before?"

Stella nodded.

"And like the good girl you are, you swiped his card when he came the first time?"

Stella nodded again.

"You swiped his card and he put in his pin code?"

"Yes, of course."

Will smiled, "So, his card's still open. You haven't closed it off."

"Yes. And no," she replied.

Will shook his head and rolled his eyes as though Stella was being dumb or worse. "So close his card off this morning, after you call the doctor. Charge him for the whole stay. Forget the cash he gave you. No one will know. Charge him from the day you swiped the card until now. It's the right thing to do. That's what you do if one of your guests pegs it, right; close the card off, charge for the full stay, and put the cash he gave you in your back pocket. Common sense, isn't it? If you don't, you'll lose out."

"What? I can't do that, it's dishonest. That's not right."

"'Course it is, Doll. But you can't reopen the card for last Monday and close it off today because you don't know his pin. The only way it works is to charge him from the day he arrived, because that was when the card was opened. If, down the road, anyone asks you, you tell them Mr Margetz asked to pay you when he got back from London, and that if he didn't return, all you would have to do was close off the card just the way you would for any guest leaving early or a guest who skipped without settling. Come on, Doll, think about it."

Stella was more than a little horrified. She'd never been to bed with a guest before. She couldn't exactly charge him for that.

Will said, "I'm going to put this bottle of grog up in his room," and left.

Stella rested her head in her hands. Margetz had stayed six weeks before he went off to London. He'd given her the £1,000; that was still in the safe in her bedroom cupboard. He probably owed her another few quid, plus a bit more for one or two shopping errands she'd run for him.

But more than the money, Stella couldn't grasp what a bloke like Margetz was doing all on his own in the flat, glacial wastes that bordered the North Sea. And at Christmas? Even the devil lacked sufficient imagination to dream up enough to occupy the idle hands of Strand folk at Christmas. If a bloke wanted to lose himself in one of those nice wooden cabins down on the Broads, a beachside chalet in California-

Will reappeared, looking edgy.

"What time do you think I'd be safe calling the police?" she asked.

"Ten-ish, I suppose. Tell them you expected him down for a Yuletide breakfast and when he didn't appear, you got nervous and tried to get him on the phone. When he didn't answer, you went upstairs, knocked on the door and then used your pass key in case something had happened to him. What did you decide about charging him?"

Stella wondered why Will looked so twitchy. "You look awful, Will," Stella said.

"Not my favourite occupation, hauling dead bodies upstairs. But, never mind me, Doll; you look as though you could do with a hot flannel and a change of clothes yourself."

He looked as though he was about to ask her another question, but then obviously changed his mind, "Listen, Doll, you charge him what you like, but don't leave yourself short. I've got to go or my Christmas date'll think I've run off with Santa Claus."

She moved to thank him for being there for her, but he turned away from her. "No need to see me out," he said. "You go and get dressed. Oh, by the way, I wiped that bottle of grog round with a towel. Can't be too careful."

Next thing, the front door slammed.

It was when Stella was standing in the shower, face up to the streams of water she hoped would wash the evidence of Margetz' body from hers, that she realised what Will had said, "Can't be too careful." It wasn't as though she'd done anything to hasten Margetz' departure. If anything, she'd made sure he'd enjoyed his last night. It was no wonder he'd fallen asleep so fast-

"Oh my god, the Nightnurse! The post-mortem!"

She wrapped the towel around her, threw on her dressing gown and dashed to the medical cabinet. Stella removed the Nightnurse, grabbed a tea towel and the pass key for his room and went upstairs. She wiped the bottle carefully and put it on the shelf next to his wash bag.

Stella locked the door behind her, went downstairs and finished changing. She took one last look around the kitchen, checking all the glasses and cutlery were put away, and went out to her office. She ran through £2,750.00 on Margetz's credit card, holding her breath and crossing her fingers in the hope that there would be no referral.

"Yes, Mr Barnes," Stella said, "you're absolutely right; it was quite the opposite of a happy Christmas. It was about as unhappy as you can get – inauspicious might be the right word. And you're right in thinking there were only the two of us staying at The Reach that Christmas, if you can call it staying. Mr Margetz missed out on the mince pies and I didn't feel much like indulging in the Christmas spirit by the time I'd dealt with the police, the doctor and the undertakers.

"Strange really, I distinctly remember wondering if they worked on Christmas Day or whether they had the time off like most people. They arrived much quicker than I thought they would. Seems people are not so prone to pass away on Christmas Day. I suppose it does put a bit of a dampener on the festivities."

Barnes nodded, "I guess it would, Ms Anworthy. I guess it would. I-"

"So, what do you think Margetz was doing up here all that time?"

He smiled a rueful little smile. He could see Stella was back to her old ways of asking the questions before she was asked them. Clearly, he didn't like it so much as admire it, "It's a good question, Ms Anworthy; a good question. I was really hoping you might be able to enlighten us."

"I'm sorry, Mr Barnes. I can't. He was very unforthcoming, kept himself to himself. There was obviously something going on in his head; I could see that at breakfast, like he was deep in thought all the time."

Barnes sat forward. "We are given to understand by his family that Mr Margetz left home with a considerable sum of money in cash." He paused, studying Stella. But, when she didn't blink, he went on, "And his family have told the local authorities that this considerable sum was not present in his personal effects when they were returned along with his body. In fact, they were not recorded as having been about his person or in his baggage by the policemen when they attended the scene of his death either. Can you tell us anything about that, Ms Anworthy?"

"Well, no," she replied. "He paid by card. The final amount would have registered on his credit card; should've been on his last statement. It was over £2,000 as I recall."

Barnes glanced at a slip of paper on the table, "£2,750.00 exactly, Ms Anworthy. In itself, a considerable sum."

Stella bristled, "He stayed at The Reach for over six weeks, nearer seven as I recall. And, unless my guests have made some arrangement to pay in cash," she glanced at Doyle as she said it, "I swipe their card when they arrive. If guests have to leave very early, as some do, or if they slip off without settling their account, it means I'm not left out of pocket."

Stella turned her attention back to the policeman, "I know it sounds a bit strange, closing their card off when they've slipped off the mortal coil, but you could say Mr Margetz was one of those who slipped off without settling up, couldn't you?"

"Indeed, Ms Anworthy," Barnes fought back a smile, "indeed you could." He began to fold his papers away, but said by way of afterthought, "So, if Margetz did have 20,000 Euros on him, Ms Anworthy, you wouldn't know what happened to it or where the money disappeared to?"

"No, Mr Barnes, I most certainly would not. Absolutely and completely I do not! 20,000 Euros! Bloody hell! Who'd have imagined?"

"It's a sizeable sum, Ms Anworthy, a sizeable sum. And we'd like to know what happened to it. You're quite sure you can't help us with what might have happened to it? You're sure now? Think carefully, please, Ms Anworthy. Think very carefully."

The silence played itself out.

Barnes said, "Thank you for your time, Ms Anworthy. If anything should come to mind, please call me." He handed her a business card: a Detective Sergeant, Regional Crime.

The woman, Doyle, stood and said, "That will be all for now, Ms Anworthy. But please don't think we are finished with this line of enquiry. I'm very unhappy with your bookkeeping. It is extremely important for you to maintain up-to-date and accurate records. And it is vitally important that you maintain a high level of awareness of all your guests, particularly in today's climate of increased terrorist activity. Good day, Ms Anworthy."

"Is it?" asked Stella, turning to look out the window at the lowering sky beyond.

"Is it what?"

"A good day, Ms Doyle! You never can tell in these parts."

10

Philip

After his lunch with Archie, Philip strolled back to his office and tried hard to recall as much as he could of his dinner at Gort's two evenings before.

He remembered sitting at the noisy table; a benign grin for an expression, the numbing syrup of enjoyment oozing through his form. But more than the physical sensations that controlled his anima, he remembered an overwhelming need for the evening to continue and never to end; a desire similar to the brief longing he encountered in the final moments of love-making.

Maja, the hostess, joined their table late on. And, as the other guys all competed for her attention, she made a B-line for Philip, sat down on his lap, draped her long, sinuous arm around his shoulder and breathed sweet nothings in his ear.

That much he'd remembered the next morning. And there was nothing unnatural about that image or the way the impression stuck in his mind. After all, who among his work colleagues wouldn't want Maja whispering in their ear?

But now, striding beneath the plane trees of Berkeley Square, he was reminded of the cool night air outside Gort's. And he remembered hanging on to Maja while he tried to flag down a taxi.

Sadly, any recollection of what happened after that had been erased from his mind by the surfeit of alcohol.

II

Hacker

Even in the dull, afternoon light, he could see the house had been recently benefitted from a lick of paint. The bright, brass lettering, The Reach, set into a wooden plaque beside the blue door wore too much lacquer and-

"Mr Hacker?"

"Ms Anworthy." The house was not the only recipient of a lick of paint.

The grey gale from offshore threatened to dismantle the landlady's tightly curled and neatly tucked brown hair. "Come in, Mr Hacker. I'm afraid the weather has not seen fit to greet you as one would like."

She paused, studying him and then turned away into the hall. "Or is it that you have brought the inclement weather with you, Mr Hacker? There is a bite to the wind that tells me it comes from the north. You have come from that way, have you not?"

Hacker noticed her voice contained no hint of local brogue; it was London, Southern or Home Counties, and she finished her sentences with a slight rise in tone as though, whether question or statement, Stella Anworthy always expected a response. He trailed in the wake of her floral perfume.

At the reception counter, she turned to face him. She was a good six inches shorter and so he found it difficult to avoid looking at her without looking down at her breasts, framed as they were by her low-cut, frilled blouse.

"I guess it is north to some, Ms Anworthy."

"You'll be pleased to know I've put you in Room 2, at the front; nice view, though perhaps not today. But you will see we've spent a good deal of time and no little expense on refurbishment." She raised her eyebrows as if to accentuate some great hardship she'd endured during the process.

Hacker found himself looking at her face for too long as he tried to guess her age. She was a shade on the heavy side; a very generous size twelve, perhaps a fourteen. The skin around her eyes was firm, if lined – no doubt from overdoing the B&B welcome smile – and her lips were full.

"Looks good to me. Certainly looks very good to me," he said.

She warmed. Her cheeks coloured and her eyes flashed a brief but gentle appreciation.

"As a result, I've had to increase the tariff of late. Not much, mind you, but an increase nevertheless." She looked down at his laptop case. "We do have Wi-Fi. The password and instructions are in your room. Oh," she hesitated and leant towards him as if to whisper – but instead of whispering, she stepped back and said, "I'm afraid I don't allow smoking in the rooms, Mr Hacker."

"I'll take that on board, Ms Anworthy."

Her face softened and warmed again. "Thank you, Mr Hacker. I'm sorry if I sound a shade formal, but it's my experience that if I don't make it plain, people are wont to take liberties." The woman relaxed and looked at him with what he supposed was an expression of some gratitude, "Erm... sorry to have to ask, Mr... er Hacker, but do you have a first name? Please don't think me nosey, but I'll need more information than merely a surname for the register? It's the revenue, you see. If I don't lodge more than a surname, they'll think I've made you up; you know, invented you."

"That's quite alright, Ms Anworthy. My Initials are C H, but everyone knows me by my surname. I'll be sure to put my correct address in the register."

She handed him a laminated sheet of rules, regulations and fire precautions. In doing so, she briefly touched his arm as if to brush away a fleck of dust.

Hacker signed the register and went up to room 2 on the right at the top of the stairs.

Even with his nicotine dulled senses, he took note of the new carpet, curtains and freshly pressed bed-linen. He also appreciated that where once there must have been warped, wood-sash windows, there were now new plastic-framed double-glazed units.

His right knee suggested he take the weight off it, so he flicked off his shoes, lay down on the bed, stretched his arms above his head and flexed his toes, just as he had done too many times before in too many similar guesthouses. He reached in his pocket for his cigarettes, but, remembering what Ms Anworthy had said, threw the packet across the room into the shiny, white wastepaper basket.

12

Stella

"C and H," Stella repeated quietly, wondering what they stood for. She noted the time of his arrival in the register.

"Now then, Will," she said as she sent him a text asking him if he wanted supper: steak and kidney pie and swimmers, his favourite.

Stella changed her skirt and blouse for her pink housecoat. She wanted Will to feel properly at home before she broached the subject of the missing money.

He pitched up just after seven-thirty, his breath heavy with honey and beer.

"How's my Doll?"

"Good as new," she replied. "How about you?"

"Oh, you know: Feast one minute; famine the next. Mmm, smells good."

"Like a gin, Will?"

"Naa, best not, Doll; got the car. Beer'd be nice though."

Stella passed him a bottle. They sat down at her kitchen table; she'd laid it nicely, even brought some serviettes in from the breakfast room.

"How's that lovely man of yours?" she asked.

"Wants me to move in with him, doesn't he?" Will shook his head solemnly. "Doesn't get the picture! Can't understand why I won't."

"Why ever not, Will? Why don't you try it for a while? See if you take to it; see if you get used to it? You'll never know, if you don't try it, m'dear."

"Precisely, Doll. Might do just that; get used to it. And I wouldn't want that." He pulled on his beer and sighed, "Cherish my freedom above all else, you know me, Doll. Need to be able to do what I want to do, not what others think I should."

She'd intended to wait until she'd fed him the steak and kidney pie before bringing up the money, but seeing as Will had hoisted the garish flag of his narcissism...

She sipped her gin, sat back and smiled, "Y'know m'dear, it's really only by spending time in someone else's company that you get to know yourself properly."

Will looked a shade bemused by her line.

Stella sipped her gin and said, "Isn't part of growing up about getting to know yourself, getting to know what you are capable of, realising your potential, understanding what it is you really want out of life, that kind of thing?"

Will frowned. "Bit heavy for a Thursday evening, Doll. Got on the mother's ruin a bit early?"

She laughed, "Not tonight, m'dear. No, I was just thinking about you today; this afternoon as a matter of fact. Someone mentioned your name and I thought: he's a wily cove that Will. I bet there's more to him than meets the eye."

"There is to most people," he said and looked up to meet her stare with his own.

"I suppose you're frightened that someone might remove your wrapper and reveal a layer of Orange Creams instead of Montelimar?" she teased. "Afraid they'll look inside and not like what they see? Is that it, Will? Or is it that you think everyone else might just be the same as you and that if they are, you know full well you can't trust them because you can't trust yourself?"

Will leaned forward and placed his bottle of beer gently on the table, "Someone upset you, Doll?"

"You could say that, m'dear. You could say that."

He leaned even further towards her, their noses almost touching, and whispered, "Tell me who's upset you, Doll. I'll have a word with them for you, quiet like. Know what I mean? Who's upset you? Come on, you can tell me, Doll."

And as if someone else was speaking, Stella heard herself say, "You have, Will."

He studied her eyes, her face and her hair, and last her form, tensed and straining beneath her housecoat. Then he sat back and laughed and slapped his thigh, "Me? What have I done, Doll? My carpentry not up to scratch? Missed out a couple of patches with my paintbrush? Bit of masonry need repointing? Can't be anything I can't fix."

When Stella didn't reply, his face darkened and the fun fell from it. "Oh," he said. "It's not that, is it? It's something more serious."

"Did you take a wad of money from that dead man's belongings, Will?"

For a second he looked like the kid who'd been caught with his fingers in the biscuit jar, but then his wicked, cheeky grin returned, "Money? What money?"

But as disarming as his smile could be, on this occasion, it sold him short.

They sat and studied each other across the kitchen table; the odours of steak and kidney pie hanging in the air, the pop and bubble of vegetables simmering on the hob punctuating two trains of thought destined to collide.

Eventually, Will's face darkened again. He sat forward, "So what if I did?"

"You-"

"It's not as though he was going to need it, him being all dead as a post as he was. And don't sit there looking like you've got a wasp stuck up your drawers, Doll, I seem to remember you feathered your nest with his credit card before you called the ambulance. And not without me having to convince you of the sense in it in the first place."

"I only took what I was owed," Stella said. "You fleeced him clean."

"Like I said: So what? Who's complaining?" Will paused. "Oh, don't tell me he was on the run from the Mafia and some po-faced stranger with a captive air pistol has come looking for what's left of their ill-gotten gains. I think we've both seen that movie."

"No, Will. They haven't. And if they had, we wouldn't be sitting here waiting for your supper to warm, would we?" Stella rubbed at the bone behind her ear. "The problem or problems I've got aren't so much like that. It's more like because of your light-fingers I've now got the bloody revenue and the police on my back. That man's family want to know where his money went and the revenue seem to think I kept it to pay you for all the work you did refurbishing this place. They say I haven't generated sufficient funds from the business to pay for it."

Will frowned, "And you think you might have to tell them I took the money to get them off your back. Is that it? Did they try the old dish us a bit of dirt and we'll ignore your little misdemeanour routine?"

"Of course they did," Stella sighed, "and they wanted to know a good deal about you, Will. Or are you Tom Martin or John Melville as they seemed to think? Bloody hell, Will! They seemed to know more about you than I did."

Will's face turned darker; so dark that his eyes seemed to disappear beneath his brow. His cheeks looked hollow and drawn, and he leant on his elbows, staring hard at her.

"If you've any stupid ideas about playing that game, you'd better think again, Doll," he said. "They talk a lot of squit. They'll offer you all sorts of carrots to get you to split on others and then they'll beat you with exactly the same stick. Mark my words, Doll. You seriously think you can trust them over me?"

When she didn't reply, when she just sat and looked at him and didn't know what to say, he closed his eyes and screwed up his face as if he was suffering an immense pain. "You don't want to lose me, Stella," he whispered.

He'd not called her by her name since that day on the beach. She'd liked that: Doll. Living Doll, that's what he'd said that first time. Living Doll; Cliff Richard. He'd never called her Stella though, not since.

"What about the other names, Will? Why do you have to use other names?"

He shrugged, "Helps avoid a bit of tax, that's all. Makes no difference to you what name I use."

"But I don't know what to do," she said. "I fobbed them off with a load of drivel, played the dimwit. Trouble is I didn't get the feeling they bought it. I mean I'll end up having to explain all of it somehow, won't I?"

"What you tell them is up to you, Stella, just so long as you remember to leave me out of it. Have you got that?"

Then he shouted so loud he made her jump, "Are you listening to me? Have you got that, Stella?"

His words echoed through the void in her head. Her eyes welled up and her legs turned to jelly.

Will, or Tom or John, gave her one last coldly menacing stare and stood up, knocking his chair over.

"You don't want to lose me as a friend, Stella," he said. Then he turned on his heels and was gone.

Stella winced, expecting him to slam the kitchen door behind him.

But he didn't. And it was only when she was righting his chair, and wondering what she was going to do with all the steak and kidney pie, that she felt the draught from the hall. He'd left the front door open.

"Oh no, he called me Stella."

13

Phoebe

Being rusticated, Dame Clarissa told her, was very different from being sent down; it didn't carry the same stigma.

After the meeting, Phoebe stumbled back to her set.

Heather looked sheepish and the boys drifted in as if to pay their respects at a wake. Yu, the very beautiful Yuichi Murasaki, put his head round the door and shot her a short meaningful stare, which didn't mean much, if anything, at all.

"Still, it's probably for the best," Heather said.

"Is it, fuck!" was all Phoebe could manage. She threw a few clothes into her shoulder bag, collected her wash bag and last couple of grams of 'drone, and didn't bother to ask who had purchased the half bottle of vodka on the sideboard – she just took it.

"See you sometime, Phoebes," Heather added, as though their next meeting might take place in the hereafter.

"Yeah! Whenever?" Phoebe slammed the door.

She handed her room key in at the Porter's Lodge and collected her post.

The train down to London took just under an hour; the faces of the passengers around her, drifting in and out of the muddle in her mind.

By the time she arrived at Kings Cross, Phoebe knew she had to put some thought into where she was going to spend the night; she didn't want to end up squatting over a drain wishing she had a dog to keep her warm.

The ATM considered her status and after a lengthy calculation deemed her suitably worthy. She couldn't remember how much money wasn't left in her current account; her student loan was surely nearly all gone, thanks to her recent demands, and her College card was no bloody good to her outside of the college.

There was a hostel on the Euston road opposite the British Library. She'd stayed there with Heather when they'd been to the University Women's Club for the birthday party of a NatSci from the College. The rooms at the hostel were clean and cheap, and though she knew she would have to share a room with a bunch of strangers, at least she knew she would be guaranteed to share their gender.

So, Phoebe ambled along the Euston Road to the hostel. Traffic thundered and hooted, and the tall pitch of red tiles and solid brick façade of St Pancras leaned down on her; the gaping entrance beneath dark and yawning like the voracious maw of a baroque mental institution.

The doe-eyed girl at reception looked no older than Phoebe and spoke in slow, Spanish-accented English: yes, they had rooms available, but they would be busy later, so it would be a good idea to reserve. A shared room would cost twenty pounds and fifty pence, but she had to pay right then and there if she wanted to make a reservation. What identification did she have?

Phoebe had her driving licence, but didn't make a reservation on the off chance she got a better offer – twenty quid was one fifth of her modest pot.

To the left of the hostel stood an O'Neill's; to the right, a Fuller's pub.

The beer in O'Neill's cost more than she was used to, but the goat's cheese salad knocked the college canteen food into a cocked hat. Phoebe perched on her stool, fed her turbulent insides, and watched the city folk pass by. The vigorous energy of their passage seemed to Phoebe at odds with the solemn apathy of their expression. They reminded her of Levi's mud puppets scuttling to their work Kommando; their place on the planet defined purely by their progress.

It was then that she remembered the post she'd picked up on her way out of college.

There were three items of junk mail and a large envelope, which, she decided by its typescript, was probably from a government department or university organisation.

Phoebe was about to put them back in her bag, when, on turning the envelope over, she noticed the return address printed on the back. The letter was from the agency she'd approached a couple of weeks before.

She resisted the temptation to open it; rather, she studied it for a minute or so before putting it back in her bag.

Soon the grey skies fell to black and the street lights came on, suggesting it was time for her to move on.

The Euston Flyer stared straight out onto the busiest stretch of road in the city, so Phoebe backtracked around the corner into the relative quiet of a side street and stole into the Skinner's Arms. It was warm and cosy, but a shade intimate and placid for her needs, so she didn't linger. She wandered on until she came to the broad Kingsway; an avenue like any other that criss-crossed every major capital in Europe. She had another beer in the Shakespeare's Head, purely because she could think of no good reason not to.

By the time she got to Covent Garden, Phoebe was a fair distance down the road to being drunk. But theatre land was gay and radiant and hectic, and the atmosphere wrested her from her gloom; having no plan meant she didn't have to be any place at any time-

Someone nudged her from behind and she tripped off the pavement and fell sprawling into the road. She scraped her right knee

and skinned the palm of her right hand on the cobble stones. However, her injuries came a distant second to her embarrassment.

"Whoa," said a voice of authority from behind. "Here, let me help you up. I'm sorry, that was my fault."

His hands were warm and strong boned, and he pulled her back onto her feet with ease. He wore a dark suit and light shirt, open at his neck, and his hair was very fair and tidy.

"I'm sorry," he said, "I really am."

A voice away down the road taunted, "C'mon, boy. Plenty of time for that later."

He waved his company away.

"I'm okay, thanks," Phoebe said. "Just banged my knee. No harm done." But when she went to put her weight on her right knee, it grumbled and she stumbled forwards again.

He put out his hand to stop her from falling a second time. "Steady. Look, I really am sorry. You might have stepped back, but I wasn't looking where I was going. Guess that makes it my fault. Are you really okay? Is there anybody with you?"

"No!" she half-shouted, trying to rub some life back into her knee.

He didn't seem to know how to take her answer.

"No, there is nobody with me," she said, "and yes, I am okay. Don't worry about it. You carry on. I'm alright." Phoebe stopped rubbing and stood up to look at him. He was taller than her by a good few inches, and he was lean of build and his suit fit him well enough to suggest it didn't come from a charity shop.

"Look," he said, "let me get you over to that bar. I'll get you a chair and a drink while your knee recovers."

"No. That's alright. I said I'll be fine. You get off back to your mates before they give you too much stick for being the proper gent."

But instead of being relieved at her releasing him from any further obligation, the young man seemed intimidated by her reply.

"If you don't mind," he said, "I'd rather make up for being so clumsy and see that you're alright first. That lot," he nodded in the direction in which his mates had disappeared, "can wait." He picked up her shoulder bag.

There was a bar a few yards up the road, a sister bar to one Phoebe drank in, in Cambridge. Probably because she knew the kind of place, she decided she would feel safe enough going into it with a complete stranger. The irony of her having just been into several unfamiliar bars all on her own amused her.

"What's so funny?" he asked.

"Nothing," she said, but her reply was lost in the hubbub of the bar as he opened the door.

Normally, Phoebe wouldn't have let anyone open a door for her, but, slightly oiled and more than a little unsettled by his action, she let him.

"Sorry, I missed that," he said.

Phoebe stood looking up at him; he had nice eyes, "It doesn't matter."

A couple vacated their seats away down the bar. He squeezed past them, put her bag down between the stools and motioned for her to follow him.

As she sat down, he half stood off his seat; a display of antique manners she'd not witnessed from any of her college dates.

"What can I get you?"

"You don't need to do this, you know," she said.

"Sorry to disagree," he shook his head, "but I do. You see, it's a rule I have: If I bump into a beautiful young lady in Henrietta Street, I have to make it up to her before she goes telling everybody what a blundering oaf I am. And besides I..."

"Thick!" Phoebe mocked.

"Who, me?"

"No," she replied. "The line; a bit thick. I bet you must cruise

Henri-whatever-it-is Street on a Thursday night looking for girls to floor just so you can pick'em up and bundle'em in here."

For a moment, he looked puzzled. But then, whatever fog it was that had strayed into his head cleared and he said nothing for a few seconds. He just sat and looked at her. "You've lost me," he said.

"You're not out sharking then?"

"Sharking?"

"Yes. You know, Sharking." Phoebe raised her hand up to her head and pressed the base of her thumb against her nose, making the shape of a shark's fin. She lowered her head slightly, unintentionally squinting a little at him as she did so, "You know: Sharking?"

He laughed, politely, and then, noticing her slight squint, he chuckled, "Out on the pull, you mean? No, I'm not. Or rather I wasn't. I'm sorry if it seemed that way. Look, I... What can I get you to drink; a glass of champagne?"

Phoebe frowned, "No thanks, a beer'll do just fine."

"Are you meeting friends?"

"No." Phoebe looked at his hands. They were indeed lean and strong. They were freckled on the back and covered in fine blond hairs. His nails were clean and even: a city boy.

He also wore a simple, narrow gold ring on the third finger of his left hand: a married city boy.

The barman appeared with a bottle of pink champagne and two flutes.

"Look, I'm sorry, but I'm celebrating. Well, in a way," he said, offering her a glass.

Phoebe was gripped by an urge to run. No one had ever threatened her with pink champagne before, not even her fabulously minted Texan, Jay. "So am I, in a way," she said. "Thank you."

"What are you celebrating?" he asked as he concentrated on filling her glass.

"Oh, that's for me to know. How about you?"

"Oh, you know, this and that."

"Mmm," Phoebe replied. "That I do understand."

"Sometimes things just don't go the way you expect them to, do they?" he said.

As the evening went on, the fizzy cocktail of beer and champagne, mixing with the residue of Mephedrone in her system, did little to restrain the more loquacious side to her nature. However, Phoebe perceived no great tingling, physical rush or nervy elation, as she had sometimes experienced on other big nights out. Rather, swept along as she was in the gentle flow of conversation and the attentions of a more mature and very good-looking man, Phoebe found herself enjoying an unusual sense of self-worth — the seeds of which soon blossomed into an even greater sense of wellbeing. The second bottle arrived without her noticing him order it.

"I'm Phoebe," she said as they touched glasses, "Phoebe Wallace."

He hesitated before saying, "Charlie, pleased to meet you, Phoebe."

Charlie told her about London, about the pubs, clubs, restaurants and bars; about the huge nights out he'd enjoyed and how the greater value of the city was to be found off the beaten track.

In turn, Phoebe described the university city of which, up until recently, she had been so fond. There was much she left out.

Phoebe bought the third bottle of pink champagne. She handed over her bank card with something approaching a casual élan, but inside she tied up in knots as she waited for the dreaded machine to acknowledge her pin.

"I know just how you feel," he said. "It doesn't seem to matter how insignificant the amount or how much I think I've got in the bank, one day I know that blasted machine's not going to recognise my card and I'm certain I won't exist as an entity from that moment on. It's stupid really."

The barman raised an eyebrow in mock disbelief and then smiled to let her know the transaction had gone through.

Phoebe heaved a sigh of relief. Charlie threw his head back and laughed.

"What about your mates, Charlie?" she asked.

"Oh, them? I expect they'll be tearing up some place in Soho by now. They won't miss me."

"Won't you get a fine or a forfeit or something?"

Charlie chuckled. "No. It doesn't work like that. Besides they work for me, so if they give me too much stick, I'll just make them suffer."

Not too much later, Phoebe began to feel a shade overcooked. When she stood up to go to the ladies, she nearly fell over. Fortunately, Charlie stood up to steady her.

An attendant loitered in the ladies. Phoebe had intended to get a quick hit of 'drone on board, just to keep her going, but realised she couldn't guarantee to snort it quietly, so she rubbed a little round her gums and sucked the remainder off her finger.

She'd been gone a while and he said, "I thought you might have baled ship on me."

"What? Just to fall prey to some other shark. No thanks," she giggled. "Bloody hell, Charlie! I don't suppose Covent Garden's exactly lacking in sharks."

The drone did lift her for a while, but the lift did not last as long as she'd have liked.

They drank more, but more slowly, and they added substance to their liquid intake in an effort to prolong the evening. However, there came a time when they both realised that the food they picked at was too little and far, far too late.

How much later Phoebe wasn't sure, but she became aware of people brushing past her towards the door and even Charlie began to look less than comfortable. There was a battle going on in his head, she noticed. His lovely eyes, the window to his mind, revealed a man at odds with himself.

Phoebe took it to mean that Charlie didn't know how to end the evening and that he was embarrassed at having plied her with alcohol only to desert her to the city streets.

"It's not a problem, Charlie," Phoebe said.

"It isn't?" He nodded his head slowly, as though he'd meant to reply in the positive, but had not.

"No," she said. "It's been a blast. And it's time for me to go." Phoebe got off the stool and lurched right into a couple walking past her.

Charlie caught her arm and pulled her back to her seat. "I'll get you a taxi."

"Yeah," Phoebe said, "that would be good."

The cool, fresh night air weakened her knees and Charlie had to grab hold of her a third time.

It felt like forever, the two of them standing on the pavement waiting for a taxi; Charlie standing bolt upright like a lamppost, Phoebe leaning against him.

In the end, one stopped. Charlie opened the door, "Phoebe, where are you staying?"

"YHA, Euston Road."

"King's Cross end?" the driver asked.

Phoebe nodded twice, slowly.

"Is the young lady going to be alright, sir?"

"Look, Phoebe, would it be better if I saw you to the hostel door?" Charlie lifted up her chin so that he was sure she could see he was speaking.

She repeated her nodding.

"Okay. Let's get you in the cab. Come on."

The taxi seemed to swing in endless circles and his neck was warm and smelt very vaguely of cypress and jasmine.

He spoke softly to her, reassuring her, telling her she would be alright.

The taxi pulled up and they both got out; Phoebe less steadily than Charlie.

The automatic glass doors to the hostel were shut when she walked right smack into them. Phoebe stood back, expecting them to open at her presence. A man and a woman sat behind the reception desk.

Then Charlie pressed the metal plate to the left of the doors and they slid open.

"Look, Phoebe-"

"Hey Charlie," she said. "'S okay. Really it is. 'S bin nice. Thanks for the evening." Phoebe did not look back at him. "Bye Charlie."

"Hi," said the girl on reception. She wasn't English and she wasn't the girl who Phoebe had spoken to earlier.

"Hi," replied Phoebe, yawning. "My name's Wallace. I came in this afternoon and reserved a room."

The girl typed and checked her screen. She had long brown hair and a bell-shaped face, "Wallace, you said?"

"Yes, Wallace. Phoebe Wallace."

"Are you sure you actually made the reservation? I don't have a record.

"Yes, I'm sure, I... Oh shit! No sorry, I didn't. I said I would be coming back."

The girl behind the desk held up her hands in surrender and smiled a weak apologetic smile, "Sorry, Ms Wallace, we are full. We have been full since about eight o'clock."

"Oh shit!" repeated Phoebe too loudly. She stood and contemplated the floor for a few seconds, a minute – she wasn't sure for how long. "Is there another place? Somewhere not too far? Somewhere I can walk to?"

The girl smiled, "We have another place at Great Portland Street. You can walk, but it's not so near."

"Could you phone them for me and find out if they have room?"

"Sure. I'd be happy to." The girl picked up the phone.

When she put it down again, Phoebe knew from her expression that the news was not good.

"Thanks anyway." Phoebe's eyes welled up as she turned round and staggered out through the double glass doors into the Euston Road and the cold night air.

Charlie was standing right where she'd left him; the taxi the same.

"You'd better come with me," he said.

Phoebe hesitated. She fought her tears; she fought the urge to ring Heather and ask her to come and get her, and she fought the urge to scream that it wasn't supposed to be like this.

But it was either go with him or find a doorway in which to spend the night, and she was neither drunk nor sober enough for that.

The taxi took them to the Barbican; a vast, concrete maze of corridors and lifts.

Phoebe trailed in Charlie's wake. "I'm sorry to do this to you, Charlie," she said, once he'd closed the door.

The apartment was spacious, but was only made to look so by the lack of anything other than essential furniture. It seemed more like a hotel room than someone's flat.

"Would you like a drink, some water, something?"

"No, thank you. I don't know how to thank you enough, Charlie."

He smiled. He seemed even taller now than when he'd picked her up off the road, "You don't have to, Phoebe. I enjoyed the evening too, you know. I'm glad to be... well, to be able to help out."

Charlie seemed nervous of coming too close to her; awkward, as though he was afraid he might come across as threatening. But that was not the message his body language spoke at all. He looked tired. There were deep shadows beneath his eyes and whereas before his blond hair had glowed in the golden light of the bar, now it had lost its lustre. But he smiled a kind of wistful, regretful smile. "I won't bother you, Phoebe," he said. "You'll be safe here."

Phoebe was aware her mascara had run and the skin around her cheeks felt puffy.

"The spare room is here," he said, opening a door for her. He switched on the light; a gold-quilted double bed dominated the room. "The bathroom ... there."

"It's nice," was all she could think of to say.

"Sleep well, Phoebe," he said, but still he would not come near her. "It was fun, huh?"

"Yes, Charlie. It was fun, thanks." She locked the door behind him.

During the night, Phoebe was aware of Charlie moving about outside her door.

14

Hacker

By the time he woke up, the grey light in the room had been replaced by the white light from the streetlamps.

Hacker got up, washed the sleep from his face and unpacked. He hung his business suit on the back of the door in much the same way as he would have hung his kit on the wall of an away dressing room. He set his laptop on the bedside table and sat down to play a couple of games of Solitaire before he went out in search of more muscular entertainment.

Before him, lay his own pitch and players; blacks against reds and spades against hearts. He rubbed his face, cracked his knuckles and briefly massaged his hands. It was a precise and long-practised routine, ingrained over too many long evenings in too many tired boarding houses. By the time he'd finished his warm-up, the machine was ready for his prompt.

And that was how Hacker passed the next hour. He played the best of threes and that grew into the best of sevens and nines. He played just one more game ten or more so times. The black nine turned against him; it was his common nemesis.

The leering face of the black centre forward from Senegal kept blocking his way. Somehow he couldn't seem to get past him, and, just when he was convinced he'd got all the black nines down, he realised he'd missed the Jack. His mood didn't improve as his losses mounted. He shut the lid.

Though the carpet had been replaced, the stairs creaked and sure enough Ms Anworthy's door opened as he crossed the hall. She still wore her warpaint, but her blouse and skirt had given way to a pink housecoat.

"Thought I'd stretch my legs," he said. "Is there a pub in strolling distance?"

"Well, since you've asked, Mr Hacker, there's recently a new landlord in the Old Tern; down the front to the right. Relief manager as I understand it. I've heard the food is not up to much. Only it's a bit of a walk and I wouldn't want you to be disappointed." Her expression was as dead pan as her delivery, but then she raised her left hand and fiddled with a curl of hair at the back of her neck, "Otherwise turn left and it's a walk into town; couple of places there. But you won't find much excitement at this time of year.

"The new front door key can be a bit stiff," she said, before ducking back behind her door.

The wind had eased, but the rain was fine and it swirled around the streetlamps like the mist from his ex-wife's perfume spray. From the darkness beyond the road, he could hear the waves breaking along the front.

Hacker looked down at his car. Some hopeful had stuffed a yellow business flyer beneath his wipers. But, as he started down the steps from the front door, he realised that his was the only car to have received such a blessing, so he strode over and took a closer look.

A parking ticket!

"What the...?" he moaned. "Oh, no!" He ripped the plastic bag off the screen and turned to look at the other cars parked near his. None of them had tickets.

He looked up at the lamppost and saw the white plaque informing him that the bays were reserved for residents' parking until 6.00pm.

"Oh, for Christ's sake!"

The Old Tern was half a mile south down the front. It too had received a makeover, although the hinges on the sign above the door cried for lack of oil.

Hacker got the impression that before the makeover he would have been greeted by the comforting suffusion of stale ale and fags, whereas now the pot-pourri floating in the bar reminded him of lemon disinfectant and freshly mown grass.

A small blackboard behind the bar bore out Ms Anworthy's suspicions regarding food and a red NO SMOKING sign peeked out from behind the optics. He got his pint, made for the door, reaching for his cigarettes in the process, and saw the polite notice requesting patrons not to take glasses outside; plastic reusable glasses were available from the bar if required.

It was the last straw. Hacker threw back his beer and left.

The night fared little better. There was a lengthy queue of refugees outside the fish and chip shop, and the idea of a kebab turned his stomach. So he walked on, found a mini-supermarket and bought a criminally expensive bottle of gin, a couple of tonic waters and a bag of peanuts.

He went home.

Home! Home to Hacker was damp sheets in musty dorms with cold floors and smelly toilets. And then later, much later on, home was a hotel room and an alcohol-fuelled party with women whose names he couldn't recall in the morning.

Then, after people had stopped asking him to grace their houses or endorse their hotels, home became the cheap guesthouse or the B&B, or even the motorway services car park, or just once in a while, if he got lucky, a swish London hotel with a free mini-bar.

The lights were still on when he got back to The Reach. The door through to Ms Anworthy's room was slightly ajar.

Before he could get halfway to the stairs, she came out still wearing the same pink housecoat, though it was no longer tied so tightly. She held a tumbler in her left hand. "So you'd be hungry then, Mr Hacker?" was all she said.

PART 2

FRIDAY

15

Phoebe

There was no window to the room and so she had no idea of the time. She checked her phone: the battery was dead. Phoebe got up, rubbing her sore knee, unlocked the door and peered into the small hallway.

She expected to hear a radio playing and smell toast burning, but instead the silence and the lack of any real scent in the apartment unnerved her.

The bathroom mirror was a little kinder to her than the evening before and as she searched for greater encouragement from her reflection, she noticed a curious lack of any bathroom accessories. The soap was still in its paper wrapper; the sachet of shower gel unused. She opened the cupboard behind the mirror, expecting to find toothpaste, toothbrush, deodorant and such, but it was empty; no Paracetamol, no Berocca, nothing. For sure there was toilet paper, but the roll sat on the cistern and not in the holder to the side. And, although there were clean hand and bath towels on the rail, they felt rough and new.

Phoebe finished washing and went back into the hall. The door to the other bedroom was open; it was similar to hers – in fact, apart from the window, the radio alarm on the bedside table and an armchair by the window, it was identical. The bedclothes were pretty much the same too and the bed was made so well there was no way anyone could have slept in it.

She turned and went into the living room. A glass coffee table sat in the middle of the room flanked by two dark brown leather sofas, but apart from that the room was bare.

Despite wearing jeans and a sweater, Phoebe began to feel chilled. The granite work surfaces in the kitchen gleamed and the floor was so clean she wondered whether she should walk on it.

"Charlie?" she called. "Charlie where are you?" Phoebe went back into the hall just in case she'd missed another room to the apartment.

She went back into the kitchen, hoping Charlie had simply stepped out to get fresh croissants. She needed a cup of tea or coffee, a glass of juice, something. Her head drummed and her mouth was bone-dry.

Then she saw a handwritten note by the coffee maker.

Phoebe stood stock-still and didn't approach it for a few seconds. "He's not coming back," she said out loud. "That was the noise I heard in the night. That was him leaving."

The note was handwritten in ink:

Dear Phoebe, thank you for sharing my evening and making it such fun. I'm sorry about the lack of breakfast and that I am not here to see you. Please make sure you have everything before you leave. I have left you a couple of pounds to make up for the champagne you bought. I hope our paths will cross again. Charlie.

He'd left her two fifty pound notes; comfortably more than she'd paid for the champagne.

She sat at the breakfast bar and tried to make sense of Charlie and his curious apartment. Clearly it was a bachelor pad; a refuge or den; some place Charlie and his mates brought their women.

It vaguely offended her that Charlie had not tried to do whatever it was that he and his mates usually did with the women they brought to the flat. But then, perhaps Charlie had brought her to this place out of pity — and pity, Phoebe knew, was reserved for those who could not climb out of the pit life had dug for them. Pity was reserved strictly for the Muselmann.

She took the letter from the agency out of her bag and opened it. She read the contents slowly and carefully a couple of times over. She hadn't heard of the town, but she knew the county – and, more importantly, she knew the station she would have to travel from in order to get there.

Liverpool Street was a fifteen-minute walk. Phoebe collected her bag, checked the bedroom and bathroom, and let herself out.

16

Hacker

He came to in his own room, the thin and all too recognisable vinegar of alcoholic remorse sluicing through his veins. His head moaned and his stomach griped at processing the uneasy mix of gin, steak and kidney pie and dumplings she'd set before him.

He fished a bulging blue file titled 'Norfolk Electrical' out of his briefcase.

His long and very healthy relationship with the company had generated a fair mountain of paperwork and the file contained all the associated information relevant to his sales. The file Hacker held in his hand also contained several sub-folders. What he was looking for was the folder marked 'Chisholm, Outsourcing Manager and Personal Details'.

Brian Chisholm held the key to Hacker's future.

Years of selling Norfolk Electrical everything from neodymium magnets, copper winding, thyristor circuits and a thousand other sundry electrical components, meant that the greater part of Hacker's annual income depended on Brian Chisholm's empathy, his loyalty, and ultimately his signature.

Chisholm was without doubt his last chance saloon, and today Hacker was going to be singing in it at the top of his voice. It was either sing, or kiss his job and his flat goodbye.

Breakfast was on the go downstairs; he could smell it.

He showered and shaved, and changed into his grey business suit. He chose a white shirt and his old club tie, which he took two attempts at tying so that the club shield and motto sat just above the crossover of his jacket lapels. Hacker had even had his hair trimmed for this trip; he needed to cut just the right dash; like he was making it, but not necessarily rolling in it.

Down in the breakfast room, Stella Anworthy had laid just the one place at the single, wide table. So, assuming it was for him, he sat down.

Hacker tapped the oak, refectory table. He'd not seen such a hefty piece in a guesthouse breakfast room before. Most places had a collection of individual tables rather than one long one, and the idea of having to swap conversation with strangers at breakfast made him feel uncomfortable.

The Reach had four guest rooms: number 1 across the hall, and numbers 2, 3 and 4 on the first floor. The breakfast room was in what would have been the front room of the house before it had resorted to charging guests. Stella Anworthy's living quarters lay beyond the kitchen at the back.

She smiled at him; not exactly a wide smile of grateful appreciation or a warming ray of sunshine in which he could bathe, but then neither was it a thin-lipped reproach for being too free with her.

"Can I get you more coffee, Cornelius?"

Her use of his Christian name paralysed him. "Thank you, yes." He sat back and looked around, and for the want of anything else to say, said, "My first time here. Usually I stay over in Cromer. You've been here long?"

"Something over five years."

"You certainly look after the place."

"Well, it was in need of a bit of TLC when I took over. To tell you the truth, I don't think the previous owners, the Watermans —

nice people though they were — had much time for it once they'd decided to go. I couldn't afford to do it up for the first few years, but I can't expect people to return if they don't like what they see, can I?"

"You must have employed a small army of builders and decorators to do this place up."

"Just the one," she replied, surveying the breakfast room as if for the first time. "My boy William is quite a talent: bricky, chippy, plasterer, painter and decorator. There's not much he can't turn his hand to."

"Sounds like a useful fellow to know, your friend William."

"He is that, Cornelius," she said. Then a cloud drifted in front of her sun and Stella was absorbed by her maudlin for a moment. "Sorry? What did you say?"

Hacker shrugged.

"I'll leave you to your work then," she said.

He read the file while he ate: Chisholm had married late, Jean, not so much iron fist in velvet glove as po-faced jailer, and they had two girls, Kayla and Kaitlyn. Chisholm's financial status was assured as long as he held his position at Norfolk; he had no other income. He was a Canary, a Norwich City Football Club die-hard, with a passion for driven shoots and gun dogs — the details ran on and on. There was even a note Hacker had written in the margin: An eye for the women. He wasn't as pure as some, but then neither was he a front line player; that was except for that one time at the club in the West End when Chisholm had stepped way over the line.

Hacker recalled all the faces as if it were yesterday; the kid, Sherri, dulled, expressionless and senseless, so drunk she couldn't have known what Chisholm had in mind; the young copper, the horror on his face as he realised what was going on; and the huge bouncer who'd wanted to tear Brian Chisholm limb from limb.

He went back to the file, more awake now that the coffee was working through his system.

Both he and Chisholm had been new to their jobs when they first met. Beasely, who'd taken it upon himself to shepherd Hacker through his first couple of months at Marchman, had introduced them to each other on Hacker's first sales round.

"Mr Chisholm's predecessor was a right proper bloke," Beasely had said that time when they pulled up outside the offices of Norfolk Electrical. "Good bloke he was; our man. We did a shedload of business with him over the years; our first and biggest contract."

Beasely hesitated before getting out of the car, "Got moved on." Then he turned to Hacker with a sad and slightly serious frown and said, "Just got greedy, I suppose. This new bloke, Chisholm, don't have much gen on 'im, so we're playing this one a bit blind like."

There was, though, only ever going to be one way to play it.

So in they had gone and employed the old double-hander, the boss and his protégé, and their reception had fallen flat.

Chisholm, a good few inches shorter than Hacker and sporting a round, squashed face like that of a heavy dog run into a closed door, told them he would happily review their order if Marchman could review their prices.

In turn, Beasely, having dragged out the history of the long and mutually beneficial relationship between Marchman and Norfolk, rested his hand on Chisholm's shoulder and showed him the lie of the land in much the same way, Hacker guessed, as the Lord must have shown it to Moses.

But Chisholm wasn't Moses and neither was Beasley the Lord.

Too late, Beasley had realised he was using the wrong tactic and all too soon it became clear that Chisholm wanted to play a more sophisticated game. Beasely stuttered and stammered away in the face of the new man, and with each new line of attack he found himself penned further and further back in his own half.

They left without taking Chisholm to the extravagant lunch they'd set up; Beasley inconsolable, Hacker faintly amused. The only words Beasely had muttered on the long drive home were "er" and "um".

But while Beasely had been busy burying himself beneath layers of marzipan, some brief flash of recognition had passed between the two new boys.

The next day Hacker took it upon himself to phone Norfolk Engineering. He was put straight through.

"Mr Hacker? Brian Chisholm. Thank you for calling. I was hoping you would."

"Look, about Beasely-"

"That tosser," interrupted Chisholm, as though he'd just trodden on a nail. "Look, we both know my predecessor and Mr Beasely were as thick as thieves. It's part of why I've been taken on."

Hacker didn't know, though naturally he'd harboured a few suspicions. After all, Beasely was a remnant of the bung-in-boot brigade. He wasn't unique, though his breed was on the wane.

"Now you," Chisholm said, "you're different. I remember watching you play a couple of times at Carrow Road. If you're like your football, and in my experience watching a man play is like looking through a window to his soul, then we'll get along. You played hard, but you played straight and fair. That's how I play it. It won't always be easy, but you will get a level playing field – that I can promise you."

"I hear what you're saying, Mr Chisholm. I'll take it on board."

"Good. That's fine. If you can sharpen your pencil for me, something I can take upstairs to show the board we're moving in the right direction, then we'll get along fine."

Hacker heard the call as clear as if his centre forward had been standing next to him. If Chisholm wanted a couple of nicely judged through balls or the odd gift in front of goal, then Hacker was only too ready to deliver that style of game. He bypassed Beasely and went directly to pricing, lopped a couple of pence off here and there, added a couple where he could conceal them in order to compensate for the reductions, and submitted a new quote to Chisholm by the close of play the same day.

And that was all there was to it. Well, that and the understanding that Chisholm, as a card-carrying Canary, wouldn't mind the odd complementary ticket to Wembley.

"More coffee? Toast?" Stella Anworthy asked.

"No thank you, Stella. That was just the job." Hacker stood up, but was careful to keep the table between them. "Now, I really must be getting on. Busy day."

"Aren't they all, Cornelius? Aren't they all?" She stood her ground and waited for some broader appreciation of her hospitality.

He couldn't remember what he'd told her or exactly what they'd got up to after the second bottle of gin, so he said, "Yes, yes they are. And thank you for your very generous hospitality. Last night was certainly... fun."

It was the eye contact she was after. It was all she wanted from him; recognition, reassurance, affirmation – perhaps one, perhaps all three. She glowed like the embers of a fire kicked over.

Hacker returned as grateful a smile as he could muster.

"Well, Cornelius, good luck with your day. I expect I'll see you later."

"Yes, thank you." He hesitated and then said, "Yes, Stella, I'll see you later. Thank you, Stella."

17

Philip

So, having fought their way through the rush hour traffic, they dropped Harry and Hattie off at Hanger Holt and neither of the children looked back as they fell giggling into their grandmother's outstretched arms.

Philip drove up past Colchester and dipped around the south of Ipswich, preferring to take them to Norfolk by the coastal route. They weren't in any hurry and a casual peace settled over them, if not between them.

The perfect intimacy of their new love had lasted only until Fiona let slip their engagement to her best friend, India, after which the news spread faster than a royal indiscretion.

By midday the next day, Fiona had rung his office ten times to ask him for the party line should her mother ring to say she'd heard the news second-hand.

Naturally, he didn't have one. Quite naturally, he hadn't looked that far ahead.

Late one evening a couple of weeks before, in the tranquil moments following an excess of glorious love-making, Fiona had sat bolt upright in bed and wiped the seraphic smile off Philip's face by asking when he thought they ought to tell her mother.

It was the first time Fiona had mentioned her mother in the

bedroom and it was the first time she'd exposed the unpleasantness in their relationship.

Still riding the crest of betrothal and so still disregarding the complexities of joining another family, Philip had brushed her question away by reaching for her hand and forcing it playfully between his legs. "Never mind your mother," he said. "She'll never know what she's missing, if you don't tell her."

But, Fiona had pulled her hand away and swept her hair back off her face. Her hair was long and as soft as silk, like the skin of her heavy breasts, but unlike her breasts, her hair hung straight down. She usually kept it tied back with a clip both sides and just above her ears. She knew it was one of the things he liked about her, her hair, and so she committed a small fortune to it once a week.

"No, Phil. We have to talk about it sometime. We can't ignore it. It'll be a problem if we don't get it right. You know what she's like."

"Yes," he sighed, "I know what she's like, but I'm not sure she's anything like you are in all the most important places."

"Philip? Please?"

And that was the nearest they'd got to having a conversation about when they would tell her mother. In himself, he knew it was a mistake, not to talk about it, but he hadn't at that time got used to Fiona's habit of wanting to talk after sex.

So her mother did not phone the morning the news began to spread, and she did not phone when Fiona knew for certain that she knew because one of her mother's neighbours phoned to offer congratulations.

By three o'clock, Fiona was a nervous wreck and Philip could no longer ignore the jaunty tune she'd programmed as the ringtone on his mobile.

"Ring and tell her," he said.

"But don't you see, Phil. You're supposed to have asked Archie for my hand first. You're supposed to have done that before everyone else knew. Christ! She'll go nuts, Phil. She really will."

"Listen, darling, just ring and tell her your foghorn of a best mate couldn't keep her trap shut for two days and that we're both going up to Hanger Holt at the weekend to break it to her."

"But she'll know we weren't. You know how she likes to know in advance if we're going up. If we'd wanted to go up this weekend, I should've suggested it last weekend."

Philip took a deep breath and counted quickly to ten, "Angel, if I had thought for a minute that I should've planned the timing of my proposal by which day of the week it would suit your mother to find out, then I would have asked you on a Saturday, wouldn't I?"

"Philip?"

He understood very well that part of the problem lay in the fact that Fiona's father had passed away before he'd met her. But, after the many hours spent listening to Fiona talk about him, he understood that she had been the very perfectly-formed apple of his very round eye and that she would always remain so, even if he could no longer see her.

Bob Davy had been a successful scrap metal dealer and as went with the territory, there was a yard-full of rumours that some of his old business partners were less than savoury characters.

Old Man Davy, as he was known, drank, gambled, womanised, refused to wear a seatbelt and drove into a ditch off the A12. Those of their friends who knew Maureen took considerable delight in joking later that she'd driven him into an early grave. But the rather unpalatable truth of the matter was that the police turned up at the house very late one night and informed Maureen and Fiona that they'd found the Old Man's Jaguar upside down near the A414 turn off. The Old Man was found lying half out of the car with fatal head injuries. They'd also found a young lady passed out on the backseat; a young lady so drunk that although she recalled being up the West End, she couldn't for the life of her understand how she'd ended up in deepest Essex, and with a complete and very dead stranger. The policeman was "sorry for their loss", he said as he handed over a carrier bag full of casino chips he'd found in the glove compartment.

Maureen Davy, or so the story went, took the bag of chips, put one in the copper's hand and shut the door.

And at the Old Man's passing, Maureen Davy found herself elevated from charwoman of Bob Davy's substantial bungalow to chairwoman and chief executive of Bob Davy's substantial overdraft. From that moment on, everyone who had until then worked for Bob, found they were working for their Matriarch — or Archie, as she became known. She'd never forgiven her parents for naming her Maureen and so had not spoken to them since she'd left home at the tender age of fifteen.

The Old Man and Archie! Both tough as nails! Well, except for the fact that the Old Man had sold off the nails and gambled away the proceeds.

Fiona said she never saw Archie shed a tear. Therefore, it was no surprise to Philip that Fiona had lived almost all her life in fear of her mother.

18

Stella

Stella finished the dishes and, once she'd heard Cornelius Hacker go out, made up his room. She checked the remaining three rooms, dusting and adjusting as she went. Finally, she ran through the register to see how much time she would have to herself before her other booking arrived; a couple by the name of Scott the woman had said, but they wouldn't be along until much later.

She was standing by the counter in reception, gathering herself, when the phone rang.

"The Reach, Stella Anworthy speaking."

She could hear people talking in the background; the muffled echo of an announcer.

"The Reach?" a woman asked. "On the front, at Strand-next-the-Sea?" She sounded nervous, as though she'd phoned a vet to find out if her dog was still alive.

"Yes. The Reach. Can I help you?"

"Please. Oh, yes please. Do you have any rooms available, tonight, I mean?"

"One second, let me see." She counted to ten, "Yes, I have a room, for tonight. Would you like-"

"Is the one on the left at the top of the stairs free?"

"Hang on, dear." She counted to five, "Yes. Would you-"

"No, that's alright. I'm sure it'll be fine. I'm coming up on the train. I'll be with you this afternoon. Thank you. Oh, my name is Poulter, Mrs Poulter. Goodbye."

Stella fished her address book out from beneath the counter and picked up the phone again.

"The Strand," a creaky voiced woman answered.

"Betty? Stella, at The Reach. How are you, dear?"

"Oh, not too bad," Betty replied. "Be nice if the rain stopped. Mind you, be nice if a lot of things weren't the way they were. How are things with you?"

"Oh, so-so. Got a couple of bookings, so I can't complain." It was all they had in common, bookings; that and the fact that they were two women running guesthouses in Strand. "Look, I wondered if you could spare me a minute. If you're not busy, that is."

Betty didn't respond immediately, clearly she was busy doing something, "Go on. What can I do you for?"

"No, I meant I wonder if I could pop round? Quick cup of tea?"

The unmistakeable clang and clatter of thin metal sounded down the phone. "No, I've not got much on, Stella. Oh, hold yew yard. It's Friday, isn't it, I'm off to get my hair fixed at eleven. Before or after?"

Stella examined her hair in the mirror; her roots needed seeing to, "Sooner would be better, if that's alright, only I'm not sure what time my bookings will turn up."

Betty sighed, "Oh, listen to you. Here we all are wondering when the next copper coin will turn up and there you are all worried about being in when it does?" She chuckled and then said, "Not a problem, dear. Pop round when you're ready. I'll put the kettle on."

Stella took off her apron and threw on her overcoat.

The Strand was the longest serving and most established of the Bed and Breakfasts along the front, and Betty Laws liked to think of herself in similar terms. She brooked no opposition when it came to proposing and settling motions at the Association meetings and was always quick to assert her self-appointed, moral authority.

She must have been waiting by her front door, as it opened as soon as Stella rang the bell.

"Come in, dear, you must be soaked," Betty said, examining her carpet. "Foul out there today. Here, let me have your coat."

Whereas The Reach was neat and tidy, the Strand was quite the reverse. Copies of yesteryear Vogue and Country Life lay untidily on the hall table, and sepia photographs of fishermen hauling nets littered the shelves. Her silverware, bright and shiny, lay strewn about the kitchen table

Betty hauled an antique Henry Loveridge copper kettle from the stove and filled a Granny Ann teapot on the sideboard.

"You like it strong, as I remember, one sugar."

"Thank you, Betty," Stella inched between the tarnished muslin cloths and tins of silver polish.

"Let's move some of this mess out of your way. Come on, you sit there," she pointed to an elm spindle, arch-back chair by the AGA.

Once the tea had enjoyed sufficient time to brew, Betty poured a dollop of milk into Meissen styled teacups and added the dark brew.

"Let's not stand on ceremony, shall we?" Betty said. "What can I do for you?"

The tea steamed before her. "Well," Stella began, "I was wondering… Well, I think it's about time I had a bit of a break; y'know, a few days away. I've got a bit of business to sort out and I was wondering if I could ask you, if it's not too much trouble of course, to keep an eye on The Reach while I'm gone. Wouldn't be too much, just pop in a couple of times to turn the odd light on and pick up the post."

Betty smiled, "How long would you be thinking?"

"Oh, not long, a week perhaps. As I said, I've got a bit of family business to sort out and I could do with a change of scenery. It's been a long season."

"I know what you mean," Betty sighed. "All work and no play makes dull beings of us all, eh?"

Stella held her peace and looked suitably glum.

"No trouble, I hope?" asked Betty.

Stella bridled, reluctant to elaborate further.

"I don't mean to pry," Betty said. "If it's private, you must say so. I won't ask."

"Well," Stella said, "it's my sister, you see. I think I've mentioned before that we don't see eye to eye and since my mum died, we've not really spoken. But before too much water passes under the bridge, I'd like to see her and do my best to put things right. Neither of us are getting any younger."

Betty Laws had no family she'd ever mentioned. Her husband had run off with a dental hygienist from Norwich and she regularly admonished Stella for not keeping in touch with her sister. A brief concern creased her brow, "Alright, is she?"

"Not sure really, I've received some mixed signals of late. Think it might be best if I went and satisfied myself she's straight. Can't get the full story from a phone call."

It was only a half truth really. The fact was she hadn't had any contact with her sister for over a year. But then, a couple of weeks before, her sister Sharon had written her that an official-looking man had come to the door asking after her.

"You let me know when," Betty said as she examined a silver teapot, "mustn't lose touch with your near ones."

As Stella got up to leave, she asked, "Seen much of Will lately, Betty?"

Betty Laws shot her a steely glance and followed it up with a lengthy, pondering pause, then, "No. Why'd you ask?"

"Oh, no reason really. I tried his number yesterday; didn't ring through. I wondered if he was away. It's just that someone down the front thought they'd seen him arguing with a bloke in the Old Tern and I just wanted to know if he was okay."

Betty stared at Stella deadpan and then said, "Take a fool to pick a fight with Will. Have you never seen him when he's angry?"

"No," Stella lied, "never. Why, is there a side to him?"

"Side? You know Mrs Hutchinson, Isla, down at the Coastal? Well, she had her car stolen. Wasn't much of a thing! A Peugeot," she said, pronouncing the name pew-gee-oh. "Anyway, it turned out your Will had been doing some work at The Coastal; fire doors, I think, 'cos you're supposed to have 'em at the stairs now. And Brian Hutchinson wasn't happy with the work your Will had done; something to do with the doors not having the correct intumescent seals. Yes, that was the word he used: intumescent." She grimaced as though she'd heard a dirty word.

"What on earth's an intumescent seal when it's at home?" Stella asked.

"Strange sounding thing; intumescent," she repeated slowly. "Apparently it's a seal that swells when it gets hot; stops smoke getting through between the door and the frame. Oh, and the doors weren't heavy enough, they didn't have cold seals or something and they weren't certificated." She paused and whispered, "And apparently after a few too many down the Tern one evening, Brian Hutchinson said he wouldn't have your Will working there again and he wouldn't be surprised if it was him who'd nicked the keys to Isla's car.

"Well, when your Will heard, he flew right off the handle, went straight round The Coastal and flattened Brian Hutchinson as if he were a child. And he's no shrinking violet that Brian; used to be in the army, he did. Apparently your Will threatened to burn the place down, which was a bit odd when you consider he'd just put the fire doors in. Frightened Isla Hutchinson something terrible! They tried to keep the whole episode under wraps, y'know, but sooner or later it gets out down the front."

"Which bit, I mean, got out down the front? The bit that Will had pinched the keys or the fact that Will gave Brian Hutchinson a pasting?"

"Both, I suppose. Wouldn't do for his business if people thought Will was up to no good. And that Brian Hutchinson still hasn't got over the affront to his masculinity, poor man."

"Oh," Stella said, "I see. I didn't know Will could be like that."

"What? Didn't know? And you being all sweet on him?"

"Oh, come off it, Betty. What would a young man like him see in an old trout like me? Even The Coastal looks better on a foggy night than I do."

The proprietor of The Strand grinned; a look that suggested all of them down the front reckoned she and Will were at it like rabbits whenever he popped round to change a light bulb.

"Betty Laws!" And yet Stella wasn't completely unhappy with her neighbour's assumption; she could live with being perceived as possessing a perfectly natural and healthy libido, even if Margetz had been the only man to cater to it in the last couple of years. And besides, a generous helping of the green-eyed monster wouldn't damage her standing with the other B&B Association members.

"Now then, I must be off. Wouldn't want to waste any more of your valuable time." She glanced at her watch, "Goodness, aren't you due at the salon in a minute?"

As Stella hurried through the rain back to The Reach, she pored over what she'd learned from her visit to the Strand: Firstly, that Betty Laws and others down the front didn't know Will was gay, and secondly, and perhaps more importantly, that her Will was given to violence.

19

Philip

The A12 skirted Woodford and wound its way through a succession of long curves up past Ufford. They were easy with their silence, even if it did seem to conjure a slight mist between them.

Philip remembered that when, eventually, Fiona took his advice and phoned her mother, Archie had refused to take her call.

"What am I going to do, Phil?" Fiona asked later when they met at a bar on the Southbank.

"Fi, there's no point in getting in a state over it. We'll think of something. Maybe she was busy."

"I've tried her three times. And I've left a message for her to call me back, but she hasn't. What the bloody hell am I going to do?" Her eyes, so normally bright and brown, had disappeared beneath her furrowed brow, "What? What are you looking at me like that for?"

"You know," he said, "some girls get more beautiful when they're angry, but you get more beautiful when you've got something on your mind; something like a puzzle you're trying to solve. It's like you're concentrating on a crossword which you know you can't finish, but you hope some knight in shining armour is going to materialise out of the paper and give you the answers to three down and five across." He paused, "You should concentrate more often. It suits you."

"Oh, for Christ's sake, Phil, you're hopeless. Besides, there aren't any woods along the Embankment these days; they've chopped them all down to stick heads on up at Tower Hill, which is where mine will end up if we don't come up with a proper plan."

Even though it was a Thursday, the place was rammed with the after-work crowd.

"How about telling her the truth? Tell her you were so excited you couldn't keep from telling what's-her-name and that you are furious with her for not keeping her trap shut."

"I can't, Phil," she said, between two hurried sips of wine. "You know how she doesn't like India. It'll be too much of an opportunity for her to go through the old I-told-you-that girl-was-no-good routine."

"Not much of a price to pay. How was work?"

"Fine."

"Oh, that good?"

"Well," she replied, sitting back, "I managed to cock up a Crème Anglaise. Couldn't bloody-well think straight, could I?"

It was why she was in a flap. It wasn't just the thought of confronting Archie; she'd had a hard time at work.

"No, can't blame India, I just can't."

"Then blame me," he said.

"Oh, no," Fiona shook her head and wagged a finger at him. "You've only met her three times."

"Only three?" he paused. "Seems like more."

"No, you've only met her three times. You know you have. Christ, I know people who've known her for twenty years or more and they can tell you exactly how many times they've been in her company." Fiona emptied her glass of wine, set it down and rested her chin on the palm of her hand as she leant forwards to stare at him. "I can't have you getting on the wrong side of her, you know. It's too unbearable to think how bloody complicated that would make it all."

Philip wondered how many more glasses it would take for her to stop worrying about her mother and start listening to him, "More Pinot Grigio?"

"Mm, right now I could drown in the bloody stuff."

As he queued at the bar, Philip remembered the first time he met Fiona's mother.

Fiona had told him it was her idea, but Philip got the impression that Fiona had been dancing to her mother's tune. It hadn't been a case of 'let's go', as much as 'we're going'.

He'd imagined some decrepit clapboard shanty in the marshy wastes of Essex. In some respects, he was right; in others, completely wrong.

The winter evening promised little but nuisance and, after two hours of nose-to-tail up the A12, they turned off at Hatfield Peverel and took the road to Heybridge. Once through Goldhanger, Fiona directed him down a narrow lane with high hedges either side.

He was surprised by the arc of ornamental gates that appeared out of the gloom.

Philip hurried over to the intercom.

A fine drizzle hung in the air and the moisture lay on his neck like a clammy hand.

Through the tall, black iron gates set with finials and urns and inlaid with copper styled monograms, he saw a long, low building fronted by a portico supported on Greek columns. Hanger Holt looked equal parts pool pavilion and southern cotton plantation; a miniature Tara-by-Marsh cast away like an embarrassing birth into the reedy meadows of the Thames estuary.

After a minute or so, the gates swung back.

He followed the gravel drive up around the lawn and parked beneath the lighted portico. A pin-clean white Range Rover, a black BMW saloon and a 4x4 so caked in mud it was impossible to identify its make, stood just beyond. No one appeared, so he looked at Fiona for a lead as he opened the car door.

"You're not nervous?" she asked.

"Should I be?"

Fiona looked away and studied her nails, "No. Well, yes, maybe. Oh, not really, I suppose. It's just that I'm always bloody nervous when I come here and I don't understand why. If anyone should be nervous, it should be you and you're not."

Philip leant towards her and kissed her very slowly, his lips full and soft. He didn't hurry; he wanted her to know she had his support.

Then he jerked back as he became aware of a figure standing by his door.

"Introductions first, I think, Mr Scott," the woman said.

Philip winced and got out of the car.

"Philip Scott, Mrs Davy. How do you do?" he asked, holding out his hand.

She took it with some enthusiasm and smiled; a very warm and generous smile. "Very well, thank you. Pleased to meet you, Philip. You must call me Archie, everyone does. Hereabouts they think I'm some kind of new-age Boadicea." She spoke very plain English with just a trace of London; her elocution was precise, though she dropped off the end of the harder consonants.

"Fi, darling," she said, turning. Mother and daughter bent towards each other and made a play of kissing on both cheeks like foreign dignitaries. "How are you, dear?" she asked, standing back and examining her daughter.

"I'm fine, thank you, Mother. Sorry we're late. Traffic was appalling."

"Well, I said you should've come up in the morning, didn't I?"

"Yes, Mother. But, like I said, we have a dinner to get back for tomorrow evening."

Philip wracked his brain; he didn't remember a dinner engagement.

Fiona's mother was studying him, "No matter, you're here now. Shall we?" She motioned towards the front door.

The beige hall ceiling curved up to a low vault; shoes came off at the door and were paired in individual wicker baskets. Muted voices came from beyond double doors and a small, white-haired dog foraged through the cream, deep-pile carpet. It sniffed noisily at Philip's feet.

"Please don't give Camilla a second thought," Archie said. "She's been in the queerest mood all day. Ignore her and she'll return the compliment. Fi, you're in your old room, and Philip, you're down this way."

Fiona scowled, indicated the double doors and mouthed the word 'people'.

Philip shrugged.

He guessed Fiona's mother was late forties, maybe good for fifty; slim and elegant.

When Archie showed him into his very spacious but Spartan bedroom, she said, "I do appreciate you coming, Philip. I so rarely get the chance to see Fi. It would appear she casts her vote in favour of the city these days; used to be such a country bumpkin in her youth. I am sure you'd like to wash your hands. The bathroom is through there." Her nail extensions shone white. "A cocktail before dinner? What would you like? We're in the drawing room when you're ready."

He'd arrived wearing cords and a sweater, but after the rather formal preamble he decided a jacket and tie was required.

Fi had decided the same.

When he met her in the hall, she was wearing a bright floral shirt and blue skirt he had not seen before; a bit high street department store for her — a look he had not pictured.

"Nice tie," she whispered, but couldn't resist adjusting it.

"Remind me where we are going tomorrow evening?"

"She's bloody ambushed us," Fiona said. "She didn't tell me this lot were going to be here."

The door opened and Archie stood back without looking at them.

"Jenny and Tom's new baby," Fiona muttered under her breath, and then sneezed loudly, "Bloody dog!"

Besides Archie, there were three others in the drawing room.

Fiona's mother introduced them, "This is Jimmy Carson, an old family friend," a short wiry man in his fifties, grey suit, slim tie, thin hair, thick glasses, "and this is Harold Barter," a heavyset, ruddy-cheeked, Bunter, "and Grace, Mrs Barter," his rather bovine wife.

They quizzed Fiona about her employers, evidently they knew one of them, and her flat, which, they'd heard, she kept spic and span. And wasn't Clapham such a lovely, villagey atmosphere these days?

Dinner was taken at a long table, finished in a high-gloss cream, and the room was decorated in a brushed blushing pink. The first course consisted of a watery, watercress soup and the second, a pigeon casserole. The white wine was dreadfully sweet and the red, unpleasantly tannic; both were served in heavy crystal glasses with long stems and tiny bowls.

Mercifully, Philip had only to smile and agree; little else was asked of him. But then, Jimmy Carson rounded on him, "What do you do, Philip?"

"I'm a quantity surveyor," he replied, trying hard to refrain from disliking the man for asking such a dull question. "I work for a commercial property company in the city."

"It's a very large company, worldwide," Fiona cut in.

Carson sat up straight, "Not by any chance where Fiona works?"

"No," replied Philip. "Though that was where we met."

"That so," Carson said, pushing his glasses back up his nose. He rather too openly studied Philip, who took his attention as an invitation to expand.

"I graduated from Kingston University with a degree in Quantity Surveying."

"Is that one of those polytechnics that awful man Blair turned into a university?" Barter interrupted.

Archie and Harold Barter exchanged disapproving glances.

"I guess it would be," Philip replied. "In the summer holidays between my second and final year, I managed to get a work placement with the company where Fi works. As part of the placement I was treated to a lunch in the director's dining room. That was where we met."

And the very first time he'd spoken to her, she'd been upset at making a pig's ear of a Hollandaise. She'd been angry and clearly wasn't afraid to show her feelings; something which, after being brought up in a house where concealing one's emotions was considered something of a virtue, appealed to him.

Later in their relationship, Philip realised that Fiona's propensity to wear her heart on her sleeve was not fostered out of any desire to be free with her feelings; rather it was that she was young and naïve and could see no good reason to conceal them. But, too late, Philip figured out that whereas he, since leaving home, had managed to cure himself of his own emotional constipation, now, he spent much of his time stemming the flow of hers.

"Actually, Philip's being kind now," said Fiona, coming to his rescue, "just like he was then. Goodness, the directors were such a stuffy bunch. It was my first week and I was really nervous. I think if Philip hadn't been such a perfect gentleman that day, I'd have thrown in the washing-up towel."

Mrs Barter beamed.

Archie bridled at her daughter's all too apparent display of affection.

Carson pushed his glasses back up the bridge of his nose and looked nonplussed at Philip, "Lucrative line of work, quantity surveying."

"It can be, but I'm only a fairly small fry at the moment."

"Opportunities for advancement are there, in your firm?"

"There seems to be a bit of a queue for that ladder. But one never knows. Early days yet; I've only been there a couple of years."

"Well, son, if you ever get stuck on one of the lower rungs for too long," Carson said, "let me know. I know one or two people in the property game." Then he said, "In fact, might even know one or two in your firm."

"Thank you, Mr Carson. I, er… That's very kind of you."

"Mr Carson introduced Fiona to the company where she works, didn't you, Jimmy?" said Archie. She smiled at Carson, but not for long. She turned back to Philip, "I'm sure Mr Scott intends to race up the tree trunk of success so that he can keep Fiona in the higher branches where she belongs, don't you, Mr Scott?"

"Mother?"

"Well," Mrs Barter chipped in, "if you start at the bottom, the only way is up, that's what I say."

Harold Barter smiled a warm, but gently patronising smile at his wife. He patted her on the shoulder the same way he patted the fluffy mongrel Camilla, "That's not strictly true, dear. We've all known a few who've started at the bottom and descended from there; especially round this neck of the woods."

"Thank you, Harold," said Archie. "Wouldn't want Fiona's new beau getting the wrong idea about where or how she was brung up, now do we?"

"Mother?" Fiona repeated, but louder this time.

"Well," continued Archie, intent on making her point, "I don't think Harold was referring to your father directly."

"Oh no," said Harold Barter, almost rising off his chair, "I didn't mean the Old Man." Unfortunately, his look of horror gave him away; the Old Man was exactly who he'd meant.

Fiona's wide eyes welled. She threw her napkin down and stormed out.

"Please don't mind Fiona, Philip," Archie said. "She always gets this way when someone mentions her father. Five years!" she scoffed as though the milkman was on holiday. "You'd think she'd be over him by now."

Fiona reappeared as they finished desert, a trifle drowned in Madeira. Her make-up couldn't hide the fact that she'd been crying, but there was now a steely resolution to her expression. Her mother resisted the temptation to goad her further.

The rest of the evening lumbered like a pregnant cow and Fiona rather too often looked over at him to see how he was faring.

He smiled back. There was little to be gained by his letting her know just how ordinary he felt.

Mrs Barter stood on tiptoe to kiss him goodbye. The fluff-ball of a dog yapped.

"Yes. Well. Isn't that nice," said Archie, without directing her comment either way.

Harold Barter said, "Good luck," as though Philip might need a generous dose of it to get through the night, and then hugged Fiona for rather too long.

Jimmy Carson stared at him, offered him a limp hand and said, "Michael Fairbank one of your main board directors?"

"I believe he is."

"Pass on my best," Carson said, even though his best did not stretch to a smile.

As she closed the doors behind them, Archie said, "Knows everybody that Jimmy does. Don't know how he does it."

"Can I help with the clearing up?" Philip asked.

Archie turned and frowned as though the dog had left a present on the carpet, "No thank you, Philip. Maria will see to that in the morning." And that was followed by an awkward silence during which mother and daughter looked at each other as though each was waiting for the other to suggest what course the rest of the evening should take.

Philip was not about to offer. He considered saying how much he'd enjoyed the dinner, but somehow couldn't bring himself to. He wondered whether he'd ever possess the patience to stomach another evening like it. And he wondered too whether Archie Davy had planned the whole charade in order to disillusion him, in which case he wouldn't give Fiona's mother the benefit of thinking she'd succeeded.

Archie held out her hand, "I expect you two must be tired what with a hard week's work and the drive up tonight. So, I'll see you both in the morning."

Her hand was cool to touch and slender to hold. Philip set his hand so that he did not squeeze hers, "Goodnight, Mrs Davy, charming company. Thank you."

"Goodnight, Philip." She turned to Fiona and was about to speak but-

"Goodnight, Mother," said Fiona, and she about-faced and marched off down the corridor in the opposite direction.

As Archie turned back towards Philip, he too turned and walked away. The dog yapped at him as though warning him not to leave his room during the night.

20

Phoebe

Phoebe forced herself to relax her mouth so that her lips would part just enough for her to breathe in. She didn't really want the stale air of the train compartment anywhere near her lungs, but she had to breathe and her nose was blocked solid.

The carriage was neither clean nor warm, and the bench seat was hard and uncompromising and chilled her bones. But, at least the train moved. It was an inviolable capsule; a vessel in motion through the fixed land beyond the windows; a secure and strangely comforting organ of delivery.

She stared through her own reflection at the fields and hedgerows flashing by; a flat, hue-less land beneath an even flatter, pallid sky.

Tears of rain herded by an intolerant wind began to streak across the window and her face shone bright against their course. As she sat back, her image growing smaller in the glass, she pictured herself as a child peacefully asleep in a pushchair, gentle hands guiding her smoothly down a broad street; the sun flickering through the leaves, projecting its white light onto her face. She rubbed her eyes with tiny clenched fists and leant forwards in her seat, turning round to look at her guardian. But whoever it was the young Phoebe expected to see, whoever it was she wanted to see, wasn't there. She never was and never would be. A couple of months shy of her twenty-first birthday, Phoebe felt it would always be that way.

For Phoebe, it was a common flashback – in fact, so common that the terror and the melancholy it provoked were now very much reduced in their concentration.

Through her pre-teenage years, the same short film had occasionally disturbed, woken and frightened her during the night. But later, through her early teens, the film trailer of her past had grown in length, clarity and frequency, and had eventually trespassed into her waking moments.

Phoebe confided in a friend at school, not unnaturally inquisitive as to whether her contemporaries suffered similar disturbing visions.

At first, the girl had lent Phoebe a sympathetic ear and had reassured her that all of them put up with such unwelcome imaginings. They were part of what her mother had described to her as the change.

Then, a few days later, and a day Phoebe remembered as starting out so bright and so full of promise, her friend had given Phoebe's secret away to the whole class and they had laughed and pointed and sniggered at her. And as they attended Elmwood Secondary School, some clever bitch piped up that Phoebe sounded like something out of *Nightmare on Elm Street*; the film series being popular with the fright-night set at the time. And that was how she became to be nicknamed Freddie, after the villain of the piece.

The boys at school couldn't resist the wicked pleasure of asking her out to the cinema and then, right in the middle of whatever it was they weren't watching, asking her why she was known by a boy's name? And was it true she sharpened her fingernails? It was as harsh a lesson in the abuse of trust as Phoebe would ever need.

By the age of fourteen, she'd learnt to suppress her occasional urges to communicate with her classmates and had stopped accepting invitations from the boys to the back row of the local flea-pit. Instead, she devoted her free time to reason and rationale; to working out why it was that this short film of her as a child in a pushchair should bother her so, and why it was that the world was such a mean and prejudicial place.

And that had been pretty much the end and the beginning of so much of it. That period she liked to think of as her Renaissance, in as much as it proclaimed the death of the infant that was her social life and heralded the birth of the adolescent who would succeed where her wheedling contemporaries failed.

It all seemed so simple now.

The train rattled and jolted across a set of points. The lady sitting opposite lurched and grabbed hold of her seat.

Phoebe rocked with the motion. It was all she wanted to do; to be rocked and to be carried along.

There were only the two of them in the carriage. And as is so often the way, they'd ended up sitting opposite each other.

The lady, a rather crisply dressed fifty or just possibly sixty-something, was lost in her very own private daydream. She had a slightly birdlike face with high cheekbones and a narrow forehead, and the lift of her straight and elegant nose suggested that she too was offended by the odour in the carriage.

She looked, to Phoebe, as though she was searching for something in her thoughts; her eyes had a glazed, distant look to them. But she did not look sad; she just looked thoughtful, in her own world and deeply contemplative of it.

Phoebe understood the woman's look. It was the motion, the rhythm, the passage without effort, the satisfaction of travel without the disappointment of arrival. It brought on a kind of curative dislocation, and that was what Phoebe liked most of all — the dislocation.

The doors at the front of the carriage opened and a chubby ticket inspector appeared. "Tickets, please," he called as though the carriage was full of commuters.

Phoebe held up her ticket.

He squinted at it. "That's your return!" he said as though she ought to have known better.

Phoebe held up the other half.

"Uh-huh. That's it. Thank you." He wheezed and shuffled over to the lady opposite.

"Staying in Strand-next-the-Sea long?" Phoebe heard him say.

"Sorry?" the woman asked.

"Return," he said, bending forward examining her ticket. "It would have been cheaper to buy a return; only a couple more quid for a return, even an open one. I can change your single if you like."

"I... um... well..." she said.

But, after an awkward silence, the ticket collector merely said, "That's fine. Thank you. Be in Strand in about five minutes."

Phoebe coughed and the lady looked up and frowned.

The run into her GCSEs became something of a formality. Freddie, as she had become known, developed an ordered and inquiring mind. Her parents, her 'rents, used to whisper to each other and their friends about how amazing it was that Phoebe kept such a tidy bedroom, kept her books in such an ordered progression and always folded her clothes just so.

And in that way 'rents have of believing that praise for their child is therefore praise for themselves, a credit recognition by association as Phoebe liked to think of it, they began to walk heads high into parent-teacher meetings. And while other children sobbed as their teachers dragged out tales of woe, Phoebe's 'rents just smiled and stifled their pride.

Phoebe found much of the procedure amusing, although she knew better than to let anyone notice. Her 'rents weren't exactly cool, but neither were they uncool; they both held down full-time jobs.

Her father worked at a local car plant: calibration or metrology or something to do with instruments. She realised, watching the grey world flashing by, that she'd never sat him down and asked him exactly what it was he did. He was a gentle man who shied away from confrontation and always seemed a little put upon, as though permanently in need of a long weekend.

Her mum was the warmest, softest, most patient and most loving mum any daughter could hope for; a diabetic – the uncomplaining, never-mentions-it diabetic; and, what with her uncontrollably frizzy brown hair, not what her contemporaries would describe as beautiful in the conventional sense. Phoebe couldn't have asked for a better mum and that was saying something when looking at some of her classmate's mums.

Her younger brother Billy was just plain cute; eyes bright like a shiny button and mind sharp as the razor he hoped he would soon need.

One or two of the teachers mentioned that Phoebe could be a shade introverted, a little self-possessed, and that it would be better for her if she joined in the discussions a little more. She even saw the word 'precocious' mouthed at one meeting. That was Mrs Sharp, the biology teacher, who soon enough changed her tune when the time came for Phoebe to drop a subject.

But Phoebe wasn't self-possessed and neither was she precocious; unless of course it was precocious to know your own mind, which she knew perfectly well she did. She may have matured mentally a little earlier than most, but in that case hadn't every pupil at every college in Cambridge? Hadn't she read that there was a much greater frequency of autism amongst high achievers? Or was it simply that she possessed a greater mental capacity than most of the other flakes at Elmwood?

She read avidly *The Diary of Anne Frank* and Primo Levi's *If This is a Man*, and read and reread the chapter 'The Drowned and the Saved' in which Levi described those who developed methods by which they could yield themselves extra rations of bread; people labelled esteemed and respected. She read Keneally's *Schindler's List* and Styron's *Sophie's*

Choice, and was mesmerised by the influence those more powerful exercised over those less fortunate. Phoebe learnt that it wasn't enough merely to be strong or individually resolute; she learned that it was up to her to make the difference in her life as to whether she prevailed or surrendered like Levi's Muselmann.

When she joined in the throng to collect her GCSE results, Phoebe did not open her envelope until she was back at home in the safety of her bedroom. She was certain that, in the face of her classmate's disappointments, she would not be able to suppress her joy if her results were as good as she hoped.

They weren't. They were far, far better.

The train creaked and wobbled as it slowed. The brakes screeched and grated like fingernails on a blackboard.

Phoebe looked up at the woman opposite who now sat bolt upright, staring out the window. She noticed a shadow about the woman's face.

The woman grew slowly aware that she was being watched and looked concerned that Phoebe might have pierced the veil of her thoughts. She turned to look back at Phoebe, but did not look at her directly; rather, she looked at the space between them.

The train came to a halt and in the silence before the doors slid open, the lady smiled and said softly, "You're so lucky."

"I am?" Phoebe replied.

And somehow Phoebe's response hauled the woman from her trance. Her eyes slowly regained their focus and fixed properly on Phoebe, seeing her as if for the first time.

"Oh, I'm sorry," she said.

"For what?"

"Oh, for staring like that. I was dreaming."

"Yes," Phoebe said, "so was I."

21

Hacker

Hacker stopped at a fuel station, ran his Ford through the car wash, and vacuumed out the inside; taking care to check the ashtray was empty. It wasn't an effort to him; it was match preparation.

Though the entrance was neatly manicured, the Airfield Trading Estate hardly drew the eye. But in keeping with so many other redundant airfields, Strand was home to a modest, modern industrial estate and a Home Park. Three large Romney huts sat back beyond the old runway and, but for the doors in the centre, resembled a row of rusty, corrugated half-barrels.

Beyond the huts, and concealed by them, stood the more modern industrial estate that was home to Norfolk Electrical; four two-storey offices and manufacturing units set in symmetrical squares, postage stamp-sized lawns out front and car parking down the side.

The girl at reception looked a little sideways at him.

"Erin. Good to see you."

"Mr Hacker?" She quickly checked her screen below the counter, "How nice to see you. Um, do you have an appointment?"

"Of course."

She glanced back down at her screen again, "Long way to come without an appointment, Mr Hacker." Erin frowned again, "I haven't got anything about an appointment down here."

"I'm sure you wouldn't," he replied, confidently. "Brian said if I popped in around ten-thirty he'd spare me a few minutes."

Erin's brow furrowed in concentration once more. She snapped the end of her pen a couple of times, picked up her phone and tapped out an extension. After a moment's silence, she replaced the receiver and smiled a polite but flat smile up at him, "Just let me go and see. I'm not sure Mr Chisholm's in this morning." She left the counter and waddled off down the corridor.

Hacker had spotted the Blue BMW with the yellow NEVER MIND THE DANGER bumper sticker in the car park. He'd even slipped over to check it was parked in the bay designated Procurement Manager.

Erin's heels clipped as she strode towards him, "I'm sorry, Mr Hacker, Mr Chisholm isn't here."

He moved to his left just enough to make it difficult for her to get back behind her counter. "That's strange, seeing as he said he'd be and even more strange considering his car's out front."

"Gone out with the MD, I believe. Now, would you excuse me?"

Hacker stepped back to his right and sighed as though beaten, "Must have been the two of them in that black Mercedes I passed in the lane, eh — the one with the fancy private number."

"Yes, that would be the one."

"Now Erin," he said, "let's be sure about this. Brian Chisholm has gone out with the big man in the big man's black Mercedes." He paused for effect and Erin began to look nervous. "Just like the one that's parked in the big man's parking space. Is that right?"

"Oh? Perhaps they went out in someone else's car and I didn't see them leave." And, as the relief of her get-out came to her, she reached to retrieve the sign-in register from the counter.

Hacker had his arm on it and wasn't about to give it up. "Look, Erin, I'll just wait here until Brian's got a couple of minutes free, shall I? Please do me the kindness of letting him know I'll wait. And please be sure to tell him, very respectfully, that I've got all day."

"Cornelius," said a voice from behind him.

There was only one bloke he allowed to call him Cornelius, "Brian, how are you?"

"Thank you, Erin," Chisholm said. "Cornelius?" He ushered Hacker smartly down the corridor and into his office, "Nice one!"

"Sorry?"

"The Citizen!" Chisholm said. "And there I was thinking the club wanted to know what I thought of the season so far."

Hacker, using the name of a reporter from *The Citizen*, the Norwich City Football Club fanzine, had phoned up the day before to inquire as to whether Chisholm might be in.

"I'm sure the club would have been grateful for your input, Brian." Hacker laid claim to the only other available seat in the office, but pulled it forward so that he sat within arm's reach of his quarry.

Brian Chisholm grimaced, smiled, and raised his eyes to the ceiling, "Suppose I should've known really."

"Nice tidy desk, Brian. New secretary?"

"No, no new secretary," he replied, the grin falling from his face like ice cream from a cornet. "In fact, no secretary at all these days. I have to share one with my sales director. A paperless office, that's how they want it run now. Everything starts and ends here." He opened the centre drawer of his desk and pulled out a silver-sided laptop, "I can't so much as blow my nose without a bloody lecture from the cleaner as to how I should dispose of the tissue." Chisholm opened his laptop and drummed his fingers, "I've even had to go on bloody office-system-sharing so I don't abuse any protocols or upset the gentile sensitivities of some faceless nerd in Accounts Overdue."

"Computers," Hacker sneered in agreement, "rather like women, eh? Can't live with 'em, can't live with 'em."

Chisholm laughed, not much perhaps, but he laughed all the same.

"Talking of women," Hacker continued quickly, "which we weren't. How're Jean and the girls? The older one, Kayla, she must be finishing school this year? How's she doing?"

"One more year. She's doing okay; not exactly given to the disciplines of academia, but she's doing okay."

"Kaitlyn?"

"Fine, thank you. Mustn't grumble. Look Cornelius-"

"No, you're quite right. You mustn't grumble. Nobody'd pay any bloody attention if you did. You're a lucky man, Brian. Mind you, it's not all luck is it. With parents like you and Jean, at least the girls have got the best possible start in life. Can't do much better than you two for parents. Doesn't your Kaitlyn play hockey?"

"Yes, she does. County runners-up this year. Got a game against the City Girls tomorrow – they're the champions. Means I have to miss out on my day's shoot, but never mind, eh? How's... er...?"

"Geraldine? Oh, you know, okay I suppose. Like I said, Brian, can't live with 'em." He studied the Outsourcing Manager; his side-combed hair a little thinner, his neck a little thicker and his cheeks a little fuller and ruddier and slacker. "Jean still running the PTA at the girl's school, is she?"

"Sadly!"

"They do that, don't they," Hacker said. "One minute they can't do enough for you and," he snapped his fingers, but softly so as not to break the spell, "the next, they don't have the time, and you're the one picking the kids up from school, cooking them dinner, doing their homework and putting them to bed. And the week after that, you'll be volunteered to dish out ten different varieties of cheap plonk at quiz night when you'd rather be watching the Canaries kick a bunch of noisy Seagulls in high definition on the telly."

Chisholm nodded in agreement, "But you haven't got any children, Cornelius. How come you know all that?"

"Oh, I've turned out at enough open evenings and seen the

expression on enough faces. Unmistakable, it is," Hacker began to mimic a master of ceremonies: "Our very special guest on this sports quiz evening, Borough's longest serving left-back, our very own Hatchet man, Mr C.F. Hacker." He shook his head in sorry appreciation, "And all the broad toothy smiles, limp handshakes and hearty claps-on-the-back desperately trying to hide the fact that, to a man, they'd all rather be somewhere else other than crammed into a draughty sports hall, trying to remember who won the first FA Cup Final and what year it was?"

Chisholm looked up from examining his blotter, "Wanderers, 1872."

"See what I mean," Hacker said, arms up, appealing for offside. "Go on then, clever clogs. What was the score and who scored the goal?"

"One-nil, Morton Betts; played under the pseudonym of A H Chequer."

"Bloody hell, Brian! Go to the top of the class."

They kicked a metaphorical football around for half an hour, but, Hacker noted, neither tea nor biscuits arrived and not even an inquiry as to whether Hacker could provide a few tickets to the next round of Champions League matches. "So, what's it to be? Who'd you fancy for the Cup this year?"

But Chisholm's face fell and his complexion darkened. "Does it matter? I won't be going, will I? Neither Marchman Engineering nor you, Cornelius, will be supplying me with a ticket this time round."

"Why not, Brian?"

"Because, Cornelius, Norfolk Electrical won't be submitting the usual comprehensive order for components to Marchman Engineering."

"Why ever not?"

"Because it appears that over the last couple of years, I've not been paying enough attention to locating alternative suppliers. That's why not." Chisholm ran the fingers of his right hand round his collar.

Left hanging by the silence, he grew fidgety, "And because, four weeks ago, I got hauled in front of the Board and asked to explain why I'd not investigated sourcing components from Slovakia." He paused to allow the news to sink in, "Would you 'effing believe it, Slovakia?"

Hacker chuckled. "Oh, come off it, Brian. You can source your components from a hundred countries between here and Japan. There's lots of places cheaper than Slovakia."

"There might be," he leaned across the desk, "But what I didn't know, Cornelius, was that one of our newly arrived EU brethren, some cheap and cheerful Yacub, who's been trucking Norfolk Electricals around the Continent, put our Sales Director in touch with some component suppliers in Slovakia – some bunch who no doubt receive state subsidies for their exports. And these bastards have undercut not just Marchman Engineering, but also just about every other component supplier in Europe and the Far East by fifty per cent!" He let the margin float in the air for a moment.

"And the worst part of it is, it turns out they'd mail-shot me via email eighteen months ago – and not once, but several times. 'Course, I'd junked the mail shots. I mean... Slovakia!" he sneered. "But our Sales Director, who's always said he could do my job better than me, showed the Board the mail-shots. Seems, as far as the Board is concerned, the bloody Sales Director actually can do my job better than me. I'm lucky to have a desk to park my arse behind after the grilling I got, I can tell you."

"Oh, come off it," Hacker repeated. "How many times has some other fly-by-night operation tried to buy its way into the business with a cheap first-time offer?"

"More times than I've had hot dinners," Chisholm replied, but his hands were shaking now and he'd broken out in a sweat. "But," he went on, "this time they not only sent over a shedload of free samples, they even guaranteed the price for the next five years."

"What?"

"You heard, Cornelius: five bloody years."

"Five years?"

"Yes. Five years! That's five years this firm doesn't need a Procurement Manager for electrical motor components." Chisholm sat back and sighed. "Fortunately for me our products need more than just a few copper wires and a couple of magnets, otherwise they'd be handing me my P45, make no bloody mistake!"

"Fifty per cent and five years, eh?"

"It's the EU and the bloody internet, Cornelius," Chisholm went on in the solemn voice broadcasters usually reserve for obituaries. "It's not a level bloody playing field anymore. Of course, they think opening up all these markets makes us more competitive, and in some ways they're right. But we're the only ones who play by the rules and, while the refs looking the other way, every Yacub-come-lately is busy kicking me to death."

"Look, my old chum," Hacker said, "maybe this isn't the place. Perhaps you are right, maybe I shouldn't've come. Perhaps it would be better if we could meet for a pint at lunchtime?"

"A pint? Lunchtime? You must be bloody joking. One sniff of the booze and you're out of here before your feet touch the ground." Brian Chisholm stared, disbelieving that Hacker could have come up with such a stupid idea. "Caught one of the old boys down the back taking a nip with his morning break last month. Sixty-three he was. 'Bin 'ere fourteen years; sweeping up, bit of maintenance. His feet didn't touch the ground. No handshake, no pat on the back and no nothing: fourteen years and not so much as a thank you. A pint, at lunchtime?"

"Well, what about this evening? Stop on the way home for a quick one?"

Chisholm shook his head, "Got to take Kaitlyn to a team talk this evening. She's got this big game at school tomorrow morning. Sorry."

"Good for you, Brian. Mustn't lose sight of your priorities. What about after?"

He shook his head, "Usually stay and watch. Not much point in going home. By the time I get back, I'd have to leave to pick her up again."

"How about we have a beer while young Kaitlyn is at her meeting?"

At the mention of his home turf, Chisholm looked up sharply. His cheeks flushed a deep red and his eyes glowed hard and dark. Then he looked down at his desk as if suffering some faint humiliation, "No. Not tonight. Jean's out tonight. She's not back till later."

Hacker chuckled, "PTA?"

The Procurement Manager nodded, his shoulders sagged.

"Well I'm sure you can arrange for a babysitter, perhaps one of the other parents can help out, Brian."

"No," he repeated. "Not tonight. I can't; definitely not tonight."

"Come on, Brian. Just half an hour. Won't take long."

"No, I told you, not tonight. I can't."

Hacker paused and said quietly, "Be at the Flyer, this evening, about seven. I've got a message from Sherri."

22

Philip

They stopped for fish and chips on the Parade at Great Yarmouth and the brume that had built up between them slowly evaporated. For the first time in a long time they held hands and he remembered how uncomplicated their lives had been before that first night at Hanger Holt.

Philip remembered so clearly being woken by a loud intermittent beeping. There was no alarm clock on the bedside table and it took him a while to realise that the noise was coming from somewhere the other side of the bedroom wall. As he showered and dressed, he could hear the sound of metal scraping and a couple of times the floor shook alarmingly.

Camilla was waiting outside his door. Philip followed the dog to the kitchen.

A short, stout woman of Latin descent ushered him to the kitchen table. "Tea? Coffee?" she asked as she wiped her hands on her apron.

"Good morning. Tea, please. I'm Philip."

She beamed back at him as she stood by his chair, "Yes. Good breakfast?"

"You must be Maria?" He held out his hand.

Her smile glowed even brighter, "Eh-yes."

Fiona came in, looking as though she'd spent the early hours at a beauty parlour. She smiled at the little woman.

"Querida," said Maria, throwing her arms wide.

Fiona went to the little woman, bent down towards her and hugged her, "Maezinha."

Both women's eyes looked to Philip a shade watery when they stood back.

"Mama?" asked Fiona.

Maria pointed to the door, "She is gone work early. She is not sure when back."

Philip didn't feel much like staying, in case his exit visa was revoked, but the breakfast Maria had prepared kept him in the house for as long as it took him to eat it.

"You no stay?" Maria asked.

"No," Fiona said, "thank you, Maria. Mother said we were to go if we needed to. And I don't know about you Phil, but I need to."

As Philip drove slowly down towards the gates, he could see in his rear view mirror the long jib of a crane standing up at a high angle behind the house. A huge, closed grabber lifted up above the roof and opened to drop its contents somewhere away in the back. Long strips of what looked like aluminium fell from the bucket.

The drive back down into London was easy and they had much to discuss. They laughed at the absurdity of the meal and their dinner partners, and almost cried with relief that the night was over.

Fiona began by apologising for her mother's habit of inviting her acolytes to dinner every time she went home. "I didn't tell you because I didn't think she'd do it. I can't work out if she seeks safety in numbers or if she invites them because she needs specialist judges at her talent show. Either way, I can't bear how they cow-tow to her; how they all look to see her reaction before they commit to showing theirs."

"Maria?" Philip asked. "Portuguese?"

"Uh-huh! My second mother; been with us for years. Sometimes I think I'd have been better off if she'd been my first mother." She quieted for a moment.

"Nice lady," Philip encouraged, but nothing more came. "Harold Barter seemed pretty harmless."

"Mother's man on the council: Gets a bit fresh now and again."

"Jimmy Carson? What's he all about?"

"Carson?" Fiona repeated. "Wretched snake in the grass is Jimmy Carson. I used to think she was having an affair with him he was about the house so often. Then I found out from Maria he was keeping tabs on my father for her. He makes my skin crawl."

"Know what you mean."

They drove on in silence for a few miles.

"Sorry you had to go through all that," Fiona said.

Philip risked a glance at her. A trickle of tears ran down her cheek and onto her lip. He wondered how long she had been crying and reached down, rested his hand on her thigh and squeezed it in a manner he hoped she would find reassuring, "Hey. It wasn't so bad."

"Yes, it was." Fiona searched in her bag for a tissue. "It was bloody awful."

They were summoned to Hanger Holt twice before their engagement: Christmas and Easter.

The painfully slow journey up at Christmas demanded as much, if not more, patience than was demanded of Philip through the two days they stayed. The flap caused by Fiona's dithering over what to buy her mother for a present, ran his apprehension a close second. But, in the spirit of goodwill, he cut Archie a yard or two of slack when she was at her most caustic. And when she was mean with her daughter in his company, he simply ignored her. He didn't want to; ignoring her went against the grain, but it was the better course.

At Easter, the usual suspects turned up. Harold Barter, Grace and other guests herded around Archie like farmhands at market. Jimmy Carson once again expressed his desire to help Philip ascend the ladder towards the higher floors, and a host of local ne'er-do-wells dressed like George Formby argued about television programmes and lounged about quoting mockney

Maria greeted Philip like the prodigal son and her eyes twinkled with mischief as though she knew for certain what he and Fiona got up to after lights out. She was cheeky, genial, affable and affectionate all at once and Philip warmed to her. Fiona had very obviously grown up in her care.

But the most important lesson Philip learned that weekend was that he could love Fiona and accommodate her mother. Easter reinforced a growing awareness in him that his feelings for Fiona comfortably superseded the low opinion he harboured of Archie. Maybe his capacity to suffer others, his tolerance for characters who didn't conform or fit in to his vision of the future, was slowly being augmented by her confidence in him. Whatever it was, he felt more complete and as such ready for the next step.

What Philip wasn't ready for was the palaver resulting from Fiona's inability to keep the next step a secret.

23

Phoebe

There was only one taxi outside and she let the lady from her carriage have it. The dull weather fostered a casual melancholy in her and she needed a walk. The school bus stop had been a five-minute walk from home; the idea of walking in the rain was not exactly anathema to her.

A grey Ford cruised by. Phoebe turned away as the car threw up a great spray, soaking her.

"You…" she yelled at the car. She saw the driver turn, look at her and mouth an apology. "Never mind sorry, you knobhead," she shouted.

No one heard. There was no one to hear. And the freedom to shout when there was no one to hear amused her. Phoebe laughed out loud; unrestrained, unfettered. She laughed in a forced, rebellious manner like a newly-released captive in the face of her jailer.

At the seafront, Phoebe turned left and walked along the esplanade into town. The sea was white-capped and the town deserted. Most of the summer season shops were closed, but, judging by the collections of gnarled driftwood furniture, barnacled anchors and sailing pennants laid out, a few of the arts and craft shops had not yet surrendered to hibernation.

After walking a good way, she came to a coffee shop.

A bearded mannequin clothed in a faded Sou'Wester bade her

enter and a bell tinkled above the door as she eased it open. The place smelt of chip fat and vinegar, but it was warm and would do.

A middle-aged waitress appeared. She had thin arms and a sceptical air, "Something to drink?"

"A tea, please," Phoebe quickly searched the menu for the beverages, but only found tea or coffee or soft drinks. "Do you have any white tea?"

The waitress frowned. "I think we've got some Earl Grey, otherwise it'll be PG Tips, love. Only the best of British here."

"I'll have the Earl Grey if you've got it. No milk, thanks." And, as she said it, the bridge of her nose itched and she sneezed violently, only just managing to cup her hands up to her nose in time. She felt a spatter of moisture on her palms, "Excuse me."

The waitress handed her a white paper serviette.

"No," Phoebe said, "thank you. I've got a tissue." Her nose felt heavy and congested.

"Wouldn't bother with your tissue, love, you'll make a proper mess of your jacket. Here, take this."

Phoebe glanced up at the waitress, but, when she looked down at her hands, her palms were dappled with blood.

The waitress studied her for a second, "Leave that. I'll sort the table. You get cleaned up. The toilets are over there." She waved her pen over her shoulder.

When Phoebe came out of the toilets, the waitress was spraying and wiping the table. She ignored Phoebe until she was satisfied the table was clean, then went away and came back with a pot of tea and a cup and saucer. "Anything else, love?" she said, confident she wasn't going to have to waste the ink in her biro.

"Could I have spaghetti, but without the sauce, just a little olive oil and some parmesan, please? I mean, if that's not too much trouble?"

The waitress bridled, "Of course, dear. I'm sure Stevie can manage that." Before she turned to leave, she said, "My daughter used to get awful nosebleeds when she was about your age. They don't last. You'll get over them."

Phoebe tried her best to smile without moving her face so much that the wads of toilet tissue fell out of her nose.

As she poured the Earl Grey from the small pot, she realised, that apart from a wholegrain bar and an apple, she hadn't taken anything on board since the goat's cheese salad and pink champagne.

Twenty years old and she'd hardly put a foot wrong; hardly ever stepped out of or over the line. She'd even managed to resist swamping her mind with alcohol until she'd got through school and college.

Most of her classmates, those who achieved three A-levels, went to whichever university would have them and spent the first few weeks getting so smashed some of them even forgot which courses they were on.

Not Phoebe! As before, she refused to open the letter containing her A-level results until she was alone at home. And again she was justified in her strangely clandestine act. Her collection of A-stars from her GCSEs was augmented by four As at A-level.

But it had been earlier in the year that her teachers had begun to whisper the words Oxbridge and Law.

So that, which to others seemed a fairytale, became to Phoebe nothing more than a natural progression. She interviewed well and was not intimidated when pressed by academics much older and wiser. She sat the L-NAT, the law test, and was not fazed when the essay question asked her to consider whether offenders should be entitled to the same human rights as their victims. She liked an argument, on paper at least, and it all seemed to go her way.

She was, perhaps just like the old lady on the train had said, "so lucky."

So Fresher's week at Cambridge was short; not necessarily restrained, nor any less alcohol soaked, but short and done with. And then it was down to work.

The first term flew by in a whirl of lectures and supervisions, and generally Phoebe found herself wide-eyed and wondrous that so many of the law books she was reading had actually been written by the lecturers: it was as if God was reading his own bible and solely for her benefit.

And it took her a while to understand the context in which her supervisor wanted her essays written, and she often found herself up all night researching and writing and hurrying to submit her work before deadline. This was a new experience for a girl who up until then had finished most of her essays just hours after they'd been set.

The boarding school style of college was a complete revelation to her. She was homesick, a little; Phoebe granted herself that luxury. But, also, she revelled in the company of those who found academic work the perfectly natural consequence of a busy mind, and that new association with her confederates more than adequately filled the hole created by the absence of her family. Gradually, the walls Phoebe had erected to protect herself from the heathen majority of her teens began to dissolve in a solution of shared intelligence and capacity; a solution common to those who knew how to yield themselves that extra ration of bread. *Well, maybe not all,* she remembered thinking at the time; *maybe not some of the Mathmos.*

And as Phoebe no longer felt the pressure to maintain her defences, she ignored them more and more. And by well into the Lent term, there wasn't much of the university social scene that escaped her notice.

"'Nother tea, dear?" offered the waitress.

"Thank you." Phoebe passed her the pot. Her nose had stopped bleeding and was beginning to itch as it dried. She looked in her handbag for a tissue, but couldn't find one. She opened her overnight bag and located a new handy-pack that had sunk to the bottom.

The waitress returned with her second pot.

Phoebe rather self-consciously closed her bag when she realised the waitress was staring at the half bottle of vodka in it.

"Anything else, dear?"

"No, thank you." Phoebe broke into a fit of coughing as her throat dried.

The waitress scowled, paused and left.

Phoebe remembered exactly at which point in her college education the first seeds of her current dilemma were sown: It was one of those Sunday evenings that glided so smoothly into Monday morning.

Pre-lash at mine, the text from Terence had read. She hadn't realised it was already eight o'clock. She finished the notes for her essay, backed them up, shut down her Mac, and rushed over to Terence's room with what was left of her vodka and a bottle of lime cordial. Pre-lash; that was how most evenings began.

Terence, Simon, Heather, Boris and the Japanese boy, Yuichi, or Yu as everyone called him, were already there. Phoebe found herself drawn to Yu. She liked the way he hung back in conversation and allowed the boys and Heather to talk themselves round in circles before he entered the fray to deliver his coup de grace.

"Freddie," he greeted her, smiling. He was the only one who called her by her old school nickname and, possibly because his race set him apart, he was the only one she allowed to. He was taller than most of the other Japanese at the university and was possessed of a perfect oval face and perfect white teeth. "Whass'up?"

"Sorry I'm a bit late. Got a beast of an essay to get in by Tuesday and my DOS wants to see me tomorrow, so I don't want to go too hard tonight."

"Phoebes," Boris lifted his head from the board, "you always say that and you always get smashed the same as everybody." Boris had more blond hair and bluer baby-blue eyes than any boy had a right to.

"Well, not tonight," Phoebe said. "I don't want to be hanging in the morning."

"Come on now, Phoebes. Let's not talk about deadlines," Terence moaned, "Mustn't let that stuff get in the way of a good night out." He got up to make room for her on his bed.

Clearly, the day had started early for Terence. He was very tall and lean, his cheeks slightly sunken, and he had hands the size of dinner plates and feet to match.

Heather, brunette, kind brown eyes, soft face and a gentle Northern-Irish brogue, glanced up and winked, "Evening m'lud."

Simon rubbed his face with his hands in something approaching exasperation, "Hello, Phoebes." He had short, ginger hair and a thing for Heather, but she wouldn't permit his attraction to develop into anything more substantial, hence they argued.

If there was one reason why the six of them gravitated to each other, it was that in each other they found exactly what they had not found in their school or college contemporaries — namely the ability to exist as a group of friends without judgement or reproach.

By the time they finished pre-lash, Phoebe already felt queasy; Pringles on vodka like autumn leaves on a stagnant Cam. So they went to McDonalds to feed before the night grew much older.

At eleven they transferred to Real, the usual club for a Sunday night. The boys stood at the bar and argued rugby and bands. Phoebe and Heather danced and danced, and danced a bit more.

"I think I'm gonna' go," she shouted in Heather's ear.

Heather leaned towards her, "Why? What time is it? It can't be late; we've only just got here."

The music thumped and boomed.

Phoebe shrugged and tried her best to move in some kind of syncopated rhythm. "I don't know why," she shouted, "but I feel like Pippi Longstocking on Prozac," and they laughed. For a while the laughter banished Phoebe's fatigue, so she carried on.

The boys stood at the bar and talked, and Phoebe couldn't understand how they could talk so much when she had to shout every time she wanted to make herself heard.

Yu seemed to be looking over at them a lot. Now and again, he smiled at her, and she, very naturally, smiled back.

Some time later, and she couldn't remember how much later because the music and the energy and the atmosphere absorbed time like water on sand, she found herself leaning against Yu, wondering how the hell she was going to make it back to college.

"Oh, shit," she moaned, "I've had it. I'm done. I'm going."

Yu leaned away from her for a moment and spoke to Heather and Phoebe was vaguely aware that he passed something to Heather from his pocket.

"C'mon, Phoebes," Heather pulled Phoebe in the direction of the toilets.

The loos were busier than the train station at the end of term, but, unusually, there was no attendant on duty.

"Come in here," Heather sat Phoebe on the toilet, shut the cubicle door and backed up against it.

Now sitting down, Phoebe realised she was drunk. The walls of the toilet stall crowded her and for a moment she felt coldly sick.

Then Heather said, "Here, close your mouth and breathe this in through your nose. But for Christ's sake, don't blow. I've only got the one." She passed Phoebe a little vanity mirror. There was a slender line of white powder on it.

Without really thinking about it, Phoebe leaned forwards and sniffed.

Not much happened.

"No, you monkey," Heather said. "Hold one side of your nose shut with your finger and then breathe in as if you're trying to stop your nose from running. Don't whiff it, snort it."

And, at the mention of the word snort, an alarm bell rang in her head and Phoebe came rudely awake. She pulled back and looked up at Heather, "What is it? Is it coke?" And then, because she assumed it would be cocaine, she heard herself say very confidently, "I won't take coke, or E, you know that. I won't do that illegal shit. I've told you before. You know that." She shook her head like an obstructive child.

Heather stood in front of her and crouched down to whisper in her ear, "It's not coke and it's not E. It's 'drone, Mephedrone, and it's perfectly legal. It'll help. Here," she offered, "take it. But don't blow; sniff it like you mean it." Heather's tone held just the right blend of persuasion and authority. "I wouldn't give you coke, like I don't do coke, and like I don't trust anyone enough to supply me with E either, Phoebes. So take this, I promise it's completely legal. God, half the people here take it."

So, boxed in the toilet cubicle and lacking in any further argument, Phoebe pressed her right nostril shut and sniffed in hard through her left.

"Shit!" she shouted and shook her head at the stinging sensation. She felt as though someone'd stuck a red-hot chilli pepper up her nose. Phoebe screwed up her face and pushed Heather roughly away. Only there was nowhere for Heather to go, so Phoebe ended up pulling Heather back to her and resting her head against Heather's stomach. "Fucking hell! Is it always like that? I mean... Shit!"

"Yes," replied Heather, bending and kissing her softly on the back of her head, "it is if you don't do it too often. Give it a while, it'll go off."

Quite why Phoebe flushed the loo as she got up and left, she couldn't think. There were no knowing looks shared between any of the other girls in the toilets, no conspiratorial nods or winks, just the noise of some girl throwing up and another spitting and swearing.

There was a look, though, between Yu and Heather when they got back. Phoebe just caught the tail end of it.

After what seemed like an age in which she just stood next to the boys and stared aimlessly about the club, Terence suggested they dance – so they did.

He danced like a crane in a hurry; like his limbs were manually operated by a puppeteer. But, strangely, it worked for him, as though he gained some synthesis with the rhythm through his continuous default.

They played a track by Journey and Boris joined them. He was far more systematic in his footwork and he looked a shade Greek when he raised his hands over his head.

Then Heather appeared with Simon trailing along behind. And finally Yu, who seemed to dance without moving at all. He just swayed with the beat, eyes closed, right into the music.

The six of them danced and blocked out others around them. And Phoebe didn't know where it came from, but she was dancing properly now, relaxed, unhindered by her previously uncooperative frame, her legs and arms released. And not in any wild goose or grotesque manner, but in a pleasing, balanced way with occasional balletic turns and spirals; movements that continued on from one graceful twist and whirl, on and on and through to the next. And she smiled and was not tired in the least. And she loved Heather and all her friends and she loved where she was, and wasn't it just the best time of her life. And she wanted to tell Yu that he was the most attractive man she'd ever met, and yet she wanted to save that for later, because for now it couldn't get much better.

They went back to Terence's room and drank more and talked more and played cards until the sky coloured and Phoebe fell asleep curled up in a chair.

The next day, she was hung-over. In fact, she felt so hung-over she couldn't recall ever feeling quite so rough.

In that, there was nothing terribly new. She had felt rough before and knew she would do so again, particularly if that was the price of such a fabulous night out. But, she didn't wake up with the jitters and neither did she have the munchies. That was the 'drone, of course, and whilst she felt guilty and a little as though she'd lost the last of virginity, she wasn't spooked.

In fact, Phoebe wasn't spooked at all. And that confused her more than it worried her.

The waitress appeared, but didn't ask her if she wanted any more to eat or drink. She merely stood by the table and waited.

Phoebe paid and left, the waitress standing watching her as she opened the door awkwardly, trying her best not to bash the bearded mannequin with her bag.

The light would be gone soon and she needed a place to hang. There didn't seem much to the left, so Phoebe walked back the way she'd come.

When she got to the road she'd walked in on, she crossed over and carried on. The wind was blowing in hard from the sea and the sky on the horizon was now slate grey in both pallor and texture.

The first few B&Bs looked a little shabby, like they might not offer the cleanest of sheets or showers. And just when the well of her enthusiasm was beginning to run dry, she came across what she hoped she'd find: The Reach. It looked very presentable, not exactly like a new pin, as her mother used to say, but promising in terms of a well made bed or a bathroom devoid of someone else's pubic hair.

24

Audrey

"You must be Mrs Poulter," said the woman.

"If you say so."

"Well," the woman continued, very quickly understanding that Mrs Poulter was not the type suited to her brand of instant familiarity, "I don't wish to presume, but we have only the four rooms and what with two of the other three being taken and you standing there with your overnight bag, I... Well, I assumed. I know I shouldn't. You'll have to forgive me. I'm Ms Anworthy."

She stood aside to let Audrey into the hall, "You're in Room 3. You said you wanted the first floor room on the left facing the front, didn't you? Here's the room key. No need to sign the register now, later will be fine." Mrs Anworthy retrieved a laminated sheet from a shelf by the alcove. "It's all here," she said, brandishing it like a sabre. "House Rules. Not many, just a few! You'll find the safety information in your room too, but I like to hand out the House Rules personally; that way I know you've had sight of them."

The landlady glanced at the brass porthole clock behind her counter.

Audrey nodded, squashed the awkwardly stiff sheet into her handbag, picked up her overnight bag and turned for the stairs.

"I'll give you the front door key when you come down then, shall I?"

Audrey Poulter closed the door gently but firmly, set her bag on the bed and sat down beside it.

Not much was as she remembered. The counterpane was olive-green and ribbed, and the bedhead something similar. The drapes were imitation Italian Damask and, judging by the way they creased, an unnecessarily cheap imitation at that.

"At least they've tried to marry some of the colours with the carpet," she said.

She studied the wardrobe immediately before her. The doors of the top half hung open exposing its cavernous inside. It was a good age; mahogany, probably Dutch but possibly Flemish, nicely inlaid. The shelves had been removed from the upper section to create hanging space, and below it lay two half-drawers and two full-width drawers with ornate, but substantial, pull-handles. Audrey was attracted to it, perhaps even liked it. It was something left behind and there was no doubt it too possessed its very own story of why it was here in this place, at this time.

Audrey got up, stood on tiptoe and ran her hand along the top of the cupboard. She studied the dust on her fingers. She pushed the doors shut slowly, as though all things over a certain age deserved to be treated with respect. However, the doors swung slowly back and it became clear to Audrey that without being locked, the doors were unlikely to remain shut. Audrey stared at the cupboard for a few seconds, then pushed the doors shut once again and turned the heavy key.

She ran the hot tap at the sink and washed the dust off her fingers. The water grew piping hot very quickly; the washbasin was nicely clean.

Audrey went to open the window, but on trying the handle realised it was locked. She searched the margin behind the curtains and the drawers in the bedside table for the key, and when she couldn't locate it, made a mental note to ask the landlady where the key was kept.

Her Gladstone bag was new. She'd spotted her bag in the market in Oxford only a couple of weeks before and had bought it on the fly. "On the fly," she said to herself.

It was in much the same way that Audrey had come to Strand-next-the-Sea; on the fly, on the spur of the moment.

Well, maybe not here exactly; not this grey, windy and rainy settlement perched on the edge of East Anglia, like a bit of pastry crust waiting to be trimmed off an apple pie.

The day before, after the postman had come, Audrey had left the small bundle of letters on the kitchen table and taken to her bed. She'd stayed there for the rest of the day and through the evening and night, unable to think straight and incapable of unravelling the bird's nest of emotions smothering her sight. She did not sleep.

But with the cold light of dawn came a desire to act; a need to do something, anything. And when, finally, she dared go downstairs, hoping upon hope that the letters would have vanished from the kitchen table, she made herself a cup of tea and sat down to stare at them.

It was the house, of course. It wasn't the letters. It was Richard's house. Everywhere she looked, she saw him and felt his presence. There was no way on God's earth she could sit in his draughty, unsympathetic, old pile of Cotswold stone and read the letters. It wouldn't do. It wasn't right. She had to go, to get out and get away. And that was when she realised she had to run away from him just one more time.

So Audrey threw the bundle of letters in her handbag and picked up the phone to call for a taxi. Having impressed upon the cab company exactly how instantly she required their services, she slammed down the phone, stormed upstairs and gathered together a few essentials.

And that, simply, was that. She was out the door and in the back of the cab, and neither God nor the Devil would get in the way of her going to Norfolk.

Thank God, she remembered thinking, *for Strand-next-the-Sea*. It would come to her rescue once more.

She drew back the bedspread and inspected the pillows and sheets for any errant hairs. She could find none; that relieved her, even pleased her.

She took off her jacket and hung it in the cupboard, slipped off her shoes, unzipped her skirt and lay down on the bed to read through the local guidebook. Five minutes rest wouldn't do her any harm.

But, Audrey wasn't really tired. She'd managed nothing other than the sudoku and the word puzzle on that draughty, rattling train. Mind you, that girl had intrigued her. She had rather strange colour hair; it was red metallic like strands of electrical wire and she had striking green eyes, and her bulky jacket seemed to be slowly ingesting her. She looked pale and tired, almost careworn, in need of a bowl of chicken soup and some bracing sea air. The girl had stood back to let her have the taxi; that had been good of her.

Water dripped from a gutter outside and a sudden gust of wind whipped a handful of pellets against the window.

She'd give the weather a chance to calm down.

The guidebook, apart from proclaiming the delights of Strand-next-the-Sea's sandy seafront and thirteenth century church, extolled the virtues of the crabs from further up the coast in Cromer and the Pleasure Beach further south in Great Yarmouth. Strand-next-the-Sea! It didn't exactly jump out of the list when it came to choosing a destination for a weekend away from it all, especially not after all those newspaper reports in the seventies about the appalling levels of pollution in the North Sea. Still, that second time, she hadn't come to the coast with the intention of swimming.

Truth be told, she couldn't recall much about her first visit to Strand either. She'd come across a postcard in a box of old knickknacks when she'd been clearing out her bedroom in the old house near Telford. Audrey decided she must have been seven or eight when she wrote it; a picture of a very bored looking donkey wearing a straw hat on the seafront and HAVING LOTS OF FUN WITH MY BEST FRIEND BRYONY RIDING THE DONKEY LOVE AUDREY very neatly printed on the back. She vaguely remembered staying in a caravan with Bryony and Bryony's parents, but the only evidence she could find that she'd enjoyed the holiday lay in those words. Only God knew what had happened to Bryony.

The guidebook suggested a local gastro-pub, the Norfolk Flyer, well known, supposedly, for local dressed crab, mussels, scallops and crayfish.

Crayfish? Wasn't that what she'd eaten that second time? Was it crayfish? And was it the Norfolk Flyer?

Audrey pressed the palms of her hands over her eyes as though shutting out the world around her might help her remember. "Do you know," she said quietly to herself, "I think it was the Norfolk Flyer at Craving. Of course, of course it was." She picked up the book and read the review again.

And it was: the Norfolk Flyer at Craving. A craving for crayfish! How could she have forgotten that tiny but significant moment? She'd wept tears of laughter as she'd tried to explain why the phrase amused her so: a craving for crayfish.

And, at the memory of how light and amused and uncontrolled she'd felt that time, Audrey began to giggle. She clutched the guidebook to her heaving stomach and let her laughter flow until the tears of her humour slowly ran out.

She laid her few spare clothes out in the cupboard drawers and placed her red vanity case on the dresser. From the case, she took her toothbrush and paste and put them in the plastic cup on the sink shelf. Next, she pulled out a small white envelope. It was sealed and the pills inside rattled as she stood the envelope up beside the cup.

She smiled; a little self-satisfied and mischievous smile that bordered, but only faintly bordered, on a smirk. Audrey was pleased with her deception. If, she decided with a twinge of guilt, being pleased with a deceit was not too great a sin.

25

Philip

Along the narrower lanes out past Scratby and Winterton-on-Sea, Fiona toyed with him; one moment pointing out the grey sea on the right and the next touching him in a suggestive and subtly provocative manner; teasing him with vague promises of what she might do to him if he fancied parking up in one of the sandy lanes that lead off towards the beach.

Philip tried his level best to concentrate, but couldn't keep his mind from drifting.

They were at his flat, midweek; he was cooking. "May I make a suggestion?" Philip asked from the kitchenette.

"If it's sensible."

Philip wondered if his timing was up to the mark. As far as he was concerned, when the food hit Fiona's stomach she was more than likely to fall asleep. If, in the minute or two beforehand, he could get her to agree to his proposition, he just might alter the course of their relationship, and for the better.

The following Saturday morning the skies hung criminally low as he crawled up to Bromley-By-Bow. The market traders and pedestrians milling about in Mile End seemed to stare at him as though they'd heard the rumour: Philip was embarked on a noble and perilous quest.

Before he left, Fiona had hugged him and wished him luck. "You'll need it," she said.

Philip noted her lack of confidence in his diplomatic skills and told her it was very definitely not a matter of luck. "Sometimes," he said, "it just falls to one to do the right thing."

Seven miles ago it had been that easy to say, but with each mile he drove he wished it could have fallen to someone else.

Half-an-hour later he was battling with the traffic through Leytonstone and Wanstead, and Gallows Corner delayed him still further.

"I shall expect you at eleven," Archie had decreed. "Please don't be late. I have to be out before midday."

Apart from that, she had reacted to his request for an audience with polite acceptance; an hour would surely provide sufficient time for him to settle the matter.

Philip knew there was a speed camera on the 414 at Danbury, but he was running out of time and so driving too fast. He missed it and it flashed him, but he made it down the lane and up to the gates dot on eleven.

Two cranes stood like vigilant sentries beside great heaps of scrap-iron behind the bungalow. Archie was waiting beneath the portico. She checked her watch as he pulled up.

Camilla yapped at him.

"Well," Philip said, "nice to know someone's pleased to see me."

Archie permitted him a brief smile, "Very droll, Mr Scott! Please don't think I'm not grateful to you for coming to see me, it's just that I've got a lot on today."

Her use of his surname was not lost on him, "Of course, Mrs Davy. I'm sure you have. But I am grateful for your time and I do apologise for this sudden intrusion."

Her look suggested he might not want to overplay his hand, "Come in then."

Maria stood in the hall, beaming from ear to ear. She was still wiping her hands on her apron in much the same way as she had been when he'd last seen her at Easter.

"We'll take coffee in the snug, thank you, Maria," Archie commanded and Maria scuttled away.

"Please," said Archie and she lead him to a side room that looked through net curtains onto the front lawn. A mahogany writing desk, the lid open and two neat stacks of letters in wooden trays either side of an unmarked, leather-edged blotter, stood in front of the window. An Edwardian Captain's Chair sat angled back before the desk and a second low stool was tucked beneath the adjacent computer workstation. If there was a surprise, it was the pair of oil paintings: Suffolk barges, Edward Seago.

Philip had not expected such style.

"Pull up a chair," Archie suggested as she sat down at the desk.

He did so, feeling a shade self-conscious like a patient before a doctor. "You said you are grateful? I mean, grateful that I've come to see you?"

"Naturally," she said, fixing him with what he took to be a knowing stare. But Archie wasn't going to give him the benefit of telling him what it was that she was grateful for, or what it was she doubtless already knew.

"I'd like to marry Fiona."

"She has accepted your proposal?"

"Yes, I'm glad to say she has."

"Then either you must be barking mad, Philip, or you must love her very much." Archie sat still, waiting.

"I'd like to think both," he said, "if you can live with that."

"Both?"

"Well, yes; madly in love? And, naturally, I think Fiona must be a little bit mad, too. I mean, mad to agree to marry me in the first place. These days, one's got to be a little loopy to want to get married."

"You can say that again," Archie scoffed, "But if you're half mad, Philip, that implies you're only half in love with Fiona as well. Is that enough... only to be half in love?"

Philip was not expecting to be drawn into a debate about love in quantity and her line took him by surprise. He spent much of his working day measuring quantities; he never imagined emotions could be calculated in similar alphanumeric terms.

"I think so," was all he could think of to say. Then he realised, "I'm not sure one knows how sufficiently in love one needs to be to want to spend the rest of one's life with another."

Archie smiled at him.

That lent Philip hope.

"You asked if I could live with that?" she asked. "Why should it be so important for me to be able to live with that? It's not me that you'll be trying to live the rest of your life with. Shouldn't it be more important that Fiona can live with the balance of your madness and your love?"

"Yes. It should," he said, "but the only way we'll get to find that out is if we try, and our life would be so much more complete if you would not only give us your blessing, but also be a part of it."

"My blessing?" she laughed and looked up at the ceiling. "Oh, Philip, you can have my blessing. That's the easy part. Although I'm not so sure I understand why you should want my blessing. I'm sure Fiona will have filled you in on the all-too-short inventory of my blessings."

He said nothing.

Archie raised an eyebrow, "Oh, I see, she has. Well, of course, that would be perfectly natural of her. But, as you have no doubt realised, my relationship with Fiona is somewhat awkward. We're quite the same in very many respects, although there is a good deal more of her father in her than she suspects."

Philip was a little confused by her remark. He wasn't sure whether his future mother-in-law was suggesting that he had yet to deal with Fiona's philandering-gambling-soak phase?

"No. That's not what I mean," she said. "You see love has a habit of blinding those suffering under its ferocious glare to anything other than what they most want to see. Love blinds us to imperfections that later become too significant to ignore; small flaws and little bumps in the road that grow into deep ravines and vast mountains, all of which require constant and tiring circumnavigation. That is, until they grow to the size where you no longer possess the energy to scale them, at which point you'll be surprised how very quickly you can lose the will to be bothered."

"We're not all perfect," Philip cut in. "I mean, I'm sure my imperfections are probably far more intimidating to Fiona than any of those I've noticed in her."

"Oh, I'm not talking about yours, Philip," Archie said with a wave of her hand. "You may possess the arrogance of youth which shrinks all obstacles to manageable proportion. That's no bad thing. No, I'm talking about Fiona."

He didn't reply. Philip was aware she wanted to do the talking for a moment.

"Or maybe her and her father," she said. "Fiona has this conveniently misty view of her father being an affable carouser, a benevolent ageing roué, good-time Johnny; a little tipsy now and then, but an attractive man as far as the opposite sex was concerned. I suppose it's easier for her to remember him that way. It is certainly a more comforting vision. It helps her to retain her affection for him and provides her with sufficient justification to hate me. After all, it's far simpler to carry a grudge against someone who is alive than someone who has moved on to a place where they are no longer accessible."

She paused and said, "In spite of what you may have heard, Fiona's father wasn't bad through and through. An uncompromising misogynist he may have been, but he wasn't a bad or particularly unkind man; although that may depend on your definition of unkind. There were just certain things he demanded that, in the end, I could not continue to supply. And I'm not necessarily talking about sex either."

Archie paused again. She seemed uncertain whether to go on and Philip wondered whether she had caught herself being too openly honest with him.

"I'm sure you're not, Archie," he said to fill the silence. "But if there's something I ought to know, you'll be better off telling me rather than waiting until later to hear me say how much I wished you'd told me."

"Oh, don't worry, Philip. I'm not about to tell you Fiona's been sectioned or has some degenerative condition she's concealed from you. I don't mean that kind of dark secret."

Maria knocked and came into the snug with a tray of coffee and biscuits. She grinned at Philip.

"What I mean is," Archie continued when the door was shut again, "some people are naturally confident in themselves, in what they do and how they treat those around them. For them it is innate, or, as I have heard it described, immanent. It is a confidence that is a part of their fabric. But, they are very rare individuals. Others display the same confidence when it is necessary, but they possess it in the same way one possesses a certain commodity. I've learned it's in no small way similar to metal. Some have it, others do not, and some have it in measure and in different forms. God!" she scoffed. "I should know; ferrous metal, nonferrous, home, industrial and obsolete scrap. I've seen it in all shapes and sizes. Believe me, I hate to say all that glitters is not necessarily gold, but I tell you, Philip, I've seen it, believed it and, though I hate to admit it, all too often fallen for it." Archie poured the coffee and handed him a cup.

"You're talking about Fiona's father," he stated gently.

"Yes. I'm talking about Fiona's father, but I'm talking about Fiona, too." She paused and sipped. "You see her father possessed confidence in abundance, even though it was not inherent in him. People round here thought of him as one who knew how to handle any problem that came his way. He was capable; a man of some metal, but in quantity, literally, not in construction.

"But I knew him as a man who ran out of metal all too often. And on those occasions, he could behave quite childishly; sometimes afraid of something as simple as walking out the front door. Over the years, I found I was able to recharge the batteries of his confidence; I thought it was what wives did for their men. I thought it was a part of the grand design that women should be the stuffing in the throne — that that was how marriage was supposed to be. But, inevitably, even I couldn't continue to resupply him with all that he needed.

"Sadly, I realised I had to preserve some for myself and I didn't need to be Einstein to know what was coming. Once I was of no more use to him that way, I knew he would fill the void with what he needed from outside of our marriage. The rest, I am sure, you know."

Archie sat back and drank her coffee; her expression flat, but for the way she studied him, as though she might bristle if his reply was inappropriate.

"And you're suggesting Fiona is the same in terms of her confidence?"

"Oh, come on, Philip." She sat up again, "Don't tell me there aren't times when you get tired of her constant need for affirmation? Why do you think I give her such a hard time? God knows, if I pandered to her every weak moment, she'd have gotten used to being picked up every time she fell down — just like her father. Just like today."

Philip couldn't see what his coming to Hanger Holt this Saturday morning had to do with some emotional flaw Fiona might have inherited from her father.

"Young man, if my daughter had rung me to tell me you were

engaged, I'd have been delighted, straight out, absolutely delighted. Instead of which, I've had to put up with hearing about it from every third Tom, Dick and Harry, and you've had to come up here today to pull her out of the hole she's dug for herself."

He was about to say she was being a bit hard on Fiona, but held his peace until he realised Archie was not going to speak for the moment. "I think it's more my fault than hers," he said. "I'm sorry you had to get the news in such a manner. I cocked up the protocol. The fault does not lie with Fiona."

Archie smiled at him; an amused, knowing and resigned smile, "And so it begins, Philip."

Archie finished her coffee, glanced at her watch and sat forward to look very directly at Philip. Her eyes were a shade darker brown than her daughters, but she shared her broad forehead and fine hair. "Marry Fiona, Philip. Marry her with my blessing and my best wishes. And if I can help along the way, you only have to ask."

26

Stella

Friday dragged.

However hard Stella tried, she couldn't banish Will's unpleasantness from her head. She rubbed at her scalp, hoping to erase his harsh imprint, but she could still hear the echo of his outburst bouncing around in her head.

She played music as loud as she dared, hoping the distraction would divert her from contemplating the jam she was in. The Beach Boys and Roy Orbison did their level best for a while, but inevitably her CD player selected Cliff Richard and 'Living Doll', and the track reminded her of Will once more.

She tried to read, but the psychopath of Arnott's novel bore too close a resemblance to the portrait of Will her mind was busy painting. Stella thought about preparing her evening meal, but all she could smell was the leftovers of the steak and kidney pie from the evening before.

Just after lunch, Room 3, Mrs Poulter, the lady who'd phoned her earlier in the day, had arrived. Stella knew she'd been a little too informal when greeting her. She didn't know why, but she thought Mrs Poulter familiar, as though she'd met the woman somewhere; as if, perhaps, she'd stayed at The Reach before.

About an hour later, she heard the doorbell. She wasn't expecting anyone else and she took a quick glance from the breakfast room window in case it was her Will come back to give her another piece of his mind.

It wasn't. It was a girl.

"Yes, dear," Stella said, opening the door. She was ready to tell the girl that she already had a very full list of charities she subscribed to, but she'd never seen such a bright red shade of hair colour before. There were a few Goths in Strand, but their hair was generally black — not bright red like a multi-filament, fibre-optic lamp.

The girl just stood and looked back at her as though she was expecting Stella to tell her to get lost. She had a big black holdall on her shoulder which resembled one of those bags the Tommy-knockers used to carry, but she wasn't in any rush to flog its contents. She just stood and looked blank.

"Yes, dear?" Stella offered again.

"This is The Reach?"

"That's what it says on the sign, yes. What is it you're after, dear? A room? Is that what you're looking for?"

The girl nodded; her hair bouncing as she did so.

"Of course it is!" She stepped back to allow the girl into the hall, but she hesitated. "Don't worry, dear. It's not a knocking shop. You'll be alright. I expect you'll be wanting to look at the tariff." But when she looked at the girl in the light of the hall, she wondered if she ought to throw her back out on the street. She looked a touch dark round the eyes and more than a little thumbed around the edges.

Instead, she heard herself say, "I'll save you the trouble. I've got the one room left; number 1. Thirty-five quid, if you'd like it. Breakfast, even if I do say so myself, is as good as you'll find. You won't go hungry." She cast a critical eye over her new and very young arrival. "And we've got Wi-Fi, so you'll be able to use your iPhone or whatever it is that you use."

Still, the girl said nothing. Stella closed the door behind her.

"Is it just the one night or will you be staying over?"

"Thank you," the girl said, "that's good. I mean, yes, that'll be fine."

"Which is it then?"

"I don't know."

"Like that is it, dear?" She looked Phoebe up and down once more, "Bad days and worse?"

"Not really, I'm just a bit tired."

Stella leant towards her. The girl didn't smoke, that was good. "Breakfast is from seven thirty. I'll give you a key to get yourself in later, that's if you want to go out. There's a pub down the way, The Old Tern. It's not much, but it's warm and what they serve is wet — if that's your fancy. Or there are a couple of places in town that harbour a bit more life; only some of it being remotely human, mind you. I'm Stella, Stella Anworthy," she said over her shoulder as she opened the door to Room 1.

"Phoebe, Phoebe Wallace. And thank you, Ms Anworthy."

"Phoebe," Stella repeated. "What a nice name."

27

Philip

Fiona's persistence eventually got the better of him and they stopped at a beach. She slipped off her shoes and ran down to the water's edge, the wind blowing at her shirt and ruffling her hair.

The months before the wedding passed as smoothly as he could have hoped. Neither of them wanted to get married in their childhood neighbourhoods, so with a clipped list of friends and relations they booked out a hotel in the shadow of the Sussex Downs.

The stag night got a little out of hand when, much against his will, he was forced to spend far too long trawling the streets of Edgware in search of mischief. And, the next day, before taking his cognac-scented suit to the dry cleaners, Fiona emptied the pockets and found a handful of business cards one of his mates had stripped from a phone booth and planted on him: Exclusive Oriental Massage, Very Personal Service and Sensual Delights 24/7.

"Not funny," was all she said. But, making up for his friend's puerile humour cost Philip a substantial bouquet of flowers and dinner in Parson's Green.

On their wedding day, even the weather gods smiled at them. Spring painted the fields and hedgerows in glorious green hues, and lamb's wool clouds drifted on a cobalt sky like party balloons on the ceiling of a grand ballroom.

After a truly predictable wedding morning meltdown, during which Archie revealed a depth of patience and tenderness Philip had not imagined she'd possess, Fiona simply radiated. She did not wear the kind of off-the-shoulder, open-fronted number he'd expected – a misjudgement for which he coldly berated himself; rather she wore white silk with lace up to her neck in a Victorian style; her hair pinned up at the back but with long curls falling behind her shoulders. He had never seen her so beautiful and if, in the few nights before the wedding, he'd harboured any lingering doubts about his love for her, he banished them the moment he saw her in that dress.

When they returned from honeymoon in Menorca, Fiona let her flat and for the first time they had money they could spend; restaurants, shows and weekends away. And very soon, Fiona was expecting.

Harry came first and all Philip cared about was that the pair of them came through the long and rather difficult birth unscathed. And when he shepherded them back to their flat, it seemed very small and the three flights of stairs up to it very steep.

Philip took to fatherhood in a way he knew his father hadn't. He was of a different generation. He wanted to prove it and wanted Fiona to recognise it and love him all the more for it. Wanting her love, as he saw it, was not merely a question of being rewarded or gaining recognition for being a good father; it was also a large part of Philip's desire to let Fiona know that although her body had, in the normal course of becoming a mother, changed its shape, he still loved her just as much afterwards as he had before. He was patient and, he liked to think, undemanding.

However, Hattie soon followed on the heels of Harry and their living space contracted even further.

So they sold her flat and gave up his, mortgaged their souls and moved up the river to a terrace in Barnes. Fiona had heard the schools in the area were good and, if anything, Philip didn't object to a slightly longer commute to his office; it lent him more time to think.

After the move or perhaps it was after Hattie had come into their lives, things were different. Where there had been order, there was chaos, and where there had been time in abundance, there was suddenly none at all.

Philip remembered one winter evening when he got home late. He'd stayed on to finish a presentation, for which he had been congratulated by one of the senior partners, but he'd refused the offer of drinks in town because he wanted to get back for Fiona. That morning, before he left, she'd told him she was so tired she wasn't sure she'd be able to manage without a break or some help.

Philip, though, was so weary when he got off the train, he almost tripped down the steep steps at Barnes Bridge Station.

Just up from the station, there stood a pub: The White Hart. He'd passed it often and would have fallen into it but for the want of some company. As he walked past, the door opened. A babble of conversation like a warm, inviting stream poured out from within.

At home, all was unusually tranquil. The hall light was on, as was another in the living room, but apart from those, the house was so quiet it might have been deserted; the air was warm and a little musty, but held no promise of food.

He noticed a scrap of paper at the foot of the stairs: *Crashed, microwave dinner in fridge, sorry, love you, Fi x*

Normally, it wouldn't have mattered. But, for some reason, and later on he decided it must have been because he was so dog-tired, he flipped.

Philip lobbed his briefcase onto the living room sofa as he passed by on his way back out the door.

The pub was one spacious, high ceilinged room furnished with chairs, armchairs and sofas. It overlooked the Thames and could have been the front room of a private house, but for the large, triangular, central bar.

Philip ordered two pints of Guinness and polished off the first in one long draught while the barmaid let the second settle. When she came back with his change and realised both pints were for him alone, she smiled.

He recognised a few faces from the street and the station platform. He nodded politely, but felt no need to engage in conversation. By the time four more pints had gone the way of the first, his appetite was stilled and he was perfectly happy with his own company. The pub turned out to be just as agreeable as it had seemed inviting.

In fact, the pub was so agreeable, he stumbled into the wrong garden on the way home and that amused him rather than annoyed him, which he deemed an improvement in his mood.

The next evening Fiona told him off for not having eaten, but he responded by lying that he'd eaten on the way home from the office, which, in a sense, he had.

Over the coming weeks when waiting for the train, he progressed past nodding terms with those on the platform he'd seen in the pub. Most of them were either property or city boys, and, if a couple of them turned up on the same train home, Philip joined them for a beer.

Fiona even suggested it was a good thing. But, like all good things, she hoped he would be able to moderate his attendance.

"What is it about the place?" she said one evening when he came home a little later than usual. She was standing in the kitchen, a prawn and vegetable stir-fry steaming on the hob.

"How was the pub?" she asked, clearly a little narked.

"Okay." He was busy trying to work out why he felt so full. "It's got a nice atmosphere and I'm doing some work with a couple of the guys I've met. You know, networking."

"I'm not counting," she said, "but that's three times you've been this week and I could've done with a little bit of help putting the children to bed. Hattie was at her worst; she's only just gone down."

"Well, perhaps if you could arrange for Hattie to throw one of her tantrums on an evening when I don't run into the guys, then I wouldn't feel so guilty for affording myself a little down-time."

"Philip?"

The moment he said it, he knew she wouldn't pick up on the intended self-deprecation in his pathos. He knew she would interpret it as sarcasm.

"Philip? You're not listening to me," she was saying.

"Yes, I am. I'm sorry you've had a tough day. I'm sorry Hattie can be a pain in the arse, but outside of giving her up for adoption, I have no better idea than you about how to get her to sleep." Philip hung his coat and backpack in the hall. Perhaps it was taking off his suit jacket that brought the thought to mind, but he realised they'd not gone to bed at the same time for at least two weeks.

When he went back in, he saw that Fiona was angry and near to tears. "Listen," he said, putting his arms around her and drawing her close to him, "you're exhausted. I know that, I..."

Fiona pushed him away roughly. "I know I'm bloody exhausted." She put her hands up to her face to hide her tears. "You don't have to tell me I'm tired; I know I am. And I know you are, too," she said through her fingers. "And you've every right to be. But what I can't stand is both of us being so bloody exhausted at the same time and when we're on our own. We're not allowed to be exhausted when we're doing all the mundane stuff, so why the hell are we so tired when we want to do something together? It's like there isn't an alternative these days." Fiona reached for a tissue to blow her nose.

Philip moved back towards her, hoping upon hope that just the one flare-up would be sufficient to draw the heat from her frustrations.

She put her arms around his waist and pulled his hips towards her so she could feel him against her.

His stomach muscles tightened.

But to Fiona, it must have felt like he was trying to pull away or shrink back from her. She sagged and dropped her head onto his chest to avoid his eyes.

"Don't do that," he murmured, "I know it's not easy. Come on, I know you're tired." He lifted her chin and held her face so that he could look deep into her eyes.

He was tired, too. "Let me get you a glass of wine," he whispered. "And then, with your permission, or perhaps it would be better if I didn't ask your permission, Mrs Scott, I'd like to take you upstairs while the house is quiet and show you just how much I still love you."

Fiona opened her eyes very slowly. She pouted a shade too theatrically for his liking, "But do you, Phil? Do you?"

"Of course I do." He kissed her slowly on her lips; his mouth closed at first. Then he very gradually opened it so that he could touch her lips with his tongue, the honey sweetness of the beer still on it.

At first she didn't respond, so he hugged her more firmly in his arms and squeezed her tighter, persuading her he meant what he'd just said. He eased her gently backwards against the kitchen table, nudged his right leg between hers and raised it so that the top of his thigh rubbed against her.

Philip held her there until he felt her body begin to yield and then respond to his urging, and he knew she wanted him. He kissed her long and hard, and could taste her need — sweet and hot in her mouth. He steeled himself against his tiredness and led her up the stairs, both of them undressing as they went.

By the time they got into the bedroom, she was almost naked and she turned and pulled at the rest of his clothes and fell on him and devoured him.

Fiona didn't care that he'd not showered or was not as clean as she liked him to be. Her only thought seemed to be that she was going to take what she needed from him. And what she needed right then, Philip understood, was to be made to feel good about herself; to be

172

made to feel that what she went through every day was worthwhile and had meaning and therefore made sense.

When he'd walked through the door, she'd been as tired as he could remember. But he realised as he made love to her that she'd settled the children, prepared a special meal, and bathed and made up for him. He scolded himself for not recognising the signs.

This time, though, Fiona seemed to be at seriously low ebb; there was desperation to her urgency. She appeared almost to disregard his identity in pursuit of what he might provide her. She seemed to use him solely as some kind of repository from which she would be able to replenish her depleted emotional reserves.

All these thoughts rushed at him as Fiona kissed him hard, searching in his mouth with her tongue and running her hands over his buttocks.

And just as she urged him down towards her, Philip felt an infection of confusion rise in his cheeks.

Was this what Archie had meant when she said she'd had to continuously resupply Fiona's father with the emotional juice he needed to carry on? Because if that was what he would continually have to supply to Fiona, how could he know whether or not he possessed sufficient reserves? Was he like Fiona's mother? Was he the provider, the host, the emotional reservoir from which Fiona would draw all she needed?

And in the moment when he knew he could not make sense of it, Fiona arched her back and convulsed and finally took what she most needed from him. And, in the moments afterwards, when Fiona breathed hard and moaned softly, drifting back and forth in her sea of satisfaction — in the moments when Philip would normally have been exhilarated and overwhelmed with a sense of self-worth — somewhere in those moments, Philip went missing.

28

Phoebe

She flopped on the bed and stared at the ceiling. The up-lighter picked out all the irregularities in the surface; all the slight undulations where cracks had been filled and sanded only to leave dull indents. Phoebe traced them as though they were rivers winding towards a greater sea.

Her first year exams taxed and stressed her more than her A-levels, but she didn't allow them to get in her way.

May Week, so long in anticipation, flew by. Two of the balls, Clare College and Downing, were amazing; the second, they all agreed, was so sick. Days slipped seamlessly into nights and back again into days in one never-ending patchwork quilt of hedonism.

But after forty-eight hours of constant partying, Phoebe began to struggle, and at the seventy-two hour mark she fell asleep on the college lawn and only woke when the chill of dawn crept over her.

There was one more ball that evening, supposedly the best, or so everyone said. Her Student Finance loan was exhausted and her Grant the same. Her College Bursary came off her College costs, so she never had the chance to get her hands on that particular pile. And even though she had a few quid on her college card, there was no way she could magic that into real money, so she was as good as broke.

To pay for her ticket to Magdalene, Phoebe had to look to her 'rents. Her request went very much against the grain; hers, not theirs.

And, as with her depleted funds, so did Phoebe need to recharge her batteries.

"Heather," she said as they compared and hitched the last of their ball gowns, "you know that stuff you gave me last term; that powder, the 'drone.'"

"Uh-huh!" Heather replied, fiddling with her knicker-line.

Phoebe didn't take her eyes off her image in the mirror. She was trying to be as cool as possible with her enquiry, "You wouldn't happen to have any more, would you?"

"No, babe. Oh, bugger," said Heather. "You haven't got a thong I can borrow, have you? I really can't do knickers with this dress and I'm not going commando, not the way Si's behaving anyway."

Phoebe rummaged through a drawer and finally came up with what Heather needed, "Here."

"Thanks, darling. Why?"

"Well," said Phoebe, pushing aside her hair and examining her rather bloodshot eyes in the mirror, "I don't know about you, but after the last couple of nights I'm hanging like a bitch. I'm battered. I'm never going to last the night on adrenalin and vodka alone. I just wondered if you had any, that's all."

"No, babe, I don't. Ask Yu. He'll have some. He buys it off the internet. It's only plant food. It's quite legal."

So Phoebe slipped on her running shoes and hurried over to Yu's room. She knocked on the door.

"Come," he shouted. "It is open."

Yu was standing in front of the mirror, a bath towel around his waist.

"Hello, gorgeous!" she said in mock appreciation.

"What do you think, Phoebes?" He swept his jet black hair down over his forehead. "What do you think? Bit too Gorillaz? Bit too Plastic Beach?"

"Not at all, man!" In truth, it wasn't a genre she liked, but she didn't want to piss him off, so she said, "It's a good look."

"You're so just saying that. What brings you to my temple? You look fantastic, by the way."

"Thanks. I just wondered if you had any 'drone I could buy off you. Only I'm still hanging from last night and I hate feeling like a limp di-"

"Dick?"

"Dish cloth, actually." Phoebe tugged playfully at his towel, but stopped short of pulling it off. "I just don't want to get there and fade too early. You know, feel like I need to be in bed when everyone else is still going."

"Who with, babe. That would be the question, wouldn't it? Who with?"

Phoebe ignored his teasing, but moved over to stand behind him. She draped her arms round his neck and looked over his shoulder so that they could stand and watch their reflection; her bright red hair and porcelain skin in stark contrast to his jet black mop and smooth, light brown chest. Clearly, he liked how they looked.

"I've never asked you this-"

But he cut her off, "What? For some 'drone?"

"No, not for 'drone. I mean, yes, but that wasn't what I was going to ask. I was going to ask what Yuichi means in English. Don't all Japanese names have meanings?"

Yu beamed back at her from the mirror. "It means First Son, Rich or Brave or Abundant First Son," he replied and flexed the long slender muscles of his arms and shoulders.

"Which one are you?" she asked. "Rich, brave or abundant?"

"Well, if you pull my towel off, you'll find out."

Phoebe dropped her arm off his shoulder and made to pull his towel away again, but he stepped quickly out of her reach, laughing.

"Really, I am all of them, because I don't, as you already know, have a brother, so I am the first and last son."

"Sounds to me like you'd be the ideal son-in-law."

"Go and fix your hair in the bathroom," he said.

"What's wrong with my hair?"

"Nothing, it looks fab. Just get out of my room for a moment. How much do you want? Enough for now or will you need some for later?"

"Oh, I get it. Sorry," she said, "enough to get me through the night would be good. I guess you'd know more about how much of that Oriental Organic Fertiliser I will need."

Yu looked down at the floor and frowned, "Actually, it's Chinese, not Japanese."

Phoebe blushed and shut herself in his bathroom.

After a couple of minutes, he called her out. Handing her a small plastic bag containing some white powder settled in one corner, he said, "Divide it up into three and eat it when you feel knackered, it'll give you a longer buzz that way. Rub what's left onto your gums." He looked directly into her face, a stark intensity to his expression as though he was trying to look deep into her soul. "Don't go chucking it about, huh; it won't be legal for that long."

Phoebe was drowning in the black pools of his eyes, her world in suspension, "What do I owe?"

Yu smiled. "Forget it, Phoebes," he said. "Next time, it'll be fifteen pounds a go."

"There won't be a next time," she mumbled.

Philip

He sat at the back of the beach perfectly happy to watch Fiona skip between the groynes, overturn the rocks and shriek in response to the life that crawled out from under. He enjoyed watching her, he always had.

Later that next afternoon, as Philip sat in his office, he decided that that was the only way he could honestly describe what had happened to him while they were making love. He had simply gone missing. And it was as though the jungle had closed in behind him and erased any sign of how he had come by his location; a place he did not recognise because he'd never been there before.

If only he had attached some kind of mental chord around him, he might have been able to retrace his steps to the point from which he'd set off. But he hadn't.

To ward off any further analysis, Philip buried himself in his work. He left home early and worked out at a gym. He took lunch in his office and cleared his desk in order to network the firm's old clients and cultivate a few new ones. On Tuesdays and Wednesdays, he made certain he arrived home on time and to help Fiona put the children to bed. And he hoped that by sticking to a more ordered regime, he would benefit both of them by providing them with the opportunity of spending more quality time together; not to mention the residual value of furthering his chances of scaling the ladder of promotion at work and earning them more money in the process.

"After all," he murmured whenever he found himself knocked back at the office, "it makes sense."

And it did make sense. It made good, earthy common sense, for a while.

Philip felt revived. His sense of self-worth returned and his libido, if it was his flagging libido that had been responsible for his mental detachment, revived.

Then a couple of months down the line, a phone call from an unexpected quarter pierced the bubble he was so busy constructing.

"Philip Scott?" said the man.

"That would be me," he replied, trying desperately to place the voice. It was thin and very nasal in tone. The rolodex in Philip's head whirred like a wheel of fortune.

The line went dead for a second. Evidently, the man expected to be identified.

Then Philip got it, "Mr Carson, to what do I owe the pleasure?" He sat back in his chair.

"Very good! Most impressed, Philip! Well, how are we?"

"Fighting fit, thank you. And your good self?"

"Very well, thank you. Not interrupting a meeting or anything?"

"No, Mr Carson. I'm sitting at my desk about to attack a rather limp ham sandwich; that's if I can work out which end to assault first." He was not inclined to describe his lunch so, but Philip was aware Carson wanted to know if he was alone, and in the meantime he was trying to come up with the name of the senior partner at the firm Carson had said he knew. "Have you seen Mr Fairbank recently?"

Carson paused and then replied in a tone that suggested he was again impressed, "Matter of fact, spoke with him last week. Gave good report of you, so he did."

"Well, that's nice to hear. Always pays to keep the boss, or bosses, on side. We must have more senior partners than any other firm in town. Mind you, we have more departments in more countries than just about any other real estate management company in the world, so it's to be expected that we should have more than the usual spread of senior partners." Philip knew he was talking too much, but Jimmy Carson unsettled him. He'd done so the first time they'd met at Hanger Holt. "What can I do for you, Mr Carson?"

"Like a chat, Philip," he said; a demand as opposed to a preference. "Gort's, tomorrow. Twelve thirty alright for you? Know where it is?"

Philip considered consulting his diary, but then decided that any humour, however subtle, would probably be lost on Carson. "Of course," he said.

"See you then." The line clicked dead. Carson's economy with words matched his thrift with etiquette.

It was only when Philip looked at the phone and put it down that he realised Carson had called him on his mobile. Either that meant Archie had given Carson his number or Carson had not wanted the call recorded by the company, which, Philip knew, they all were.

What Philip didn't know was Gort's. He'd read reviews of the restaurant and had tried to book a table more times than he cared to remember. One of the guys with whom he used to drop into the pub on the way home had told him that even a Black Amex card couldn't get you a table at Gort's.

For the first time in his short career, Philip lied in saying he was taking the afternoon to visit a prospective client. One of his contemporaries tapped his nose knowingly as Philip walked towards the lift at midday.

He paid the taxi driver and stood for a while studying the shabby facade of the three-storey pub. Gort's, just off the Farringdon Road in Clerkenwell, squatted uneasily between two much larger and more modern buildings. The restaurant leaned like a practised drunk, who, but for the support of two younger and sober friends on either side, would likely as not slide to the pavement. And in keeping with the quintessential drunk of so many cartoons, new and gaily coloured flowers cheered from the window boxes like carnations on a tired lapel. The front door had once been red, but its frosted glass inserts were spotlessly clean.

Immediately inside stood a front desk manned by a striking blonde with a broad, welcoming smile.

"Sir?"

"Philip Scott."

The woman didn't bother to consult any list, she merely smiled, "A table with Mr Carson?"

"Yes," he said, relaxing.

She picked a menu off the desk and motioned for him to follow.

The room was oak panelled, the tables partitioned in the manner of stalls in a livery stable.

The particular stall she showed him to was empty. Philip checked his watch; he was, right on time.

Just as he sat down, Jimmy Carson walked in, but from the back not the front. "Punctual! Sharp! Speaks well of you. Hope you've an appetite, Philip?"

"Always."

"Good. The Porterhouse is the best in London. Hate it when people call it a T-bone; sounds rather too carnivorous. How'd you like it?"

Carson sported a grey suit, white shirt and dark tie, and what with his thick spectacles, sharp features and shiny, thinning hair, could have passed for an undertaker or perhaps a passport clerk.

"Medium'll be fine, thank you."

"Drink?"

"No thanks, not at lunch. Well, leastways, not during the week."

Carson looked miffed by Philip's reply, "You sure? I'm paying." When he received no response, he turned to the waitress, "Large Gordon's and tonic.

"How is Fiona?"

"Top form."

"Children?"

"Noisy; Hattie is enjoying more than her fare share of the terrible twos, if you know what I mean."

"No," said Carson, "haven't got kids. Not my thing. Work?"

"Flat out."

He looked straight at Philip, "So I gather."

They talked sport for a while. Carson was an Arsenal season ticket holder, had been for as long as he could remember; didn't like the nags, as he put it, but liked the dogs; Walthamstow, Romford, sometimes Crayford, but never Wimbledon — too far west; did lots of things, fingers in the strangest pies, not much he wanted to talk about though, most things, different things, anything with a sensible margin. And he knew a lot of people; some who'd made it big, others who hadn't, but whose day was yet to come.

Fifteen minutes later the gulf between them was no narrower, but, thankfully, the food arrived.

The restaurant filled up. The low murmur of conversation warmed the room, but because of the partitions the conversation from other tables did not crowd theirs.

Carson took wine and even though Philip was tempted, he politely declined. And, while Philip struggled, Carson ate as though it was his first meal in a year. There was still an obscene lump of strip loin lounging on Philip's plate when the man sitting opposite placed his own knife and fork neatly together.

"How many people work in your firm, Philip?"

"UK or worldwide?"

"Let's start with the home market," Carson replied.

"Twelve hundred and fifty, give or take."

"Two thousand five hundred and that's only the home market."

Philip was surprised. He allowed it to register in his look, but added a light sprinkling of doubt for good measure.

"Your department? What do you spend most of your time on?"

Philip had a feeling Carson already knew the answer, but he had little alternative other than to play along and see where the conversation was headed, "Construction Management and Project Controls. Sounds rather grand, but it isn't really."

"Quite specialised, though?"

"You could say that."

"So," Carson carried on quickly, "while you're keeping your head down with all that construction supervision and scheduling and so on, there's other people attending to the preconstruction project controls, the design management, the sustainability planning and consultancy, the risk and value management, the technical diligence, bidding and procurement, and the investment appraisal, too. Correct?"

"Sure."

"They keep their heads down in their department — their noses to the grindstone, if you like — and you keep yours down in your department?"

"That's how it works," Philip agreed. "But that's how it works in most companies of our size. There is some interdepartmental crossover, but on larger projects there is an overall project manager who coordinates the relevant departments." He was preaching to the educated and he knew it. Philip could have replied with a simple yes or no, but he felt, given Carson's apparently considerable knowledge of a subject that ought to have been Philip's domain, such a response might be deemed inadequate. Then, a light began to glow in his mind. "But if what you're driving at is that by concentrating in our own specialised areas we're forfeiting our ability to work on a broader scale, then I'd have to agree with you."

"Good," said Carson. He smiled, very obviously appreciating that Philip had joined him on his journey. "That's partly where I'm going, but only a part."

Philip carved off a final morsel of the steak and closed his plate.

If he was going to have to think, he wanted to remain clear-headed and coherent, not gorged and ruminant.

"Now, how many people work in your firm worldwide?" Carson asked.

"Upwards of twenty thousand."

"And how many of those twenty thousand are Quantity Surveyors or of similar qualification? What's the rough percentage?"

"I'm not sure I know that," Philip did, however, know that a wild guess would only expose his ignorance, "but I've got a sneaking feeling you're going to tell me."

"Forty-one per cent, Philip. Over eight thousand five hundred people! That's one hell-of-a-lot of QSs in one company." Carson waited for the numbers to sink in, then he said, "And if eight thousand four hundred 'n ninety-nine of them are trying to stand on your shoulders to get a leg up onto the next rung of the ladder, unless you're superman, which okay I'm sure Fiona rightly thinks you are, all you're likely to end up with is a bill from the osteopath. Make sense?"

Philip was beginning to find Carson's abbreviated questions a little irritating. "Naturally it makes sense. But, just because there's an extended workforce, it doesn't follow that there are no prospects for advancement or that one has to assassinate one's colleagues just to get in the frame."

Jimmy Carson fell silent. He watched Philip with a kind of vacant intensity.

The waitress came, cleared their plates and swept the table.

They ordered coffee.

"Let's look at this from another angle, shall we?" Carson said, leaning forwards, elbows on the table. "The girl on the front desk: Maja, Polish." He nodded towards the door as though Philip had forgotten where he came in.

"The blonde?" Philip asked. "Pink shirt, black skirt? Nice smile. Good-looking girl."

"Very polished; no pun intended. Very clever girl! No fool!" Carson pushed his glasses back up and rubbed the bridge of his nose briefly. "While you were busy clocking her assets…"

Philip frowned in mock disapproval.

"Wouldn't worry about it, son. They're there for a reason and it's nothing to do with what most of us are thinking. They're there so that whilst you can't take your eyes off them, she's working out if you are expected and if so who you are here to meet and whether you are the kind of customer they want back here. If she hadn't thought you were here to meet someone, you'd have been out on the street before you could have said Wodge."

"Sorry?"

"Wodge! It's where she's from in Poland. Wodge: L-0-D-Z. It's pronounced Wodge. Don't ask me why. It just is." Carson carried on. "She won't be here for long," he scoffed. "She'll be somebody's PA inside of a month. She's not just eye candy; she's sharp as a razor and just as keen on the strap."

"Okay, I get it," Philip said, risking a look over his shoulder; she certainly was a good-looking girl. He turned back, "What you're suggesting is that she's using Gort's as a stepping stone and maybe I should be doing the same thing."

"Yes," Carson said, but he stretched out the confirmation to imply he wasn't quite finished. "Now, let's look at where you are right now and where you want to be in five years or maybe ten." Carson laid his napkin on the table and reached into his jacket. The gold pen he produced was thin like his tie. He started to sketch details on the linen napkin.

Philip raised an eyebrow.

Carson looked up, "Don't worry; I've thrown enough money at this place over the years. They're not likely to cancel my membership over a serviette. He scribbled away: words and figures, some brief addition and subtraction.

The coffee arrived.

Philip took his time to look around the restaurant. The deep oak panels lent the room a comfortable atmosphere and the wall lights cast a gentle ambience that balanced with the conversation floating upon it. The floor was blocked in solid oak, but to a matt finish, not waxed and shiny. Although exclusive, Gort's was not pretentious like some of the other city eateries Philip had been treated to.

"Now then," Carson said, handing him the napkin, "have a quick look at that and tell me whether it's accurate."

Set out in black ink on the white linen was a spread of Philip's finances: his current earnings, his mortgage, his outgoings and his savings. Below that was a similar spread but projected forward ten years. Some of the figures were disconcertingly accurate. He read both sets of figures twice and then looked up, more than a little angry. "How do you-"

Carson waved away Philip's objection, "Now, before you get out of your chair, I've guessed some of those figures; guesstimations sure, but estimations nevertheless."

"I don't accept that, Mr Carson." Philip was annoyed. "Did Archie put you up to this?"

"No, Philip. She didn't." Carson tapped the napkin. "Those figures are what I would expect from a young man in your position. Your earnings, they're easy to find out. Your mortgage is an educated guess, but you had to sell Fiona's flat to make up the deposit for your house in Barnes and they don't come cheap. Your outgoings aren't difficult to predict; one income, two kids. As far as your savings go: well, I didn't need to ask Archie if she'd bought you the house, that's not her style. And I gambled on your parents not providing you with a trust fund in Jersey. If they had you'd be living in a big house on Putney Hill, not a terrace in Barnes." He paused. "Believe it or not, Philip, London's full of young guys like you – heads down, providing for the family."

Philip didn't know whether to get up and hit Carson or strangle the anger that was rising in his throat. "You're not going to tell me I need life insurance, Mr Carson? I somehow don't get the feeling you're regulated by the FSA."

"No," Carson said, "I most certainly am not."

There was an awkward silence while Philip read the figures again. He was trying to work out Carson's motive for producing such a detailed map.

"Look, Philip," Carson said, "can I ask you to do me a couple of favours?"

"I don't know, Mr Carson. But I suppose there's no harm in asking. Fire away."

"One, please call me Jimmy. The last person to call me Mister was a magistrate. And two, have a glass of wine and stop seeing dragons just because you can feel a hot wind on the back of your neck."

"That's three favours."

"Okay," he spread his arms wide, "three."

Philip looked across the table at the short, wiry individual. Logic recommended that he should listen to the man. Archie Davy did and she was nobody's fool. And he needn't go back to the office; that had been a fall-back.

"Sure. Okay. Why not," Philip said and breathed deep, unsure of the water he was going to find upstream. "Where do we go from here?"

Jimmy Carson smiled and as he did so his face relaxed. It took on a whole new attitude, a depth and warmth that the previous poker face had not hinted at. He ordered a bottle of wine from the waitress without, as far as Philip noticed, informing her of which particular wine he wanted.

Where they went for the next hour was the paradise Philip had always dreamt of occupying: a place where he, Fiona and the children would be comfortable.

The hostess Maja brought the wine: a bottle of Hautes Côtes de Beaune, 2002. She presented it to Jimmy for his approval and when he nodded, opened it and poured the contents into an elegant and simple Burgundy decanter which she placed beside him on the table.

"I like to pour my own wine," Jimmy said. "Hate all that prissy waiting-for-the-waiter crap." He contemplated the brick-red liquid for a few seconds. It had a faint violet tinge to it. "Like wine, do you, Philip? Or are you a beer man?"

"No, I don't think one can ask for much more than good company and a bottle of wine. I like a beer, too, but if I had to choose, it would be the wine every time."

"Good man," said Jimmy, "I'm what you might call a Burgundy freak. I don't pass up claret, but I prefer a lighter red. Here, get your laughing tackle round this."

With the glass at his lips, Philip breathed in slowly; a profusion of red fruits danced up his nose. He sipped it and held the wine on his tongue; silky, sweet cherries set on dry leaden minerals.

Jimmy Carson had his eyes closed in appreciation. "Burgundy for Kings," he quoted.

Philip nodded. He'd heard the expression.

"Know a thing or two about wine, do you, Philip?"

"Not much," he replied. "Basic stuff, really: Good wine ruins the purse; bad wine ruins the stomach, that kind of thing."

Carson eyed him. "You do like to hide your light under a bushel, don't you, Philip? I can see by the way you drink that you know a thing or two about the noble grape. Where'd you learn? Come on?"

Forty-five minutes later, the gulf that had divided them at the beginning of the meal was solidly bridged. The curious property of wine to either amplify or shrink differences between people, in this case, provided them with a middle ground on which to cultivate their mutual respect.

And towards the end of the decanter, their conversation wound its way back to the subject of Philip's aspirations. He found the wine released him from his somewhat cautious definitions and he grew more voluble in trying to describe exactly what it was that he wanted out of life. Spiritual goals were, after all, very personal and not always so easy to put into words.

With Jimmy's enthusiastic blessing, Philip ordered another bottle of the Burgundy.

When Maja appeared with the bottle, she also brought a fresh decanter and this time set it down beside Philip. She smiled at him and afforded him the time to smile back before she turned away.

"I hear you've been doing a bit of networking yourself, Philip," Jimmy said, diverting Philip from his more carnal attractions.

"Sure. It's important to show willing."

Jimmy nodded, "I couldn't agree more, Philip. But, and please correct me if I'm wrong, you've done more than show a little willing recently. You recently hijacked a fairly lucrative contract from one of your competitors: Mason Marberg Associates? Ring any bells? Well, Howard Marberg is an old mucker of mine and he was very cheesed off with having that contract nicked from under his nose. You might say it put his nose out of joint."

Philip reddened with embarrassment and then grinned with satisfaction, "Don't tell me he wants to break my legs?"

"No, Philip, he wants you to go and work for him."

30

Audrey

The taxi driver was an Asian gentleman; a full moustache tied back and netted, heavy glasses and a grey turban.

Audrey could neither understand what he said, nor quite see his lips when he was speaking. She felt uncomfortable at the way he glanced at her in the rear view mirror and she found it hard to understand why he should fiddle so with his Tom-Tom when they were travelling but a few miles.

They passed beside the high sea wall, through low reed beds and by the entrance to what looked like an airfield. The neighbourhood seemed a good deal sleepier than she remembered.

They arrived at The Norfolk Flyer just before seven-thirty and she paused at the door, taking a couple of long, deep breaths. It had been a long time since she'd walked alone into a... well, into almost anywhere that wasn't a shop.

Of course it was Richard's fault, wasn't it? Everything was Richard's fault.

Three couples seated at the low tables all looked fairly well dressed and two suited gentleman sat at the back, buried in their own conversation.

"Now, what can I get you?" the waiter asked.

Looking around as if studying what the other patrons were

drinking, Audrey caught sight of the Specials board, and there they were: Crayfish; boiled, fried, smoked, Bordelaise, Mornay, or just as a plain and simple cocktail. She could have cried.

"A large glass of Sauvignon Blanc, please; Bordeaux would be nice."

"As you wish. Please find a table. I'll bring your wine over."

A log fire burned in the inglenook and Audrey, perching at the table nearest to it, tried ever so hard to look as though she was used to going into pubs on her own. Maybe the other diners would think she was waiting to meet someone. But then again, perhaps they might feel sorry for her when her rendezvous didn't show. That, she couldn't bear.

"Your wine," said the barman, placing the rather large glass of pale, almost straw-green wine before her. "And would you like to order now or would you like a little more time to study the menu?"

"Well, I..."

"Not a bother. You take your time," he interrupted when she hesitated.

Bordelaise would be too rich for her, also the Mornay. The smoked was not really her thing. Fried, she would consider, but then fried anything was not, strictly speaking, healthy. And as a cocktail; too much like a prawn starter. "The crayfish, boiled, please," she said as he was turning away.

"An excellent choice, if I may say. We don't over-season them; just salt, onion and lemon," he added, more probably to ensure that Audrey would understand exactly how simple the Boiled Crayfish would be served.

She took off her jacket, laid it on the seat beside her, sipped her wine, sat back in her chair, and tried to recall how the place had been when she'd last set foot in it.

The fire had been there then; although it was summer, so it had not been lit. Goodness, hadn't they had a lot of rain that year; floods down below the village, she remembered. The pub was darker back then; the beams painted black or dark-brown, the ceiling in between yellowed, smoke-stained. Of course they all smoked back then, even her: Rothmans. Grief, what a bloody fool! And Baileys! That was a new drink at the time. They'd drunk Baileys by the bottle and belted out 'Waterloo' as if it was the only song that had ever been written. Still, the seventies were much milder than the sixties, weren't they? Oh the sixties, she scoffed and looked round self-consciously. In the sixties, every brother and his uncle was trying to get you to smoke pot; it scrambled your brains and your legs fell apart. Who needed conversation?

"You'll be needing these," said the waiter, laying out a string place-mat, cutlery and napkin.

Audrey frowned and then she realised the barman would not have been born before the eighties, so she forgave him and smiled back at him.

No, she had not liked the sixties; they'd confused her.

And, why wouldn't they? At eighteen St Dominica's had done with her, and after ten years of incarceration she was thrown like a spring lamb to the wolves. Sadly, she hadn't shared her patron saints extraordinary gift of not being harmed by the many wild beasts; not by a long chalk! Still, it had been either suffer a bit or suffer the consequences, and being socially beheaded in the late sixties was probably just as bad as being physically beheaded in the third century. Poor Dominica, what would she have made of all those dope-heads?

No, when she had last been to Strand-next-the-Sea in seventy-four, she'd sat in the exact same seat and the room had somehow been darker, but darker in a different way. The lighting was different or maybe it was the layout of the bar.

The seventies: Well, they had been another matter entirely. Politically, Audrey had matured late; she recognised that now. But then, what with Watergate and the nuclear tests in Nevada, she'd fervently believed that it was up to her to make the world a better place before it was too late.

But too late for whom? Too late for the people of the rest of the world before they disappeared beneath a shroud of atomic dust, or too late for Audrey Crichton, before she forsook her future for that scion of the Lloyds community, Richard Poulter; a man who, curiously for one involved in marine insurance, didn't like waves?

So, they argued.

Audrey sipped her Sauvignon and fixed her eyes on a Tea Clipper forging through the foam on the wall opposite.

"What of it?" he'd asked. "Everybody argues!"

Well, the what of it was that nobody ever argued with Richard Poulter. It just wasn't humanly possible. He possessed that wonderfully selective hearing which granted him a form of benign ignorance. If he didn't like something, he appeared not to hear it. And if he did hear something that he could not avoid disagreeing with, then he would browbeat or bully his adversary into submission. He would be gloriously contentious, effortlessly dismissive and even openly base in his disrespect. But, like so many of those public school boys who'd suffered at the hands of brutish, older pupils and merciless, pedantic masters, he concealed a soft side which, once she had glimpsed it, she rather liked. His plaintive, sad moments appealed to her more nurturing instincts; instincts which, like her increasing cup-size in the early seventies, she'd found profoundly unsettling.

He'd been part of that burgeoning, new-city crowd who frequented the Kings and Fulham Road restaurants of early seventies London; large and colourful characters who became larger and more colourful with every glass of claret; broad-shouldered individuals who, when they weren't playing rugby, were blasting defenceless birds out of the Cotswold skies, losing their shirts at Ascot or careering down pistes in the Valais. They were many things they ought not to have been, but the one thing they weren't was dull.

And Audrey had happened upon one of those restaurants quite by chance.

She was born late to older parents, who'd despatched her, aged eight, to St Dominica's as though they had not known what to do with their strange and discomfiting addition.

But in spite of her abandonment, Audrey soon got used to convent life. There was, after all, little else she could do but get used to it. At least as a boarder she'd permitted herself to feel as though she was one rung higher up the celestial ladder than the day girls. Celebrating Saints days, helping Sister Grainne out in the kitchen and the affection of Sister Colette, her French teacher, were the high points; Morning Mass, mortification and sanitary towels, the lows.

Some Sundays her parents would come and take her out to lunch. Her father would be impatient, occasionally grumpy; her mother, gracious, but more often than not distant. She didn't hold it against them. They'd lived through the war and expected her to be grateful for their sacrifices. But if St Dominica's taught her anything, it was that life was how it was and there was little point in questioning it. It was just something that one got on with. Everyone did. Even her namesake St Audrey the Abbess of Ely, she just got on with perpetuating her virginity much as she was directed to by her god. Obedience was, after all, divine; only Satan was permitted sufficient intellect to question.

For their family summer holidays they would stay at the Carlton in Cannes on the Côte d'Azur and, whilst her parents took their afternoon nap, Audrey would sneak out to wander the Rue Félix Fauré and the Quai Saint-Pierre and linger in the flea market between. In the cool shade of Palm Square, idle thoughts of Sister Colette fostered her love for most things French. And thanks to the gentle Sister, Audrey had learned the language and studied the art, so she felt comfortable amongst strangers who returned her smile with their own.

Sadly both her parents passed away whilst she was still at the convent; the wounds her father had sustained during the war finally overcame him, and her mother, Audrey believed, never recovered from losing him.

They left her a Tudor Manor House near Telford; a pile in the middle of nowhere, as she liked to sing. But at eighteen Audrey had no idea what to do with such a pile, so her trustees disposed of it.

After honing her secretarial skills at Pitman's and cultivating her culinary talents at Tante Marie, she felt ready for just about anything. What that anything was though, she didn't have a clue.

Initially she took a job with a wine merchant in the West End, her French helped, and she answered an ad in the Evening Standard regarding a one-bed flat in Fulham. The agent described it as bijou, and the word intrigued her. The flat turned out to be small, but adequate, and above a restaurant called Fed's.

A few weeks after she'd moved in and having grown used to the constant clash of crockery and the heavy perfume of stale cooking oil, she asked the owner if there was any chance she could supplement her income by waiting table at weekends.

It was a dimly-lit but cosy bistro of twenty or so covers, with, as far as its identity was concerned, a sprawling and confusing menu. Fed's catered for every cosmopolitan palate and in doing so, pleased few.

Six months later, Federico asked her to look after the place for a couple of evenings each week; he couldn't devote as much time to the place what with his wife being ill.

Over time, Audrey persuaded Fed to introduce a more Mediterranean, Elizabeth David style menu and she gave the place a coat of paint. And in return for a share of the business, she invested some of her savings in a more significant and essentially French cellar. That was the key. That was what opened the door to the sharp suited city crew, the poodle parloured property boys, the old-school motor dealers, the wannabees and would-bees, and the prototype Sloane

Rangers. Fed's began to attract so many of the aspiring seventies set that some whispered the restaurant sat over an enormous style magnet. And, soon enough, if you hadn't booked...

Naturally, a young woman in her early twenties managing a trendy Fulham Road eatery did not lack for the attention of her male, and, on the odd occasion, female patrons. But Audrey never had and never would consider herself to be beautiful or glamorous in the conventional sense.

One evening, a party of diners, suffering under the glaring misapprehension that they knew Audrey much better than they had any right to, told her she bore a striking resemblance to Audrey Hepburn. She remembered feeling quite taken aback, almost angry. Considering her reddish hair, she was certain they must have meant Katharine Hepburn, not Audrey. God, it wasn't as though a drunk would describe her nose as dainty! And, God, how much money would she have given to actually look like Hepburn?

She also remembered thinking she ought to have known better than to react so; she ought to have been more professional. After all, the idiots had been drinking Wolfschmidt long into the evening and from the caraway and cumin-flavoured Kummel, she and Fed made a healthy turn.

So Audrey had not been short of suitors, even though she found out one night that the word on the street was that she was frigid.

However, that only seemed to foster an increasingly intense competition amongst her suitors as to who would be the first to bed her. And that led to her having to be quite forthright, and sometimes quite physical with them. On those occasions, St Dominica, her suitably convenient Catholicism and the vows of her namesake were never far from her mind.

Then, late one night as she was closing up, she noticed the usually genial Richard Poulter fast asleep or, perhaps more accurately, comatose at the table in the back corner. His fellow pleasure-seekers, bleary and weary devotees of the grape, apparently uncaring that they'd left their even blearier and wearier chum behind. And she found herself feeling strangely charitable towards such a rumpled beast and wondered whether she might be clever enough to iron out a few of his creases the way the laundry would soon iron them out of the table cloths she was collecting.

"Here we are," said a soft voice, interrupting her train of thought. "Would you like another glass of wine?" The waiter put the bowl of crayfish down on the place mat.

Audrey hauled herself from her reverie, nodded and smiled. When he came back with her refilled glass, he also bought a finger bowl, a larger serviette and a plate for the crayfish shells.

She studied the crayfish for a moment and then set about peeling them delicately and methodically. As she picked each one from the bowl, peeled it and then dipped it in the mayonnaise, she realised she was at the same time retrieving memories from deep within her mind, examining and garnishing them, so that they might seem more suited to her purpose.

Surely the crayfish had been a deeper red? But they were as delicious as she recalled and the flavours gave rise to a rainbow of sensations.

An image of Richard emerged from her wine as she gazed through it into the yellow flames of the log fire.

He hadn't minded when she asked him to wait until their wedding night to go the whole way, as he termed it. In that respect, he was wonderfully chivalrous — a quality she found both disarming and heartening, and a quality that set him apart from the other, baser beasts. But by behaving in such an understanding, patient and gentlemanly manner, he made for her a bed so comfortable that she never properly considered refusing it.

It was only later, after she had given up the restaurant, that Audrey began to lose her bearings.

With time on her hands, she read more and more, and she grew more self-aware and more politically active. It was as though when she became a housewife, the time left to her to expand her mental capacity was going to run out; as though once married, that particular form of cerebral activity might become inappropriate and so lost to her forever.

Within a few months, Audrey had transformed from good-time, free-thinking, easy-going restaurant manageress into angst-ridden, conscience-driven, Campaign for Nuclear Disarmament activist.

Looking back, some of her views had been far too trenchant, even by modern standards.

Maybe it was that, for her, marriage implied children, and that children were entitled to a future. And their future required direction, and she, Audrey soon-to-be Poulter, worked out that she needed to have some attitude to or some control over that direction.

And nuclear hadn't been the way to go. It had, after all, wiped out generations of youth in the forties and threatened to do the same in the sixties.

Well, that was how she looked at it then and, discarding the luxury of hindsight, whether that was a true appraisal of the events or not no longer mattered.

At first, Richard found her metamorphosis amusing. At first! But soon enough her new-found convictions began to wear a little thin on some of the others of their dinner party circuit and one or two invitations went by the way. Soon enough, Richard grew increasingly irritated by her reluctance to let her crusade drop.

So they argued and Audrey upped-sticks and fled to France. Well, to Bordeaux to be more accurate. She took the boat-train to Paris, the wagon-lit to Bordeaux and finally the *tortillard* along the northern estuary of the Gironde to the humble village of Braud-Saint-Louis. There, in the backyard of the world's premier wine makers, Audrey joined the local farmers in their demonstrations against the construction of the nuclear power station planned by Électricité de France.

And it was there that she met Laurent.

Audrey dipped her hands in the finger bowl, dried them on the serviette and took a long, slow sip of wine. The Sauvignon Blanc transported her back to Braud as if she were on a magic carpet. She could hear the farmers cheering and smell their dark tobacco and the diesel fumes from their tractors as they barricaded the road. She could see their crude banners waving and the blue uniforms of the po-faced Compagnies Républicaines de Sécurité as they cheered and charged and tried more than once to break the demonstration. And she could see Laurent's young, tanned face, his curly brown hair and the way it fell over his brow. Audrey remembered the taste of wine on his tongue almost the way she could taste it now.

A disagreement from the other side of the room distracted her for a moment. The two men in suits were arguing. It annoyed her; they'd punctured her trance. She took another sip of wine and held it in her mouth, playing the dry essence lightly back and forth over her tongue.

After four weeks of washing in a bucket and squatting behind cow sheds, Audrey was dirty, dishevelled, flea-bitten and hungry. And when the *forces d'ordre* eventually came to break up the demonstration, she cursed and spat at them. She kicked out at their riot shields, their *bouclier antiémeutes*, and sobbed and stumbled beneath the barrage of their tear gas, their *gaz lacrymogènes*. The CRS were not gentle with her. Perhaps they were even more brutal with her. It certainly seemed like it at the time; it mattered not to them that she was British.

Luckily, she'd kept her passport safe.

When she got back to London, she stayed with a friend rather than go directly home. Audrey could not allow Richard to witness the welts and bruises on her arms and legs. They would only encourage him in his view that what she'd done was childish. After all, Richard was eight years older than her and she was beginning to understand only too well how he saw her.

And then there were the psychological scars; the marks left by those, even more painfully raw than the physical. It was as though Laurent had torn a wound in her side; a deep and sweet wound which she was unwilling to allow to heal too quickly. And as the days stretched into weeks, Audrey would scratch away at her wound; she would aggravate it and peel back the scab as it formed, anxious that it should never repair. She liked it, adored it, even loved it; that dull ache that reminded her of just how alive she had felt with Laurent.

But girlfriends cajoled her and his friends told her how much Richard missed her, how she had been the best thing in his life and how it would be a good life for her with him. So she agreed to meet him for dinner at Fed's. It was a mistake and she knew it, but she did not, or possibly would not, keep from going.

It had been a kind of laziness. She knew that now; a treacherous combination of what was right and what was easy; a fatal cocktail of options, like alcohol and sleeping pills.

Then, two weeks before their wedding, while Richard was on one of his protracted and, or so the rumours suggested, unpleasantly carnal stag weekends, the door intercom buzzed.

And it was Laurent.

Audrey knew full well what it was that she was going to remember next, so she quickly closed her mind to it. There were other, less savoury memories she needed to recall before she could allow herself to remember her second time with Laurent. There would be time for intimacy later, she'd promised herself that.

She sipped at her wine without realising there was nothing in her glass, and her bowl was empty but for a couple of quarters of lemon and the crayfish shells.

She started to rise to go to the bar. God knows, she didn't exactly need any more wine.

But just as she knew she had not been going to stop thirty-seven years before, nothing this evening, neither the lack of wine nor the other people around her, and certainly not the last vestiges of her widowhood, was going to stop her from giving herself absolutely and completely to Laurent.

Another glass of Sauvignon wouldn't go amiss.

She sat back down, sipped, stared at the fire and was calm for a while. There was much she wanted to remember, but some of it was not for the moment; not for now.

"How were your crayfish?" said the barman. She hadn't notice him approach.

"Just as I remembered them, thank you." She knew her eyes were glazed, but she was beyond caring.

"So you've been here before…?"

"Could I have the bill, please?" she said. "And would you be kind enough to call me a taxi?"

The rain had ceased, but a gale still blew. The taxi driver was the same bespectacled Asian.

"The Reach, please," she said.

He nodded and Audrey got in. But when she sat back in the rather squashy seat, she realised she wasn't quite ready.

"Excuse me?" Audrey leant forwards and, when the man braked to a halt too quickly, she was thrown forwards against the back of the front seat.

The taxi driver turned his head, but did not speak to her. He simply waited for her instructions.

Audrey sat back and regained her composure, making the man wait for her instructions and so pay for his clumsiness, "Please drop me on the front by the traffic lights, thank you."

31

Phoebe

The longer she stared at the oblique patterns in the ceiling, the more Phoebe saw the soft, slanting lines of Yu's face.

Of course there would be a next time and perhaps that was what he had been wondering when he'd stared at her with those dark, fathomless eyes.

She looked forward to the start of her second year. A set with Heather, rather than a room on her own, meant more and better social, and life seemed pretty straightforward until Phoebe found herself on the receiving end of a curve ball — as the American post-grad, Jay, she was seeing, called it — a text from Billy asking her to phone home.

"It's your mother, she's in the hospital," her father said. "I've just got back. She's okay. But she's on a dialysis machine. She's got something called Established Renal Failure; something to do with her kidneys."

"Yes, Dad, I do know what renal means."

"Sounds awful, I know, but I expect she'll be alright in a couple of days. They had to keep her in for observation. She's on this machine; a dialysis machine."

For someone who worked with precision instruments, her father could be ever so vague, so she asked, "Have you got a number for her at the hospital, a ward name, anything?"

"A number? Oh, I see. Er, wait a minute, I wrote it down somewhere, African sounding name the ward was. Hang on, I'll..."

"Oh, for Christ's sake, Dad, is Billy there? Put him on, would you?" The line went dead for a couple of seconds.

"Phoebes?"

"Where is she, Billy?"

"Elmwood General, I should wait until after six. They were just putting her on the dialysis machine when we left. Her hands were all itchy and her breath smelt grim." Billy paused. "She looked bloody awful, Sis, legs all swollen, a bit dopey too, like she forgot where she was a couple of times."

"Alright, Billy, I get the picture. You okay?"

"Yes, I'm alright," he replied, but then added in a whisper, "Dad's a bit upset though."

Phoebe got the hospital number off the internet and rang that evening. After some confusion as to which ward her mother was on, she got through. Her mum sounded right as rain, didn't know what all the fuss was about, and was sure to be back at home in the morning. Other than that, Phoebe might as well have been talking to a newly bricked wall her mother was so miserly with any real medical information.

After a quick, but inconclusive chat with one of the med students in college, Phoebe sent Dame Clarissa an email explaining her situation and caught the train home. Billy, being the intelligent brother he was, had left a key out for her and she climbed into her own bed at midnight relieved and exhausted.

The next morning, Phoebe caught the bus into Elmwood. The senior nurse wouldn't let her on the ward to begin with; visiting hours were now after six o'clock in the evening. But Phoebe was patient and charming and explained she'd come a long way...

Her mother, apart from her ankles still being a little swollen and her hands dry and inflamed, looked better than she had a right to look in her hospital gown. She had colour in her face, light in her eyes and an intravenous drip in her arm.

"Don't you feel embarrassed being in here, looking that well?" Phoebe asked.

Sarah Wallace frowned and lowered her head. "I know," she swept her greying hair off her face, "mind you, they," she pointed at the beds opposite, "they think they've witnessed some biblical miracle; a resurrection of Lazarean proportion, they insist on calling it. Though really, Phoebe darling, I think it was all a bit of a storm in a teacup. I'll be back up and running in no time, you'll see."

It was so typical of her generation to pass off her trip to hospital as merely a momentary lapse in her otherwise robust health.

She tried to find a doctor who might be able to give her a clearer idea of her mother's condition, but, as the nurse kept telling her, they were out and about on their rounds. The nurse suggested that the renal failure, though it was sudden, was not to be seen as life-threatening. But Phoebe knew only too well that the nurse would tell her Lazarus was about to be discharged if it would get her to leave.

Hadn't the medic in college suggested that CKD or ERF, she couldn't remember which, if not correctly treated, could lead to end-stage kidney disease?

They chatted for a while and her mum told her she shouldn't have missed her lectures on account of a slight medical hick-up. But when time came to leave, her mum's eyes welled up, which upset Phoebe, so they both ended up sharing a little cry and a hug.

Back at college, Phoebe pestered all the medics and grew weary surfing the web looking for relevant diagnoses and miracle cures. The only thing she learned was that kidney transplants were not uncommon.

There wasn't much she could do, being so far away; she had to hope that Billy would keep her up to speed.

A few days later her mother was discharged, but with the proviso that she maintain regular dialysis. Phoebe wasn't to worry, her mother told her; it would all sort itself out soon, she would see.

But Phoebe did worry.

Eventually she came across an article on the web regarding a mother who had successfully donated one of her kidneys to her daughter, and it set Phoebe wondering whether the reverse might be possible.

She sought out a Medical Fellow; Nicholls, a senior lecturer; a broad, bearded man. Phoebe latched onto him at one of the very rare Formals when the High Table had stooped to invite the lower tables to pierce their normally armour-plated coterie. And when she broached the subject of daughters donating kidneys to mothers, he told her that in essence it was feasible, but that there were three principal criteria. The first prerequisite was that the donor had to be of a blood type compatible to the recipient; the second part involved tissue matching, which determined the number of antigens common to the donor and the recipient – the more the better; and the third part involved cross-matching, which provided information as to whether the recipient was likely to reject the donor kidney.

"In most cases," he concluded, "if you do have a compatible blood type, it's about what some refer to as histo-compatibility." He narrowed his eyes. "But, there is also the physical and psychological wellbeing of the donor to consider. Donating an organ may be the greatest gift it is within one's power to grant, but it should not end up being a bequest. If you need any help, you know where to find me. My door is always open."

Phoebe rang her dad that evening. Her mother was in the hospital again. "But don't rush back," he said, in that same absent-minded tone, "your mother and I don't want you to fuss."

"Fuss?" she shouted at her phone. "Next minute you'll be telling me she's about to meet the grim reaper and not to fuss. Bloody hell, Dad!"

"Now, there's no cause for bad language-"

"Oh, get a grip, Dad. Did you speak to the doctor yourself? Today?"

"Well, no, I... Well, yes, in a way."

"Why not, Dad?"

"Well, by the time I got there he'd already seen her."

"Jesus, Dad! How many times have I got to tell you, you must speak to the doctor? Mum'll never tell you the whole story. You know only too well she'll tell you exactly what she wants you to know and nothing else. Christ, Dad!"

It was just as well Phoebe didn't get home until after midnight, if she'd found her father up she might have throttled him.

The next morning Phoebe dragged as much information out of Billy as she could and then went to the hospital and demanded to see her mother's doctor.

"You need to see the renal consultant," the nurse at reception said, "Dr Blessing. He'll be along."

Two hours later, a tall, elegant and very black man in a very white coat swept through the doors.

Phoebe watched him come and go, and a while later noticed the nurse talk to him and point at her.

He strode up to her, a brown file in his long slender right hand. He moved gracefully and confidently, like an athlete approaching his starting blocks. His face was smooth, almost polished; the curve of his cheeks rounding perfectly to the corners of his mouth.

"Miss Wallace?" But before she could answer, he said, "Please, come this way." He led her into a side-room; beige carpet, floral Alpine prints and sombre atmosphere.

"Please, sit down." The doctor paused. "I'm Julius Blessing, your mother's renal consultant. You'd like me to talk to you about your mother?"

"Yes, please," Phoebe replied. "I'm afraid I've tried to talk to my father, but he gets a bit tongue-tied. I understand my mother is suffering from kidney failure, but so far no one has given me any real information."

"I see. Well, I have spoken to your father and I'm not completely surprised he hasn't kept you up-to-date. He... I... Well, it's not all bad news," he added, hurriedly.

Phoebe felt a huge rush of air escape from her, like the bursting of her breath when she and Billy used to hold theirs through a long tunnel.

Dr Blessing smiled, revealing even white teeth and tiny crow's feet at the corners of his eyes. "Oh, I see," he said, his face softening, "because your father hasn't given you all the details regarding the state of your mother's health, you've assumed the worst. You shouldn't, absolutely you shouldn't."

Dr Blessing smiled and passed her a box of tissues from a side table.

"There is good news and bad news," he continued in a matter of fact monotone. "The bad news is that your mother is suffering from Chronic Kidney Disease which has brought on her kidney failure; Established Renal Failure, as we know it. Initially we thought this might have been caused by Pyelonephritis, an infection. But the signs are, and because it is both kidneys that are affected, that her condition is a result of her diabetes whereby the little filters in her kidneys have become irreparably damaged by irregular sugar levels. Slightly less than half of people suffering from diabetes develop some form of kidney disease in later age, but only very few go on to develop renal failure. Unfortunately, your mother is one of that small number. Now that all sounds rather pessimistic and dramatic, which in some cases it can be."

He paused for a moment and looked up as if he'd forgotten to mention something important. "You're at Cambridge University, aren't you? Your mother has told me. She's very proud of you, you know. Remind me please, what are you reading?"

"Law."

"Thank goodness. For a moment I thought you were going to say medicine and I didn't want to appear patronising."

That relaxed Phoebe a little. She smiled and warmed to the very good-looking, young doctor. "You're not being patronising at all, Dr Blessing. Please, go on."

"Because your mother's kidneys are failing, we have had to put her on dialysis until we can sort out which is the best way forward for her."

Phoebe blew her nose and mumbled through the tissue. "And just what are her options?"

"Principally, your mother has four options. In some cases we can manage this condition with various medicines and supportive care, but your mother's kidneys may be too damaged for that. We're not certain yet, but it looks probable at this stage. She can have haemodialysis, which would mean her coming into the hospital three times a week, or peritoneal dialysis, which involves a catheter and which she might be able to manage at home. Or she can go down the transplant route, but that of course involves finding a suitable donor, and, as you probably know, the waiting list is fairly long."

Phoebe nodded. "Would it be fair to say that by and large the most suitable donors are found closest to home?" she asked. "I mean, through the patient's relations."

The doctor smiled, "Generally, that is the case." Then his face became more serious, and the lines about his eyes grew deeper. "Ms Wallace, as you probably understand, your father is a fair bit older than you mother, and while that doesn't preclude him from being a donor, it does increase the risk to his health significantly."

"I know. I've done some research."

"Yes, I'm sure you have. Forgive me if I was being presumptuous." Dr Blessing sat back in his chair, rubbed his bottom lip and looked at Phoebe in much the same way as had the Medical Fellow Nicholls. "Your brother is young," he continued, "and although there is no minimum age limit in the UK, I would have to counsel very strongly against him even considering this course of action." He paused and then added, "You are thinking you might be a suitable donor?"

Phoebe smiled a weak, but coy smile, "I can't see why not. I know it has happened the other way round; mother to daughter. I'm sure somewhere it must have happened this way round, too."

"Yes." Dr Blessing exhaled loudly as he spoke, "I can see why you would think that."

The good doctor then echoed what Nicholls had told her regarding the various requirements that she would need to meet, "But, first off, do you happen to know your blood type?"

"No, but I'm sure it'll match my mother's." She smiled at the doctor, a knowing, confident smile that suggested providence would not possess the nerve to proscribe against her.

Dr Blessing hesitated, then looked down at the floor for a moment. "Please bear in mind there is the possibility that your blood type might match your father's. But if you do match, you would then need to undergo a medical, surgical and psychological assessment." He emphasised the word psychological, paused again and proceeded to detail a few more prerequisites.

"What I would ask you to do, Ms Wallace, is to go home and think this over for a while. Your mother is in no immediate danger and what you are suggesting may have very far-reaching consequences for a young woman not only of your age, but also for you at this time of your life. How many years do you have left at university?"

"I've just started my second year."

"Please," the doctor replied, "please don't take this the wrong way. It is extremely important that you commit the necessary thought to this step. It is not to be taken lightly. What may appear to be appropriately altruistic now, when you come to have children and there is the chance, however slight, that you develop a similar condition, may prove with the benefit of hindsight to have been unwise."

"Yes, Dr Blessing. I get your message. I understand this is not the simple decision it might at first seem."

"You must promise me, Ms Wallace, that you will consider this with all the tremendous mental faculties I have been led to believe you have at your disposal."

"Of, course, Dr Blessing," Phoebe summoned her most deferential smile. "I promise."

Dr Blessing's face broke from the pressure he had endured in maintaining his stern and rather deliberative countenance, "Good. In the meantime, I wish you and your mother all the very best. Come back in two weeks or longer, if you need more time, and we will talk again."

A gigantic wave of joy broke upon Phoebe. She felt dizzy with elation and was gripped by a desire to kiss Julius Blessing. Instead, she heard herself say, "Just one more question, Doctor?"

The doctor hesitated from the door and turned back to her.

"Out of interest, what is my mother's blood type?"

Without looking at the file, Dr Julius Blessing replied, "Your mother is A-positive, Ms Wallace; A-positive."

32

Hacker

The road out to the Norfolk Flyer wound its way between high sand dunes; there were no streetlamps, only the vague shadows cast by the security lights from a caravan park.

They met at seven, after Chisholm had dropped his daughter at school.

Hacker had met him at the Flyer before and usually about the same time. "Glad you could make it," he said, laying a familiar hand on the shorter man's shoulder.

Chisholm turned his shoulder so that Hacker's hand dropped away, "Didn't have much bloody choice, did I?"

They took their beer to a low table in the alcove furthest from the bar. "Didn't recognise the place," Hacker said, looking around, appreciating the décor. "New owners?

"Gastro-pub," Chisholm sneered as though the title went hand in hand with some vicious strain of food poisoning. "Owned by some Private Equity Group; bought out a load of places up this way. Old landlords couldn't afford to look the gift horse in the mouth. Not many of them making the kind of money they used to; 'sides, beer's too bloody expensive."

"Come on, Brian. Cheer up. At least I'm buying."

"You've got a nerve, Cornelius."

"A nerve? You don't pay any lip service to the niceties, do you Brian?" Hacker had been expecting the aggressive opener, so he spoke slowly and clearly, as if reading from a warrant, "I think you're the one with the nerve, Brian. Look at it from where I'm standing. The first FA Cup Final at the new Wembley, Chelsea and Manchester United, a hospitality suite, travel expenses, hotel, dinner and a night out at a club. Do you know how much that set us back?"

"I didn't ask for it, did I?"

"Didn't ask for it?" Hacker feigned surprise and then continued raising his voice just loud enough that Chisholm would not mistake the intention in his insult, "No, Brian, you are quite right, you didn't ask for it. And you didn't ask me to pay off that bloody enormous bouncer who wanted to tear your head off either. You didn't ask me because you were so bloody drunk you didn't know what time of day or night it was, or what you were doing." He paused to let his words sink in.

Chisholm glanced nervously in the direction of the bar and lowered his head towards Hacker, "What I mean is; I'm not ungrateful for all the many favours you afforded me over the years. Don't get me wrong, I'm very grateful – particularly for everything you did for me that night." He paused, remembering, "God knows what would have happened if you hadn't been so sharp."

"And the copper, Brian," Hacker reminded him gently. "I had to deal with that young copper, too. If he'd had his way, you'd've been banged up for the night. And that would've opened a can of worms even I couldn't have kept the lid on."

But Chisholm wasn't going to lie down quietly. "So you bought off a bouncer and fobbed off a copper. Don't tell me you've never had one over the eight and lost your bearings. For Christ's sake, Cornelius, you lot were well known for it."

At that remark, Hacker silenced. The muscles in his shoulders twitched as he fought the sudden urge to ram his glass into Brian

Chisholm's doughy face. His lot were not his lot. They were the same lot as any other lot. Footballers were just better news, that was all; just bloody good copy – a means by which some low-life tabloid hack or loitering paparazzi could justify his P60.

But instead Hacker said, "Room for another?" grabbed both glasses and went to the bar.

He passed the barman their glasses. "Same again," Hacker said, "these'll do."

"Sorry. No can do," replied the barman as he picked a pair of clean pint glasses from the shelf. "It's the taps, see."

Hacker frowned, not understanding.

The barman looked nonplussed, but continued, "If germs from your old glass get on the tap, they can be passed into someone else's beer." He shrugged his shoulders. "Not my fault, sir: EU regulations."

Back at the table, he handed Chisholm his fresh glass.

Both had used the break to consider their positions; the only difference between the two being that Hacker had anticipated their arriving at this crossroads, and he now knew where he stood and what he would have to do if he was going to show Chisholm the way.

But it was Chisholm who tried to seize the initiative. "You see that was all part of the business," he laid a heavy emphasis on the word, "the business we used to be a part of. And that business has changed. So even if you did offer me another round of your very generous hospitality, I couldn't accept it. I had to go on a course last month in Norwich; Regulatory and Obligatory Risk and Compliance, Workplace Ethics, Racial, Sexual and Age Discrimination, the FSA... Four bloody days spent listening to some pimply-faced youth tell me that I could only accept gratuities up to the value of twenty-five quid; that I could accept one bottle of wine and not two; and that if I was out for dinner and I wasn't paying, I could accept a first course, but if I wanted to have a main course or desert, I would have to phone my supervisor to get clearance. My supervisor!" he repeated, tapping the table.

"I tell you, Cornelius, the world's gone stark raving mad. My grandfather lost two brothers in the Great War, and my mother her father in the second. And now we all labour in the sun while the very same fascists stamp their jackboots all over us in the name of Corporate Governance and compliance. It's got so as you can't do your job without having to ask permission from a bloody Europhile."

He stopped to draw breath and allow the tide of his resentment to recede. "So even if you could guarantee the Canaries a place in the Champions League final, seats in the box with Michel Platini and a tip on who's going to score the first goal, there's bugger all I can do about getting Marchman Engineering's order back on track. I'm sorry, very sorry, but there it is." His voice tailed off a little towards the end, but then, as if to promote some kind of empathy with or sympathy for his partner across the table, he pointed at Hacker and said too loudly, "We're right royally bloody screwed; you and me both, Cornelius, right royally bloody screwed."

The pub had gotten busier while Chisholm delivered his eulogy and a couple of the older customers turned at the word screwed.

Chisholm glared back at them and swept the loose strands of hair up over his head.

Hacker took his time. It was one thing for the red-faced, balding Outsourcing Manager to front up to a few pensioners in a pub, but Hacker doubted he would cut such a confident and aggressive figure before his board of directors. "I can see I'm going to have to spell it out for you, aren't I?" he said, quietly.

"Go on then. I'm all ears."

"Well, Brian, you need to come up with a way to convince your board that Marchman Engineering is still a partner they want to stay in bed with; a partner they can rely on and a partner who can still provide them with high quality components for their high quality products. And, at a price where that high quality is not sacrificed on the altar of alternative, sub-standard parts, manufactured by some second rate, Eastern European Yacub-come-lately-on-the-block, who in a year's time won't give a toss what the quality of his merchandise is like, and, furthermore, won't give a toss because he's got you all bound up in a watertight, extended contract."

"Slovakian," Chisholm said.

"Alright, Slovakian. You know as well as I do, those extended contracts don't add up. They start out supplying you with reasonable quality goods, then, because they've slashed their margins to get the order, they have to find ways to shave their costs. They can't alter their production techniques so they end up making their components out of cheap materials. The end result of all that is a couple of years down the line, your next door neighbour won't buy another widget manufactured by Norfolk Electrical, because they fall to bits three days after the warranty expires."

Chisholm shook his head, whether in disagreement or abandonment it wasn't clear. "There's a quality control clause welded firmly into the contract. You should see the agreement. I can barely make head or tail of it, it's written in such legalistic jargon. Cost us a fortune just to have it deciphered." He took a long pull at his beer and sat back.

"I tell you, Cornelius, the only people making money out of this new contract are the bloody lawyers. We'll probably be paying the saving we're making directly to the firm of lawyers we've hired to produce the bloody contract in the first place. It bloody well doesn't add up!" He pushed a few loose strands of hair up over the crown of his head again and blinked rapidly.

Hacker, too, had arrived at a destination of sorts. "You know, Brian, if things don't add up, perhaps you would be well advised to mix a little imagination in with your arithmetic."

"Oh, how so?" His eyebrows raised in the manner of a confident bully.

"Well, Brian," Hacker lowered his voice, "that first FA Cup final at the new Wembley. Do you remember how long ago it was?"

Chisholm scoffed, "I was wondering when you were going to bring that up again."

"Well, do you remember? It's important. Come on, you're good at remembering dates. When was it?"

"May the something, 2007, one-nil, Drogba, in extra time. That good enough? You see I was sober for some of it."

"Sober enough to remember what happened later?"

"If I must?" Chisholm moaned.

"Well?"

"Dinner at some fancy Italian: Mozzarella something, pasta something else and far too much Montepulciano."

"After that?"

Chisholm leant forwards. "Get on with it, Hacker. I know where you're going with this and it won't make a blind bit of difference. I told you, the contract's been signed. It's all over."

"Highlights?"

"What, the girl?"

"No, Brian," Hacker replied quietly, "the club, Highlights — bit of a young crowd for us. Tequila and champagne! You know, Royal Slammers at the bar, and you thinking you were John Travolta. Only trouble was that your partner was too young to've heard of Olivia Newton-John."

The ruddy face got ruddier and Chisholm seemed to shrink a little into his grey suit jacket. "So? Grease isn't everyone's favourite musical. What's that got to do with the price of eggs?"

"You're not listening to me, Brian," Hacker hissed. "Let's go at this another way. You said the month was May, and we're now in October. And, as you so correctly pointed out, the year was 2007. That puts it at nearly three and a half years ago. Never mind that I got you your tickets for last year. I'm not bothered with that. I'm talking about three and a half years ago."

"Okay. So what? So the last three and a half years have not been that kind to me," Chisholm said. "I didn't take to being fifty as easily as some."

Hacker reigned himself in and sat back to take a sip of his beer. He didn't want to go off half cocked; he needed to stretch his play out. "Well, I found myself back in the very same club about this time last year: big private party in one of the side rooms. The bouncer wasn't going to let me in 'til my fifty quid note jump-started his memory. Guess who was at the party? Go on. Oh, I bet you can."

"I suppose you're going to tell me that girl Sherri was there."

"Well," Hacker sipped his beer again, swirling the sweetness around in his mouth. It tasted good, as good as any beer he'd ever drunk. He swallowed another mouthful of beer and said, "You're right of course, Brian. That nice young Sherri was there."

Chisholm's curiosity was pricked and a slight leer infected his expression.

Hacker didn't like the look, but he managed to suppress his revulsion. "Actually, Brian, it was that nice young Sherri's birthday party."

"Oh," said Chisholm. "Sorry I missed that."

"I bet you are, Brian. I bet you are: All those nubile bodies, all their prurient charms on display, and most of them sufficiently drunk not to care who they were displayed to."

Chisholm retained his leer, but his brow was now ever so slowly corrugating and his face draining of its ruddy complexion. Against the run of play, he said, "I bet she's quite the young London debutante, that Sherri."

"Interesting that you should choose that turn of phrase, Brian."

Chisholm's bid to break out of defence barely made it to the halfway line before he realised he was completely isolated, "For Christ's sake Cornelius, get on with it, man."

"Interesting, because not only was it young Sherri's birthday party; it was young Sherri's eighteenth birthday party."

"Oh, I see. Well, I hope she didn't mind you crashing her eighteenth, not after... What," Chisholm asked, "are you looking at me like that for?"

The pub seemed to have gone very quiet as though the other customers were ear-wigging their conversation. All Hacker could hear was the sound of his own very controlled breathing and the squeak of the handle as the barman pulled a pint.

"You're still not with me, are you, Brian?" he said quietly. "You're not singing from the same hymn sheet. Think about it or do I have to paint it in letters so large the rest of Strand-next-the-Sea will be able to read it?"

Chisholm stared back at him. A trickle of sweat ran down his forehead and he began to rub the palm of his left hand as though it itched. "I don't follow you."

"Eighteenth, Brian; this time last year!" Hacker leant even further forward across the table so that he could feel the other man's breath on his face. "May 2007 was three and a half years ago, which means that you, Brian Chisholm, had your hand up the skirt of a juvenile. She wasn't sixteen, three and a half years ago." He sat back as if to allow his calculation enough room and time to sink in.

"Oh!" Chisholm blinked and rubbed his right ear. He frowned, winced and then cringed all at once. He reached across to adjust the spare beer mats into a quartered symmetrical pattern. "Oh!" he repeated. "What a shame." Then, "What the bloody hell are they doing letting fifteen-year-old kids into a bloody nightclub like that?"

But Hacker wasn't going to allow him the luxury of a casual deflection. "Fake IDs," he replied. "Can't do much about it, can they?"

"Well, if they don't know, how was I supposed to know?" he pleaded. "Especially considering the state I was in." Chisholm stared at his poisonous messenger. The colour coursed back into his cheeks, but as it returned it ripened from the sunset warmth of gentle embarrassment through to the fire-brick red of anger and frustration.

"Are you trying to blackmail me, Hacker, because, if you are, I'd like to remind you of a couple of salient points that may have escaped your bloody convenient memory?"

Hacker sat up a couple of degrees straighter so that Chisholm would have to look up at him, "As you said earlier, Brian, I'm all ears."

"One: I wasn't the only one of the pair of us who had his hands firmly in the honey jar that night. And two: I can't think of a single miserable sod who would be remotely interested in malicious gossip being pedalled by some should've-could've-would've second rate, washed-up ex-pro-footballer like you." Chisholm banged his knuckles rather too loudly on the table, "Can you?"

Hacker had expected the counterattack, although for a moment he was impressed at the speed with which his prey had put it all together. "No, Brian, you're dead right. A tabloid hack I am not and I don't suppose the Citizen would be interested in printing this style of smutty story." He paused, and having closed Chisholm down, went hard into the tackle, "But Norfolk Electrical might be."

"Oh, so now you've tracked down some stringer of a sleazebag who just happens to have a couple of snaps of us in flagrante delicto? And what about your misses, Geraldine: Won't she be just as interested in seeing them?"

This time it was Hacker's turn to lean forward, "Not much, Brian. The former Mrs Hacker is, and has been for over a year, the ex-Mrs Hacker. I don't think it would be news to her." He paused. "And besides, I didn't need to track any sleazebag of a stringer down. I've got the pictures. I've got the only pictures. Here, have a look for yourself." He pulled his mobile phone out of his pocket, tapped it a couple of times and handed it to Chisholm.

The squat, sweaty lump that was Brian Chisholm squinted at the screen. Then he searched his jacket pockets and pulled out a pair of glasses. Once he'd focused properly on the picture, he blinked and rubbed his ear again.

"Oh no," was all he said as he studied the photo of him with his hand up the very short skirt of a very much younger blonde, whose breasts were clearly visible through the armpit of her purple foil crop-top.

"There's more," whispered Hacker, "and worse on my laptop and hard-drive."

Chisholm gripped the mobile phone tightly and banged it slowly and repeatedly against his forehead. "This phone wasn't around in 2007," he said.

"Correct," replied Hacker. "I took them with my old phone, downloaded them onto my laptop and uploaded that one onto my new phone. Stop snatching at straws, Brian. Marvellous thing technology, particularly when it works for you. It's a bugger when it goes the other way though."

Hacker couldn't conceal the triumphant edge to his tone. "With this little beauty, I can have pictures of good old Brian Chisholm and his jailbait all over Norfolk Electrical in minutes. Now that would make the board sit up and take notice, wouldn't it?"

Hacker paused again. He was aware he sounded as though he was enjoying himself, which he was a little. But he couldn't resist a last pop, "'Course the images might appeal to one or two or your main board directors, and one or two might even be proud that their trusty old Outsourcing Manager was capable of such lewd behaviour. Might find some encouragement in it, I dare say." He paused. "But, I doubt it, Brian. I very much doubt it."

Chisholm marshalled whatever remnants of his team had not departed to the dressing room, "We're not living in the Cold War now, you know, Hacker. This kind of thing is all a bit smoke and mirrors for my lot. They'll think it's just plain sour grapes coming from Marchman."

Hacker nodded. "Good point. They might. They just might." He paused, "But then again, they might not, might they? They just might not."

Now it was Chisholm's turn to hiss, but he hissed like a snake in response to a careless foot. "I always thought you were a bit grubby, Hacker, but I wouldn't have marked you down as pond life. I've seen you put in some hard tackles, but I always thought of them as part of the game; tackles that needed to be made. Get in early, do the job and get out. But, I would never've put you down for this. D'you know what your problem is, Cornelius?"

"No, Brian, but I'm sure you're about to tell me."

"I am, Cornelius. You're bloody right I am. It's the same problem you had on the pitch. In many ways, it's a most admirable quality and one which, I noticed, was sadly lacking in many of your contemporaries. I suppose it's one of the most difficult qualities to possess in just the right measure: too little of it and you might as well not put your boots on, and too much of it and it's perfectly obvious to every season ticket holder that one day it will be your undoing. It's always been your Achilles Heel, Cornelius: You never know when to stop. You stupid, sad bastard, Cornelius, you never know when you're beaten." Chisholm dropped the phone on the table.

They sat in silence for a minute. Neither drank their beer, they just sat and looked at each other. One man uncertain, agitated and fidgeting; the other sure, composed and curiously tranquil.

Of course, Hacker was not really as tranquil as he made out, but he was very definitely sure and he knew he had to be composed. He never allowed himself to look unsettled, not even when the rest of the team dropped their heads. He always made sure he looked as though he was up for it, right to the bloody end.

But blackmail was completely new to him. He didn't like it. In fact, he detested it. But, if Norfolk Electrical, embodied as it was in the chubby frame of Brian Chisholm, was going to fuck up his life, then he felt the absolute right to employ whatever methods he had at his disposal to fuck up theirs.

That was the way it was: If some other bastard chopped you down on the field, then some other bastard would know Cornelius Hacker was duty-bound to repay the compliment.

That was the way it was, that was the way it had always been and that was the way it was always going to be.

33

Audrey

When they arrived at the seafront, the taxi driver said, "Very windy," as though through his observation he might make up for his lack of conversation.

"Yes. Wonderful, isn't it," replied Audrey, handing over a ten pound note and walking away.

"Now then, Richard," she said as if he was standing next to her and she had something important to discuss with him.

That first time she noticed him sleeping at the table seemed like an opening sequence to an alternative life.

She remembered trying to wake him, resting her hand on his shoulder and feeling the weight of it. It was firm in a resistant, independent and enduring way.

He was as far the other side of thirty as she was shy of it, and his hair was fair, shortish, straight and thinning, promising a shining bald pate to come.

At first he would not stir, so she left him and continued with closing up.

Then the last of the kitchen staff went home and she had no alternative but to rouse him. She rubbed his shoulder with her right hand and placed her left on the back of his exposed neck, hoping the warmth from her palm would help him wake gently. It was an overly familiar gesture and she realised theirs could've been mistaken for a rather intimate scene; the two of them alone in the deserted restaurant; silent witnesses looking on: Redford, Fonda, McQueen and MacGraw; faces she knew, people she did not.

Perhaps it was because she was tired from the long day, but, standing behind his sleeping form, she was reminded of her bed. Not necessarily her bed with him in it, and then not necessarily without him in it either.

He stirred, his head coming upright. "Good grief!" he mumbled for want of anything better to say and followed it up with, "I really am most awfully sorry." He rubbed his eyes, "Big day! Bit played out this evening. You must think..."

"I don't," she replied. "Not at all."

"I'm not, er..."

Drunk, he had been going to say. It was the standard defence from one of a crowd who measured the merit of their evening by the bottle count.

Audrey felt the need to relieve him of having to articulate the rather vulgar suggestion, so she said, "No, I didn't for one minute think you were." She paused, removed her hands from him, and walked round the table.

Richard ran his fingers through his hair. "I must be going."

"Another big day? Tomorrow?"

"No," he said, and stared at his hands for a moment. "Friday, isn't it, today?"

"Yes," she said, glancing at him, "of course it is. It's just that..."

"Well," he replied, gathering himself together in that way men do of checking all their body parts are still properly attached and not about to fall to the floor when they stand up, "I'm sorry. I mustn't impose on your hospitality."

She couldn't remember anyone ever apologising for something they hadn't yet done. It had been a tough lunchtime and evening, and she could recall a few of the other diners who'd been less cooperative than this charming man. So Audrey accepted his apology and added, "Would you join me in a nightcap?"

He looked up and smiled a sheepish, got-away-with-it smile, as though he'd expected to be summarily expelled from her presence and considered himself very fortunate not to have been, "If you're sure? Not too tired, I mean?"

His eyes were grey; they didn't promise much. And yet the longer she looked into them, the more she perceived a capacity for reason – like this one, this man, might just be a thinker rather than one of those boys held hostage by their baser instincts. But then, he was older than the other boys.

Her pause confused him. He took it that her offer of a nightcap amounted to her being polite and that she was now pausing to offer him a get-out. "No, really," he said. "Thank you, it's been a great evening. I mean: good food, good wine, good company. What more can a fellow ask for?"

"You're sure about the last part, are you? Good company, that is?"

At first he didn't quite get her drift, but then he realised what she meant. He scratched his head nervously and gazed at the as yet unpaid bill on his side-plate. "Oh, the other chaps. Well, their idea of a joke I suppose. My fault for dropping off. Means I pick up the tab; probably would have lost the spoof anyway," he noted, referring to the schoolboy guessing game they usually played to decide who would foot the bill. "Any chance I could buy the nightcap?" he asked.

"No," she said firmly, "you may not." But Audrey liked the way he offered; liked the way he tilted his head and raised his eyebrows when asking – a bit like her father's Labrador, Monty, when he hoped there might be seconds.

She opened a bottle of Remy Martin.

They talked about something and nothing for a while; about people they knew, others they would like to know and a few they wished they didn't. They discussed the rising cost of living, the increasing inflation, the talk of a Three-Day Week, whether the IRA were behind the King's Cross and Euston bombings, the merits of finally becoming members of the EEC, and what were the chances of Princess Anne actually marrying that fop from the Dragoons – for surely her first boyfriend, that Parker-Bowles fellow, was much more fun. And having exhausted the home news, they moved on to Nixon, to the Watergate Tapes, and on to Kissinger and Vietnam.

And then a policeman knocked on the window of the restaurant and Audrey had to go out and explain that she was the manageress and that she was not holding any kind of after-hours drinking party and that, yes officer, thank you, it's not a problem, you are very kind, no, we won't be long.

The Remy was finished and soon the chef would be returning from Billingsgate with the day's fish. So they went up to her flat and talked until the brandy wore off and they fell asleep on the sofa.

In the morning she woke up cold but for the warmth supplied her by Richard's ample frame.

And in the days that followed, he frequented the restaurant so often that it seemed like every time she turned round he was there, sometimes in company and occasionally alone. She knew that his kind of oppressive attention should bother her, but it didn't. And she told him on another evening when they sat and drank Remy, that she wouldn't go all the way with him until they were married. She wouldn't. She just absolutely wouldn't. That wasn't her way and if it wasn't to be her way, then it was not going to be any way at all.

What Audrey singularly failed to mention in her edict to Richard was that, probably very strangely for a twenty-five-year-old female managing a trendy eatery in the Fulham Road, she was still a virgin.

But before she knew it, people were congratulating her on the wonderful news of her engagement, and did it mean she would be leaving the restaurant?

And, no sooner was her leaving the restaurant mentioned than she began to find an increasing number of reasons why she should not stay there a moment longer.

Audrey began to find the staff irritating and over-sensitive, the unremitting paperwork a heavy chore, and the clientele mostly tiresome and quite often just plain rude. And the idea of substituting a poky little flat on a busy road in town for a roomy house in the country, in addition to her poky little flat, very quickly began to appeal to her.

So Audrey threw Richard a very lavish birthday party: blinis, smoke salmon, cream cheese and caviar, Krug; almond trout, Puligny-Montrachet; filet de boeuf au foie gras, Chateau Lafite. It was all a little heavy for Elizabeth David, but Audrey hoped she wouldn't begrudge the new Lucrezia a little garnish for her conspiracy.

And sure enough, when she mentioned to one of her wealthier patrons that she was thinking of selling up, he immediately offered to buy the restaurant, lock stock and barrel, and for an irresistible sum. With her share, she bought her flat outright.

Fed was overcome; he'd never dreamt of such reward. Even Richard was impressed.

Audrey walked on down the seafront. She wasn't hurrying, but then neither did she dawdle. It would be another ten minutes or so before she got back to The Reach and she still had a few details to call forward. She wanted certain matters to be clear in her mind; she wanted to be straight with certain things.

A couple of kids swaggered down the promenade towards her, their cigarette ends burning bright in the dark, their shirt tails flapping in the breeze.

She harboured no fear of them. On the contrary, she had some sympathy for them; not only for the mistakes they would make, but also for the harvest those mistakes would surely reap. Mistakes like those she'd made. She hadn't found life perfect; neither would they.

Richard's home turned out to be a quaint and rather rundown Cotswold Stone house halfway up the hill by St Mary's church in the Oxfordshire village of Charlbury.

She understood now that she fell in love with the house as much as the man and she drew just about as much pleasure from getting to know the one as she did the other. If a man can resemble his house in the same way it is said that owners resemble their dogs, then both Richard and his house shared much in common; the only apparent difference being that Richard was rather larger than his house.

At first Audrey could not understand why such a tall and broad individual would live in a house with such a narrow front door, but once inside, though the ceilings were low, each small door opened into yet another small, peaceful, but rather draughty room; rooms that had clearly not enjoyed the warmth of a feminine hand for some time.

The chill of the flagstone floor and the glacial draught that hung around the dormant Aga discouraged her from any great culinary enterprise, and the dark wood of the furniture was so long cold it did not answer when questioned by her touch. Richard used only two of the rooms; the cold living room, which was only really adequately large enough to be termed a snug, and his even colder bedroom. The frame of his wrought iron bed being so gelid she considered it not merely uninviting, it was more a threat to her health. And the loo in the very rudimentary bathroom clanked loudly when she pulled the long, heavy chain. The house had been left to grow old, as though by being deserted it had atrophied.

Richard's house demanded colour; colour and life. And so did Richard.

Audrey trod carefully for the first few weeks of her occupation. She bought a couple of sweaters from a local shop and wore them both as she set about pulling the house round.

The new broom needed to sweep very clean, but not in a destructive manner, she reasoned as she washed, hoovered, polished and tidied. And Audrey tried to resist the temptation to nose through Richard's jumble of work-related papers and managed, whenever the need arose, to turn a blind eye to some of the more masculine glossy editions she found stuffed down the back of the sofa. She understood men should have their way and, after all, she was ultramodern, if not emancipated within limits, and it was his house and therefore it and he deserved a measure of mutual respect.

Richard went off on Monday morning and came back on Friday, though every so often he returned unexpectedly on a Thursday. He liked his work. He liked his chums. His beaming smile and fierce hug suggested he loved coming back to her and being with her for the weekend.

Audrey watched him stride off down the hill to the station and welcomed him by meeting him off the train when the weather was foul. She got to know the neighbours. She even went to St Mary's Church and smothered her Catholicism in order to fit in with the congregation. And she learned to cherish Richard's ways; they were all the confirmation she needed to know that, in him, she'd made the right choice.

In the early days whenever Audrey tired of the silence, she took the train into London and caught up with a few girlfriends or drove up to see those of her parent's friends still hanging on by their bootstraps in Shropshire. There were jolly dinner parties in Town and some with the shooting circuit in the country. Life wasn't a continuous social whirl, but there was more than enough to be going on with.

Audrey stopped and stood still. The Reach was not more than a hundred yards away and she wasn't ready yet. She was warmed by her exercise and comforted by her course. She gazed at the blinking lights far out to sea.

So what had changed her, she asked? What had abducted her from what so many had described to her as such an idyllic existence? Had it started in the church?

No, not in any sense was the church responsible. It wasn't simply a matter of Anglican or Catholic, although the church did provide her with a platform from which to launch her crusade.

Audrey learnt from reading one of the local parish guides that the bright cold waters that flowed along the meadows at the bottom of the hill belonged to the River Evenlode; a river which, curiously, already flowed through her veins.

For thousands of years the Evenlode had wound a gentle path from the limestone Hills of the Cotswolds through to the Thames at King's Lock just outside Oxford. But more important than its course was the fact that Hilaire Belloc had blessed and acclaimed the river in one of his poems.

At St Dominica's, in preparation for her English Literature A level, Audrey had produced a lengthy comparison between the poets Wordsworth and Belloc, born as they were a hundred years apart. Though one was not the political animal the other came to be, they both shared an association with France. Wordsworth's first child was born to a French mother and Belloc's father was of the same nationality. The similarities between the two were not manifold, but Audrey had filled the paper with a certain lyricism that had delighted her tutor. And yet, her research fostered a deeper interest in Belloc, both politically and spiritually, and more particularly his attitude towards Catholicism and War.

So the spring of '74 found Audrey picnicking beside the Evenlode and falling in love with Belloc's poetry.

His world, a world Audrey found she had time to learn about, seemed so strong to her; so set in stone, so absolute and indestructible.

Whereas this new world, a world in which the French obliterated Mururoa Atoll and the Indian Government dressed their nuclear experiment up as a Smiling Bhudda, would likely as not go to hell in a handcart. This new world seemed so delicate and so fragile, so ill-prepared for the abyss into which it was rushing headlong. For the first time she realised that just as Belloc had chosen to sanctify the Evenlode with his poetry, it now fell to her to ensure that the river would continue to flow. For if the world disappeared in a cloud of nuclear Armageddon, there would be no more water meadows in which to picnic with the children who would surely follow from her sleeping with Richard on their wedding night.

The next time she picnic'd by the Evenlode, Audrey bought a copy of the *Guardian* newspaper and procured for herself a copy of Carter's *Political Theory of Anarchism*.

Oh, she had understood it all so well at the time; how it wasn't her fault and how the blame for the ills of the world lay squarely at the feet of those pompous windbags in government.

Looking back on it now, Audrey had no problem with viewing it all as a cause célèbre; a tunnel through which she had to pass before she could emerge into the colder light of common sense. Oh, she was sure there were a barrow load of shrinks who would have diagnosed her rapid descent into anarchy as a convenient flight from the confinement that was her virginity; either that or some kind of punishment from her God for a minor infringement of her vows; an escape, perhaps a denial.

And maybe it was. What and to whom did it matter?

Well, it mattered and it mattered to her. Audrey needed to make sense of it. She needed to understand what it was that had driven her to behave in such an unforgivable manner.

They had argued, Richard and her, not now and again, but more and more often. And he tried so damnably hard to accommodate her. He tried so hard to help her believe that her feelings, her intentions and her directions were all so very natural; that everyone felt something of the same about it all and that intelligent and ignorant, rich or poor, ordinary and extraordinary people alike shared her misgivings about the nuclear age. But the greater the obstacles he tore down for her, the faster and higher she rebuilt them and fixed them in his way.

He accused her of being a closet disciple of Ayn Rand, of her needing to find her own personal road to happiness at the expense of his feelings.

She accused him of being a paid lackey of the establishment, of peddling a system that protected and perpetuated its own obnoxious elitism.

Oh, how she wished she hadn't said that. It had been so mean of her; so, so mean.

Audrey remembered the look of utter despair on Richard's face when he realised he'd lost her.

Then came Braud-Saint-Louis and Laurent, and soon after that Laurent and Strand-next-the-Sea, and then her long crawl back towards the light and finally her wedding night.

Though dreading it, Audrey rather surprised herself. When the fumblingly hilarious moment came, she enjoyed it. She'd played along at first, wary of what she should say if Richard realised she was not a virgin. But, fortunately, somewhere between the bright smiles of the well-wishers, the gallons of champagne and the casting off of her deep-seated inhibitions, not to mention his more conventional cautions, a ship called Future slipped noisily from its moorings and Audrey, who used to be Crichton, forgot all about it.

As the next years flew, so did the stork appear: James followed soon by John; nappies and broken nights, emotions both great and occasionally ghastly, so much that stood out and the odd moment to be forgotten. They moved, a purchase which absorbed all but the last of her shares and savings, to a Queen Anne house round the corner. And they were forced to reappraise their idea of heaven; a scare with John's eyesight, a heart by-pass for Richard, another chance for them all. They battled prep school and soon would battle public school. They cheered and consoled, laughed and cried, and then Richard came home late one night looking as though he'd been standing in the shadow of a tall building when it collapsed.

The Piper Alpha disaster in the summer of '88 nearly broke him. He was lucky, he said, it was bad and it might even break him, but there were already 167 lives that would never be put back together. She admired his fortitude, his resilience and his resolve. The loss ran into millions for his syndicate alone, but somehow he survived.

Then, in early '89, the super-tanker Exxon Valdez ran aground in Alaska and bled three-quarters of a million barrels of crude oil along a thousand miles of the most beautiful coastline in the world.

Richard came home that evening, strode straight to the drinks cabinet and drained the better part of a bottle of scotch before he acknowledged her.

At least this time, no one had died, she told him; it wouldn't be so bad. The damage to the environment was just too wretched to contemplate, she agreed, but at least no one had died.

He said nothing.

There was an aura about him that night. He did eventually speak to her, but he said little. She made him dinner, but he did not eat it. He wasn't rude to her, neither was he dismissive, but he shied away from her comfort when they got into bed that night and she could tell he barely slept.

The next day he came home from work and behaved as though the cloying tar and struggling wildfowl on the television were as nothing to him.

Fortunately the boys were away at school, so, apart from Audrey, there was no one around to badger him about the news.

And over the years she had learnt to read his signals, and now all his peculiar semaphore suggested that she should leave the subject well alone. There was no doubt his libido suffered and he grew somewhat distant from her. But it was nothing she had not seen in some of their friends; so rather than worry that it might be something she'd done, that this new way of their being together, being together only not so, was just the way it went when one got older.

Richard left for the city each Monday morning and came home every Friday evening. His unexpected returns on Thursday evenings ceased.

Then one breakfast he suggested they didn't need the flat in town now that he was working as a consultant; he said he could commute and bunk down with a chum when the need arose. And even though she liked to meet her girlfriends in London every now and then, take in the odd show, do some shopping and had hoped that it would make a nice pied-a-terre for the boys when they were older, she agreed.

"'Course it won't be easy to sell and we won't get much for it what with the blasted recession," he said.

Curiously, that poky little flat, that place Audrey Crichton had called home for the gayest period of her life, sold very quickly and, to of all people, a foreigner. It wasn't that she hated all foreigners, but, for some reason, signing the place over to one made her think of Laurent and the flat was where she'd received the occasional letter from him. Once the flat was gone, so would his letters cease.

She'd never written back, of course. Never!

Well, that wasn't exactly true. She'd started many letters; how many she couldn't remember, but it was many and she'd never got as far as finishing one.

Richard believed they were from a friend from what he liked to call her Green Period, which in a sense they were. And the more Richard dismissed them, the more she looked forward to receiving them. They were her secret; her weakness.

So Audrey cried about the flat in private, away from the family, and managed to temper her emotions when Richard presented her with the papers for signing.

She also supported him when he suggested they cut back on holidays. After all, two boys at public school was a considerable financial burden and, in order to maintain his consultancy qualifications, there was the extra expense of those bloody residential courses he had to attend every few months.

In '93 James finished school and went directly to Bristol University, and John was in his final year at Bruton. Richard went off to work on the early train and came home on the late. Audrey didn't like him working such long hours, but she loved him for his commitment to the family and so was wont not to query him when he sometimes returned a little the worse for wear.

Their social life slowly withered. It didn't bother Audrey at first; she was busy writing to the boys, sending them food parcels and doing anything that might help smooth John's passage through his time in that wretched institution. And she was busy with St Mary's, the local Women's Institute and Lest We Forget, the latter charity being close to Richard's heart as his father had also been lost to him soon after the war.

One bright and fine summer's day, Audrey received a call from an old girlfriend, Pippa Ward.

She hadn't seen Pippa since the flat above Fed's had gone, though they'd swapped Christmas cards every year. They arranged to meet and go to what had been Fed's in the Fulham Road; a trip down memory lane. But, much like Pippa's maiden name, Fed's no longer existed, though Audrey was sure she'd heard that somewhere. And neither of them could remember what it had been renamed, but they would meet there anyway. Richard had gone off early and she was alone in the house; no one would miss her.

They met in the Fulham Road, but didn't like the look of what used to be Fed's; it had gone all pink and Malaysian. So they ate in a department store restaurant up in Knightsbridge. They discussed children, milestones and old friends. But they shied away from introducing either of their husbands into conversation until Pippa mentioned in passing that she'd glimpsed Richard on the beach at Perranporth in Cornwall. "Easter weekend," she said. It was what had set her to look Audrey up again.

It couldn't have been Richard, Audrey told her, he'd been away at

Easter; some brain-storming, leadership course in the Midlands; named after an animal, white wolf or black bear or something. Such a bore for him over Easter!

The Galician Salad was delicious, even if the Hearts of Romaine were a shade limp and the Chocolate Fondant, though such a treat, proved a shade too gooey. Pippa very kindly insisted on paying. It was a grand day, they both agreed. They would do it more often now that they'd made contact again.

After lunch, Audrey decided to walk across Hyde Park to Paddington Station rather than suffer the expense of a taxi. The sun warmed her back as she wandered up through Kensington Gardens towards the Serpentine and she marvelled at how good life had been to her. Audrey had so much to be grateful for, really she did; Richard, James, and John in particular. And wasn't it so nice of Pippa to make the effort to get in touch and then pay for the meal, too?

Richard really had achieved so much for them.

It was early for him to be leaving town, but she wondered, if she could locate him, whether she might persuade him to get off early or take her out for dinner; the bottle of Gavi she'd shared with Pippa had left Audrey feeling a shade adventurous and, if she allowed herself to admit it, even a touch mischievous. She wondered, just wondered... Sadly, she hadn't been able to persuade Richard of the benefits of carrying one of those new portable phones; he was too much of a Luddite for one of those new fangled gadgets; he still listened to Sunday Service on the wireless in the drawing room.

And that was when she saw him, sitting on a bench.

She carried on walking, thinking her eyes must be playing tricks.

But, they weren't.

Audrey stopped still, watching. She gripped her handbag with both hands out front, hanging onto the rope straps as though they were her only physical attachment to the world — as though if she let go of her earthly anchor, she might float away and never come down.

She wondered what on earth he was doing in Hyde Park at three in the afternoon. Besides, Richard absolutely loathed Knightsbridge.

A kid on a bicycle brushed past her and she flinched.

She knew she should be pleased to see him, really she should. It was amazing! Just like one of those stories he was always telling over dinner about how he was forever bumping into people when in the most out of the way places, or abroad.

Well, now it had happened to them.

She made to surprise him, but instead of moving towards Richard, Audrey found herself rooted to the spot. A cold and withering doubt infected her mind.

Something was wrong. Her body began to tremble just ever so slightly and Audrey realised she was afraid. Indeed, something was very wrong. Her stomach liquefied and the bones within her legs turned to jelly. She felt dizzy and faint.

He was with a woman. And the woman was kissing him.

Audrey stood, transfixed, certain but uncertain, seeing but not believing.

She was younger than Richard, clearly, and by a good few years. But then Audrey was younger than Richard by eight years and the woman looked younger than Audrey. She dressed younger and her hair was thicker, longer. She was laughing, posing like a model, throwing her hips out at him, teasing him, daring him.

For a moment, she wondered whether the woman might be a daughter he hadn't told her about.

But then, daughters didn't kiss fathers the way the woman had just kissed Richard.

Richard was tall and balding, a slightly heavy man; he was fifty-four. He wasn't exactly playboy material, not exactly a ladies' man or a womaniser. For sure, he could play the ageing roué when he wanted to, but Audrey didn't mind a bit of that; all men were allowed to dream.

But as Audrey watched, her husband got up off the bench and ran, yes, ran the few steps to the woman and embraced her and then kissed her again.

It was all the kinds of kiss only lovers kiss; deep and intense and it went on for far too long.

In fact, it was still going on when Audrey managed to tear her eyes away from them. She turned and walked; the image of it, of them, seared onto her mind like a brand on the flank of a cow; the smell and taste of the smoke from the branding iron lying heavy and thick upon her tongue. She felt sick in her throat, dizzy, so dizzy, and weak, and cripplingly awkward at her knees.

Before she realised it, Audrey had arrived at the Albert Memorial. She was going the wrong way.

She stopped. A passer-by, a Philipino woman pushing a pram, touched her jacket and asked her if she was alright.

"Mmm? Thank you, yes," was all she could manage.

She walked towards Alexandra Gate. She'd get a taxi, get away and go anywhere, but where? She no longer felt the sun on her back; she felt naked, naked and cold, and naked like everyone could see her through her clothing; see the loose, spare flesh as it hung down the back of her upper arms, see the sagging limp flesh of her buttocks and see the wrinkles left by the stretchmarks on her belly. And she was convinced they could all see, every one of them; the taxi driver, the station porter, the passengers on the platform, on the train, the people driving past her as she walked across the meadow from the station, and even Belloc, as she staggered over the bridge across the Evenlode. Even Belloc stood witness to her nakedness.

Audrey slammed the front door so hard she shattered a pane of glass.

34

Philip

They found a windbreak between the dunes and lay down on a rug she had thought to pack. Fiona gazed at him, her expression crowded with questions, but Philip smiled and closed his eyes, preferring, for the moment, not to hear them.

Three months after his lunch with Carson, Philip took up his desk at Mason Marberg Associates. No longer was he a small fish swimming in the large ocean of an open-plan city office; Philip now found himself sitting at a broad partner's desk behind a solid oak door, overlooking a bustling West End square. And when he wasn't going out to lunch with one or other of his colleagues, his secretary brought in for him.

But aside from the rather ostentatious trappings, Philip's day-to-day existence also altered immeasurably. He now found himself swimming in a completely different sea; one unrecognisable from the open sea he'd recently inhabited. His new sea was far more intimate; everybody seemed to know everybody, and if they didn't, then somebody very definitely knew someone who knew the very person he needed to know. And soon enough, Philip knew most, if not all, of them.

Understandably, his previously rigid adherence to his domestic duties fell by the wayside. He justified it by the swell of their bank balance and the elevation of their social sphere, though more than once he overheard Fiona say that she missed some of their old friends.

He was invited to driven shoots in Sussex and weekend breaks skiing. They were provided with concert tickets, which mollified Fiona somewhat, and ate in more fashionable restaurants.

If there was a downside, it was that Philip found less time for Fiona and the children. He wasn't always happy with work overriding his commitment to his family, but to query the direction down which this new avenue took him seemed, to him anyway, barking mad.

So, Philip closed his ears to Fiona's occasional discontent and carried on striding smartly towards the rewards promised at the end of what was becoming a much stylised pilgrimage.

Though he still loved Fiona and Harry and Hattie as much as he could remember, Philip was aware that he was learning to love his progress just as much – and that, he recognised as he staggered like a pic-stuck, long-bled bull around the bed one night, was not healthy.

Philip understood that it was imperative for him to act, because if he didn't and the gulf between them continued to widen, there was every chance he would lose sight of them before long.

As bad luck would have it, work intervened.

A contract Philip had been working on, a second and much more prestigious supermarket chain with a large home improvements arm, came to fruition. It was, by some way, one of the biggest supermarket contracts Mason Marberg Associates had ever pitched for and certainly, Howard Marberg informed him afterwards, one of the largest they had ever achieved.

The celebrations began with champagne in the office and led on to dinner at a restaurant of his choice.

Philip shunned the more predictable West End venues and surprised his directors by opting for Gort's in Clerkenwell.

Even though none of his colleagues had been to Gort's, one or two were reluctant to go up the City when there was easier fare round the corner. But it was Philip's choice and Howard Marberg pointed out that the new contract would keep them all in Porsches for a year or two.

He rang Jimmy Carson and asked if he would sort a table for them.

Much to his surprise, Maja was still at the front desk.

"Mr Scott, we would have expected to see you before this. You must be a very busy man. Please, gentlemen, this way."

His colleagues who had carped about having to suffer the taxi to Clerkenwell forgot their grievances the moment they set eyes on Maja and began to view Philip with a more rounded admiration.

Much of the rest of the evening disappeared in a blur.

The next day he remembered some had demanded champagne and others claret, but, perhaps to honour Jimmy Carson, Philip had ordered Burgundy, silencing his critics by quoting Jimmy in full: "Burgundy for Kings, Champagne for Duchesses and Claret for Gentlemen."

Late on in the evening, Maja appeared and sat on his lap. She smelt of roses and jasmine, and told him her favourite perfume was called Pani Walewska and that if he went to Poland he should buy her a bottle – a little blue bottle.

Outside of clinging to Maja on a very deserted pavement, finding it difficult to count off the ten pound notes to the taxi driver when he was woken up at his door and struggling out of a champagne-soaked suit halfway up the stairs, Philip remembered very little else about the evening.

He made it in to the office the next day. Others did not.

"It was a fine evening," he said to an equally grey Howard Marberg. "At least, I hope it was."

"Certainly was," replied Marberg. He was a tall and broad and barrel-chested, and had, even at fifty, a full head of hair. He was no stranger to late nights wading through swamps of alcohol, "Come into my office for a second, would you?"

Philip immediately wondered what faux-pas he had committed the night before.

In Marberg's plush office sat Geoffrey Mason, a short, squat and unamusing man who most of Philip's contemporaries steered clear of.

Marberg closed the door.

Neither spoke for a moment, both looked serious, perhaps grave.

Then Marberg held out his hand and said, "The deal with Crawford's Supermarkets really is a blinder and we're both very pleased with all the work you've completed since you've come to us, Philip." He smiled. "This offer normally doesn't get extended to a junior until he's been with us for six or more years, but Geoffrey and I would like to offer you the opportunity to become a partner in Mason Marberg Associates."

Howard Marberg didn't so much shake Philip's hand as pump it dry. When Philip got his hand back, Geoffrey Mason took his turn. And what with the ringing head, the crushed hand and the offer of becoming a partner in a West End property company, Philip didn't know whether to laugh or cry.

Marberg had a fridge in his office; from it, he produced a bottle of Roederer Cristal.

Later, the three of them went out for lunch.

"You'll need to get your hands on £150,000, that's all," Mason said, as though he expected Philip to go and retrieve it from an ATM. "Beg, borrow, or steal it. It doesn't matter where it comes from, but get it whatever you do. This is your big chance. Most people would murder for an opportunity of this magnitude. Don't miss it." Mason studied Philip for a while. "Here," he said, "have another glass of champagne; it'll make the amount seem smaller."

Philip fell asleep on the train on his way home, overshot Barnes Bridge and got out at Mortlake. Given the area's charnel history and his corpselike pallor, he chuckled at the irony that he should return home from Mortlake with such uplifting news.

Fiona was brief with him when at last he stumbled through the front door.

He parked his weary frame in the front room and debated the best way to tell Fiona the magnificent news. Philip knew he was in the doghouse, and he knew she had every right to be bleak with him after his late and clumsy return the night before. But he could hear the children thumping about above him, and his offer of becoming a partner, though they couldn't possibly understand the significance, would have as much bearing on them as it would on Fiona.

As Philip took the stairs two at a time, he called out, "Hello kids. I'm home," and for the next hour, the unrestrained glee of their innocent youth matched their father's joy. He read to them both before they slept.

Unfortunately, no such enthusiasm penetrated the kitchen.

"I can only hope you feel as rough as you look," Fiona said, as she poured stock onto a risotto.

He disliked risotto. She knew that. But he hadn't the energy to object and he knew the slightest reference would only provoke her to greater anger. "I'm sorry," he said. "I should have phoned."

She did not look round at him. "You did. Small surprise you don't remember."

Philip hadn't checked his mobile in case he'd made any highly spirited calls the evening before. Thank God he'd remembered to call her. He didn't remember doing so and wondered what else it was that he couldn't remember.

"Yes," he sighed, a picture of Maja sprung rudely into his mind, "a big night!" Half of him wanted a drink; half of him didn't. His natural reaction was to put enough distance between them until she grew tired of rejecting him. And he knew that if he tried to dilute her disdain with humour or play the wounded soldier, he would only annoy her and she would grow even more determined to give him a hard time. Above all, he wanted and needed to tell her the great news about Marberg's offer. But he wanted her to be in the right mood to appreciate it and not merely to accept it, as if it was some kind of compensation for the offence he'd dealt her. After all, the proposed elevation of his status was as much down to her efforts at home as it was to his efforts at the office.

"I'm sure it was," she replied. "It sounded like you were having a whale of a time."

"Well," he began, then paused, realising that he had to lead up to his news rather than blurt it straight out, "we had what you might call a good day at the office. I managed to close the Crawford's Supermarket contract."

Fiona carried on staring at her risotto as if it held the promise of better company, but said, "I had to go and see Mrs Carpenter, the woman who runs Harry's playschool; seems he's been fighting with another of the boys."

"Oh," Philip replied, stretching out his reply to display his concern. He moved around the kitchen island a little closer to her.

Fiona put down her spoon, took a tissue from her pocket and blew her nose loudly.

"Darling," he moved closer to her, "I didn't-."

"Don't!" She held up her hand to ward him off. "I don't feel very approachable right now. Just give me some space, would you?"

"When did this happen? With Harry, I mean?"

"Yesterday," she said and reached for another tissue. "He came home yesterday with bite marks on his arm."

"Bite marks?"

"Yes, Phil. Bite marks!" she said and blew her nose again. "That bloody Beaton sod, the one with the stroppy mother who's always banging on about how her Tommy has a hard time because he's much taller than the others. He's a pain in the bum."

"Harry seemed fine just now. I didn't see any bite marks."

"No. You wouldn't, would you, Phil?" she said, returning her attention to the risotto. "You wouldn't notice if he came home minus an arm or a leg."

"That's a bit harsh, Fi."

"Oh, is it, Phil?" She turned to look at him, wiping the tears from her eyes with her fingers. "When was the last time you bathed either Harry or Hattie, eh?"

He tried to think quickly.

"The week before last, Phil: That was the last time you managed to squeeze bathtime into your busy schedule. In fact, apart from this evening, that was the last time you put the children to bed or spent any time reading with them."

He'd walked them up to Richmond Park on Sunday morning while Fi had prepared lunch, but he knew what he did with Harry and Hattie at the weekends didn't count when balancing the scales of duty.

"Yes, Fi, that's true. And I know it doesn't count for much, but I've been working on the tender for the Crawford's Supermarket contract and it's taken up more of my time than I'd imagined. It's a huge contract."

"Oh, of course it is, Phil," she dismissed. "They're always huge or gigantic or the next biggest thing. And I know," Fi said, softening for just a moment, "that you've got to commit the time to the office. But," she continued, hardening and building to a crescendo, "why is it, the very bloody evening I could have done with a little bit of extra moral support, you have to go out on the lash and come home at three in the morning?" Her spoon landed with a jarring crash in the sink.

They waited for a reaction from upstairs, but none came.

Philip breathed deep. He'd been here before with her. Doubtless, he'd be here again in the future. But tonight, when they should be celebrating, with Fiona patting him on the back for engineering their passage from poky Battersea flat to God knows where they might want to move to now that they would be able to afford it, Philip found himself having to chuck an extra shovel-full of patience into the well of his composure to stop it rising up and overflowing into a loss of cool.

"It was a work dinner," he pleaded. "I got the contract. Me." He pointed at his chest. "Philip Scott. I got the company the contract. Howard Marberg asked me to choose the restaurant to celebrate. Five of us went out to dinner. It got a little out of hand. And then…"

The sound of Hattie crying filtered down from upstairs.

They glowered at each other across the island.

Fiona looked completely washed out, if lividly defiant. Her hair hung lank and in need of colouring, her eyes shone red and teary, and her lips were cracked and dry. She looked every bit as exhausted as she sounded, but he realised she was going to make him sing for his supper or throw it at him if he got the tune wrong.

However, before he could openly capitulate, she leant against the island, the aggression in her stance evident and not to be mistaken for one of her casual aberrations, "And then…" Fiona went on as Hattie's very audible and growing objections heightened the tension, "And then, just when I get Harry settled from his crap day getting bitten at his office, I get you on the phone so rat-arsed I can only just recognise you. And then I get some Eastern European slapper telling me that I shouldn't worry about you because she'd look after you, but that she wasn't sure when I would see you again because you'd just told her that you loved her."

Philip looked guilty. He knew it. He'd always been lousy at denying any accusation that possessed the faintest ring of truth. He'd never got away with it; it was why he didn't do it. But the recollection of being ticked off at school merely for thinking of misbehaving caused his mouth to split into the briefest nostalgic smile.

The risotto pan ricocheted off his shoulder and slammed against the wall.

35

Audrey

When Richard came home that night, Audrey lied as if her day had been perfectly ordinary. Pippa had paid the bill at the restaurant and Audrey had paid cash for the train and taxi, so there was no trail from her trip to Town.

So she lied when she told him she'd had a nice day and she lied when she told him she hoped he'd had a nice day. And she lied and lied, and lied when, after an evening that seemed as though it would never end, she said "Goodnight".

Every now and again, she cleaned and dusted his study; his sanctum sanctorum as he liked to call it. She was careful not to disturb any of his papers, because he insisted that he'd never be able to find exactly what he wanted when he wanted it if someone else was to interfere with any of his orderly disorder.

Audrey had worried years ago that her flat in Fulham might be a convenient pad wherein Richard could conduct some illicit affair. She knew other women who suffered under such arrangements; other wives who lived with their cheating husbands rather than live without them. So when Richard sold the flat, Audrey reasonably assumed he was not one for that kind of dalliance.

The next day she read through both his business and personal papers, and Audrey found he'd had no alternative but to sell the flat.

The purchaser's name was a Mrs Lentz — yes, that was it, she remembered now, a strange name; German, maybe Austrian. And Richard hadn't gilded the lily when he'd told her that it wouldn't fetch much. It hadn't.

Richard had been right when he'd told her the Piper Alpha might break him. It almost did. But the papers she laid out on the sofa showed her he'd hung on and fought. He'd returned from the brink and regained his foothold in the very competitive echelons of marine insurance.

The Exxon Valdez, though, did finish him. From that cataclysmic disaster, there had been no return. He'd even kept the hate letters, the death threats and the obsequious, grovelling pleas; some from the Names, others from employees.

The holidays had gone by the board, but not because they couldn't squeeze them within their budget. They'd gone by the board because they'd had no money at all; it turned out that Richard's uncle had stumped up the rest of the funds for the boys' education.

She could find no evidence of the many business courses Richard disappeared off to so regularly.

Of course, she was a fool! Of course she wouldn't find any. Nothing existed. He'd been with her. HER! That woman! Over Easter! It was true. Pippa had seen him. That was what Pippa had been trying to tell Audrey in her roundabout, subtle way.

"Damn you for your kindness, Pippa," she said beneath her breath.

And now she would look at those other wives who put up with their husband's infidelity and know what they felt; that chiselling blade that each day chipped away at the woman who had once been so whole. That was their look, wasn't it? A she-thinks-it-won't-happen-to-her look — not exactly patronising, rather more pitying. Now she would be just like them; tarnished glass, no longer cleaned and no longer able to be clean.

So, he went off every day on the train to London, but not to the

London he wanted her to believe he was off to. And most evenings she cooked him his dinner.

The business had gone down the tubes in what? She looked back through the file: '91. What the hell did he do all day? And for three years? What the hell had he been doing every day for the last three bloody years?

Well, Audrey had finally found out. All the while she was washing his clothes and putting them on his back, that woman was indulging in their contents.

"No wonder he'd showed no interest in me," she shouted into the empty hall. "He was too busy fucking her!"

Then she cried so much she gagged on her tears and was sick.

So, Audrey lied again. And every day she lied a little bit bigger and a little bit more often. She lied to him and she lied to the boys, for she could not bear to think they might know. But worst of all, she lied to herself from that moment on and throughout the years that followed.

Audrey hadn't ever really understood why she'd made that decision to lie. She knew now. But, like much of her life, it only made sense to her when she was able to look back on it: She lied because she didn't know what else to do.

She had been forty-six years old and was by no means ready to be thrown on the scrapheap.

She tried her best to give it a go with a young man she met near Witney. A puncture had forced her to stop on a fast and dangerous section of the A40. It was raining hard and she felt pathetic and wanted to scream for help. A young man in a beaten-up Renault stopped. He was quite handsome in a boyish way; slim-waisted, fresh and eyes that reminded her of Laurent. And when his hand slipped on the wet wheel-brace and he skinned his knuckles, she gave him her handkerchief.

Her spare was flat, too. He was soaked. They called for a

breakdown truck, and when it came and took her car off to the local garage, he offered her a lift home. Audrey took it, jumped at it; a reaction, she realised later, born more of want than despair. And if only he'd known what she was thinking as she'd squirmed in her seat next to him. But that was all Audrey had done; think, imagine, and shrink from her feelings — nothing else.

That was the first time in a long time her mind was turned to Laurent. Curiously, she'd not even remembered him when she first discovered Richard's infidelity. So why should the young man make her think of him again? After all, her brief moment in the sun with Laurent was not strictly an infidelity.

Memories of Laurent, and her short spell of lewd imaginings with the young man who'd rescued her, prompted Audrey to review the boundaries of her own faith. But, after a tortuous period of self-examination, and with absolutely no help whatsoever from any higher power, she decided such prayer and contemplation were not for her. No one would or could change the facts. Only in one's mind's eye, she realised, could Belloc preserve the idyll that was the Evenlode.

On the eve of his sixtieth birthday, she plied Richard with VSOP for old time's sake and hid a carving knife in the drawer of her bedside table.

Audrey got up just after midnight. She turned on the bedside light, took out the knife and stood watching him like a spectre from a nightmare. For a good few minutes, she held the knife tight to her breasts and luxuriated in her power over him.

But the brandy had anaesthetised Richard and he looked so pathetically defenceless as he lay sleeping that she could not bring herself to harm him. She blamed the rather bizarre nocturnal aberration on her menopause. Well, she had to lay the blame somewhere; she wasn't mad.

Next morning over birthday cards and boiled eggs, Audrey went to ask Richard to pass the salt, but instead said, "I'd like a divorce."

Richard didn't even look up from the papers. In reply, he merely said, "Of course you do, dear," and passed her the salt.

It was never spoken of again.

But, he didn't go to Town so often after that. She didn't know why. She didn't like to ask or really need to know why. She simply assumed it was because he was retired.

He sold the big house and they moved back to the confines of his original house halfway up the hill.

Two years later, Richard was dead.

She'd always believed he'd die of Cirrhosis of the Liver from his drinking, or Atherosclerosis from smoking, or perhaps even old-fashioned consumption from too much rich food. But, he didn't. Cancer claimed him.

That took him away from her for good; first that woman, then Cancer.

At the end, it was so slow; much slower than the doctors had suggested it might be. There was nothing she or they could do for him; nothing at all. That grotesque witch, Cancer, was not for driving out.

She wanted to believe Richard had simply strolled off into the early morning rime that suspended about the Evenlode. The notion sounded acceptably prosaic in her head and she hoped that when Richard met Belloc on the riverbank, Belloc might forgive him for that which she could not.

But all she could remember about those final days was not his inert, cool, wasting frame; rather it was the carrier bag of medicines she'd been left to dispose of; the inhalers, the powders, the tablets, the gauze swabs and the papier-mâché urine bottles.

And she remembered having to inject him with Diamorphine when the palliative care nurse had been absent and he could no longer swallow the Oramorph. The injections; they very nearly did for her. But then she remembered injecting Kummel into strawberries when

251

she was at Fed's, so she imagined it was a similar procedure, although she didn't have to go through the rigmarole of coating him in chocolate afterwards.

Dr Chalmers provided her with something called a Syringe Driver; an innocuous looking device about the size of an electric whisk, though without the whisks attached, of course.

At first it looked innocuous, but when the District Nurse attached the syringe to the top of it, it looked to Audrey like an instrument of torture and she could barely bring herself to listen to the simple instructions: Check the battery daily. Avoid using your mobile phone closer than one metre to the device. Don't use the Syringe Driver without first understanding the instructions. Don't get it wet. Don't take it from a cool place into a humid atmosphere...

She remembered glazing over.

Oh! What did she say? Was it something about strong magnetic fields? "Sorry. Yes. Oh yes. Of course I'm listening."

This device would mean Audrey could accurately administer controlled doses of Diamorphine over a much longer period than she could by injection.

She didn't like the machine; she didn't entirely trust it. But, if it meant she didn't have to glance at her watch every five minutes to keep herself from forgetting Richard's medication, and if it meant she didn't have to think of Kummel Infused Strawberries Coated in Chocolate, then maybe she could get along with it.

The blue labelled Hourly Rate Syringe Driver would also free up some time for her. For of the many and curious idiosyncrasies Audrey had noticed about death, perhaps the most obvious was that the last part of the process seemed to take such an awfully long time.

One day, she needed to pop into Oxford. There was a rather natty clothing shop in the city which was bound to have just the right coloured sweater for John on his birthday. He'd been a bit down recently, though God only knew what he had to be down about. But unlike James who had Sian to attend to him, John was not married and now and again needed a little fillip to bolster his confidence. And, if she set the machine up to look after Richard, she'd have enough time to stop by Waitrose on her way back and get herself something nice for dinner.

She recalled filling the syringe with the correct volume of medication and she remembered connecting and filling the infusion line, checking the air was completely expelled. She measured the distance from the empty line to the plunger, divided it by the number of hours she required the medication to be administered over, and set the rate in the window. If she remembered anything clearly, it was that she set the rate to 04. She was certain of it. Certain! The plunger of the syringe would move forward 4mm every hour. She needed two hours for her trip into Oxford, but set the rate for twelve hours just in case something happened to her; something unforeseen like a tree falling on her which might stop her from getting back before the District Nurse came in at eight.

Audrey put the syringe on top of the driver in the recess and ensured the finger grip of the barrel was secured in the slot. She pressed and held the button on the side of the actuator and slid it into the correct position, making sure the button fitted firmly into the slot. Then she checked the line was properly secured to Richard's IV, hooked the rubber strap over the syringe barrel and the phone rang.

"Fish-hooks!" she said. "Sorry Richard." Audrey kissed him on the forehead and pressed the start button on the side of the Driver.

His eyes were closed; they had been most of the morning.

"Be right back," she promised.

Audrey nipped into the hall and grabbed the receiver off its mount, "Hello?"

"Hello?" said a voice somewhere down a long pipe. "Hello? Is that Mrs Poulter?"

"Yes. Mrs Poulter speaking."

"Mrs Poulter, this is Dilip-"

"Look," she said, "I'm a bit tied up right now. Could you call back another time?"

Audrey put the receiver down, threw on her coat and drove swiftly into Oxford.

She wasn't long. She knew that for certain because she listened to the Archers on the drive back and so it can't have been much after two-thirty. Richard would be listening to the afternoon play and she was pleased with herself; she'd found a nice college-style scarf for John and had treated herself to a delicious Love Life Lasagne for dinner.

But, Richard wasn't listening to the afternoon play. He was dead.

She sat beside his bed for a whole hour before calling Dr Chalmers. She remembered feeling as though her head was encased in a huge church bell which clanged and clanged and clanged. And all she could see was the lack of movement in Richard's chest; no rhythmic rising and falling, no nothing, just a person who looked like Richard, but not him; a corpse, inert, vacant.

Eventually the ringing abated and her eyes settled once more to focus.

When Dr Chalmers arrived, he briefly examined Richard's body, expressed his condolences and asked Audrey whether she'd made any plans with a local undertaker.

"Of course bloody not," she replied angrily, and immediately hated herself for being so ugly. "I mean no, I haven't."

"I'll just remove the Syringe Driver," he said and moved back to the bed.

That was when they both noticed the syringe barrel had not been properly strapped to the actuator. It was lying on top of the device, at an angle, and it was empty.

Dr Chalmers looked at her long and hard.

Richard had received the whole syringe of Diamorphine in less than three hours as opposed to twelve.

Dr Chalmers was weighing Audrey as if she were on the scales in his surgery. He was older than Richard, quite a lot older; if it was possible to be older than someone who was just an hour ago dead. He wore a sports jacket and club tie. "Now, Audrey..." he said.

"I've killed him, haven't I?" she whispered. She had to. It was what she was thinking and, judging by the look on his ruddy face, it was exactly what he was thinking. If she showed no remorse now, how guilty would she look? "I've killed him," she repeated a little louder.

"No, Audrey, you haven't. There's absolutely no way we can ever know whether the Diamorphine tipped him over the edge. We just cannot know."

Audrey saw in her mind's eye a video of her shoving Richard's lifeless form over a chalk cliff, legs and arms flailing as his body plummeted towards the rocks below. "Are you sure?"

She was back at The Reach now, standing beneath a lamppost, and staring out to sea as though she was expecting a boat to come in. It had begun to rain; a fine, hanging rain that whirled and spun in slow eddies beneath the light.

"Morphine," she said quietly to herself. "What idiot left me in charge of a machine that dispensed Morphine?"

She remembered the envelope of Oramorph pills sitting on the bathroom shelf upstairs in her room. God knows why she'd kept them! But then, God knew why, too. HE was just as capable as anyone of scheming; after all, hadn't HE invented it?

She was nearly finished. The end was not so far off. She would be able to go inside soon.

Over the days following Richard's passing, Audrey found herself dealing with a distended clutter of widow's debris: probate, pensions, utility bills and other papers whose newly altered headings sought to erase Richard's name from her life. And, as if she didn't feel sufficiently reduced by his fading, the bank sought to reduce her standing further by recalling her credit card. She had no credit rating, James informed her; she was the supplementary and not primary card holder. Richard had been the primary. It was as though she didn't exist.

And didn't it just cost more to bury him than to keep him alive? £1,200 for the funeral, £400 for the hearse, £300 for the coffin, and £700 just to keep his body on ice until all and sundry were present to commit him to the earth! The carrion crow had a field day.

But it was the funeral that finally buckled her.

She found Richard's memorial service at St Mary's a curiously surreal and strangely procedural affair; a cluster of faintly amusing recollections from a colleague, the odd promise to stay in touch, an occasional tight hug from someone she knew she ought to recognise.

Thankfully and mercifully, the woman she had seen kissing Richard that day in Kensington Gardens did not appear. Audrey had been vigilant. She was sure she would have noticed. And she remembered thinking that perhaps the tone of a funeral was governed as much by the absence of some as by the attendance of others.

She tried her best to hide from the All-seeing Eye of her albeit waning Catholicism, but she knew deep down hers was a hopeless lot; there was and would be no escape from her fatal misdemeanour with the Syringe Driver. Half of her wanted to be brazen in His sight and yet half of her knew she was being watched by others, or at least Audrey understood that her conscience intended for her to feel that way.

The boys were brilliant until late on when she realised they were both very drunk.

James's wife wanted to take him home. Audrey didn't blame her.

Sian, blond and freckly, was no fool; a bit of a Sloane, but smart enough to realise that James was not for moving, so she persuaded him up to the tiny spare room. Sian would make a good mother when the time came; though what she saw in James was anybody's guess.

John grew very maudlin at never having been able to communicate more openly with his father. But, then again, he always had been swift to regret.

As the clock on the mantelpiece counted down the evening, Audrey knew exactly what John was on about, but she also knew better than to scold herself for what she perceived to be someone else's shortcomings. It was too late for that. And though she tried to be at her soothing best for John, she could not keep him from getting lost in a fog of self-pity. He harboured demons similar to those she had harboured before she met Richard; he was like her.

In the end she hugged him, dried his eyes and tucked him up on the sofa.

The next day, as Audrey was clearing away breakfast, she overheard the boys discussing their father. They were in the snug. The door was open.

"'Course she must have known," she heard James say.

"No," replied John, his voice hoarse, deep and hungover, "I'm telling you she didn't. Mum would never have put up with that kind of behaviour from Dad. I'm telling you, she didn't."

"No? Come on, John. Wake up and smell the coffee. If she didn't know she must have been blind or bloody stupid."

"James?" pleaded Sian. "This is neither the right time nor the right place for this-"

"Well," said James, "either she knew or she's dimmer than I thought."

"James?" Sian repeated. "She's in the kitchen. Keep your voice down."

"Well, what are we going to do about her? At least she had the good grace not to turn up at the service. She wasn't there, was she?" John asked.

Audrey didn't mind the boys thinking she was dim if that was what it took to maintain their affection for her. Even though it was unkind and wide of the mark, she could live with that. And she was equally rewarded to hear that her vigilance at the funeral had not been suspect.

She knew it was wrong to stay and listen. She absolutely knew she was going to hear something that she would rather not. But, she was mesmerised by their conversation and, rather like scratching at an irritating insect bite, Audrey couldn't help herself.

"So, what are we going to do about her?" James asked.

"Oh for goodness' sake," said Sian in something above a whisper. "Your Mum will get over losing your Dad. She's a tough old bird. Granted she may have to get some part-time job to make ends meet, but she'll get by. And you forget she's not exactly alone."

"No, not about Mum," James said, "about HER."

"About who?" asked Audrey, appearing at the door.

The dam was breached; the fury behind it unleashed. She knew bloody well who they were talking about. And after all that had gone before, the one indignity she would not suffer was having her sons express concern about her husband's mistress in her house. She glared at James, "About whom, James? Oh," she turned from him for a split-second and rested a withering look upon Sian, "and thanks for the vote of confidence, Sian, I'm sure I'll get by."

Audrey looked from James to John.

James was strangely defiant, like he would defend until death whoever it was he was talking about; that or deny his knowledge of the person he was talking about. It mattered little; either way he was condemned.

John didn't know where to put himself.

The snug was cold, almost as cold as the spring day on which Audrey had first walked into it.

Then she shouted in a controlled and commanding tone, "Come on, about whom?" Audrey knew John would not speak up. He would rather do anything other than upset her. So she moved half a step towards James and focused her fury on him. "Dim as you clearly think I am, James," she yelled, "who are you talking about?"

James's face seemed to bob from side to side, his eyes turned towards the floor and he rubbed the hair on the nape of his neck. His head dropped, "Maria, Mother. Please don't say you didn't know about her. You must have. I'm talking about Maria, Mother, father's mistress."

The image of James and John standing there looking at her with the same shadowed expressions she'd seen on the faces of the mourners at the funeral would haunt Audrey through the rest of her days. The picture of their sorry, forlorn, pitying faces, their subtle confusions of contempt and sympathy, Audrey knew from that very moment on she would see every time she looked across the table at her sons and their families; at New Year, Easter and Christmas; at births, christenings, birthdays, graduations, marriages and, yes, probably at other funerals too.

And like the tears she'd shed all through the autumn of her life, the sadness of her sons dissolved into the darkness of the North Sea before her.

With their images went Richard and that woman, Maria Lentz; the woman to whom Richard had all but given her flat above Fed's; her home, her only real home, which had been soiled and trodden underfoot like everything else in her life.

The images all faded away like walkers in the rain, consumed by the vast darkness of the night and the sea. With them too went the pictures of a life lived by someone she had once known; a widow who had never delivered her fellow beings any disservice or discourtesy. Audrey knew she had been a good friend to some and never really the slightest nuisance to others.

"Oh, but they won't see it that way, will they?" she said.

But she could live with that. Or, rather, she could leave them with that. It didn't matter now; the contempt of her sons had seen to that.

She turned across the road towards The Reach.

Audrey was tired. She would go to her bed in the same room in which she'd stayed with Laurent all those years ago. And that was precisely why she'd had to dredge up all that sour history; all that stuff and nonsense she'd been forced to put up with over the years, all that pain and sorrow meted out by those who ought to have known better. Surely, putting up with all of that was sufficient to justify Audrey her one, final infidelity.

36

Phoebe

Among the elusive shadows chasing across the bedroom ceiling, Phoebe made out the face of Dr Julius Blessing. And she wondered whether, if she'd tried harder, she could have driven her future in any other direction. She felt blown down the road like a speck of dust before the wind, for both Dr Julius and Yu had guided her towards this temporary destination and yet neither of them had ever possessed the slightest intention of forcing her towards it.

After her meeting with the doctor, Phoebe had looked in on her mother. She was asleep. Phoebe wanted to wake her mother up and reassure her that everything was going to be okay, that Phoebe would sort everything out, and that there was nothing her mum should worry about. But, she didn't have the heart. In fact, it was probably just as well her mother was asleep, there would have been no way Phoebe could have contained her excitement.

But Phoebe did feel good. She felt so, so good.

Back at college, she threw herself into her work with a vigour born of her renewed confidence. Phoebe set herself two weeks in which to weigh up the pros and cons of giving her mother one of her kidneys. After all, she'd promised the very good-looking and charmingly earnest Dr Julius that she would do so. And if he were to oversee her donation, she should at least afford him the respect of doing what he'd asked and what she'd promised.

Phoebe excused herself from socials and, in her spare hours, walked the winding path beside the Cam into Grantchester. There were no punts out on the river; no Chinese tourists crowding together for photographs or bumping up against the students hoping some of their intellect might rub off. The water meadows were still and quiet, and provided her with exactly what she needed: a vast, uncluttered space in which to give free rein to her emotions. Lingering in the deserted Orchard Tea Garden, Phoebe wondered what those Bloomsburys and Grantchesters, Woolf and Brooke, would have made of her plight.

Curiously, Phoebe didn't feel inclined to consult those closest to her. She knew her father would object, so there was nothing to be gained by asking a question she already knew the answer to. And besides, she was now old enough to do with her body as she saw fit. And if that meant redistributing an organ, then...

But what she found most curious was that she didn't feel inclined to consult Heather, or Yu, or Terence or Boris or Simon. Phoebe wasn't necessarily anxious they might discourage her, it was more that she wanted the decision to be hers and in no way theirs. If later on, as Dr Julius had pointed out could be the case, her decision came back to haunt her, Phoebe wanted to be the only one to be haunted; she did not wish such a haunting on her friends.

By the end of the second week, her mind was made up, again. Granted she felt as though her final decision was little more than a logical progression from her initial one, but Phoebe liked to think she had given over a suitable period to due diligence and that she had employed all the mental faculties at her disposal, as the good doctor had put it.

And like the high-powered commercial lawyer she hoped one day to become, Phoebe reasoned that now the deal was concluded, she owed it to herself to get out and let off a little steam.

I need to go out, she texted Heather.

Sorry got a beast of an essay tomorrow. Where have you been, came the reply. From Yu, she got no reply. Terence had a rugby game the next day. Boris was all loved up with a Land-Ec Fresher. And Simon, she didn't bother to bother — he was so not going to come out to play without Heather.

She called Jay, the very tall American post-grad she had been seeing when she first heard about her mother's condition.

They met in the Eagle in Benet Street. It wasn't her favourite place; it was expensive. But, like many of whom Phoebe referred to as the tourist post-grads, Jay liked the rather kitsch history of the RAF pilots' signatures on the ceiling of the bar at the back. When she phoned, he never so much as mentioned her recent absence and she put it down to his being American and rather pleasantly feckless. He was taking an MPhil in Finance at The Judge and they didn't have all that much in common, but he was easy fun. The only other advantage Jay had going for him was that he was certainly big and tall enough for her to hang on to, should the need arise later.

By eight, Phoebe was fed up with the King's crowd in the Eagle, so they moved on to Bar Room Bar where they ate Americana pizza and drank Hurricanes. She liked Jay more as the evening grew; he was a good listener. And though she never discussed her mother or any of the many puzzles that had occupied her mind over the last few weeks, Phoebe found she had plenty to say.

But by eleven thirty Phoebe had reached her zenith, or so Jay decided. He tried, at first gently, then firmly, and finally rather physically to manoeuvre her towards the door, but Phoebe would have none of it. She was going to go down gloriously, just like the *Titanic*, or so she told him, and, big as he was, he wasn't big enough to stop her.

Jay was on the verge of abandoning her when Yu walked in.

If the evening had been steady up until then, when Yu pitched up it descended to a whole new level of depravity and destruction.

The next day, sometime around three in the afternoon, Phoebe woke up in Yu's room, in Yu's bed, with Yu.

The slightest movement of her head pained her as though she'd been beaten in the face with a bat, and she couldn't understand why there was any way she could have slept when her heart stomped through her brain like a clumsy giant in hobnail boots.

She sat up very slowly, dressed, and stole out of the room. At the door, Phoebe stopped and forced herself to look back at the quietly sleeping Yu. He lay on his front, his face turned to the wall, his skin strangely pale and smooth in the afternoon light.

Back at the set, her head and heart still thumped. The front of her face felt stiff and full.

Phoebe staggered into the bathroom and studied her face in the mirror.

She felt awful, but great; although, if she was honest with herself, she felt more awful than great. There were dark rings under her eyes, her red hair was matted and knotted, and, when she examined her nose more closely, she noticed a small crust of white powder coating the rim of her nostrils.

Phoebe splashed her face, wiped around the inside of her nose with her little finger and noticed a residue of powder stuck to the inside of her nail.

"Oh Shit!" she breathed at the mirror. She splashed more water up her nose. She flared her nostrils in an effort to clean them as thoroughly as she could without making herself gag. Phoebe all but sniffed the water in, probably in much the same way as she had snorted the 'drone the evening before.

"That wasn't very bloody clever," she moaned at her reflection.

That evening word got round that Phoebe had been seen in Crystie's with Yu, and that she had. . .

Heather came back to the set about seven. Phoebe was in her pyjamas, tucked up in bed, clutching a cup-a-soup.

Heather grinned, but said nothing to begin with. It was only later, when they were watching a movie on Phoebe's laptop, that she slipped the goss' into their conversation, "So, Yu's the man, huh?"

Phoebe didn't reply immediately, but after a lengthy pause said, "Would seem that way."

There was more silence until Heather said, "Look, babe, what you do, you do-"

"Guess so," Phoebe cut back.

Heather wasn't to be fobbed off so easily, "But if there's a bit more going on just now than getting hammered in Crystie's with Yu will solve, then perhaps you'd be better off sharing whatever it is that's bothering you with your closest mate, eh?"

"No. I'm okay. Leave it alone."

But, again, Heather wouldn't let it go, "Like bloody hell I will, Phoebes. In case you'd forgotten, we live virtually in the same room and this last two weeks you've been playing like the silent apostle, ruminating with the livestock down on the water meadows, and communing with the spirits in the tea garden. And then you go and behave like a complete twat with Yu in front of most of the second years in Crystie's." Heather studied Phoebe for any reaction.

"Yea," said Phoebe, "so I got a little out of hand. It's nothing you haven't done before."

"Granted, Phoebes," Heather replied, raising her eyebrows and rolling her eyes. "But, babe, when I do it, it's nothing new; when you do it, it's completely out of character. And I know you, and so do the guys, and therefore none of us have to be too clever to work out that something in the world of Phoebe Wallace is wrong, very wrong."

That did it. That broke Phoebe. And that was the problem: Heather had put into words exactly what Phoebe couldn't understand, namely why was it that everything in Phoebe's world felt so right when it all seemed so wrong?

For the next two hours, Phoebe could not hold back from drawing

265

out the whole saga of her mother's illness and her wanting to donate one of her kidneys. And then there was the bare fact that she'd slept with Yu and that she'd taken Mephedrone when she'd sworn blind that she would never poison her body in such a way again.

When Phoebe had run out of steam, Heather went out and returned with ice cream and vodka, and they got into Phoebe's bed and talked and talked and talked.

By the early hours both of them realised that, perhaps for the first time in her life, Phoebe's emotions were commanding her reasoning and not the reverse.

"When do you have to go back to the hospital?" Heather asked.

"Day after tomorrow."

"You might want to check all that 'drone has gone through your system. Nobody's quite sure how long it hangs around."

"How the bloody hell do I do that?" Phoebe asked.

Heather stared at her. "I tell you what, they're collecting blood – the blood transfusion service, or whatever it's called – down at the Methodist Centre at Christ's Pieces tomorrow. Why don't you go and give them a drop of blood. If there's anything wrong with it, they'll tell you."

Phoebe looked at Heather as though she'd gone stark raving mad. "And what if there is and word gets back to college I've got a river of 'drone flowing through my veins?"

"They won't tell anyone," Heather dismissed. "Look, if you're that worried about it, pretend you're someone else. Give them someone else's name, DOB and address. It's simple enough. Don't look so worried, it'll be a breeze."

The next morning, and feeling as though she'd resumed partial control over her mind and body, Phoebe strolled over to the modern Wesleyan Methodist Church on Christ's Pieces and signed up to give blood.

There was nothing a child couldn't grasp in the Welcome Folder and she was able to tick every No box in the health check. Okay, so she'd slept with Yu, but she hadn't done it for the 'drone. Registering proved simple; fictitious name, date of birth and address. The Health Screening nurse checked her details through and asked her a few pertinent questions. Phoebe did not have to lie when asked if she'd indulged in any banned substances in the last seventy-two hours: The 'drone wasn't yet illegal. Phoebe signed the consent form. The nurse cleaned her finger with a sterile wipe, pricked it with a lancet and collected the drop of blood that oozed from the puncture with a pastette. She took the sample off for testing.

After a short wait, Phoebe was shown to a donation bed where a nurse cuffed her right arm, found her vein, cleaned the area with a sterile wand and inserted a needle.

Phoebe got a bit tearful when she realised this was just the beginning of the physical process that would lead to her giving her mother her life back, and the nurse was concerned that she might be going into shock until Phoebe reassured her otherwise. She wanted to tell the nurse exactly why it was that she was giving her blood, but decided that might complicate her impersonation of the Fresher whose identity she'd used, so she didn't.

Just before she left, Phoebe was given her new donor card. Nobody mentioned any unusual substance showing up in her screen, so she guessed she was clean enough to go back to Elmwood General and see the gorgeous Dr Julius.

Phoebe walked back to college in a happy daze. As she walked, she flicked the donor card absentmindedly between her fingers.

She stopped to look in a shop window, debated buying her mother a present; chocolates wouldn't do, flowers she could get at home, maybe a nice nightshirt for when she went to hospital.

Phoebe dropped the donor card and, as she picked it up, she noticed her blood type had been written on the card: B negative.

B-negative?

That wasn't right. Dr Julius had said her mother was A-positive. *There must be a mistake,* she thought; *there must be.* Perhaps they'd given her the wrong card. She checked the details; the false name she'd given was right there on the card.

Phoebe looked up at her reflection in the shop window and didn't recognise herself.

"B-negative? I can't be."

37

Stella

If midday had dragged, the afternoon and evening slowly petrified.

Stella sat, listened to music and drank gin; too much gin and too quickly. She wished the world would go away and leave her alone. But she was waiting for her last guests, the Scotts.

The meeting with Doyle had left her feeling invaded and vacant as though some dreadful witchfinder had opened up her insides and hung them on display. She wondered if that was how those Tudor-beathan dandies felt when they were hung, drawn and quartered — much like they were on that programme she'd seen the other night.

It was, she decided as she poured herself another three fingers of gin, all so wretchedly unfair. She hadn't done anything her neighbours hadn't done.

The television coughed up a frothy brew of puerile drama; strained faces, risible stunts and papier-mâché sex; nothing that would prick the bubble of her downbeat mood. And by the time the weatherman predicted more wind and rain, Stella was sufficiently moved to throw one of her slippers at the screen.

She switched the useless machine off and surrendered to Buddy Holly. He would keep the hounds of her depression at bay; he never let her down.

38

Phoebe

"Fine," was all she could manage when she got back to the set, "Good idea, H, thanks."

Phoebe simply refused to allow herself to believe that she might be a different blood type to her mother. She hadn't entertained the possibility that she shared her father's. But, if she did, she wouldn't be able to donate her kidney to her mother, and that she just didn't want to contemplate.

By the time she got home that evening, her father was in bed. And when she looked in on Billy, he was asleep, which was just as well as Phoebe felt very uncertain of the coming days. She wouldn't have wanted Billy to see her that way; for him she needed to appear confident and in control, just as she'd always been.

The next morning, Phoebe made sure she was up and ready to catch her father. He rose very early, breakfasted early and left early; always had.

"I didn't hear you come in," he said by way of welcome.

Phoebe put her arms round him and kissed him on the cheek, "Morning, Dad."

"Oh," he stepped back, "thank you. What brings you back here and gets you out of your pit so early?"

"Well, I wanted to catch you before you left. I'm going to see

Mum and I have to leave straight after. And, besides, we never get the chance to talk properly on the phone." She decided he looked older, much older than the last time she'd seen him, "How's Mum?"

"Talk, eh? Mum? She's as well as can be expected. The doctor..." Brian Wallace filled his mouth with toast.

"Dr Blessing?"

"Mmm, him. He says she should be able to come home in a few days. She'll have to go back three times a week for dialysis though."

"Yes," Phoebe said, pouring herself coffee, "that's what he told me. Have you spoken to Mum about a transplant?"

"Me?"

"Yes, Dad: You!"

She'd worked out that for her to be B-neg and her mum to be A-pos, her dad had to be either B-something or AB-something. That gave him an even chance of being a match.

Her father finished his toast. "I believe the doctor has discussed it with her," he said, wiping his mouth on a napkin. "She told me he'd told her a transplant would be a viable proposition." That was all he said. He got up from the breakfast table, cleared away his mug and plate, and bent to load them in the dishwasher.

"Dad? Dad, don't you think it would be a good idea if you spoke to Dr Blessing yourself?"

Brian Wallace turned from the kitchen door and looked back at his daughter. He paused before he spoke; it was his way of suggesting she should wait in line for his reply and not expect it immediately. "Mmm... Yes. I should, shouldn't I?" Then he turned away.

"Oh, Christ, Dad!"

"Phoebe," he growled from the hall.

"Well really, dad," she said, dropping her head onto her chest in defeat, "sometimes I really bloody wonder." Phoebe heard the front door open. She got up and rushed into the hall. "Dad, have you given this any thought at all?"

Brian Wallace turned back to her again. His shoulders, crowned by the porch light, sagged. "Phoebe, you know I'm a little past prime donor age. Do you not think I'd give your mother one of my kidneys if I thought it'd help?"

Phoebe felt like throwing her coffee cup at him, "Dad, there is no upper age limit on organ donation. And, if there was, I'm sure it would be way over sixty-two."

He turned round, looked directly at her and said, "I just don't see it as an option, Phoebe; as an option for me or for your mother."

"You don't see it as an option?" she shouted at him. "This isn't about you, Dad. It's about Mum. It's about all of us."

He winced, no doubt concerned about waking up the neighbours. But he didn't reply.

Phoebe, on the other hand, wanted to see some fight in him. She was desperate for him to show her that he had the willingness or ability to intervene, to help, to contribute, just to do bloody something, anything rather than mope about accepting Fate like a Muselmann awaiting selection.

"I bet you don't even know your own blood type, do you, Dad? Has it crossed your mind to ask?"

He didn't react to her taunt, though. He just paused a while longer; a sad, slightly reduced figure from the hardy father she'd known in her youth.

She moved towards him, fearing she'd wounded him too deeply and wishing she could take back her words, but he turned away from her.

"I told you," he said into the misty dawn, "it's simply not an option."

"Dad?" she asked again, but more softly this time. "That wasn't what I asked you. I asked you if you'd even bothered to find out what your blood type is?"

"Er, no," he replied, his voice drifting towards the road, "I... sorry," and he was already closing the gate.

Phoebe wasn't sure whether she wanted to run after him or stand there and abuse him. Initially, she plain didn't understand her father's inability to act and wondered if she'd ever really known this man whom she worshipped.

She knew she had to act even if he wouldn't. She would persuade him to make his contribution if it was the last thing she ever got him to do.

But first, she had to find out his blood type. There would be no point in dragging him to the hospital to see Dr Blessing if her dad was not compatible in the first place. She wasn't going to make the same mistake with him that she'd so stupidly made with herself.

Once Billy had left for school, she went very methodically through all of her father's papers, but there was not one scrap of paper that would give up the secret of his blood type.

Phoebe sat on the floor and picked out an old black and white newspaper photo of her father standing beside a rather delicate, single-seater racing car. It wasn't one of those sleek, winged beasts the boys watched on the TV in the college café on Sunday lunchtimes; this was diminutive in body, but with wheels that stuck out like big ears. The picture may have faded, but his smile was bright, just like Billy's after he'd scored at football.

It was then that she remembered his racing overalls would have his blood type on them. In her mind's eye, Phoebe recalled them being stitched somewhere on a pocket. They were stuffed in a plastic bag along with all the other dressing up costumes.

Phoebe replaced the photographs and the various files just as she had found them, and then rushed upstairs.

The large supermarket bag was buried behind Billy's cricket kit in the overhead cupboard above the sink in her parent's bedroom. Standing on tiptoe on her mother's vanity stool, Phoebe eased the carrier bag gently out from beneath the others.

Her father's white racing overalls were exactly where she remembered them.

Phoebe tugged them out of the bag and hung them up against the cupboard door. "There you are, Phoebe Wallace," she said. "If you needed proof of your fabulous intellect, here it bloody well is."

The overalls were back to front. As she turned them round, she said, "Now, Dad, let's see if you are a match for Mum. If I've got this right and I'm B and Mum's A, then you must be..."

She examined the black stitching on the left breast. "No, that's not right. You can't be," Phoebe muttered quietly and looked again. "No way: O-neg? That can't be right. You've got to be kidding."

39

Philip

"Are you alright, Phil?" she asked, stroking the back of his neck. "You've gone a bit pale." Fiona rested her other hand in his crutch, but didn't move it further. "Not petrified at the thought of just the two of us alone in a hotel bedroom, are you?" she giggled, leaning forward so that she knew he would see her teasing her lower lip.

Philip made a play of looking for directions. He needed a couple of minutes to cloak the many unanswered questions that suspended in his mind. He felt protective towards her, loving and wanting to love her more. And yet as soon as he projected Fiona to the forefront of his thoughts, the spectre of her mother took shape beside her.

40

Hacker

Stella Anworthy's door was shut when Hacker slipped back into The Reach. Buddy Holly warbled from behind it and so masked the creak of his footfall. It wasn't that he wanted to avoid her attentions; it was more that he couldn't guarantee his reactions should she offer them.

He noticed that his hands were trembling and he felt hollow and weary. He'd fronted up to far tougher opponents than Brian Chisholm in his time. He'd had to; that was the nature of the game. But he'd never stooped to threatening someone, anyone, in such a manner before. Sure, marking the other team's forwards, squaring up to them and daring them to take him on had been a fundamental aspect of his game. And there had been a certain psychological edge to that, too; bravado, confidence, and an inherent and flagrant desire to assert himself over the man opposite were all necessary elements of his game. But, threatening a miserable specimen like Chisholm did not come naturally to him. He felt mean and cheap, and the feeling purled uneasily in his stomach as he got into bed.

41

Phoebe

Phoebe wasn't sure what time it was. She lay tangled in the bedclothes and, like a psychiatric patient in evaluation, forced herself to retrace the steep and slippery incline of her descent into purgatory.

She remembered thinking when she saw Dr Julius Blessing that last time that he wasn't quite so good-looking.

After her conclusive blood test at the hospital, Phoebe returned to college and began to worry that the bedrock of home might not be as solid as she had always perceived it to be. And for the first time in her life, Phoebe's concentration was forcibly hijacked from her academic work and focussed on a situation over which she was powerless to exert any influence. This new and very alarming impotence undermined her nerve and fuelled in her an anxiety she had not suffered since her early days at school.

Essays were not completed before deadline, supervisions were missed and her DOS called her in for a cautionary review. This assault on her academic propensity only served to chip away at her previously impregnable acumen.

Soon Phoebe found herself burning the midnight oil merely to get essays finished, never mind get them finished on time.

Heather was sympathetic. The boys listened and either encouraged or soothed, but none of them could do the work or attend the supervisions for her.

She called Yu aside one evening while they were eating early in the canteen.

"You alright, babe?" he asked, looking down at her.

"Yea, I'm fine," she replied. "I'm just tired. Listen, I've got shit loads of work and I can't seem to keep my eyes open, but I want to go out later, got any 'drone I can have?"

Yu looked at her with the same intense, searching expression he had when she'd asked him the identical question on the evening of the Magdalene Ball. They'd never discussed the night she slept with him; never mentioned it. "Sure," he said, "but if you want to stay awake for work, Ritalin will be better. I can let you have some of that."

"No, thanks, I'd rather have some 'drone, if you don't mind. I'll need a bit of a lift later, that's all. I only need enough for tonight," Phoebe said hurriedly.

Yu, in the act of turning away, hesitated and looked back at her, his face stern and unforgiving, "We only ever need enough for tonight, Phoebes."

That was the first night, or, if she was honest with herself, it was really the fourth night; the first one being in the club, the second in May Week and the third just a couple of weeks before in Crystie's. But this night was different from the other nights, for this was the first night in the sequence of nights that led to her overwhelming.

And it wasn't just the sequence of taking 'drone either that became her problem, it was that the sequence progressively extended to a catalogue of wretched consequences.

The first was that she slept with Yu again and the second was that he refused to sleep with her at all. Yu had realised what she knew, namely that she was only sleeping with him in order to get her hands on a regular supply of 'drone.

So, without Yu, she had to procure her own 'drone off the web, which worked for a while. But the sudden increase in a certain type of mail was sure to make the Porters suspicious. To get round that she asked Heather if she would mind receiving some of her mail. Heather didn't mind to begin with; a little 'drone saw to that. But when Heather realised how much Phoebe was getting through, she quickly closed off that avenue. So Phoebe took a Post Office Box in town to circumvent the need to have the stuff delivered to college and that made life just too easy.

Their set took on a perfume all of its own, like she'd spilt a jar of honey somewhere, like the carpet-vac was saccharine powder and not the usual freesias.

Next, she was in Crystie's one Wednesday night, too many vodkas and too much 'drone, and she was waving her arms in the air and twirling like a spinning top and yelling at the top of her voice in what she believed to be perfect tune with the music. Only it wasn't. When the others wanted to leave, Phoebe wanted to carry on and got ugly with them when they wouldn't stay. And much, much later, Phoebe had to call Heather to come and get her because she was too frightened to walk home on her own.

A few nights later, Phoebe found out that the others had gone out clubbing without her.

She so wanted to understand why, but found she could only hate them for it.

On the odd occasion when she ran out of 'drone, she slept for two days and was pathetically unresponsive when Heather tried to wake her.

She missed lectures and supervisions, and to finish an essay was to climb an enormously steep and slippery slope. All too soon, Phoebe found that in order to maintain a similar rate of climb as that of her fellow students, she had to resort to time and effort-saving mechanisms, and occasionally mechanisms that were strictly forbidden.

The internet grew to become her only friend and it was only a short time later that the corrosive liquid of plagiarism began to permeate her submissions.

One of her supervisors suggested she was being miserly with her references. A second even went so far as to question her integrity and the authenticity of her work. And a third took her aside and pointed out to her that she had purchased much of one essay directly from a fairly well known essay bank, and that it would not do. It would not do at all. And, like a helpless bystander, Phoebe watched as her every effort drowned in a flood of plagiarism.

Her DOS emailed her: A summons.

The room was warm and intimately welcoming. The large opalescent glass bowl suspended by three brass chains from the ceiling cast a warm Dickensian glow over open bookcases. There were no pictures hanging on the walls; Dame Clarissa Hale had no room for imaginings. In her world, there were only written papers and definitive judgements. On any of the few horizontal surfaces, red and brown leather-bound tomes and bulging grey files lay tempting the dust, motes of which floated in the air above the light like eagles soaring on thermals.

"Please, Phoebe, let's sit down around the fire," Hale said. "The closer one's proximity to the window, the colder one gets." Two leather club chairs watched over a settled coal fire. "Tea?" she asked as much as ordered.

"Coffee, if that's alright?"

"Coffee it is. Milk? Sugar? Just plain black? Fine. I find it hard to drink coffee after lunch. Seems such a morning refreshment to me. But then these things are a bit personal, aren't they? A bit like men not wearing brown after the sun has gone down."

Phoebe marvelled that Clarissa Hale was even remotely proficient in the art of making tea. Rumour had it that she was wedded to the Faculty of Law the way Opus Dei are wedded to their Prelate, although nobody went so far as to suggest Dame Clarissa actually self-flagellated. At first meeting this tall and elegant, if slightly sharp-featured woman had seemed stand-offish and aloof, and in public she was famous for her very open displays of stark inflexibility regarding the college rules. Until now, Phoebe's supervisions had tilted towards the informal; how's the term coming along, how's the workload, got the social under control... But Phoebe knew there existed a dispassionate side to Dame Clarissa's nature and that was the face Phoebe expected to see now.

They sat beside the fire and watched the steam rise from their cups.

"I do so dislike this time of year," Dame Clarissa began. "I know there are those who would say the early evenings lend themselves to long periods of reading, but one can have too much of a good thing. Is that not true, Phoebe?" She sipped her tea, closed her eyes savouring the taste, and issued an extended, grateful sigh.

"Yes, Dame Clarissa."

"How is your mother?"

"Fine, much better, thank you," she lied.

"Now, Phoebe," the Director of Studies looked up over the brim of her cup, "I think today we'll dispense with the vestments of office. You address me by my first name and I'll carry on as normal. Agreed?"

"Yes, Clarissa. Thank you."

"Oh, don't thank me, Phoebe. Someone else saw fit to bestow upon me a title which I certainly did not ask for, and now I have to wear it like an unwieldy and often ugly chain of office about my neck. Rather not have it, if I'm honest." A lively, mischievous smile played across her face; a look the woman evidently guarded from the public. "You see, Phoebe, it's not about how others see you, for that's not always within one's control like my wretched title; it's more about how we perceive ourselves and how we crystallise our perception that matters."

The meeting was not following any standard course. "I understand that," said Phoebe, though she was sure her expression mirrored her puzzlement.

"And one of the challenges we in particular face is that Law can be a weighty and often awkward yolk to support whilst being at the same time a surly and cumbersome beast to drive." Clarissa smiled again, but this time she arched an eyebrow and pursed her lips, demanding or at least suggesting she would like a reply.

"Yes," Phoebe agreed, relaxing. "I feel that way often, but, if you'll excuse the cliché: you pays your money and you takes your chance."

Clarissa raised both her eyebrows this time. "Don't we just, Phoebe. Don't we just." She paused, sipping her tea. Then she set her cup down on the arm of her chair and asked: "So tell me, Phoebe. What is it that's making this chance, or these chances, so difficult for you to take just now?"

Phoebe flinched; she hadn't expected such a raw and frontal assault after such a gentle entrée.

But before she could answer, Hale went on, "Your first year was such a good year, too; you didn't seem to suffer from any problematic homesickness, high 2:1s right across the board, all your tutors comments so positive, no indication in any of your supervisions that there was anything amiss. But this term is a very different story."

"I can't deny it."

"Oh, come off it, Phoebe," Clarissa scoffed, her cheeks colouring a little. "You're not in court now. This is not a Q&A." She paused, evidently hoping her young charge would open up to her.

But when no further reply came, she shifted awkwardly in her chair and said, "Very well, Phoebe. Let me put it to you this way: Nothing has changed here in the interim. The Glittering Spires do not glitter more brightly now than they did last term. Your workload hasn't increased exponentially; if anything it has eased a fraction, and besides, you should be finding it less taxing after your first year. And by all accounts, your social circle hasn't suffered any seismic shift. My point is that clearly the landscape of college hasn't altered, which only leads me to conclude that some part of yours has. What is it, Phoebe? What's changed?"

But Phoebe felt herself withdrawing, felt the room closing in around her, like the shell of a clam shutting about her, squeezing and compressing her view of Dame Clarissa Hale into one tiny, thin image.

"I don't think anything's changed," she replied in a voice so confident she couldn't conceive of where or from whom it came. "It may be that I'm going through one of those late adolescent tunnels I've heard people speak about. I sometimes wonder whether I didn't allow myself the time to get through them when I was at school, because I had my nose so buried in my books. I'm sure I wouldn't be the first college student to think they'd given their youth over to a kind of blind academic devotion." Phoebe allowed a pinch of frustration to seep into her spiel.

"No, you wouldn't, Phoebe," her DOS replied. "You most certainly would not be the first. Nor the last, I suspect. But is that really what is bothering you, Phoebe? Or is it something more fundamental? Though I'm sure a forsaken youth deservedly falls into the category of fundamental." She picked up her tea again, sipped from her cup slowly, and then set it back down.

"But, Phoebe, and unless I'm very much mistaken, one of your great strengths has been your ability to rationalise, not necessarily to compartmentalise — more to reason why certain things are absolutely as they are and equally why other things are not. And by that, I don't mean you have a blinkered or predetermined view. No, quite the reverse. You possess a very considered and philosophical attitude to reality and its value. That is what drew me to you when you first came to college."

"I'm flattered. Really I am."

But Phoebe's response clearly annoyed her Director of Studies. Dame Clarissa sat more upright in her chair and leant forward a little way, "Phoebe, I'm not the hard-hearted bitch some in the college like to think I am. Believe it or not, I am here to help smooth your passage through this extraordinary seat of learning. But, neither am I a fool to be trifled with. I wasn't paying you a compliment so much as asking politely for your honesty. Please do me the kindness of affording me that."

The air in the room stilled.

"I apologise," Phoebe said, looking down at the grate beside her feet, "I didn't mean to be flippant." She paused, but not for so long that her pause could be misconstrued. "I'm not finding things easy just now. It's not just one thing though, it's many."

"Please," clipped Dame Clarissa, "indulge me."

"I do find myself swimming in the dark socially; not all the time, just at odd times and unfortunately at the most unwelcome and personal of moments. I sometimes wish I'd allowed myself the time to make the same mistakes I saw others make at school, so that I wouldn't have to run the risk of appearing so naïve now."

Dame Clarissa interrupted, "Don't be so sure your contemporaries are not still making the same mistakes you now find yourself making, Phoebe. It's called growing up." And as if to prohibit the conversation progressing down too personal, or possibly too sexual a line, Dame Clarissa carried straight on, "There is no set timetable for discovering many of life's more intimate secrets, Phoebe; no timetable at all. Go on..."

"Then there is the whole concept of Law in terms of working for the common good or working against it. Does one practise Law to further the common good or does one practice it in order to become just another bondservant of corporate greed? Stupid thing is, I'd like to think I would've had this all sorted out by now." Phoebe didn't want an answer to her quandary, but she hesitated in case one was coming.

When it didn't, she carried on, "But I haven't. I find myself wandering in some kind of disenchanted wood, in a place I would never have imagined existed. It's not a predicament I've anticipated and it isn't one I've the first idea how to approach."

284

Dame Clarissa nodded, a shrewd and sage expression settling on her face. "The problem with Law," she pronounced and sat back again in her seat.

Phoebe beat about the bush for a while longer; quoted by example a few haphazard incidents from her youth and invented a couple of related paradoxes. But, because of the lack of response from the pillar of the college community opposite, she found little alternative other than to proceed with her monologue. And all too soon, Phoebe found herself rebutting her own arguments and contradicting the hastily invented specifics of her very individual plight. Gradually her voice began to surrender its solid conviction, and, like an echo dying at the bottom of a hollow, she quieted.

"Phoebe, I am informed the ogre of plagiarism has crept into your work," Dame Clarissa said as though nothing Phoebe had said previously was of any great relevance.

"I won't deny it."

"It would be unwise of you to do so. Breaching academic integrity is not a trifling matter, Phoebe." Dame Clarissa did not bother to sit up; she just spoke up in a hard and unforgiving tone, "You're far too bright to go dashing your tremendous ability on the rocks of some blessed paper mill. Phoebe, you must desist from this course of action. And you must desist right away. You must not take someone else's work and pass it off as your own."

42

Philip

They arrived outside The Reach. They were late and it was dark. Fiona walked off to see if they needed a parking ticket while Philip unloaded the car; two nights and Fiona had brought her entire wardrobe.

Ms Anworthy was pleasantly welcoming, but Philip was surprised when she didn't ask them to sign the register. She looked a little anxious and a lot drunk. She continually toyed with her neat and very tightly curled hair.

"Number 4," she said, "upstairs on the right. Breakfast from seven-thirty or earlier if you would like. And please don't hesitate to let me know if there's anything I can get you. If you're going out and will be returning late, I can give you a separate front door key."

Philip wasn't sure whether there was a slight glint in Ms Anworthy's eye as she handed over the room key.

"Thank you, Ms Anworthy," replied Fiona, swinging the key on her finger and grinning at Philip.

"Seems like a nice lady," Fiona said as she closed the door behind her.

"And if she hadn't been?"

"Then…" she leant against the door, looking up at the ceiling and swinging the key around her finger again. "Then I wouldn't care if she was going to be bothered by the noise." Fiona put the key on the bedside table, unzipped her case and produced from it a bottle of champagne, "Not cold, I know, but better than not at all."

Philip smiled, "Glasses?"

She frowned. "No."

"Won't taste right in those plastic cups," he said.

Fiona stepped round the bed towards him. She held the champagne up to her cheek and grinned. "Why don't you hop in the shower and I'll pop down and ask that nice lady for some ice?"

Fiona grinned like a naughty child and kissed Philip very unexpectedly, forcing her tongue provocatively between his lips. "I won't be long, lover."

He was in the shower when he heard her come back into the room. Philip finished and towelled himself down. As he was rubbing his hair dry, the towel covering his head, he heard the loud pop of the champagne cork, quickly followed by a shriek from Fiona.

Philip flinched. The popping of the cork from the champagne bottle jarred with him. He shook his head as if to clear an unpleasant memory and hesitated before going back into the bedroom.

He tied his towel round his waist and forced his feet to move the two paces through the arched entrance to the room.

Fiona was lying naked on the bed, dark patches on the sheets from the spilled champagne.

He stood watching her. Her breasts were still as large as they were when he'd first met her, but now they were settled, not exactly collapsed, but neither did they stand up so proud, so firm, and the nipples were now darker and larger than before. Her hips were broader than before, but perhaps that was only a perception. After all, he'd witnessed both their children being delivered from between them.

Philip watched and hoped she would not mistake his appraisal of her form for any kind of criticism.

"Like what you see?" she asked.

"Since when didn't I?"

Fiona lowered her gaze to the towel about his waist. "My turn," she said, arching her eyebrows playfully, not taking her eyes off his crotch.

Philip teased her, delaying for a couple of seconds before he responded. Slowly and intentionally overplaying the burlesque, Philip unrolled the towel from his waist and let it drop on the floor.

"My god, Phil," Fiona whispered slowly. She lifted her hand and held it palm towards him, ordering him not to move. "Has it been that long?" she chuckled.

Philip lay down beside her and made to kiss her, but Fiona sat up and stretched across him to grab the bottle of champagne from the bedside table. She grinned at him in the same mischievous manner with which she'd looked at him just a few moments before. She pressed her breasts into his face, lingering to feel his mouth against them.

Then she sat up and raised the bottle to her mouth.

Fiona took a sip of champagne, smiled at him without opening her mouth, and buried her face in his groin.

A sharp, cold, but not altogether unwelcome pain invaded him, causing the muscles around his groin to flex involuntarily and his torso to jerk upright.

But Fiona held him down with her outstretched arms and the pain very quickly turned to a burning pleasure as the heat of his pain was soothed by the cooling fizz of bubbles. He was aware of the champagne dribbling between his thighs, and... and... and he knew he'd encountered such a catalogue of sensations somewhere before.

For a moment, Philip was confused. He felt a sudden urge to pull away from Fiona and ask her to wait while he gathered his thoughts.

He couldn't understand why he should recognise this strange feeling; why it should feel so familiar.

Fiona had not done anything like this with him before. She'd never been afraid of experimenting, especially after they'd got to know each other's likes and preferences. In fact, Fiona's imagination and her coy willingness to put her fantasies into practice had always been one of her greater attractions. She'd always been ready and willing to engage in a broad range of erotic activities; activities which, as far as the rumours went, were not included in much of the literature read by the wives of his colleagues.

But this was a bit off the wall, even for Fiona.

Philip felt as though he was going to be carried away on a cool, frothy tide towards an ocean of wellbeing.

Then an iron hand grasped him by his neck and jerked him back from the pull of the current.

Maja! It was what Maja had done.

He could see her blonde hair and smell the jasmine in her perfume. And he could see her head in his lap and he understood why his clothes had been so wet and so stinking of champagne.

Philip twitched and tensed and felt an extra hardness seize him as though the devil had stabbed him in the groin with a cattle prod.

Fiona was encouraged by his reaction. She took it as a sign that her sensual ingenuity was drawing the very response she wanted. Briefly, she moved her head more vigorously and more urgently upon him, and she gripped him tighter and tighter.

But the more control she assumed of him, the more Philip could only lay back and see Maja's image. And the clearer the image grew, the more he began to hate himself for seeing it. And the more he began to hate himself for seeing it, the more he began to despise himself for having allowed himself to get into such a state that he could let Maja do such a thing in the first place.

Philip tried to sit up, but very commandingly Fiona pressed him back down. He did not possess the will to fight her. He was overwhelmed and consumed by Fiona whilst thinking of Maja. He felt awkward and embarrassed and ashamed. He felt as though he was being watched and felt humiliated that these emotions and perceptions could be orchestrated by these two women; one who he loved and the other who he wanted to forget.

The idea held no foundation, but he worried that Fiona might somehow be aware of Maja's presence in the room and that only served to increase his anxiety.

Fiona must have sensed the change in him, for she released him and moved her body up and lowered her hips onto him, guiding him and drawing from him what she wanted.

And yet again, Philip wasn't sure whether he was purely subordinate to her desires. As she pulled and ground at him, he wondered whether her desire was more fundamental than his contribution.

She began to moan and frown and tease her bottom lip in that way she did.

But Philip was detached, not only from her visceral reactions, but also from any possibility of his joining her in them. Though he was now trapped inside her, he perceived himself to be on the outside of the bubble in which Fiona was feeding her appetites.

Fortunately, before his reduction became too obvious to her, Fiona tensed and gripped and smothered and moaned and swore at God and lay down and cuddled herself to him. And she buried her face in his neck and breathed her hot breath of satisfaction on him.

They lay quietly for a while, Fiona wallowing in the sensations that lapped at her limits, and Philip falling slowly through his own private void.

Fiona rolled onto her side and rested her head in the dip between his arm and his chest.

He felt the brush of her eyelashes against his skin and the movement of her lips.

"I thought you were so close," she whispered sleepily.

"I was." He kissed her on her glowing forehead and paused before asking, "Where in the world did you get that very exotic idea from?"

She put a finger to his lips and pouted at him playfully, "Oh, you'd be surprised, Philip. You really would. It's called Champagne Head. But I didn't get it out of the pages of a *Cosmopolitan* or an Ann Summers catalogue, if that's what you think. I just happened to read about it the other day. Thought you might like it. You know; something a little different." She paused again.

Philip could hear her marshalling her thoughts. He tensed at what he knew was coming.

"So, what did I do wrong?" she asked.

"Nothing," he replied. And it was true. He knew it. Fiona had done nothing wrong.

And, neither had Maja.

And if neither of them had done anything wrong, then Philip had no hope of reconciling himself, because he realised the confusion must lie within him.

"No, tell me," she said, gently. "What didn't I do right? Come on. Be straight with me for once. We haven't made love in...? Do you know I can't remember?" She was waking up now, but didn't lift her head.

"You did nothing wrong," he whispered, stroking her hair.

"Didn't you like what I was doing?"

"Like it? I loved it."

"But, if you loved it, why didn't it work for you?"

Philip searched the ceiling for a response, "I don't know."

"You don't know?"

He felt her tense. He wanted to ask if it mattered that he did not achieve the same release she had, but he knew too well that, to Fiona, it did matter.

"No, I don't know. Maybe it was such a new feeling, such a strange and extraordinary sensation that I didn't know how to react to it."

"But you said you loved it?" Fiona leant up on her elbow. She reached over and turned his head so that he had no alternative but to

291

look at her, "You said you loved it. So how come you loved it, if it didn't work for you?"

Philip knew his lack of response would be taken as a response in itself. What he needed was to give her something, anything, that would appease her and he wondered, not for the first time, whether that was how it would always be. Fiona had received what she'd wanted from him both physically and emotionally. She should be satiated, but what he had supplied to her hadn't been enough. She wanted all of him; every fibre and every last drop of his being. She wanted it all and then some.

He wearied and lowered at her demand and yet he knew she would not be happy until he had answered her. "Listen, it did work for me. I loved it."

"It," she whispered as she rolled away from him and sat up on the edge of the bed. "It? You loved it?" Fiona studied him, expecting, wanting and needing him to tell her that he loved her, not it.

And for the first time, he knew he did not possess the reserves within his red heart necessary to satisfy the unrelenting and limitless emotional hunger of the woman sitting beside him.

"I loved it," he repeated, looking straight into her eyes. They seemed somehow warmer and darker now that she had nourished her form, "And I love it that you should do such a thing for me. I love it that you should love me enough to want to do that for me. But, and I know this will sound strange, I loved it in a different way from a lustful, carnal, erotic way."

43

Phoebe

Phoebe stared at the ceiling and saw the benevolent features of the Grande Dame of the Law Faculty staring back at her. She worshipped, respected and revered the woman. And yet, if she was honest, she despised her a little too, if only for the intellectual concentration camp she represented.

Dame Clarissa had put Phoebe under watch, which meant that every time she missed her supervision or was not seen at lectures, her absence was noted. This constant surveillance, the guards observing her every move from their watchtowers, soon undermined Phoebe's feeble attempts at changing her ways. She felt strangely claustrophobic and unclean. But, and perhaps more importantly, she also detected in her own attitude an increasing apathy, as though life had shackled her and there was nothing she could do about it.

In an effort to quiet the dissenting voice from within, Phoebe proceeded to drown her punctured senses in whichever bar would support her presence for the longest period without interruption. With thirty-one colleges and somewhere around five hundred under-grads and post-grads in her college alone, finding a quiet corner locally in which to pander to her longing for anonymity was not simple. In time, Phoebe found she had to go further afield to preserve her solitude.

Also, in order to support her increased intake of alcohol and to bolster her flagging spirits, Phoebe resorted to consuming more Mephedrone. And pretty soon, the spiral of the mutual support for her vices surged down and out of control like a slinky springing down an endless staircase.

To make matters even worse, in one of the lesser known watering holes, the management had wiped the horizontal surfaces in the toilets with bleach.

Too late, Phoebe found out. The next line of 'drone she sniffed off the ledge behind the loo was corrupted with it. She fled the pub desperately trying to staunch the flow of blood from her seared nostrils.

Under the weight of such a craven master, her Law studies very naturally suffered. She used a plagiarism check site off the internet to sanitise her work before submission and began to take a singular delight in the deception of her tutors. In fact, Phoebe soon found herself as devoted to her methods of deception as she was to the results her deceptions achieved.

For a short while her deceit and her reliance on the Mephedrone ran in comfortable tandem, but only until Dame Clarissa issued Phoebe with her second summons.

In recalling the meeting of the day before at which the Dean of the College was present, Phoebe felt the bile of rejection rise in her throat. The acid residue of shame soured her mouth and smelt stale on her breath.

She got up and cleaned her teeth. They ached and she reminded herself it was because she was grinding her teeth at night. Even Heather had said she could hear it from her room, even with the doors closed. Phoebe supposed that that too was a side effect of the 'drone.

But the 'drone wasn't the problem. It was just a disastrous lift which had helped her along the road to her current location.

But she hadn't buckled under the weight of Dame Clarissa's cross-examination, though she had truly, really, and absolutely wanted to.

She cast her mind back to the information the tracing agency had provided and the many questions that information now forced her to confront. Curiously, the easy part had been locating the tracing agency; that she had done on the web. The hard part would be coping with what it was they'd turned up. A plague of possibilities swarmed through her mind only to leave a barren wasteland in their path.

What if she, her birth mother, turned out to be someone Phoebe didn't like or couldn't stand or even hated? Would she be able to throw the letter away and return to how things were before? Was she strong enough to do that?

And besides, Phoebe was painfully aware of the distress the letter would cause her family, particularly her mother. It would, likely as not, knock the last nail into the coffin of her failing health. But, whether or not Phoebe could come to terms with all that she'd learned was Phoebe's problem; hers alone and no one else's.

44

Philip

Okay," she said, "so how many different ways of loving are there? You seem to be the expert. How many?"

"That wasn't what I meant," he replied and rubbed his face in frustration. "Why do you always have to take everything I say so literally?"

"I don't," she said, nettled by his rebuke, "but surely love is exactly that: love. It doesn't recognise type. It's not defined by boundaries. It doesn't exist by degrees. It's not to be confused with some species of animal or make of car or character of person."

"That wasn't what I meant either," he said. But, curiously, it was exactly what he meant. He couldn't say it, of course; not now she was setting out her stall.

It was that habit she had of transforming simple, mellow post-coital conversation into contentious debate. But what irked him most was not the futility of her exercise; rather it was that she would go on to repeat their conversation at some later date, usually deep into the evening around a dinner table, in the hope that one of her girlfriends had consumed sufficient wine to want to endorse her view and thereby bolster her fragile ego.

He hated that.

Philip hated few things, but he hated that.

But he couldn't tell her that now. So he said, simply, "There are those who might disagree with you."

"Not you, though? You wouldn't take issue with it, would you?" Fiona raised the pitch of her voice towards the end of each question like a reporter interviewing an inept politician.

Philip sighed. "Well, you love Harry and Hattie in the way a mother loves her children, and that is considered to be the strongest bond; the bond between a mother and child. Isn't that maternal love?"

"Yes."

"And the love a child has for his or her parents; isn't that what people call filial love?"

"Yes."

"And my love for the children is what is referred to as paternal love. Am I right in thinking these are different forms of love?" He was careful not to use the word type again.

Fiona sulked for a moment, her head deep in her pillow. "Oh, why do I get the feeling the only thing you truly love is being right all the time?"

"I don't love being right, but..." He played his fingers softly down her exposed back as if the vertebrae of her spine were the keys of a piano. He was going to add "I love you", but he didn't. It was what she was expecting and he did love her, but the words would not come to him when she was being so impossible to appease.

There were times when she was like a corrosive solution which had spilled against him; something acid that needed wiping away instantly before it left an indelible mark. And there were other times when she was like a work in progress; his work in progress, like a half decorated room which he knew he had to finish before he could move their love into it.

In keeping with the frustration caused by a half-completed task, Philip began to feel angry. The skin of his forearms itched and his face coloured.

"But what?" she asked raising her head from the pillow and turning to look at him. "But what?"

He turned onto his side and leant up on his elbow to face her. "Well, the way you love your friends is surely different from the way you love your family. And the way you love some of your family is different to the way you love others of your family. These are different forms of love. Love, nevertheless, but different forms of love all the same."

"That's so just like you, Philip," Fiona replied with a heavy dose of resignation. "Everything in its proper place. That's just how it's got to be with you, hasn't it: pigeonholes, labels, boxes, files? This friend is closer than that friend. That job is more important than this job. So-and-so's house is worth more than someone else's house. Must you qualify and quantify everything?"

"Fi, don't change the subject just because you won't allow yourself to acknowledge what I'm saying."

When she didn't respond to his taunt, he continued, "There's also brotherly love, romantic love, courtly love, pragmatic love, erotic love, religious love, Sapphic love – the list goes on and on. They're all the same thing only they're different in some small way."

"Trust you to bring up Sapphic love," she bridled.

"And," he carried on, his temper swelling, "there's being in love and loving. They're different. That's all I said." He lay back down and stared at the ceiling.

Fiona now sat up and pulled the sheet away from him. She hugged her knees up to her heavy breasts. Her long, straight, light-brown hair fell across the left side of her face as she turned to him, her expression still serious, still demanding.

"And which of these many definitions applies to the love we have for each other, Philip?" she asked quietly. "Is it love in abundance or love in equal measure? Does painting it as a commodity fit more comfortably into the practical landscape of Philip Scott? Is love little more than a commodity; an emotion you dish out whenever the need arises?"

"I don't know, Fi, but if love is a commodity, exactly how much of it do you think I'm going to need?" He closed his eyes.

PART 3

SATURDAY

45

Philip

Philip was aware that she cried during the night. But when he woke, she was already out of bed and dressed.

"Fi? What's the matter?" he asked, stifling a yawn.

"Nothing." She sniffed quietly.

He rubbed the sleep from his eyes and watched her as she studied her mobile phone. Philip groaned inside. Perhaps he had been too philosophical for her the evening before? She never liked it when she could not follow the thread of his logic. "Come on, Fi. What's up?"

She sat down at the foot of the bed, "Nothing. Really!"

He knew she wanted him to sit up and reach for her, so he did. Philip pulled her against him and stroked her hair, "What have I done now?"

After a few seconds, Fiona let her head drop against his chest. "It's not you, I promise," she moped.

"If it isn't me, what is it then? You didn't sleep well, did you?"

She sat back upright and blew her nose. "It's not you, Philip. It's me. Do you realise this is the first morning I've woken up without the children? The first time!" She gazed at him through teary eyes.

"And you miss them?" he added for her. "That's absolutely natural."

"I know it's perfectly natural. It's just it's so stupid. And it's not just that, it's because it's also the first time I've woken up without the children but with you. And do you know what my first thought was?"

She searched his face for some understanding, but when she didn't find it she said, "You see I wanted to wake up on our first morning alone together feeling light and bright and fun and carefree; excited about doing whatever it is that we want to do, together, today. Instead of that, my first thought was about the children. Not you or me or us: the children. It's so unfair," she moaned and blew her nose again.

"Of course it's unfair," he said softly, "it's absolutely unfair. But it's all part of being a mother."

"And not a father?"

The capricious imp of Philip's frustration wriggled and sighed. "No, it's also a part of being a father."

Fiona, noticing the edge in his tone, got up from the bed and drew back the curtain. She studied her phone once more.

"Look, Fi," he said, "why don't you give me your mobile? You know only too well that bad news travels fast and if Maria has the slightest doubt about what's right for the children, I'm certain she'll be on the phone to you like a shot. So here, give me your mobile. I'll keep it so you aren't tempted to check it every minute of the day." Philip held out his hand.

She turned from the window and looked down at him. She didn't reply and she didn't hand him her phone. Her expression suggested she was weighing up whether or not she could trust him with the lives of their children.

Philip wore her gaze for as long as he could before the imp prodded him once more.

He lifted his feet off the bed and sat up. As he did so, Fiona threw her phone down beside him.

46

Audrey

For Audrey, Saturday dawned a special day!

She'd decided on the train journey up to Strand-next-the-Sea that she would be Princess for the day. Only she wasn't to be appointed Princess by her parents as she had been in the Cannes of her youth, when she used to make straight for La Maison Paul in the Rue Meynadier, humming Frère Jacques, skipping through the shadows thrown down by the broad plane trees in the Pantiero. On those days, she had known what she wanted: Tartelette Framboises! Choices had been simple back then.

Today, though, it wasn't about her having the right to choose from the patisserie counter, it was about her having the right to think about whom and what she liked.

At breakfast, a man sat opposite her. He was in his thirties; his hair prematurely greying at his temples. He was tall and muscular and rugged, perhaps a little too rugged for her, but there was an air of assurance about him which suggested to Audrey that he was used to being observed.

Ms Anworthy fussed over him, but there seemed a curious distance between them, almost as though they were pretending not to know each other.

The man looked up from his generous plate and smiled; a smile which Audrey returned. But then, without thinking to ask her to pass him the pepper grinder, he rudely stretched across the table and grabbed it.

Audrey started to giggle. In stretching across the table like that, the man had reminded Audrey of her mother!

Her parents had taken her to Sunday lunch close by the convent. She recalled the dining room of the pub; all mahogany and heavy silver cutlery and starchy napkins and everyone talking in whispers. The solid silver salt cellar caught her eye and she reached across the table for it, at which point her mother tut-tutted and quipped something about a boarding house something. Audrey was certain that was what her mother said: a boarding house... reach. That was it! "That's a boarding house reach, Audrey," she said. "We'll not see that at table again, thank you. I would have hoped they'd be teaching you better manners at St Dominica's."

Audrey tried to strangle her chuckle, but in doing so she choked on a piece of bread and coughed and spluttered.

The man glanced up again.

Audrey patted at her lips with her serviette and glowered at her plate as though it alone was responsible for her outburst.

The couple at the end of the table had clearly had a row. They kept their distance from each other like cats in an alley. He was very attractive; she, a little on the heavy side and rather curiously wearing sunglasses at the breakfast table, which suggested she was the woman Audrey had heard crying during the night.

The opposite end of the table in the room was empty. The red-headed girl who'd let Audrey have the taxi was absent.

After the rather heavy breakfast, Audrey took a long shower, put her face on, and dressed as best she could with the few clothes she'd brought. Outside the wind still blew and it turned out to be colder on the front than it looked. She was glad she'd bought her head-scarf, otherwise her hair would have been a mess by the time she came to the café.

The life-size dummy of a fisherman at the door cheered her. He was a jolly fellow, weatherworn and in need of a little touching up, but cheery nevertheless. "Good morning," she said to him.

A tinkling bell announced her entrance and the door rattled as she shut it behind her. A motley collection of youth and senility looked up.

The waitress was welcoming – friendly, if a shade inquisitive; her eyes reminded Audrey of the robin that used to watch her while she gardened.

Audrey ordered a pot of tea.

Four young men sat a couple of booths down from her; their hair heavily gelled and their suits hanging stiff on them, as though they had been stored flat rather than hung upright. Pink carnations sagged at varying angles from their lapels.

Audrey was immediately reminded of her wedding, but in the same way she had closed her mind to thinking about Laurent the day before, now she closed her mind to thinking about anything other than Laurent.

He was younger than her by a couple of years; perhaps more than a couple, she never found out.

She remembered the first day she saw him, standing on top of an upturned cart, shoulders back, chest puffed out, swearing at the gendarmes, goading them; Juan Belmonte before his bull or revolutionary youth by Delacroix; proud, defiant, committed.

His home lay deep in the vineyards of the Alsace and he'd come to Bordeaux on a student exchange to broaden his understanding of viticulture. He was working in the great vineyards of the Left Bank; St-Estèphe, Pauillac and St-Julien – vineyards that would, after centuries of producing the best wine in the world, be threatened by the uncontainable energy from the atomic power station that would generate electricity for a new and greedy world far away.

He was impressed by her knowledge of the many grapes; the

Merlot, the Cabernets Sauvignon and Franc, and the Petit Verdot, the Malbec and the Carménère. Laurent on the other hand championed the Riesling and the Pinot Gris. They debated Left against Right Bank, Cabernet Sauvignon against Merlot. They discussed the merits of Chaptalisation, and debated the historical legitimacy of feet over the commercial necessity of machines. He stuck firmly to his belief that the way forward was to be found through the co-operative whereby all the growers could realise their potential. Audrey disagreed. She hoped the smaller, independent houses would survive and told him they were the ones who would perpetuate the caractère of the wine.

And Laurent respected her view. He might not have agreed with her, but he did not dismiss her out of hand. In that one respect alone, he could not have been more different to Richard.

Audrey told him about her childhood at St Dominica's and how she'd come by her wonderful little flat; a red door down the side of a busy restaurant off the Fulham Road.

Every now and then she was sure he'd stopped listening to her and wondered whether she was boring him. But it wasn't so, Laurent just sat and smoked and listened and waited patiently for her to finish.

At first she'd reckoned him brash and too self-assured, insouciant and overconfident to the point of cocky – when, apart from his looks, she couldn't understand what it was that he had to be cocky about. His attitudes were charmingly parochial and he was, to Audrey, the antithesis of the capital sophisticate, which was perfectly acceptable considering he'd never set foot outside of his home village until he'd come to Bordeaux. And yet he seemed to know the order of things; the world seemed to fit around him like a well-tailored coat, like it belonged to him.

And then there was his casual indifference to sex; as though it was, to him, an irrelevance; as though any kind of intimacy between them was perfectly natural, not compulsory. And for the first time in her life, Audrey found that it was she who had to restrain herself from going all the way. But, whereas one moment the sensation threatened to overwhelm her; the next it was gone, leaving behind only guilt and regret and confusion.

That was pretty much how it was with Laurent and his leaving her.

The demonstration seemed to fade away like the early morning mist on the broad Gironde. It was part broken up by the CRS and part negotiated by the farmer's union. The other disparate bands of protesters, who had in the early days seemed so resolute, simply faded away.

Audrey couldn't understand why Laurent was so chary of the CRS, but then, as she soon found out, she did not fully understand what animals they could be. Fortunately through those final hours at Braud, St Dominica watched over her and prevented her from serious harm. The same charity was not afforded Laurent though.

The snatch squad came for him one night as they slept in the eaves of a barn. He said nothing. He just stared deep into her eyes and kissed her so hard she was frightened he would suck the very essence of her soul from her.

But then, he was gone, ghosting away.

Audrey poured her tea. She never forgot the intensity of that kiss. It stayed with her on her journey home and during those first weeks back, much like the bruises from the boorish police. But, unlike the bruises which discoloured and faded and eventually stopped hurting, the kiss lingered.

And Audrey remembered standing in the kitchen of her tiny flat a few weeks before her wedding and thinking of that kiss when the door intercom buzzed.

It was Laurent.

She all but fell down the stairs in her race to get to the door.

He looked tired and drawn, and he wore a week's stubble and his eyes were dark and pained. And yet... and yet, he looked magnificent.

But she couldn't have him in the flat, not so close to the wedding. Tongues would wag.

So Audrey threw a few necessities into a bag and hustled Laurent onto a number 14 up to Hyde Park Corner. She bought him lunch in the Hard Rock and a change of clothes in Marks and Spencer at Marble Arch. They took the tube to Liverpool Street and the fast train to Norwich. And when they ran along the platform to make the rattler for Strand-next-the-Sea, he must have assumed she knew where she was going. But she didn't, not really. The name of the town just happened to appear on the information board and Audrey remembered it from her holiday with Bryony. She didn't really care where she was going as long as she was going with him.

She chose The Reach because the name implied some kind of hope, like a man stretching out his arm to prevent a woman falling.

"Hope!" she whispered. "Surely, in our youth, we all hoped for something better?"

Audrey winced; the pain of remembering was sharp.

As Laurent showered, Audrey washed him with the flannel in much the way a mother would wash a tired child. He was lean and the hair beneath his arms and between his legs dense and unusually soft. Laurent was bruised in all the places she had been. They were fresh bruises too, but they showed less because his skin was tanned, almost almond and so much smoother.

She realised it was the first time she'd seen him naked. Before, in Braud-Saint-Louis, they'd always been clothed or partially clothed even when they were alone. But he looked exactly how she'd imagined he would look; adult and yet child-like; muscular and yet supple and forgiving.

And he'd wanted to make love to her there and then.

And she'd wanted to, but she was nervous and awkward, as though even though they had transferred themselves from Braud to Strand, their intimacy had not so readily followed.

Just like that time when she'd been so ready to throw caution to the wind and to give herself to him completely, Audrey stepped back. In Braud, the pair of them had been unclean beneath their grubby clothes and rarely separated from the other protesters; a soiled sleeping bag in a squalid corner of the barn and the noises of others sleeping. Here in the seclusion of The Reach, they were clean and naked and alone and with all the time in the world.

Laurent must have sensed her confusion. He dressed and suggested they go out. And it was then that they had tripped across the Norfolk Flyer at Craving.

Perhaps it was the simple act of sharing the crayfish that reminded her of how easy she found it to be with him, like sharing the walnut-cheese or the *Marc* in Braud. And yet, perhaps, it was simply that Audrey needed to reassure herself that the beast in him would not harm her.

When they returned to The Reach, there was no longer any division between them.

Although Audrey felt once more that what she was doing was wrong, she came rapidly to the conclusion that she'd put up with the burden of her virginity for too long. After all, St Dominica had lost her life not because the wild beasts refused to harm her, but because men like Richard had denounced her and murdered her purely because she'd exposed her soul to them.

But Laurent was not like other men. So, Audrey allowed him into the cave where she had for so long concealed her soul and she clung to him as he tempted her spirit out into the light.

With his hand over hers, he coaxed her soul out and released its essence up into the air to burn like phosphor – a scorching, bright pain that multiplied into unparalleled pleasures.

And then the moment was over; the pleasure rushing away before Audrey could hold on to it, so swift in emergence and then so quickly disappeared.

She looked at Laurent and wondered if she would ever feel such brief ecstasy again.

Laurent stared back at her and smiled. He glowed, he radiated, and he looked deep into Audrey's eyes. He knew everything about her; knew how to kiss her, where to touch her and when to be firm and when to be gentle.

That night she was not able to leave Laurent alone until she realised he was asleep.

She lay eyes wide in wonder and surveyed the new horizons in her mind. They were vast and sunny and warm and promised her a life of... But the longer she looked down from the high peak to which he'd led her, the more the view, instead of liberating her, confused her.

Audrey could not understand why feeling so good should leave her feeling so bad. For if feeling so good took so much effort and yet served only to confuse her moral compass, then perhaps there ought to be another way. Perhaps, she wondered, she was not suited to the twists and turns of the labyrinthine path up which she had so recently struggled. Perhaps the price of her physical happiness was beyond the means of her mental purse.

This paradox, this feeling of feeling good, but feeling bad, Audrey had never come to terms with; it was what Audrey came to think of years later as her crown of thorns. They were the persistent doubts that pricked the bubble of her conscience and they were what held her back throughout the rest of her life; these confusions of feeling good and yet not so, as though she had always done what was right because she had always been instructed to do so.

While she watched Laurent, she was taken with a sudden urge to bathe; to wash away the evidence of her immersion in his flesh.

Audrey sat up in bed. He looked so still, so beautiful and so at peace, and yet... and yet she was in such turmoil — such ugly, bewildering turmoil.

The rest of the night proved long and cold and strangely, considering Laurent lay sleeping like a baby beside her, lonely.

Finally, as the rest of the world was stirring from its slumber, Audrey drifted into hers.

The next day brought a welcome relief Audrey had not expected. She woke deaf to the voices of doubt and no longer at odds with the pleasures of her flesh.

When Laurent woke, he smiled.

They bathed and dressed and ate and talked and walked and laughed. And she bought him a Pocket Instamatic from a shop in Cromer and the breeze blew her hair across her face, and she smiled so much her face hurt.

Audrey could not remember another day when she had smiled so much without understanding why. The only time she didn't smile was when Laurent kissed her, and even then at times she had to push her lips against his to stop from breaking into yet another beaming smile.

By the time they returned to The Reach, the pressure of their proximity burst upon them and drowned them in a warm froth of pleasures.

But later, after, when they came up for air, Audrey looked at Laurent and waited. She smiled at him again with her eyes and her mouth, with her breasts and her hips and her hands and her love. And she wanted to tell him that she loved him, but could not think of the right expression in French, so she whispered, "I love you, Laurent," and waited for him to reply.

Laurent merely smiled back and closed his eyes.

Then Audrey remembered the one and only other time she'd opened and trusted her heart to another, and wondered whether, if she employed the same code that briefly unlocked the iron safe in which Sister Colette's heart was interred, she might provoke a similar response from Laurent.

"*Avec tout mon coeur*," she whispered, "*Je t'aime avec tout mon coeur*." She waited for him to open his eyes and tell her the same.

But Laurent did not. He did not react beyond a slight broadening of his lips.

When Audrey had said the very same to Sister Colette all those years ago, the good sister had told her that she too loved Audrey and loved her with all her heart.

Laurent said nothing.

Audrey saw it all so clearly. She saw through the thick clouds of doubt that had, through her youth, cloaked the expectation in her heart.

It was all so simple.

She loved Laurent in a way she would never love anyone else; neither man, nor woman, nor god. She loved Laurent and she'd given him all one person could give. There was nothing further of spirit or greater of substance to give. She had given him everything.

Before, she had not understood what love was or what form it would take. Even when she agreed to marry Richard, she believed in the idea of love and believed love would come to them in the same way she had seen it come to others. But now she recognised it and felt it and knew for certain what love was. It was spirit; it had substance. Love was more than a state of mind: it was a way of being.

Audrey knelt up in the bed and lowered her face over him until she could feel his breath against her cheek.

"*Je t'aime avec tout mon coeur*," she whispered and waited again.

But again, Laurent did not respond.

And the longer she waited, the more Audrey tried to come to terms with his silence and convince herself that he did not have to reply. It did not matter to her what he felt for her; it mattered only that she felt so much for him.

Audrey kissed him tenderly, but his lips were soft and yielding and without promise of reply.

And Laurent didn't wake and he didn't reply.

So Audrey tried one last time, *"Et pour éternité, Laurent; pour éternité,"* and kissed him lightly.

Audrey left Laurent while he slept. The sheer intensity of her love and the magnitude of its weight she knew she would not be able to bear, so she ran while she still possessed the strength to. Audrey ran and didn't look back.

That had been both yesterday and thirty-seven years ago.

"Can I get you something to go with your tea?" asked the waitress with the beady eyes.

"No, that was quite enough, thank you."

47

Phoebe

Sleep of a restless mind eventually claimed Phoebe. She woke often; once startled and terrified, another time completely disorientated.

But she no longer noticed Yuichi Murasaki or Julius Blessing or Dame Clarissa Hale observing her from the ceiling. The dawn had driven their shadowy faces before it.

She got up, washed and dressed and touched up her make-up. She didn't look too good, but then neither did she look too bad; just a bit pale and wan, as her mother used to say.

The odour of full English Cholesterol lay heavily on the air and the clash of cutlery on china from the kitchen suggested breakfast was over. It was just as well, Phoebe did not have the stomach for breakfast and certainly not breakfast round a table with a bunch of inquisitive strangers. What she needed was fresh air and lots of it, and as cold and as fast as it could come.

She didn't see Ms Anworthy on her way out, but she did bump into the driver of the Ford who'd soaked her the afternoon before. He was a tall man, probably in his thirties even though the hair around his temples was greying. He fancied himself, she could tell.

He held the door at the bottom of the stairs open for her without realising she'd come out of Room 1 on the ground floor.

When she shook her head at him, he didn't know how to respond

316

and simply stood there holding the door open. After a few seconds, he said, "Not getting this right, am I?"

"Not so far," Phoebe replied, even though she hadn't meant to encourage him.

He let the door swing back. "Hacker," he said, holding out his enormous hand for her to shake.

Phoebe didn't take it at first, fearing she would lose her hand if she allowed it anywhere near his. "Just Hacker?" she asked.

"Yes, just Hacker. That's all I'm at liberty to reveal at this stage." He paused. "Listen," he began as she turned away towards the front door. "I want to apologise for... What I mean is, I didn't mean to..."

"Phoebe," she replied, shaking his hand quickly to ensure he couldn't trap hers. "And that really is all I'm at liberty to reveal, ever. It wasn't a problem, Mr Hacker. It was only water." She spun round and hurried out of the front door.

On the front, the wind whisked in from the sea with enough force to dislodge even the deepest-seated cobweb. It wasn't that cold or if it was, Phoebe didn't notice. She thrust her hands deep in her pockets, set off along the front and soon enough she came to the path along the sea wall which stretched northward in a long, lazy curve towards Cromer.

Two young lads were flying kites down on the beach and she envied them their simple task. Surely, they were not aware of anything other than their shared aim of keeping the kite aloft.

Strand-next-the-Sea was some distance behind her when Phoebe was taken by an urge to run, and run as fast as she could and away from everything and from everyone; run, like the kite which was now flying up and away. She wanted to be disconnected from the ground; wanted her feet to move so fast she would not feel as though she was attached to any part of anything so firm. She wanted to feel the rush of life, not the gravity of it.

But there was no point or profit in doing so and, besides, she knew she'd look a bit daft in her jeans and jacket, running like a tearaway from a less than certain present towards an even more uncertain future.

The hills challenged her. They tired her and stole her breath, and yet she felt better for the exercise – somehow lighter. The wind was sharper now and blew her hood back off her head.

48

Stella

Saturday morning hurt, and hurt a lot, and even her hob would not forgive Stella her excesses of the evening before.

As she washed the dishes, doing her best not to clatter them as she stacked, Stella decided there was no point in leaving things the way they were between her and Will. He was her friend and if friends couldn't survive a little tiff now and then, then they'd best not be friends in the first place. The brush of her convenient logic swept aside the real reason behind her wish to bring about some form of reconciliation with her Will: namely the problem with the revenue and the police.

All of her guests had gone, including that strange girl, which allowed her to get through the day's housework without interruption.

Stella drove down the front and turned left at the far end of town. The overnight rain had moved on, but the stiff wind buffeted her little hatchback.

The caravan site, or The Reserve as the sign at the entrance boasted, lay hidden in a sand box created by several huge, grassy dunes set back from the sea wall.

During the summer months, most of the fifty or so caravans were let out to holidaymakers and The Reserve blossomed into a hive of activity and colour. Out of season the site lay bleached and deserted but for her Will, who carried out the maintenance and kept up the grounds. His caravan lay round the turn inside the entrance on the right.

Stella pulled up beside it. Will's car was absent, but that did not necessarily mean he would be too.

She knocked on the door: a jaunty rat-tat-tat-tat. She wanted to get off on the right foot and if that meant she had to bend a little, then so be it.

Stella knocked again a little louder, though not so loud that her report could be mistaken for impatience. She listened hard and was sure she'd heard something, but when no one came she put the noise down to the wind.

Clearly, Will was out. She would wait a while.

A comedy half hour on the radio lifted her spirits, but the car began to mist up, so she decided to stretch her legs. Stella pulled on her sheepskin jacket and wrapped her scarf around her head.

She'd only been to the site once before and all she remembered of that evening was an eerie tranquility; the caravans, sitting in rows, waiting patiently for the footfall of new tenants.

When Stella reached the furthest row, she turned back towards her car and, as she did so, she heard a plaintiff cry carry on the wind.

She was about to start out when she heard the cry again.

She tied her scarf a bit tighter beneath her chin and turned back to walk up the side of the dune.

The wind at the top was harsh and she had to lean into it to stay upright. The light was uncommonly clear for autumn and she could see a couple of hardy souls working their way along the sea wall.

What she'd heard was a flock of seagulls squabbling over a bit of flotsam over towards the sea wall. "A squabble of seagulls," she muttered.

Stella turned to walk back down the slope into The Reserve and as she looked down to check her footing, her attention was drawn to a large object lying in the slack of the dune beside her.

It was a car, or what used to be a car. It was rusted and its windows, windscreen and tyres were missing.

She picked her way down the dune towards it.

When she got closer, she realised it wasn't rusted. It was burnt out, completely. What salt and the wind hadn't managed, petrol and a match had.

Stella walked around to the front of the car. It was a hatchback, like hers. The paint was scorched and scarred, but there were no seats, nothing inside it. It was as though the interior had been stripped clean or melted. The badge on the bonnet was pretty much melted too, but she could just make out the shape within it.

It was a cat of some kind

Stella bent down to get a better look and froze. It was a Peugeot.

She looked closer. It was, or had been, green. She could just make out a small patch of green paint behind the headlight that had not been scorched. And when she stood back upright, she noticed a few flakes of paint dotted about the sand.

Isla Hutchinson's Peugeot had been green.

"Oh Will," she whispered. "What have you been up to?"

The number plates had melted too; she couldn't read those, but she was sure the Hutchinson's car had been green.

"Oh Will," she muttered again. She felt unclean, as though she'd aided and abetted a theft. She looked around nervously, worried that someone might have seen her; worried that Will might be watching her.

"Oh Jesus, Will," she said louder.

Stella walked briskly back over the dune and through The Reserve. Her chest heaved and her heart thumped all the way to her car. Her hands shook and her knees knocked together as she put the key in the ignition.

She started the car up and selected first gear instead of reverse and nearly drove into Will's caravan.

"Calm down, Stella," she said and immediately felt daft for talking out loud to herself. But the sound of her own voice reassured her.

"I'm alone," she said. "No one has to know what I've seen. I don't have to tell anybody. It's not my business. Got that straight, Stella Anworthy? It's none of your bloody business."

She turned the radio on. She'd given herself a talking to, now it was someone else's turn.

Before she turned left out of the Reserve, she changed the radio channel. She couldn't be doing with a dull play; she needed something more vibrant. Stella tuned in to Radio North Norfolk. A happy chappy was chatting about football...

"Football? Oh Stella! You idiot!" she groaned. It was Saturday. The Canaries were at home; her Will would be at the game.

49

Hacker

He'd slept well. He always had and always would, or so he believed.

At breakfast the next morning, Stella Anworthy seemed lost in her own thoughts. She neither scolded him playfully for not knocking on her door and nor did she offer any weak innuendo concerning what he might have been up to elsewhere; she merely served him carbonised black pudding and soggy tomatoes, and left him to his own devices.

An elegant, fifty-maybe-sixty-something lady with a slight smell under her nose, sat across from him. She was trim for her years; slender, but with a good figure. She giggled to herself, which he found rather charming.

To his right sat a young couple. The woman, light brown hair, pretty, though a touch buxom for his taste, curiously wore sunglasses at breakfast; the man, blond perhaps close to ginger, fit and rangy, read the paper. There was an air about them; strangers and yet not so, married perhaps, but maybe not to each other.

At nine-thirty, he left the guesthouse and drove along the front. "Hockey," he muttered, "in this wind?"

Hacker found the left turn signposted 'Strand-next-the-Sea School for Girls' and guessed the sports ground would be close by.

Sure enough, the pitch lay beside the school behind a tall, wire mesh fence. The school was modern, almost penitentiary in appearance and though there was a handful of cars and a minibus in the car park, Hacker pulled up a couple of hundred yards down the road. He didn't know much if anything about hockey, but reckoned the game would start about ten.

He sat down in his seat, turned on the radio and waited patiently.

Sure enough, a couple of minutes before ten, two teams of girls jogged out of the school and onto the pitch. Cars began to arrive, one of which he noted was Chisholm's blue BMW. Jean, his wife, was with him.

Chisholm, hands buried deep in his duffle coat, stood near the halfway line stamping his feet, while his wife marched up and down the touchline exhorting her team.

Hacker got out of his Ford and walked up to the wire. He was freezing and wished he'd brought a heavier jacket.

After five minutes, Hacker saw Chisholm turn towards him. He raised his hand in acknowledgement. But if Chisholm saw him, he showed no sign of it.

Hacker walked up to and in through the gates of the school. When he got to the pitch, he received the customary sideways glances reserved for away team parents. The home side substitutes wore blue gilets with their names printed on the back; the Norwich City girls the same, only their gilets were yellow. The scoreboard suggested the home side were being taken to task, and one of the City girls – a tall, willowy brunette wearing 5 – seemed to have the ball every time Hacker looked up. At halftime, the girl shrugged into a gilet: Suzy, or so the gilet suggested. He had not noticed anyone cheering her on.

Chisholm cowed in the face of his wife's lecture on the shortcomings of the Strand tactics, and now and then a pretty girl in the home team huddle glanced nervously towards them in much the same way as Chisholm occasionally glanced towards Hacker.

The second half went the same way as the first. Hacker froze and the Strand side fell further behind.

He bided his time before approaching Chisholm, but as he was about to set off, he saw Jean Chisholm bark at her husband and stride round the pitch towards him.

"Not going your way today," Hacker offered.

"What was that?" she replied as though he'd poked her with a sharp stick. She wore an imitation Barbour and a deerstalker.

"I said, not going your way, is it?"

"Too bloody right it's not going our way," she confirmed. "Seems to me," she went on, "that every time we go to pass the ball, we pass it to one of the opposition. Bloody coach has got them playing too far apart for these conditions. It's simple really."

Hacker studied her as she watched the game.

Jean Chisholm was attractive; a touch square-jawed for his tastes and perhaps a touch too lean. She strode efficiently, but without breaking into a trot.

"I've not seen you here before," she said, without shifting her attention from the pitch. "Must be a City father, are you?"

"No, sadly. Friend of Suzy's family. Said I would come along."

"Their centre? Tall, brown-haired girl?"

"Mm," Hacker replied. "Handy, isn't she?"

"Handy? Suzy Perry?" queried Jean Chisholm. "Handy? She's only the England Under 16 captain. Oh, sorry, I suppose you would already know that." And as if to make up for her pointing out what she presumed was perfectly obvious, she carried on, "Good-looking girl, isn't she, your Suzy? Some people get all the right genes."

"Mm! They do. Mind you, your Strand girl... the centre back," he prayed he'd interpreted her position correctly. "She's pretty handy too."

"Our sweeper?"

"Yes."

Jean Chisholm beamed, but again did not look away from the pitch. "Yes, she's not bad, but the coach is playing her out of position.

She's a better midfielder than sweeper; that's her normal position. Kaitlyn might be able to do something about your Suzy if she was playing in the right part of the field."

Hacker could see Brian Chisholm hopping from toe to toe. Whether he was trying to keep warm or revving himself up to come and see what Hacker and his wife were talking about, he couldn't tell.

"Yes, I bet you're fidgety," he muttered.

"What was that?" Jean asked, turning to him. She had brown eyes and proud cheekbones, and was probably too old for him. But, she was not the harridan her husband made her out to be.

"I said it's colder than a fridge out here."

"Yes. It is," she replied. "Too bloody cold to be out here playing, especially when we're being trounced the way we are. Rather be playing. Not that I'd make a difference to the score line, if you see what I mean."

"Mm," Hacker replied again, "I'm not so sure about that."

"Anyway…" Jean Chisholm replied, uncertain of his rather oblique flattery, "must be on the move. I always think that if they see me standing still, they'll be inclined to do the same. Nice to meet you!" And with that she marched off, belting out instructions; rousing, cajoling, sympathising, berating.

Hacker watched her stride away down the touchline. No, she was no harridan; headstrong, a woman of her own mind perhaps, but definitely no harridan.

It didn't take long for Brian Chisholm to make his move.

Whereas Jean Chisholm marched, her husband stumped. And the nearer Chisholm came, the more forthright grew his step, as though he was herding his dark thoughts before him and getting close by journey's end.

"What the bloody hell are you doing here, Cornelius?" he hissed.

But Hacker recognised the approach all too easily. He'd seen it often enough; a short, stocky centre forward hell bent on getting into the box with the sole intention of making a bloody nuisance of himself. There was only one thing to do with his kind.

"I must say, Brian, I take my hat off to you. Bloody freezing out here, it is. Put up with this most weekends, do you? Still I suppose it goes with the territory, eh, what with Norfolk being flat as a witch's tit and all that; nothing to get in the way of that wind between here and the Baltic. I hear it can drive you mad, the wind. Must be hardy people, you lot; either that or mad. You're not mad, are you, Brian?"

"Cut the crap, Cornelius. What the bloody hell were you talking to Jean about?"

Hacker waited until Chisholm was about to speak again and then cut him off, "Nothing much, we were just admiring the many and varied talents of Norwich schoolgirls."

"I said, cut the crap, Cornelius. What were you and Jean talking about?"

Hacker paused and slowly and very obviously turned his attention back to the pitch. He wanted to teach Chisholm how the game was going to go; there was no hurry, the game still had a few minutes left to run.

Again, just before Chisholm was about to speak, Hacker cut him off, "I told you, Jean and I were merely discussing the merits of young Kaitlyn's opposition. If you must know, we were talking about their tall centre, Suzy. Pretty girl, isn't she? Under sixteen too, Jean tells me."

The silence that followed was broken only by the shouts of encouragement and shrieks of despair as the City girls scored again.

"Capable girl," Hacker said. "Bit taller than young Sherri. Bit prettier. Probably a bit brighter too."

Brian Chisholm began to reply, but thought better of it. He flexed his jaw and stretched his neck as though it ached.

"Fancy that," Hacker said, "not yet sixteen and looking like that."

Still Chisholm wouldn't bite. He balled his fists and his shoulders began to twitch, but his head was still in place and it was his head Hacker wanted him to lose.

"Get your juices going does it, Brian," he paused, "watching all these nubile young creatures in their sports kit? Remind you of anyone?"

Chisholm flinched, drew back his right hand and started to swing it. "You bloody bastard, Cornelius. I'll-"

Hacker stepped in, denying him the room to throw his punch. "You'll what, Brian? Cause a scene? Two parents from opposing teams engaged in their own distasteful brawl on the touchline? Questioning looks from parents and masters? Jean wanting to know what on earth was going on, and you, Brian, trying to convince her that a couple of months banged up at her majesty's pleasure isn't really as bad as losing seven-nil to the City School? And then there's Kaitlyn's schoolmates asking her why her dad doesn't turn up to watch the games anymore, and is it true what the local paper says, he's signed up to the sex offender's register? Still, I suppose Norwich gaol is pretty convenient for visits."

Chisholm looked up; outrage, hatred, anger and frustration all bubbling up in his ruddy face.

But what Hacker had not expected to see was the steel in Chisholm's eyes; a steel he hadn't bargained for. It both impressed and unnerved him.

He knew that look. He'd seen it often enough before. For a moment, he recalled the same look on the face of that big bastard from Senegal who'd kick-started the end of his career. It was the same look that haunted Cornelius' nights and ruined his days. But then, Hacker decided, there was a world of difference between a raw boned Lion of Teranga and a stubby, overfed, middle-aged East Anglian with a passion for blowing harmless wildfowl out of the sky.

Brian Chisholm breathed hard and stared back up at him. "You won't get away with this, Hacker. You won't. You've crossed the bloody line."

"Crossed the line, Brian?" he scoffed. "Crossed the line? I've only just started. I'm not messing with your cosy little life, Brian. I'm going to destroy it in just the same way as you and your friends at Norfolk Electrical are doing your level best to destroy mine."

"Have you no conscience, Hacker?"

"Have you?" he replied quickly. "I've been good to you, Brian. In fact, I've gone the extra mile to sustain your cosy little existence. And at no little risk and no little expense, I might add. You owe me, Brian."

"Owe you? Owe you?"

The referee's whistle sounded. The Norwich City girls cheered in triumph; the home team hung their heads.

Hacker stepped back out of harm's way. "Call me on my mobile. You know the number. But if you don't want to do this over the phone, I'm staying at The Reach down on the promenade – I'm sure you know where it is. You've got until tomorrow morning to come up with a solution. After that, your future is very definitely in my hands."

Chisholm stepped back. "You won't get away with this, Hacker. I won't stand for it. I can't."

"Sure you will, Brian. Because if you can't, you just cut along to the police station and explain what you and Sherri were up to that night, and how the bloke who tried to stop you from molesting a minor has come to his senses and decided to let the world know what a raving paedophile you really are. I'm sure they'll be most understanding. I'm sure they'll bend over backwards to accommodate you in exactly the same way you'll be bending over forwards to accommodate your fellow inmates – and probably for a couple of years at the least." Hacker paused, pretending to think. "In fact, I've got a better idea. No need to go to down the nick all on your own, I'll come with you."

Chisholm straightened his back and shrugged his shoulders

upright. He shook his head slowly and as he turned away, muttered, "The Reach, you say. 'Course I know where it is."

As the shorter man walked off up the sideline, Hacker couldn't help himself, "Sorry about the game, Brian. Better luck next year; if there is one."

50

Philip

Fiona had decided they would go to Felbrigg hall: a grand Jacobean pile set in parkland just to the south of Cromer.

Philip, whilst not particularly drawn to either the architectural or horticultural delights of the National Trust, understood that as his mother had given them a family membership of the Trust the previous Christmas, he couldn't object. He did, though, manage to keep the relief from his face when they arrived to find the main house and bookshop closed.

"Well, we are a little late in the season," he said in an effort to apply a balm to Fiona's irritation.

"That's alright," she replied. "The walled garden is supposed to be very pretty and there's a walk out to the church through the estate. If the leaves haven't all dropped, that should be pretty too. You did bring your walking boots like I suggested?

"Lucky I remembered them then," she said.

Fiona was punishing him; he knew that, but he didn't possess the will to alleviate her colic.

The clouds hastened by and the bitter wind beat at the long grass. A murder of crows cawed and wheeled around them, driving them across the broad, open field down towards the small church of St Margaret's.

As they approached the square, grey tower, Fiona slipped her arm through his, nervous of the herd that grazed beneath the trees in the lea of the graveyard wall.

Philip dug his hands deeper into his jacket pockets, clamping her arm tight against his side, and led her through the small porch set against the south wall.

The small church was deserted; the flagstones and cream-painted wooden box pews frigid to touch. Yet the nave was bright and airy and lent the church a vague, or perhaps only a vain, hope of warmth. The roofline at the east window followed a curiously Byzantine curve down around the font.

"There's no stained glass," Fiona remarked. "I wonder why?"

But Philip was thinking of the children as he pretended to a fascination for the brasses of Simon and Alice de Felbrigg standing tall in the wall of the sanctuary.

The last time he'd set foot in a church had been at the children's christening. "Probably ran out of Cousin's Rose," he said.

She moved up beside and again linked her arm through his. "Cousin's Rose?" she asked.

Philip wondered what it was that Roger, son of Simon, had been up to in the late fifteenth century in far off Prussia that it should have brought about his demise. "A bit late for the Crusades; a bit early for the Thirty Years War," he muttered, and wondered too whether Fiona had brought him to St Margaret's as part of some carefully conceived plan she had cooked up to get him to recall his wedding vows.

"Cousin's Rose?" she repeated, tugging on his arm.

"Sorry?"

"You said they probably ran out of Cousin's Rose. What on earth is that?"

"Oh, I see. It's a stain they used for flesh tones in the glass."

"Philip Scott, you are full of the most useless information, but I do love you for it." Fiona pulled him round, raising her face to his for a kiss.

Philip obliged, but pulled back when she opened her warm, sweet mouth and demanded more. He glanced a shade self-consciously back towards the aisle.

Fiona sighed, tightened for a moment and then let him go. She turned away from him and said, "Do you think if we'd got married in a church like this, being together would mean something more to us?"

"I suppose so."

"You suppose? You can only suppose, you can't imagine?"

Now it was his turn to sigh. But not wanting her to realise his ambivalence for what it was, he added hurriedly, "I guess you'd better ask Alice de Felbrigg." He nodded at the large brass figure staring down at them.

She glanced at the lady in her lace. "I wasn't intending to, Philip. What I meant was, do you think being married in the sight of God creates a closer union?"

"I guess," he hesitated, "if God means that much to you, you might feel more compelled."

"Compelled? In what way?"

Philip could not see Fiona's expression, but was fairly certain it held no wry amusement. He knew his choice of words was all that stood between them and yet more argument; one careless or casual expression and he knew she'd turn on him.

"I mean compelled to maintain the union because of God, rather than because of what the union means."

"Because of God?" she asked.

"Sure, yes. Because of god! If the union fails, one or the other, or both, is deemed to have failed in the sight of God; not failed through some perfectly natural or reasonable cause."

Fiona did turn to face him, her contempt sharp like the claws of the lion at de Felbriggs feet, "Is that why you think marriages fail, Philip?" Her words filled the cold void of the church. "Do you really think they fail because of some perfectly natural or reasonable cause? Like it is a kind of organic process that is just another part of life? Like being born, growing up, breeding and dying; that kind of natural and reasonable?"

He didn't want to be drawn. "No, that's not what I'm saying at all." Philip wasn't sure what he was saying. All he knew was that Fiona, wanting a quarrel, had decided that St Margaret's Church in Felbrigg was the ideal location in which to have it.

Philip softened his expression to one of what he hoped she might read as tender and moved towards her.

But Fiona stepped back instantly.

"Look, Fi…"

The door to the south porch opened and an elderly couple walked in, stamped their feet and shut the door noisily behind them.

They looked up, surprised to see Philip and Fiona facing each other down in the centre of the aisle. They could not help but notice the electricity charging between them, so they stood transfixed like the brass images of the de Felbriggs and waited to see what the unhappy couple would do.

Fiona embarrassed and frustrated at being startled in mid flow, turned and stormed out of the church without waiting for Philip.

"Good morning," he said as he squeezed past the couple.

By the time he caught up with Fiona, she was through the kissing gates and down the slope by the lake, marching like a woman who'd left the washing out in the rain.

Philip knew there was little point in trying to bring her round when she was in such a funk, so he matched her stride and filled his lungs with the chill Norfolk air.

They walked on through the beech and sweet chestnut trees, and passed by the great Sessile Oak and the dome of the ice house. Fiona eventually slowed by the sycamore at the threshold to the two avenues of beech trees, but only, he realised, because she wasn't certain which of the divergent paths would lead them back to the car park.

Philip took the left; Fiona, after due deliberation and with no little reluctance, followed him.

They de-booted and threw their coats in the back of the car, and Philip ran the engine for a moment to warm up the interior.

He giggled. He knew he shouldn't, but he remembered that whenever Hattie was in one of her foul moods, they said it was because she was low on carbohydrates.

"Carbo-low?" he asked, trying his best not to laugh.

"Fuck off, Philip!"

51

Audrey

The bell tinkled as Audrey pulled against the door to prevent it from slamming shut behind her. A post van hurried past and lurched to a halt just up the promenade.

Audrey set off in the same direction.

The first of Laurent's letters she'd found on the doormat of the flat in Fulham a few days before her first wedding anniversary. She'd gone to meet Pippa there before going on to a show in Town.

When she opened the door, she nearly trod on it; a cream-coloured envelope addressed in a delicate hand, a Philippe de Champaigne painting of Cardinal Richelieu for a stamp.

For a moment, she feared it might be an unpleasant vestige of her ill-fated sojourn to Braud. In a way, it was.

Turning it over, she saw the sender's name and address, and her heart missed a beat. She dropped the letter.

Audrey studied the letter lying at her feet. She wanted to pick it up and open it, and yet she wanted it to disappear.

Eventually, she retrieved the envelope, took it into her kitchen and opened it carefully, as if it contained a fine powder. She sat down on the floor.

Le 16 Octobre 1974
Maison des Vins
Route de Colmar
68150 Ribeauvillé
France

Chère Audrey,

 I apologise for what it was I have done to make you to fly from our bed. I cannot think what it is I have done. I think perhaps I have hurt her? Have I forced my love on her? I think not, but it is possible I make an error. I had great tiredness and perhaps I did not show you respect. During the last two years I think of you all the time. I try to chase you from my heart. I try to say that I should respect your desires and if they do not include me then I must understand and I must respect you. But this is very hard for me now because I am yet very much in love with you. I ask you to respond to my letter, please.

 Je t'embrasse très fort,

 Laurent

Je t'embrasse très fort, the phrase completely undid her, and it wasn't until she realised Pippa was about to arrive that she dragged herself up off the floor.

She recalled sitting through the musical, the letter burning a hole in her jacket pocket while she tried so hard to concentrate on Sondheim's beautiful music and lyrics.

"You enjoyed that then," Pippa said afterwards as they hummed their way out of the Adelphi.

"Send in the Clowns. Yes."

Of course, she didn't answer the letter; it was a year too late. At least that was what she kept telling herself.

But a year or sometime during the next year, she couldn't remember exactly when, another, similar letter arrived.

The second letter was less passionate, but no less sentimental. The greater part of the text concerned what he was up to, where he was working and what plans he had for the future. It was only towards the end of the letter that he lamented what he termed his bad luck for losing her.

To that letter she wrote a lengthy reply; a long, philosophical diatribe encouraging Laurent to put what happened between them behind him and to get on with his life; to learn to look forward not back; hope and not be hopeless.

But, when she read through her letter, she decided she sounded like a school mistress reassuring her pupil that if he occupied himself with more important matters, he might not have the time to cultivate such a futile fixation; that his was nothing more than a passing crush, which, given time, would fade.

She ripped up both his letter and her attempt at a reply and consigned them to the swing-bin, the liner of which she immediately removed, tied and put in the dustbin outside.

Through the years the letters continued to come and in time Audrey learnt to keep from looking forward to them; she learnt not to hope there might be one on the doormat whenever she went down to Fulham.

Then her flat was sold and, because Audrey had always destroyed Laurent's letters immediately after reading them, she had no record of his address. She couldn't, therefore, send him a change of address card and she couldn't very well ask Richard to ask the new owner to forward her the letters from her French... pen friend, brief amant, passing fling; the man who'd plucked her virginity from Richard's grasp.

After that, Audrey tried not to think about the letters, reasoning that if she didn't think about them, she wouldn't think about Laurent so much. And that worked until she saw Richard with that woman in Kensington Gardens. From that day Audrey didn't care if she found herself thinking about him. But, sadly, by that time she'd stopped receiving the letters.

Without noticing, she had walked far past the jetty and was now out beyond the shops and houses of the little town. The path ahead lay up onto the sea wall and she didn't fancy the effort, especially in the face of such a cold north wind.

She turned round and started back, only to find the girl with the strange red hair walking towards her. She wondered what the girl was up to out on the sea wall, all alone but for an old woman who had loved once.

As the path narrowed where they met, they both stopped and hesitated. The girl stood back to let her pass.

"Thank you," Audrey said and smiled.

"A pleasure," the girl replied.

But as Audrey was about to step past her, she stopped and said, "I meant to thank you for letting me have the taxi yesterday. That was kind of you."

"Kind? I..." but her voice deserted her and she simply stood and studied Audrey's face.

The girl looked cold and tired, and more than a little lost. And, in spite of her rather brassy red hair, Audrey felt the urge to hug her, to reassure her. Instead she reached out and touched the girl's shoulder, and was warmed when the girl didn't shrink from her.

"Yes, kind," Audrey said. "You see, it's the small kindnesses that count. For, in a way, what you do for others, you do in part for yourself, and I appreciated your kindness. I just wanted you to know."

She smiled once more, dropped her arm from the girl's shoulder and turned away to carry on walking.

Audrey didn't know why she'd held back from hugging the girl. She'd wanted to repay the girl's kindness in some currency of comfort, looking all alone and cast out as she was. But, though certainly not misplaced, Audrey worried that her sudden familiarity might have been misconstrued.

The girl had been kind. Others, though, had been unkind.

She turned her mind to the letters in her bag back at The Reach. Their presence did not only mean that Laurent still held a candle for her; they held a far greater significance than simply that one, wonderful message. What was more, but dreadfully more significant, was that some of the letters were open, which meant that Richard's whore had read them. And if she'd read them, then she would almost certainly have told Richard of their contents, or probably even shown them to him. And, therefore, if he'd read them, it was entirely possible he'd told the boys. He would very possibly have done that if by doing so he thought he might justify his own infidelity.

Of course the boys had known about Lentz, they'd spoken of her the day after Richard's funeral. And they had spoken of Lentz as though she was familiar to them, as though they'd expected her to appear at Richard's funeral and as though they'd expected Audrey to accept her as nothing more than her husband's concubine.

And, even more so, they would have expected their mother to accept their father's mistress if they thought their mother was conducting a similar affair. That was obviously why they thought they could discuss the Lentz woman as though she was entitled to some strain of familial respect.

"Oh my God," she said, "they must have known! That was what Sian meant when she said I was not exactly alone, wasn't it? That was what Sian said: not exactly alone."

The Reach was now in sight. The wind was blowing even stronger than before and Audrey had to lean back now and again to keep from being blown over. She stopped for a moment and hung onto the iron railing that ran between the road and the beach, and fought back her tears.

The sadness of it was that the woman had held on to Laurent's letters for all those years after Richard's death. The strangely amusing irony being that Richard had died in their bed, with Audrey by his side – or fairly close by his side. And then there was the ghastly issue of whether Audrey had done for Richard by misusing the Syringe Driver. In that way she had at least denied the woman the luxury of any kind of closure with him.

So the woman had retained the letters out of pure spite; that much was clear.

But if Audrey had continued to receive Laurent's letters, would she have fled to France to begin again with Laurent after all this time? How long would they have had? Ten years, until now? Would she have traded the last ten years of her solitude for ten years with a man she had not seen for over thirty?

"Of course," she shouted at the wind. "Yes, you bet I bloody would; even if you are fat, ugly or bald, Laurent; even if you were all three. I'd have traded it all."

Audrey shook against the railings and shouted, "You bet I would!"

She would write to Laurent. She would throw herself at his feet and beg him to forgive her the wrong she had done him by leaving him while he slept. For Audrey realised that leaving him simply because he had shown her a glimpse of a life she was not sure she could live, was surely as great a wrong as the wrong delivered her by Richard. In that way, she had denied Laurent his future in exactly the same way as Richard had denied her hers.

52

Stella

Stella stopped off at the supermarket and stared at the meat counter until she remembered she was going to have fish for dinner. She was so distracted she even managed to forget the black pudding for the guest's breakfast and had to go back in for it.

By the time she got back to The Reach, she was a ragged bundle of nerves – the tails of which she kept tripping over.

Her mobile phone rang and she didn't know whether to drop the shopping bags or which pocket her phone was in. In the end, she dropped the shopping bags on the living room floor and found her phone.

"Now listen to me, you nosey old bag-," Will said.

"Oh, Will. Thank goodness you've called-. Nosey old what did you call me?"

"You heard, you nosey old bag..." His voice was flat and hard, and there was no mistaking his venom. "Last night I told you not to go losing me as a friend and today I find out you've been making yourself all busy, snooping around the reserve and poking your nose into what doesn't concern you. I can see you need to learn the rules, Stella." The line clicked off.

"Oh God," she said. "He called me Stella again."

53

Philip

Even though there was precious little traffic on an October Saturday afternoon, the drive into Cromer seemed to take an age.

Fiona sat and fumed.

"Come on, Fi," he began as they pulled up in the public car park, "let's go and find a pub."

"You need a drink?" she scoffed.

"No," Philip paused, "I need something to eat," adding as he walked away down the slope, "and besides, I'll get more conversation out of a plate of fish and chips..."

"Philip?"

"Come on," he said more softly, taking her hand and pulling her to him. "Look, let's not fight. Since when did we get the chance to be just the two of us together, eh? Not since..." He wanted to say not since the children were born, but knew that if he mentioned them, she would only fall into an even darker and more unmanageable mood.

At first, Fiona didn't yield. She just stared at the pavement and waited for the genie of her wisdom to decide whether she should accept his olive branch.

Philip lifted her chin up so that she could not avoid his eyes, and kissed her slowly and tenderly. Her mouth, he noticed, had lost its accommodating warmth.

Fiona stood, waiting. Whatever the kiss meant to her, she wanted more and wanted it to mean more.

Philip lowered his face back to hers and kissed her again, this time with some passion, pressing his cold lips hard against hers and reaching round behind her so that he could hug her closer to him.

He was aware they were being watched by a traffic warden. "Come on," he whispered into her ear so that she could feel the warmth of his breath, "let's find somewhere out of this biting wind."

But, Fiona hesitated. "Oh, let me have the car keys, would you, please, Philip. There's something I meant to bring with me. I'll catch you up."

She joined him as he got to the bottom of the road and slipped her arm through his. He steered her past the old Town Hall, it's carefully detailed, green-fringed heraldic shields promising more colour than the afternoon seemed capable of delivering. And, in a daze, Fiona stepped straight out onto the pedestrian crossing without looking, forcing a car to screech to a halt.

Philip mouthed an apology at the driver and stepped off the pavement.

The cake shops, cafés and bistros glowed warm and inviting beneath the leaden sky. They advertised the kind of gentle hubbub in which two unspeaking souls might defrost their egos and soften to conversation. But, a dark and vacant Woolworths and the numbing grey flint of Cromer Parish Church soon cooled any promise of a thaw in their mood.

He guided Fiona around the church and down a narrow street to a pub overlooking the front.

Before them the pier stretched out from the esplanade like an ornate, upturned spoon, the slender shaft of which was supported above the muddy waters of the North Sea by a row of skinny rods. Groynes tracked down into the surf like sturdy men hauling on thick ropes, and away to the north a wind farm, a grid of whirling limbs, shone bright and white for a few seconds before dissolving back into the dismal hue of a passing squall.

They stood and watched for a while; the wind salty and cool on their lips, the callous sea slapping at the solid wall below them.

Philip led Fiona inside and ushered her to a small, round table by a window with a view of the pier.

"Vodka and tonic, please," Fiona said in answer to his questioning look.

He went to the bar.

A pint of Blackfriars Old Habit later, his taste buds stimulated by the roasted flavours of the beer, Philip felt considerably more human, if not quite properly prepared for whatever it was that Fiona was going to throw at him next.

They shared a bowl of Brancaster mussels, then Fiona chose a crayfish and haddock chowder, and he, a trio of pork sausages.

He gazed at the pier as he ate and wondered how on earth it withstood the relentless assault of the waves.

Fiona was talking; he'd been dreaming. "Sorry," he said, coming to.

"I was merely pointing out," Fiona repeated, "that you always have sausages on a Saturday when you're at home."

"Yes, I do, don't I?" he replied, watching a child in a red coat do her level best to slip between the railings.

"I thought you might try something different. You know, an alternative," she said.

"Force of habit, I suppose; conditioned response, something like that." Philip found it hard to take his eyes off the child who, had it not been for the grip of her seemingly indifferent parent, would doubtless fall to her death.

Fiona was talking again and he wasn't concentrating; or rather he was, but on the young girl, not on Fiona.

"Beats me how you can be so detached, Philip. Sometimes it's like living with a bloody stranger. Or if not a stranger, then someone I once knew who now lives at the same address as me." She paused to provide him with the opportunity to refute her accusation. When he didn't, she put down her knife and fork, deciding to take another mouthful out of him rather than her chowder. "Sometimes, Philip, it's like you live on another planet."

54

Phoebe

In Cromer, Phoebe walked the length of the pier, all the while repeating the phrase over and over, and remembering the irenic look on the woman's face as she'd said it: "What you do for others, you do in part for yourself."

Phoebe swung round the lampposts and hid herself in plain sight of the many tourists, taking comfort in her anonymity. She read plaques about strangers; strangers who could no longer judge her; men like Lord Suffield, who once lived in the Hotel de Paris – the grand, red brick edifice which loomed above the pier like an imperious guardian.

Sometime later, she found herself sitting on a bench, looking down on the pier from a curved apron outside a busy pub. She wasn't thirsty and neither was she in need of alcohol, but her recently acquired habit of hanging out in the pubs of Cambridge urged her inside.

The pub was warm and a reassuring perfume of hops and cooked food hung heavily in the air. She waited patiently for an opening at the bar and ordered herself a coca-cola. The purple-nosed barfly beside her couldn't take his eyes off her hair and the barman popped a red straw in her glass.

Phoebe turned and stepped back from the bar to make way for

other customers waiting behind her. She turned round to look for a seat and was faced with-

Charlie?

He wasn't wearing the dark city suit and his fair hair looked more ginger, but he had the same long, slender, freckled hands and he was just as lean and good-looking as she remembered.

Phoebe stood and stared at him.

But there was something different about him; some new dimension Phoebe had not noticed in him two nights before; a look, or rather not a look, more like he was sitting beneath a stormy sky waiting for the heavens to open.

"Charlie?"

His mouth hung open in astonishment. "Phoebe," he said, "I..."

The air in the bar cooled as though someone had left the front door open.

He was with someone; a county-dressed, solid looking woman with shoulder-length, light-brown hair. There was a way the woman was sitting with him, a way she was relaxed in Charlie's company; her thigh touching his, their plates close together, as though they were perhaps brother and sister. No, not like a brother and sister; like...

Phoebe scolded herself: The wedding ring, the apartment no one lived in, the bed no one slept in, the bathroom no one used; and, of course, the reason why he was not there in the morning.

"What was that?" the woman looked up and was saying to Charlie. "Did that girl just call you Charlie, Philip? Do you know her?"

"No, I..."

Phoebe simply stood and continued to stare at Philip. Of course, there was that too. He wasn't Charlie, was he? He was Philip.

When the woman failed to gain a response from him, she turned her gaze upon Phoebe, "Excuse me? Did you just call my husband Charlie?"

Phoebe looked through Fiona as if she wasn't there. For even though Phoebe had guessed from his wedding ring that Charlie was married, she didn't want to know what his wife looked like. She wanted to see Charlie the way she'd seen him in the bar on Henrietta Street two evenings before; Charlie, not Philip, blond and fun, with inquiring eyes and freckles and clean fingernails. Charlie: A goodtime Charlie with a taste for pink champagne; a man with a flat in the Barbican, a boy who didn't leave her legless and homeless in the big city night.

For a second, a chill voice commanded her to run; to drop her glass and run, run as though she'd stood witness to some morally repugnant crime. But the voice belonged to her chafed ego and where it came from she didn't know. But, in the brief but curiously slow period that followed, Phoebe realised the decision to react was hers and hers alone. He might deny any knowledge of her. He could. And why wouldn't he? For him, what possible gain was there to be had by acknowledging her? It wasn't as though they'd done anything. After all, he, Charlie, had not come knocking at her door, expecting or demanding any form of sexual favour in return for his kindness. He had simply provided her with a refuge in which to lay her weary head for the night; a safe haven, a harbour similar to the one she remembered as home, a home which the extraordinary events of the last few weeks had sought to reduce to a collection of confusing emotions.

No, she decided, he had done her no harm. Charlie had left her to sleep and had asked nothing of her. His brand of kindness was rich and gentle.

"No, I'm sorry," Phoebe said, focussing her eyes hard on the woman in the hope that her denial would be taken seriously, "My mistake. I thought he was someone else. Sorry."

And she turned, stepped back and placed her half-full glass on the bar. "Thank you," she said to the barman and walked out, being careful to turn left out of the door so that she did not pass in front of the couple sitting by the window.

55

Philip

"Strange girl, calling you Charlie like that! You sure you don't know her, Philip? Absolutely positive?"

And when Philip didn't answer, she shook her head and said, "Close your mouth, Philip, you look stupid."

Fiona placed her cutlery neatly in her bowl, wiped her mouth and hands on her serviette and sat back, upright.

"What is it, Fi?" he asked.

"Get me another, would you? Make it a double; I think I might need it."

When he came back, Fiona was trembling and close to tears, so he sat down beside her and put his hand on her thigh.

She moved her leg away.

"Okay," he said, "let's have it. What's on your mind?"

"I'm sorry, Philip. I need to apologise. Something's been bothering me."

"What has, darling? I can't think of anything you need to apologise to me for. What's up?"

"It's this weekend," Fiona began and then blew her nose. "You see, I wanted everything to be so perfect. I wanted it all to be so warm and so soft and loving; just the two of us, no children to get between us, no diversions and no excuses. Just us."

"And it is, Fi. It is just us."

"But it isn't, is it?" Fiona reached over, took his hands in hers, and held them to her cheeks briefly. "You see, it really wasn't my idea to come up here to this funny little place, it was Archie's." She paused.

He'd known, of course. But rather than admit to his clandestine audience with her mother, an audience at which she had offered to assure their future as though she was some magnanimous sugar mother, he merely raised an eyebrow and bridled his mouth to suggest that if it was all the same to her, then he had no issue with it.

"Well, it was Archie," she went on, "who told me about this place. She said she and my father had enjoyed the odd weekend away up here. And she thought if they, knowing what a complete pig's ear they made of their marriage, could have a good time up here, then she thought we might be able to do the same-"

"I'm not sure I'm too happy with being compared to your father, but go on."

"I'm not comparing you with him, Philip. I'm not." But as she said it, her expression changed from a thoughtful frown to a look of complete horror, much as if she'd been shown a thumbnail of a dark and unpleasant future. She took a long sip of her vodka, "Leastways, I hadn't intended to."

"So, you want to apologise for your mother's ever-present hand? I wouldn't worry; I've learned to live with it."

She breathed deeply for a few seconds. "No, I need to apologise because although we are on our own, I may have brought you up here on a false pretence. You see, I'm not sure we are properly alone."

Philip looked in exaggerated fashion around the bar, leaned towards Fiona and asked, "She's not here, is she, your mother?"

Fiona sat back away from him and put her hand up to her brow in frustration, "Oh Philip, why do you always have to make fun of things when I'm trying to be serious?"

"You're right, I do. I'm sorry. Please, carry on."

"No, it's nothing to do with my mother. It's about you and me, and about how we feel about each other." She paused and looked very directly at him. "You see, I can't help but get the impression that there's no longer just the two of us in this relationship."

Philip held up his hand, "Whoa! Hang on a minute-"

"No, hear me out, Philip. I've listened to the gospel according to Philip Scott for long enough, now it's your turn to listen to me." She waited until she was certain she had his full and undivided attention. "Seeing that girl just now, and seeing how you looked at her and how she looked at you. Well, if you think I'm dumb enough to believe hers was an innocent case of mistaken identity, you've got another think coming. You even knew her name. You said it out loud, in case you thought I hadn't heard. But I didn't need to hear you speak her name, did I? If her eyes didn't say it all, yours spoke bloody volumes.

"So who the hell was she, Philip?

"Come on, Philip. Share it with me. Who was she? And don't expect me to buy any of those lame excuses about a drunken snog with some secretary bird at a Christmas party, or how she was an intern who got a bad dose of boss fixation. If it had been any of that rubbish, you'd have introduced her and tried your best to slide out sideways." Fiona leaned forward and whispered, "If only you could see yourself. Philip Scott, the rabbit caught in the bloody headlights."

"Thursday night," he began, gazing out the window at the grey sea and sky, "with the boys from the office. We had cocktails in Martini's. We'd landed another contract and I'd promised to stand them a few drinks. I was going to come home, but the guys persuaded me to move on with them, get something to eat in China Town. You know how it goes."

But Fiona sat, sipped her vodka and listened.

"I was walking down Henrietta Street after I'd paid the bill in Martini's and then I knocked this kid flying. I didn't mean to, naturally. She just stepped off the pavement and I cannoned straight into her. I couldn't leave her there; I had to make sure she was alright."

"Go on. I'm all ears," Fiona said.

"I suppose that was where I made the mistake. She'd banged her knee quite hard and I wanted to make sure she wasn't too hurt. I took her into All Bar One and bought her a drink. We got chatting. She's a university undergrad from Cambridge and she needed someone to lend her a sympathetic ear. That was it." He paused. "That was all there was to it. I forgot what the time was. I know it sounds rather far-fetched, but there was something about the way she was that reminded me of my time at university; mid-term blues, I suppose. Only I could see her situation was more complicated."

When Howard Marberg had given Philip his set of keys to the company apartment, he'd told him there was no way he could ever acknowledge its existence to anyone — period; not even to a priest on his deathbed.

Philip held his peace and waited.

Fiona didn't smile, not even with a touch of amused scepticism. "So, let me get this straight: You, Philip, having told her your name was Charlie, sat and stilled poor Matilda's troubled waters like some beneficent angel from a Frank Capra movie. And for the entire evening? Oh, pull the other one, Philip."

"Mmm, somehow I knew the truth was going to be less credible than the fiction."

"Truth? I don't want to sound like the state prosecutor, Philip, but surely even you can do better than that?"

"It's exactly what happened, Fi; exactly what happened."

"Firstly, Philip, any idiot knows All Bar One closes at eleven-thirty and, in case you were so addled you can't recall, which I don't remember you being, you didn't come in 'til four-thirty." This time, Fiona allowed a little impatience to creep into her tone, "Oh, Philip, think quickly, and while you're thinking, get me another vodka, please."

So he got up and ordered, and while he waited for the barman to pour his third pint of Old Habit, he wondered what he could do to convince Fiona nothing remotely sexual had gone on between him and Phoebe.

When she'd taken a sip of her vodka, he, like a naked man confronted by a cold river, leapt right in, "I left her at the bar and caught the guys up at a club. They were all pretty trashed by then, but I couldn't persuade them to leave until the place closed. So I got us a taxi and, being the most sober, I made my stop the last. There's really not that much to add. It was all pretty standard stuff." He took a long pull at his pint, rather than try to keep a straight face.

Fiona studied him. "Do you know that sounds pretty reasonable, the last part. That's the kind of thing you would do, Philip. I can see you making sure all your troops were safely back in their barracks. But bumping into the girl, lending her your sympathetic ear for the whole evening; that, I find hard to take." She was still remarkably composed; her expression a shade judicial.

"So, Philip, are you intending to see young Matilda again?"

He noticed his glass was nearly empty. "No, we didn't exchange numbers. Not that we were about to."

"Ah, yes, Philip; telephone numbers. Funny how one trips over them when you least expect them," Fiona teased.

"I don't know where you're going with this, Fi, but can you get to the point, if there is one?"

"The point is, darling; I need to ask you if there is something or someone stopping us from being together at the moment? It's just that for the last few years I've cooked our food, washed our clothes, cleaned our house, mothered our children and pandered to all the flights of your sexual fancy. Oh, and to be even-handed, a few of mine too. But for the last few months, I've begun to notice a... a distance between us." As Fiona spoke, her tone grew harder and more clipped, "So, I hoped that by coming up here, away from the children,

354

the telephone, the house, out of the home zone if you like, that we'd be able to forget about all the clutter that occupies our life and find some time for just the two of us. You know, reclaim the ground we used to share before there was nobody around to crowd us out of it."

"And it has," he said, turning to reassure her. He reached over to put his hand on her thigh, but for the second time she moved away.

"No, it hasn't, Phil," she bared her teeth like a kicked dog, "that's the point. It hasn't. I've tried my best to tell you gently, but either you don't, or else you won't, listen to me, Philip. It's like I'm sleeping with a bloody stranger. When we're in bed making love, having sex, call it what you want, it's like you're only half interested in what's going on; like you're only partially connected to me and the rest of your attention is focussed elsewhere —"

"You didn't seem to have a bad time of it last night!"

Fiona screwed up her face and banged the palm of her hand on her forehead, "I'm not talking about me, Philip, for Christ's sake. I'm talking about you; you and your weird separation. This detachment that comes to you the moment we're alone, right when we're supposed to be closest to each other. I can't explain it any better than that; I wish I could. It's like I'm making love, but doing it with you on my own."

She watched him think for a minute; watched his eyes search the table for an answer.

"It even happens when I try to do something special; something exotic." Fiona looked self-consciously around the pub. "Look at what I did for you last night," she whispered. "I couldn't even command your proper attention when I was doing that. God, Philip! You nearly lost concentration while I was right in the middle of it. What the hell were you thinking about?"

Her reminder of the stunt she'd pulled with the champagne drew two simultaneous reactions from Philip: His groin twitched involuntarily and an image of Maja leapt into his mind.

But Fiona was ahead of him, "I'd like to bet no one's ever done that for you."

Philip sighed and rubbed his face in an attempt to mask his expression. He wasn't sure, in that moment, he could rely on it not to betray his thoughts.

"They haven't, have they, Philip?" Fiona said, grinning and nudging his leg with her knee. "I bet they haven't, eh, Philip Scott?" She paused. "You're sure about that, Philip, completely sure? I'd like to think you might remember that particularly exotic performance if it had happened to you before, mmm? You're absolutely positive nobody's ever done that to you before? Hand on your heart? Come on, Philip, swear to me you've never done that with anyone before?"

Philip chuckled, perhaps a shade nervously for his own good, but there was no way he was going to admit to having enjoyed the same treatment at the hands, or rather the mouth, of Maja; it would surely secure his death warrant.

"No," he lied, still chuckling, "that surely was a first."

"Then explain this, Philip," she said, retrieving something from her handbag. "Kindly explain this."

Fiona handed Philip a business card; a creased and worn white business card, which looked as though it had spent too long in a pocket; the usual litter she found in one of his suits before taking it to the dry-cleaners.

And as he examined it, Fiona got up and pushed between him and the table. As she started to turn right, away from the direction in which he expected her to turn, he pointed over his shoulder and said, "Ladies, through the doors, there."

Fiona looked down at him and the heat from her glare seared the side of his face.

He glanced up at her, questioning, wondering what it was that could have provoked such embarrassment. He jerked his head back to look more closely and saw that hers was not embarrassment, it was hate.

"I don't need the bathroom, you bloody shit, Philip Scott. I'm going out for some fresh, clean air that, I hope, won't pretend to be something other than exactly what it is."

The door banged so loudly behind her that the half dozen drinkers at the bar turned in surprise, first at the door and then at Philip.

He looked down at the card. He was confused. It didn't look out of the ordinary; just Gort's written in large red lettering, and the address and contact number.

Then Philip turned it over and on what should have been the clean, white, reverse face was scrawled a message.

Philip held the card nearer the window. The writing was a shade washed out, but, sadly, all too legible:

Philip, Champagne Head for my Champagne Lover, Maja X

And beneath that was scrawled a telephone number. "Oh Christ, Maja! You didn't?"

56

Hacker

As he sat in the car and contemplated what to do next, it dawned on Hacker that Brian Chisholm might, just might, be a man of substance after all. Maybe Chisholm possessed a touch of Napoleon like some of the strikers he'd met; guys who more than made up for their lack of height in obstinacy; guys who hoisted their colours the moment they got into the box by making sure they trod on you in the first tackle or nutted you on the back of the head the first time you went up for a cross. But it didn't really matter what attitude Chisholm adopted, Hacker knew the little man's game could go only one of two ways.

And at his recollection of the sporting metaphor, Hacker's muscles tightened, his feet and hands itched, and he realised there was only one place to go on a Saturday afternoon in Norfolk: Carrow Road, Norwich.

He checked on his phone to see if the Canaries were playing at home. Then he checked to see who they were playing, in case it was one of the bigger teams and therefore tickets would be hard to come by.

Hacker set off south towards the city. Even if the game was sold out, which it was likely to be now that the Canaries were playing in the premiership, he still knew a couple of names he could try to blag a ticket off.

57

Audrey

The pack of letters was still in her handbag back at The Reach.

The front door key Ms Anworthy had provided her with was stiff in the lock and the guesthouse appeared empty.

Once safely behind the door of her room, Audrey took Laurent's letters from her handbag and sat down on the bed.

The letters that were already opened felt sullied, as though, because other eyes had danced over them, they were no longer suitably clean for reading.

She noticed from the franking that the last unopened letter was dated the year Richard died, so she began with that one.

Laurent's style was much as she remembered from his first letters. The theme was conversational; written as though he was talking directly to Audrey over a cup of coffee. The business, the vineyard to which he referred as though he was the proprietor, was flourishing: They had endured too much rain than was good for the grapes, but the harvest had been abundant and the wine had turned out better than expected. He'd taken a holiday abroad and was looking forward to the coming year with some confidence. He was thinking of her and missed her and hoped she was well. And even though he knew there was little hope of a reply, he also hoped she still remembered their brief time together. It was signed in exactly the same way he'd signed his previous letters, *Je t'embrasse très fort.*

Audrey pressed the letter to her face and breathed in the musty smell.

The second letter read pretty much the same. Even though there had not been sufficient rain through the year, the pressing had produced a significant quantity of wine and the fermentation had progressed well. Laurent had again holidayed abroad and wished he could show her all the many places he'd visited. The letter was signed with the same sentiment.

By the time Audrey removed the final letter, she felt as though Laurent was sitting on the bed beside her.

The most recent letter was something of a departure from the others. The hand was hesitant and in places Laurent had begun sentences and then crossed them out to start again. It contained less news about the vineyard and no information regarding his annual vacation. Some of his expressions reverted to his native language.

Laurent said he had suffered *une crise cardiaque*, which was happily *peu sévère*.

"Oh, poor Laurent," Audrey said out loud. "A mild heart attack."

He said that he had not been able to work and that his sister and her husband were now looking after the vineyard. He had *temps devant moi*, time on his hands she supposed, and he wished he could spend this time with Audrey.

"Oh, Laurent," she mumbled again, "My poor boy."

Only he wasn't a boy, was he? He would be like Audrey, in his sixties.

The news that he had been unwell saddened Audrey, but her sadness passed quickly, much as might a pain one receives from bumping into a piece of furniture. She no longer had the time for such small inconveniences; there were issues of greater importance. If Laurent was ill, it was up to Audrey to help him recover. If Laurent needed nursing, then who better to nurse him?

The letter grew a shade maudlin towards the end, but, thankfully, she observed, he had signed it in his usual way.

Now that she had his address once more, Audrey knew what to do. She would write and tell him that if he was ill, he could hardly be expected to travel, so it would be up to her to go to him. She would go back to Charlbury, put the house on the market and move to France.

It was all so simple; all so clear.

Of course the boys would probably object and think her rash or worse. They'd probably think she'd lost her marbles; probably diagnose her with some form of dementia, or even early Alzheimer's and have her committed.

But, she could give them some of the proceeds from that draughty, cold house and they could visit her in France if they wanted to. James? Well, he would probably be pleased to get her off his plate. John? Well, she wouldn't feel completely at ease deserting him, but...

Audrey stood up and looked over at the occasional table that twinned as a desk. There were no writing papers or envelopes on it. The Reach wasn't exactly Claridge's. But then she remembered a postcard rack on the reception counter downstairs and wondered if a card from Strand-next-the-Sea would melt Laurent's heart the same way the idea of sending him one was melting hers.

"Oh, no," she said aloud, "not his heart. I mean..."

Audrey went downstairs, rang the reception desk buzzer and waited.

No one appeared, so she rang the buzzer again; a shade more impatiently the second time. She stepped over to the white door that led into the landlady's quarters, but she could hear nothing; no radio, no humming and no shuffling of feet, only the porthole clock ticking away on the wall.

Audrey stepped back to the revolving postcard rack on the counter. She could pay Ms Anworthy for whichever card she chose later.

After a couple of minutes of looking through the many coastal landscapes, beached fishing smacks and medieval churches, Audrey found a sepia photograph of the Norfolk Flyer at Craving. Though she hadn't been looking for it, it was exactly what she wanted. It would do very nicely and she hoped Laurent would remember their evening there.

Back in her room, Audrey sat down to write.

She thought to begin with an apology, but realised such an opening line might sound casually flippant or might be too easily misinterpreted as cynical. She considered writing in French, but then realised that because she'd neither spoken nor written the language for so long, she was more than likely to employ the wrong syntax and therefore confuse the dear man even more. She tried to imagine what she could say to Laurent that might go some way towards making amends for their thirty-seven years of lost opportunity, but she couldn't.

She balled her fists, lifted her hands to her face and rested her forehead against her knuckles. "Come on, Audrey girl! Think!" she said. "What to say?"

After an hour or more of soul-searching, she realised there was little point in her being either too formal or too guarded, and as she had never replied to any of his previous letters, there was no way Laurent would know whether she had ever received any of them, so she wrote;

Cher Laurent,

I have at last received your many letters. Thank you for continuing to send them all this time. As you will see from this card I am in Strand-next-the-Sea where we stayed all those many years ago. In your last letter you said you have been unwell and I hope you are recovered. If you will permit me, I would like very much to come and visit you in France. Please write to me at the address below.

Je t'embrasse avec toute ma tendresse,
Audrey

She included her home address and, though her sentiment encouraged her otherwise, managed to resist the temptation to sign the card with a kiss.

She wondered how long it might be before she could reasonably expect a reply. She addressed the card to Laurent at the Maison des Vins in Ribeauvillé, which, she remembered, was still the same address as his earlier letters.

It sounded so wonderful, so beautiful: Ribeauvillé.

All she needed was a stamp.

Audrey glanced out the window. The light was going, the weather was still rather ordinary and the shops would soon close. She wondered if Ms Anworthy had returned and hoped the landlady might let her have a stamp.

Then, that same wave of doubt washed over her once more. That doubt like a wave; a wave which sweeps you towards the shore one minute and then drags you back further out to sea the next. She stared out at the grey sea and wondered if she could keep from tearing up the letter before she posted it.

"No. I mustn't let that happen this time. I mustn't change my mind," she whispered. "This one I simply must post. I owe us both that much."

Audrey remembered seeing a small, red cardboard box on the reception counter marked POST. The Reach might very well not be Claridge's, but at least that nice Ms Anworthy provided the service of posting her resident's letters and cards.

She would ask Ms Anworthy to post her card to Laurent. "Good idea, Audrey girl," she murmured to her reflection in the window, "Why didn't you think of that all those years ago?"

But Audrey knew why. It because all those years ago she hadn't been sure that answering Laurent's letters was the right thing to do. Now though, she was sure.

"At last," she whispered, holding the card to her lips, "I am sure."

58

Philip

Philip put the card in his pocket. He didn't remember Maja planting it on him and couldn't understand why on earth she would do so.

He remembered her doing that thing to him with the champagne. And he remembered thinking, too late, that it was wrong, but that he'd been too far gone to stop her. And afterwards he'd stumbled to her bathroom to wash himself at the basin, and when he'd come out, Maja had been standing there, holding out his trousers like a naked valet. He'd dressed. She'd laughed. He'd left. She could have slipped the card into his pocket at any time.

He picked up his glass, but, when he got it to his lips, he realised it was empty.

Fiona had gone off in a huff; if huff adequately described her mood. She'd come back when she cooled off.

Philip got another beer, figured it would definitely have to be his last, and settled their lunch bill.

Fat drops of rain began to spatter the window and the foam-topped, muddy-grey sea surged and crashed against the stanchions of the pier.

He glimpsed a figure in a dark overcoat down at the pavilion end of the pier.

He made to stand but before he got fully upright, sat, or rather slumped back down on his chair. If he left the rather too agreeable confines of the pub to chase Fiona, she might return and think he'd deserted her. But, if he stayed and waited, Fiona would return and hate him even more for not chasing after her.

Philip knew he had to convince Fiona that the problem and therefore the blame lay with him, and not with her; that it was his reaction to her that was the problem, not how she behaved towards him. And yet, he knew she would blame herself. Fiona would surely lay the blame for his infidelity at her own door; her innate sense of inadequacy would see to that.

That other girl, Phoebe, was not to blame. She was merely one of those pale coincidences that pops up out of nowhere and bites you when you're least expecting it. Nice kid though she was, she was a symptom, not the cause.

And Maja? She was, though vivacious and unquestionably attractive, nothing more than a reward; an avenue down which he had been able to pander to the spoils of his success.

Maja wasn't the problem either. It was him. It was he who had slipped away from Fiona.

Perhaps, he wondered, it was that he was the casualty of his own success. And he wondered, with a touch of irony, whether it was purely and simply the tide of his advancement that had swept him too quickly and too far from the home he'd worked so hard to construct. Perhaps he'd lost sight of what he had been working so hard for: Fiona, the children, his family, himself?

Philip hadn't realised he'd been sitting with his head in his hands. The barman was watching him. He sighed, wiped his sweating palms on his jeans and sat up. He was pretty sure it was Fiona he'd glimpsed down on the pier.

59

Hacker

The afternoon proved something of a dead end for Hacker. The couple of faces he'd known at the Carrow Road ground had long since retired and nobody seemed the slightest bit interested in when and where he'd played.

He fought his way back over the River Wensum into the city, parked in St Stephen's, followed his nose along All Saints and took a chance up Timberhill. He was just getting to the stage where he'd have killed for a pint when he stumbled across the aptly name Murderers; a sports bar. It seemed a good enough spot in which to lose himself for a couple of hours.

Like a man waiting on a date, Hacker checked his phone every few minutes. He ate cod and chips, sank a couple of pints of Ghost Ship, and came to the conclusion that there was little else Chisholm could do to resurrect Marchman's contract.

So Hacker sat and considered his options. Perhaps it was the golden, malty ale that was diluting his indignation at not being recognised by the box office clerk at the ground. Perhaps it was the food that was satisfying his appetite for retribution. Or perhaps it was the uncomfortable, furtive glances Kaitlyn Chisholm threw her parents at halftime that caused him to stop and think. He didn't know what was responsible for his change in attitude, but he perceived his previously solid resolve slowly dissolving.

If he was honest with himself, he hadn't stopped to estimate the havoc he might wreak. Sure, he'd threatened Chisholm with releasing some photographs. Sure, he'd predicted to Chisholm the disastrous results releasing such photos would have. But, in truth, Hacker had never really taken the time to consider the fallout from anyone else's perspective. The idea of damaging Chisholm in some small way had sat extremely easy with him. After all, Chisholm had damaged him and that was the unwritten rule of the four-across-the-back union: Do unto others before they get the chance to do it to you.

But, just because some Senegalese newbie had shown him no mercy, did that mean he had to show the lack of same to Jean and Kaitlyn and Kayla? Hell, he didn't exactly have a reputation for showing much in the way of mercy to the opposition. But, he was forgetting that other great unwritten rule: What goes on on the pitch, stays on the pitch. Was involving Chisholm's family, taking it off the pitch?

He finished his pint and stepped outside for a cigarette. Hacker lit up and hitched the collar of his jacket higher up the back of his neck.

An old boy, creased, brown leather jerkin, threadbare red corduroys and scuffed saddle shoes, stood rocking on his toes. His wire-grey hair was tied in a ponytail and the whiskers of his moustache hung down below his chin, framing the roll-up glued between his lips. He eyed Hacker for a while as though he was suspicious of him.

Hacker, in turn, thought he recognised the man.

"Didn't know you smoked, Hacker?" the old boy said.

"What's it to you?"

The man smiled a slightly crazy, leery smile. "See you've lost none of your aggression then," he said, nipping the thin fag from his mouth and flicking the ash off the end so that it danced away down the street like a firefly. "Mind you, I thought you left that on the pitch; thought it was only the unfortunate few who couldn't leave it where it belonged."

"Piss off."

The old boy grinned at Hacker. He was well-spoken, in spite of his bedraggled aspect. "As you wish," he said.

Hacker went indoors, rubbing his numb hands.

He watched as the old boy came inside and realised, as he limped up to the bar, that he must have a prosthetic leg or, if not, a leg that was next to useless.

The barman evidently knew the man as a regular.

Having got his beer, the old boy hobbled over to the fruit machine and began to feed it from a stack of coins he placed on top.

Hacker stepped over to the bar and, when he'd managed to attract the barman's eye, asked the old boy's name.

"Barney. He used to work down at the football stadium: Came here from Borough a few years ago. Used to play a bit, or so he's not tired of reminding us."

Hacker banged his fist on the bar. "'Course it is: Barney the Borough Bear. How could I forget?" The barman waited for Hacker to order his pint. "Oh, another pint of Ghost, one for you and tell me, what's Barney drinking?"

He carried the beers over. Barney carried on feeding the machine and pressing the tabs.

"Didn't recognise you, Barney, sorry. Surprised you recognised me."

Barney concentrated on his game.

"Got you a pint," Hacker offered.

But whatever he felt at Hacker's insult, Barney was not inclined to let Hacker off too lightly.

Hacker recalled the man, dressed up like a pantomime bear, lurching round the touchline at the Borough ground, wind-milling his arms to rouse the all too often docile crowd. He'd played for

Borough in the days when most players earned boot money as opposed to a living wage.

He'd not seen Barney play, that had been before his time, but he knew the story of Barney breaking his leg and playing on 'til the end of a league match that saw Borough promoted to the First Division. Playing on had finished his career. He'd been part of the Borough folk lore; part of the fairy tale that surrounded the Borough teams of the sixties.

And Barney had always singled out Hacker for special applause. He'd always wished him luck before the game and congratulated or commiserated with him afterwards. Then, one day, Barney disappeared.

Damn, Hacker swore silently, why of all the weird and wonderful characters did he forget Barney? He supposed it was that terrible bear costume.

"Didn't start smoking until I stopped playing," Hacker said, "Stupid, really."

"Nope, not really," Barney replied, still not shifting his eyes from the machine, "Most of us need to fill the hole with something."

Hacker knew the hole he was referring to. It was the hole in the week when you no longer trained; the hole in your gut once filled with butterflies and adrenalin and pheromones. But most of all it was the hole in your life which used to be filled by regular draughts of applause from children and adults alike. He knew it sounded vain and he knew there were few who'd own up to feeling the same, but it had never left him.

"Knew it was you the moment you stepped out the door," Barney said, "Can't mistake the way you stand. It's your body language. You always had your own; like it'd have to be metal, and heavy metal at that, before you'd let it past."

"Sorry about not recognising you, Barney."

"No matter. Thanks for the pint."

"How's the leg?"

"Mustn't grumble."

"Doing alright?"

"The same."

They drank slowly.

Eventually Barney ran out of change, so they sat and chewed the fat; players they knew, players they loved and, above all, players they respected. Conversation came light and easily to them, much as though they sat and tossed the chaff every Saturday afternoon in the Murderers. They watched the football results and moaned and groaned and muttered and griped. Of course, it wasn't like the old days, but both of them managed to keep from pointing it out. They managed a few clichés, but they managed to resist the temptation to lapse into too deep a nostalgia. They drank more beer, Hacker the Ghost, Barney the Once Bittern, and they shared a smoke outside.

Eventually the light dimmed and the colour of the beer turned dark in the glass.

"You were good, Cornelius, my boy," Barney proclaimed a little too loudly for comfort.

Hacker decided it was time to leave; spending the afternoon in the company of a bar fly, even one as affable as Barney, risked exposure to that dangerous and very contagious disease, lethargy.

"Oh, don't give me the flannel, Barney."

"No," Barney slurred a shade, "you could; really you could. You had it all."

"I hate to think," Hacker drained his glass.

"No, I mean it, son." He tapped Hacker affectionately on his knee, "I mean it. You were hard in the tackle, always ahead of your man, quick, good in the air, never got dragged out of position, had good skills on the ball, and you were never afraid. You had it all."

"So where did I go wrong?"

"Wrong?" he repeated. "You never knew when to stop, that was all. Didn't your mother ever tell you that? You knew it all except when to pull out of the tackle. That's why you ended up being flattened by that whass-is-name from the Cameroon."

"Senegal."

Barney rocked back on his seat. "There you go! Just as I said: You could've let me off the hook with that one, but, no, you 'ad to pick me up on it."

Hacker grinned.

"Er, talking of picking up, Barney," Hacker feigned to glance at his watch, "I've got a date and sitting here basking in the warmth of your compliments won't get me ready for dinner."

Without knowing it, Barney had not so much touched a raw nerve as stamped on one. Hacker had never got away from that one glaring weakness in his game; even Beasely and Brian Chisholm had remarked on it. Hacker had never known when he was beaten. All his coaches told him it was the only aspect of his game that let him down and the only aspect that would prevent him from playing the game at the highest level. He'd never learnt that no matter how hard you tackled, how fast you ran, how high you jumped, how hard you worked or how sharp you were, sometimes the game beat you and you had to hold your hands up and accept it. Sometimes, as the saying went, you were just plain lucky to get nil.

"Go on, Cornelius," Barney said. "Bugger off and have a good evening. You deserve it."

It was what Barney used to say to him when he'd played a good game. He used to say "You deserve it" even when Borough had lost. He was an old stager, Barney. He knew there would be other games to play.

60

Philip

Force of habit and a thirst for Dutch courage saw Philip finish his pint. He went to the bar, checked that the pub was going to remain open all afternoon and gave the barman his name, adding that there was an outside chance a woman, the woman he'd lunched with, might come in and ask after him. If she did, would the barman be good enough to ask her to hang on as he'd be back in... he checked his watch, half an hour?

"Four o'clock," he murmured at the door as he pulled it back. "Where the hell did those three hours go?"

He was fairly sure Fiona would've walked over the apron and down to the Prospect. He hadn't seen her, his attention had been taken by the card she'd handed him, but he figured it was the most direct route down to the pier and therefore the most likely she would take back up.

The steep steps curved round and down onto the esplanade; the railings cold and wet beneath his hand. The oriel, the box sash and the bow windows all bore silent witnesses to Philip's purposeful stride. The pantile roofs, the gable ends and overhanging eaves, the yellow and pink stuccoed walls, and the cast iron lampposts all leaned back out of his way. And the waves broke against the flint walled bullnoses of the sea defences, heartening him and spurring him on towards the pier.

But when he arrived at the entrance, there was not a soul to be seen. The gift shop was dark and deserted, and the restaurant peaceful.

Philip walked out towards the Pavilion Theatre. The wind whistled in from his left and the heavy wooden planks underfoot shone slippery with airborne spray.

Just as he got to the Pavilion, a woman in a dark coat appeared from the main door. "Sorry, dear, nothing on tonight; the band've baled. It was in the papers," she offered by way of explanation.

"Is anyone inside?"

"No, dear. Couple of grumpy security men, but the theatre's closed. Won't be anything on 'til next weekend now. They won't be letting anyone in. Be more than their job's worth."

Philip realised she was the woman he'd glimpsed from the window of the pub. "Thank you," he said, not really knowing what for.

The woman fiddled with her umbrella once more, then looked up at the sky and marched off down the pier.

Philip swore quietly to himself, then turned on his heels and followed.

He paused to study the great stone compass set in the pier forecourt, hoping upon hope that it might lend him a clue as to which direction he ought to take. But the strange granite lines all pointed out to sea and served only to make him more aware of his dilemma.

It was true; he was all at sea, and probably worse. But, as the granite lines noted the direction in which the lifeboat had set out to rescue those in peril on the sea, Philip knew one thing for certain: he couldn't expect to be thrown a lifeline any time soon.

So he took the steps back up to the pub two at a time and found, to his irritation, that he was out of breath by the time he reached the top.

The barman shook his head.

And as Philip headed for the door, the barman muttered sarcastically and mostly for the benefit of his audience, "She ain't got a mobile phone then?"

Philip turned and whatever expression he wore it inclined the barman to take a step back. "Funnily enough, no, she hasn't."

There was little else he could do but try to second-guess where Fiona might have got to.

He hurried back down the steps.

To the south-east, the Prospect curled between the seawall and the Lifeboat Museum until it petered out into the path that led up the hill and eventually along the coastline to Strand-next-the-Sea.

It was possible that she'd walked off back to The Reach. He hoped not; she knew as much about the route as he did, and he knew nothing. The light would soon be gone and, what with the bitter wind from offshore, it was getting colder by the minute. He tried to remember if she was still wearing her walking boots, but then recalled her taking them off before they'd left Felbrigg.

To the north-west, a fairly busy road climbed steeply out of Cromer past a tall terrace of red brick Edwardian houses. The Prospect, though, followed the waterline and stretched as far as he could see.

They'd just had lunch so it was unlikely she'd have hidden herself away in one of the cosy bistros; a coffee shop, maybe, but a bistro?

"Oh, Fiona," he murmured into the wind, "where the bloody hell are you?" and set off along the prospect to the north-west.

He resisted the temptation to run, knowing it would only increase his frustration and, if he came across her, leaning against the parapet of a bullnose like a sailor's wife longing for the grey waters to give up her man, he reckoned he would need all the composure he could summon. Being out of breath wouldn't help.

Out in the vast wastes to the north, the whirling white blades of the wind turbines emerged from between the curtain of cloud like ghosts on a parade ground, and a squabble of seagulls wheeled and shrieked, arguing over some scrap of bait tossed aside by a line fisherman down on the beach.

61

Phoebe

Phoebe stood before the white door marked PRIVATE, took a deep breath and exhaled slowly. She knocked and waited for a response. She could hear seventies pop music coming from the room beyond.

She waited a few seconds and then knocked again, "Excuse me, Ms Anworthy?"

Nothing happened.

Looking round, she noticed the buzzer on top of the reception counter. Like the door through to Ms Anworthy's quarters, the buzzer presented itself as a threshold over which Phoebe was nervous of stepping.

She breathed deep, then walked over to the counter and pressed the button.

The buzzer sounded beyond the door and the music silenced.

Stella Anworthy appeared, "Yes dear? Can I help you?"

"I'm sorry to bother you, Ms Anworthy, but I wondered if you could spare me a moment?"

"Of course, dear, what can I do for you?"

Phoebe stood and studied Stella Anworthy. When she'd arrived at The Reach the afternoon before, she'd not wanted to stare too hard, just in case the lady thought her strange and threw her back out on the street.

She stood about the same height as Phoebe and the reddish roots to her light brown hair needed colouring. But, more than that, they betrayed the red of her hair. And her eyes were a pale, watery green — if anything, a shade lighter than Phoebe's.

"I was wondering if I could get a cup of tea, if it's not too much trouble."

"Well, you have got a teasmade in your room, dear. Isn't it working?"

Phoebe remembered the shiny plastic machine and cringed. "Yes, I know. It's just that there's only ordinary tea and because I don't take it with milk, it's a bit strong for me. I wondered if you had some other tea, some fruit tea perhaps."

The landlady twiddled a curl at the back of her neck and stared back at Phoebe, mulling over her request.

"Well, normally people ask for plain tea or coffee, so I don't offer anything more exotic." She paused. "I might have... Oh, pop in the breakfast room for a moment, there may be some in the tray. I'll have a look in the kitchen all the same."

Phoebe sat down at the table. The room was warm, the chairs cushioned and comfortable; the place settings already laid for the next day's breakfast.

After a minute or so, Stella came in from the kitchen. She carried two small cartons of teabags; one a fruit selection, the other a green jasmine tea. "I'm afraid this is all I've got. The green jasmine might be a bit fresher than the fruit; I usually have a cup once a week, supposed to be good for you; lots of antioxidants, so they tell me."

She held them out and waited for Phoebe to choose.

But Phoebe wasn't looking at the tea; she was studying the woman's hands. Her nails were neatly clipped, but her cuticles were bitten red and rough, just like Phoebe's.

When Phoebe didn't choose, Stella withdrew the tin and set it on the table.

"Is everything alright, dear? You look all in; a bit pale, if you ask me. I know they say the sea air is good for you, but on a day like today you can catch a chill quicker than a bus down the front." She paused again and watched Phoebe intently, "Are you sure you're alright?"

Phoebe didn't realise she'd been staring at the woman's hands for quite so long. "No, I'm fine, thank you, Ms Anworthy. I'll take a green tea, if that's okay?"

But Ms Anworthy decided it wasn't okay. She was looking a little sideways at Phoebe. "I tell you what, kid, you call me Stella and I'll put the kettle on. How about that? Won't hurt to stop what I'm doing for a few minutes."

A smile spread slowly across Phoebe's face, bringing a little colour back to her cheeks. "Yes, that would be nice. I mean, if it's not too much trouble?"

"No, dear. No trouble at all." The landlady disappeared into the kitchen.

"Here we are," she said, reappearing with a tray loaded with a teapot, cups, saucers and biscuits. After she'd transferred the service onto the table, she asked, "Weak or strong?"

"As it comes. Weaker, if I'm honest."

"Might just as well be; honest, that is. Though sometimes I think being honest lays one open to more trouble, if you know what I mean? Sometimes it pays to be a bit economical with the truth." She sat down opposite Phoebe and began to pour her tea. "Bit too weak, that! I'll leave it for a minute. What's your name, love? First name, I mean? It's my fur brain, you see, I can't remember from last night."

"Phoebe," the girl said. "Phoebe Wallace. Pleased to meet you, Stella."

They shook hands rather formally, Phoebe hanging onto Stella's hand for a little longer than was polite.

"You got cold on your walk," Stella said. "You must've walked a long way?"

"Into Cromer."

"Nice walk, up past the Royal – the Royal Cromer Golf Club, that is – on your left just before you get into the town." Stella giggled. "Well, it would hardly be on the right, eh; nothing but North Sea all the way to Scandinavia on the right."

Stella poured the tea and passed Phoebe a cup.

"No, I suppose not," said Phoebe. "I bumped into a couple of your guests in Cromer at lunchtime; couple in their twenties, I guess."

Stella nodded, "The Scotts."

"They seem like a nice couple. I've met him before but he didn't remember me." Phoebe recalled the look of surprise on Charlie's face. She'd expected to feel at least some small anger, not only towards him because he'd lied to her about his name, but also towards herself because she knew she ought to have felt embarrassed at being taken for a fool. But, she didn't. She couldn't. He'd rescued her. She'd merely returned the kindness. After all, it had been her decision to turn and walk away, not his.

"Strangest thing when you think you know somebody and you find out you don't really know them at all," Phoebe said, realising immediately that she was thinking of her adoptive parents and not the woman who'd just passed her a mug of fruit tea. After all, how could she begin to think she'd known the woman opposite her when she'd only ever met her wandering in her subconscious?

The adoption contact registers were all very helpful; sometimes a little patronising, but generally very helpful. They seemed rather too focused on the negative consequences of Phoebe locating her birth mother and father, and dealing with the fallout; the devastating shock, as one had called it. They all talked of irretrievable alterations, of sorrow and loss, and questioned whether Phoebe would be up to coping with the inevitable confusion and anger that finding her birth mother would generate.

In fact, what Phoebe learned from them was that until recently she'd lived in a dark, uncompromising conspiracy of silence. And yet now, every new voice seemed only too keen to tell her to continue with the same. So, after a skinful of platitudes, she'd resorted to a tracing agency. They'd achieved what the others hadn't and without half the chat.

"Do you know them, the Scotts?" Phoebe asked.

"No, not really, dear; much as I know any of the people here, I suppose. I do have my regulars, of course, mostly in the summer. You know: the bucket and spade brigade. But this time of year we get all sorts."

Phoebe winced.

"Oh, don't get me wrong. There's nothing wrong with all sorts; bit like liquorice," she giggled, "Do you like liquorice, Phoebe?"

She nodded. She didn't much, but she was inclined to take whatever was on offer, especially if it would prolong their conversation.

Stella went to the kitchen and returned with a carton of All Sorts. "Go on. Help yourself. A little bit of what you fancy does you no harm, that's what I always say."

"I would imagine it gets a bit lonely running this place all on your own," Phoebe said, rolling a log of liquorice around in her mouth. "I mean, unless you're married. I'm sorry; I don't mean to pry." She handed the box back across the table.

Stella peered into the carton and picked out a light-blue sweet shaped like a cardigan button. "No, I'm not married," she sighed, "I was once. It didn't work out. Not his fault, if I'm honest. Not really mine either."

"Did you have any children?"

"N..." she hesitated and then turned her attention to the ceiling as though she might be judged for a liar by an all-seeing eye. "No, dear, not with Vernon. More tea?"

Phoebe nodded. Stella refilled her cup.

Curiously, Phoebe mislaid her voice. She'd caught the slight hesitation in the woman's answer, "not with Vernon". That was what she'd said. It wasn't exactly an outright denial of motherhood, "not with Vernon". Did that mean she'd had a child, or children, with some other man — a man to whom she was not married? But before Phoebe could form the words in her head into a less brutal but equally coherent order, the woman interrupted her thoughts.

"Do you have any brothers or sisters?"

"Yes," replied Phoebe, I..." but her voice dried again. Strictly speaking, Billy wasn't her brother, unless of course her parents had managed to pick him up off the very same supermarket shelf. "What I mean is..."

"Come on, dear. Surely you must know whether you've got brothers or sisters, or were you out in that wind too long?"

But Phoebe didn't know how to answer. She understood that in denying Billy, she would in essence be repeating her adoptive parent's denial of her own birth mother. For if Billy was not a brother to her, then what was he: a half-brother, a bosom buddy, a boy thrown up by fate to accompany her partway along her journey through life? It didn't really matter, because whatever Billy was to her, she was a sister to him and sisters didn't disown brothers any more than mothers disowned daughters.

"I mean..." she began, but didn't finish.

No, Billy was more than any of those things. She loved him as much as she could ever love anyone. He was in her heart. He was as much a part of her as any other singular being and if she denied him, he would be nothing more than the next entry on the potentially long list of casualties brought about by her actions. And that was exactly what the adoption register counsellors had said: He would be an elemental component of the irretrievable alteration. That was another term they had employed in their efforts to talk her out of her search for her parents; irretrievable alterations to elemental components was what they'd said, as though she was inanimate, a machine, a car or dishwasher, or just another electron in search of a neutron.

And if Billy was in her heart, then so too was her mum, Sarah. And Phoebe couldn't deny her either. Was it only a couple of months ago that she'd been so desperate to sacrifice her kidney for the one person she wanted to preserve above all others? Was it fair of Phoebe to add her adoptive mother to the list of irretrievable alterations; a sick woman who had worked so hard and gone without so much for her?

Her eyes teared and her heart thumped. "Yes," she answered finally. "Yes, I have a brother: Billy, he's a few years younger than me."

"There there, dear. Don't worry." Stella left again for the kitchen, returning this time with a box of tissues.

"Here, help yourself." She placed the box beside Phoebe. "Trouble at home?"

"Yes and no." Phoebe sniffed, aware of how inelegant and confused she must seem.

"Difficult things, families," Stella declared.

"Not their fault. I can't blame them," Phoebe replied. "It's pretty much all of my own making. You know, master of my own destiny, old enough to know better." She sniffed again.

"Yes," Stella said. "I do know something of what you mean. As I see it, the world expects you to be prepared for whatever it can throw at you, when the truth of the matter is there's no rule that suggests you should be. Here," she passed Phoebe the plate of Bourbons, "have a chocolate biscuit. You don't look as though you've had a square meal in a month."

Phoebe blew her nose, wiped it and, in the absence of a waste bin, put the used tissues in her pocket. She took a biscuit and nibbled it.

The chocolate flavours danced on her tongue and roused her taste buds; her recent diet of 'drone and vodka had not only stilled the small voice of her appetite, it had flattened her palate.

There was, though, only so much she could blame on the 'drone. The burning anger kindled by her rejection at birth and the guilt she buried when she understood that her course would hurt those she loved, were hers alone to deal with, and such a potent cocktail of emotions had caused Phoebe to lose the balance of her mind each and every time she'd sipped from the glass.

But her head had not been level to begin with; the 'drone had seen to that. It had been like too much pre-lash before a party or like being drunk before an exam. The wretched drug had conjured up the extrovert, triggered the exhibitionist and unchained the lunatic in her. It had made her wilful and deceitful and lazy and had cultivated in her a need to plagiarise. And it had made it all too easy for her to use and abuse her friends, and ignore the advice of the doctors and later the charities. But, worst of all, the Mephedrone had turned her against her family.

And the result of her unrestrained indulgence was that Phoebe Wallace had become the very person she had for so long fought not to become. Through her unrestrained indulgence she had sentenced herself to the very camp she had worked so hard to avoid; a psychological concentration camp the like of which she'd read about in the harrowing narratives of Levi, Mandelbaum and Wiesel. Without realising it, she'd become just another hollow submissive to a merciless kapo who went by the name of Mephedrone. She'd allowed him to dehumanise her and, in the end, mark her out for selection. Phoebe had permitted him to make her his very own Muselmann.

But, she had perceived a fresh breeze of confidence stirring within her on her walk into Cromer. The old lady she'd met on the train and then again on her walk had, through her simple observation, breathed new life into Phoebe. And, her measured response to Charlie's denial of her had empowered her both physically and mentally. Together, Charlie and the woman had helped her regain the control the 'drone had wrested from her.

She looked up at Stella and studied her face. "You said you didn't have children with... was it Vernon?"

"Mm, I did, didn't I?" Stella replied in a resigned tone. "No, I didn't have any children with Vernon." Then she quieted, obviously mulling over the significance of their lack of children. "It's as I said; not with Vernon."

But her deliberating, her reflecting, persisted, and quite out of the blue she said, "I did have a child; a long time ago. I was very young: too young. Too young to understand what it all meant. Too bewildered to grasp what it might mean and too innocent to imagine how much pain it would cause me later."

Phoebe noticed the woman's eyes begin to water and her face redden in embarrassment.

"Look at the two of us," Stella said, stretching across the table, "sitting here, weeping about our lot in life. Not much to be gained by it, is there?"

Phoebe assumed the woman was reaching out for her, so she leant forwards and offered her hand. But, all of a sudden, she realised Stella was merely stretching to take a tissue and so she quickly moved to pass the box over instead.

She could feel the pain in the woman's form as though it was being transmitted to her through some exclusive frequency. And she wanted so desperately to open her heart and tell her that she didn't resent her for giving her up, that everything had turned out well and that she was as much loved as any child could be. But, she didn't. It was in her power to, she knew it, but she didn't.

Phoebe gazed at Stella and tried to find herself in the woman's eyes. She was not poring over her the way she had pored over so many of her essays; assimilating, consolidating and editing in search of an acceptable balance between content and context. And neither was Phoebe concerned with whether some Darwinian hiccup in her DNA was responsible for her recent fall from grace. She was no longer interested in the mistakes that either or both of them had made.

And for the first time Phoebe began to come to terms with her part in the order of things. That she had regained some control was evident, but perhaps what she needed more than that was to measure her control against events that happened beyond her influence; to fuse the two worlds so they could coexist and overlap in some harmony.

She, Phoebe, was a misconception; a child born of an act committed through ignorance. She was what they used to call a mistake. And mistakes happened because people lost control; in her case, not one mistake, but two, because it had taken two ignorant, out of control people to complete her wonderful and awful conception.

And then she saw herself, a child peacefully asleep in a pushchair, gentle hands guiding her smoothly down a broad avenue, the sun flickering through the leaves, projecting flashes of its white light onto her face. She woke, rubbed her eyes with tiny clenched fists and leant forwards in her seat, turning round to look at her guardian. But whoever it was she expected to see, whoever it was she wanted to see, wasn't there. She had been there once, just once a very long time ago, but she would never be there again. Phoebe knew it now and knew, as she knew for certain that her future was hers and hers alone to map out, that what she was about to do would be for the best.

"It must have been hard for you," Phoebe said tenderly, "giving up your little girl like that."

Stella sniffed once more and reached for another tissue. She blew her nose noisily and sat quietly examining her hands as though they had recently betrayed her.

"Oh, it wasn't easy, that's for sure. Not at the beginning and not at the end. But, perhaps it was for the best. You see, it wasn't up to me. I didn't really have any control over it."

The phone out on the counter rang.

"Won't be a minute, love," Stella said.

62

Philip

An hour later, and after a walk that led him almost all the way to Runton, Philip had still not found Fiona.

He checked back in at the pub: nothing. So, like a military policeman in search of a deserter, he scoured the pubs, bistros and tea houses of Cromer. In frustration he felt like putting his shoulder to the door of the Parish Church when no one answered to his knocking, and, after asking a passer-by if there was another church in the vicinity, he peered like a prospective thief in through the opaque, lead-quartered windows of the Baptist Church.

And as the day slipped away and the streetlamps flickered into life, Philip started to toy with the idea that Fiona was, very possibly, no longer in Cromer.

He knew his doubt was born more of his not finding her, and yet he could not escape the feeling that this time she might just have gone off and left him.

For sure, she'd played the melancholic card before, usually at one of those country house weekends where everybody drank so much that argument became inevitable; Fiona in her party frock, running away down the lawn into the darkness, hoping he would pursue her and clutch her to his manly chest and tell her that he really, really did love her and that it would always be so. And, true to his form and his love for her, he had always pursued her and told her exactly what she needed to hear.

But this time, Philip wasn't convinced the circumstances pointed to that curiously ridiculous, yet rational behaviour. This time, it was very different.

For the first time, she'd walked and not run away from him. And for the first time, it was not the alcohol giving vent to her frustration, it was sense and reason. But more important than either of those was the fact that before, she'd always run only so far that she knew he would be able to find her — whereas now, he could not. In fact he hadn't the first clue where Fiona might have got to.

He made his way back to the car park, hoping Fiona might have left him a note tucked under the windscreen wiper.

She hadn't.

He fished in his pocket for the car keys and at the very same moment remembered Fiona had them.

He leant up against the car and banged his hip against the door in frustration.

The alarm went off, startling him.

Philip walked around the car, trying his best not to look nervous or self-conscious as it shrieked in alarm. He couldn't see if there was anything missing from inside.

It took him a couple of minutes to locate the number of The Reach on his phone.

"Ms Anworthy?" he said as soon as she answered. "Philip Scott here."

"Oh, good evening, Mr Scott. What can I do for you?" Her tone was a shade terse, as if he'd interrupted her or she'd been expecting someone other than him to call.

"It's just that my wife and I... well, we've... Well, we're in Cromer and she went off shopping and we seem to have lost touch. She's not where we'd agreed to meet and I wondered if she'd found her way back to you. She's not there by any chance, is she?"

"I don't think so, dear, your front door key is still with your room key on the rack. But just a minute, I'll go and knock on the door."

The phone went quiet but for the muffled sound of the fire door opening and closing.

Then he heard her call out, "Mrs Scott? Excuse me, Mrs Scott? Are you there?"

There followed another pause and then Ms Anworthy came back on the line, "No, I don't think she's there and both your room keys are in the rack. Where are you, dear?"

"In Cromer."

"Might I suggest you ask down at the taxi service on Church Street? It's just round the corner from Mount Street. They'd be the most likely."

"Sure. I will. Thank you, Ms Anworthy," he replied. "Oh, and Ms Anworthy?"

"Yes, dear?"

"Would you be kind enough to ask her to be sure to call me when she comes in? It's just that I think her phone is in our room, so I can't call her."

"Of course, Mr Scott, be happy to," she replied in a tone that suggested she understood there'd occurred a domestic of some nature and she would, if she could, do her best to smooth things over. "I'd be inclined to try Bolton's on the Runton Road; nice place. It's where I like to meet people."

Philip had poked his nose in there earlier.

The landlady understood, instantly, "Or the Red Lion, or the Wellington." The lack of response told her all she needed to know. "I'm sure Mrs Scott will turn up soon. Don't worry, dear," she added, "but if she comes in, I'll be sure to ask her to call."

"Thank you, Ms Anworthy. I'd be most grateful."

"Oh, one more thing, Mr Scott: If you don't get back by ten, don't

387

worry. Just ring my phone, not the doorbell – this phone – and I'll let you in."

"Sorry?"

"The front door key, Mr Scott? As I said, your room and front door keys are both on the rack here." Ms Anworthy paused long enough to let her information locate a ledge on which to perch. "These situations are not always as simple as one would hope. Just call me and I'll let you in. Never mind the time, dear, just call."

"Oh, of course, yes. I see what you mean. Yes, thank you, Ms Anworthy." He rang off.

Philip walked down the road, turned right at the end, passed the town hall and carried on round the corner and up the slope. The station lay half a mile along the Holt Road in the direction of Felbrigg Hall; they'd passed it on their way into town.

63

Stella

Stella went out to reception and hesitated before answering the phone. For a moment, she worried that it might be her Will calling her to tell her he was on his way round to teach her a lesson.

"It was Mr Scott," she said as she sat back down, "seems he's mislaid his wife."

"Where was he?"

"Still in Cromer. More green tea?"

"No, thank you."

"Well," added Stella, "that's put some colour back in your cheeks, Phoebe." She paused and smoothed her skirt. "Now, what's a young lady like you doing in a cold and windy spot like Strand, eh? Clearly you're not from these parts, you've got that nice middle England way of speaking, like you're from everywhere and nowhere all at once." She sat back, pleased, like she'd spread a winning hand at Canasta.

Phoebe hesitated as though she had to think before answering, "Oh, I'm from Elmwood, on the Staffs-Derbyshire border. No reason why you would have heard of it. It's one of those urban sprawls you drive past on the motorway without ever knowing it's there."

"Have you left school or are you at university, or what?" Stella felt she had an advantage over the girl, a right perhaps. She'd answered the girl's questions about her private life, now it was only fair that the girl should answer hers.

"I'm at university."

"Oh, good for you, love. Which one? I mean, where? Not that it would make much difference to me," she scoffed lightly, "It's not as though I was ever going to university."

"Cambridge."

"Oh, you lucky thing," Stella said and stared dreamily at Phoebe for a minute. Then, as though she realised she'd committed a terrible faux-pas, she added, "I don't mean lucky, as if it's just luck that gets you into a place like that; you must be bright in the first place, I know that. I mean lucky as in lucky to have the brains in the first place." She paused again, and then raised her eyebrows, mocking herself. "I'm making a right hash of this. Look, what I mean is, I'm sure it's been a lot of hard work, but... Oh, I don't know what I mean, do I? Your parents must be so proud of you."

When the girl didn't respond, Stella followed up with, "The greatest seat of learning in the land."

"Oh, Ms Anworthy," Phoebe said, chuckling, "you are so... so..."

Stella giggled nervously, "What are you studying?"

"Reading, Ms Anworthy. It's called reading not studying."

"Sorry, dear, didn't mean to be rude."

"No, you're not being rude; it's just that we spend most of the time reading; that's why we call it reading a subject. Believe me, I wish it wasn't. Studying was what we did at school. It all seems so simple now; studying that way we used to; learning by rote."

Stella sat up. "Right," she said, "so I'll ask my question again. What's a bright young lady like you doing so far off the beaten track?"

"I don't know," Phoebe replied, "I really don't know. I was looking for something without really knowing what it was. Does that make any kind of sense?"

The girl looked so directly at her that for a second Stella felt completely unnerved, almost as if the girl had shouted at her but without raising her voice. She shut up for a bit, staring at Phoebe, sizing her up, wondering if the girl was taking her for a fool or if there was something else, something so personal or more fundamental to her that she didn't want to tell Stella what it was.

But the girl continued, "I suppose I've been trying to find myself. It sounds a bit biblical, doesn't it, but it's that kind of thing. Know thyself! Wasn't that what Plato or Socrates or the Oracle of Delphi or someone said? But, in a way, it's exactly what I've been doing."

"Yes, dear," Stella replied, "even I can understand that. It's not uncommon to lose touch with yourself, but why here? Why this godforsaken margin of the Saxon world? You could've gone to London and had twice as much fun as coming all the way up here."

"No," she replied, shaking her head, "I tried that. I tried losing myself amongst all those people. It didn't work. There was too much noise. I needed to get lost somewhere where I could find the peace to think before I could hope to find myself. I couldn't do that around all those people who knew where they were already."

"But what about your family and your tutors or dons or whatever you call them?" Stella asked. "Won't they be worried if you've gone on the missing list all of a sudden? What about them?"

"My family," the girl said. "Mm, yes, of course; my family."

Stella knew she should have told Phoebe to mind her own business when she'd cornered her about having a child. Perhaps it was all the trouble with Will. Perhaps it was the grilling she'd put up with from that woman Doyle, and then that policeman Barnes reminding her of all the dreadful palaver with the fellow Margetz. Whatever it was, Stella hadn't possessed sufficient energy to lie to the kid when she knew she should've.

It was true, though, she hadn't had any children with Vernon.

As regards children with any other man? Well, there was that unfortunate incident with the lad from Kemp Town. That lad, that...

God, she couldn't even recall what he looked like or remember his name. She'd never seen him again, of course, not once he'd done up his pants and scooted out of the house shouting how he was late. That had been the way it was. That quick! That stupid!

And then she was the kid lying in the Royal Sussex Infirmary, skin flushed pink against white sheets on a white metal bed; a young girl, limp and exhausted from labour, alone and confused, the cries of other's newborns carrying on the air, the contractions in her belly sheer and sharp and tying her up in burning knots. She was crying out in pain and calling out for help, and yet no one came. That was what she recalled so clearly: No one came. And the next minute, there was new life in all its gory glory desperate to get out from between her legs and Stella not the first clue how to help the poor thing along.

Her mother told her she was young of heart and mind, and given time she would be able to start again, as though life was a race and all that had happened was that Stella had begun running before the starter fired his pistol. Except that Stella worked out she'd been entered for a race separate from the one in which her friends ran. Her figure changed and she knew that she could no longer expect to compete with the others. Her hips widened at every appraisal, her breasts all too obviously grew heavy and lost their firm texture, and she put on so much weight so quickly that her once slender waist disappeared in as many months as it took her to finish school.

She studied Phoebe for a second. There was something about the girl; something she'd said that didn't make sense to Stella. And she couldn't for the life of her understand why this slip of a thing should call forth such painful memories. But she left Stella feeling curiously short-changed, as though she, Stella, had bared her soul, but the girl had concealed hers. She felt sure there was more to her than met the eye. But, she liked her; perhaps liked her even more now that the girl had confirmed she had a brain and wasn't just another one of those doe-eyed heifers who hung around down the front. But something wasn't right. As sure as God made little apples, Stella decided, something wasn't right.

Then the phone rang for a second time. Only it wasn't the reception phone this time, it was the house line in her living room.

"Excuse me, dear," she said, "don't go away."

64

Philip

Cromer station, Philip was dismayed to see, possessed no manned ticket office and, as far as he could make out, no ticket machines either.

He looked up at the list of departures and then checked his phone. The next train left in ten minutes.

He walked smartly onto platform one and proceeded to check every carriage. A flock of scantily clad girls shrieked in one and a few pensioners stared dreaming into space in the others.

Philip contemplated asking the guard if Fiona might be hiding in the toilet, but realised that his own thought train was beginning to verge towards the paranoid.

He walked back to the concourse and studied the larger timetable on the wall: the earlier trains had departed at four, five and just after six. The most direct route back to London lay through Norwich, but the whole journey took the better part of three hours. Upset as Fiona was, he couldn't imagine her saddling herself with that. There was a train to Ely, but...

Wherever she was, she wasn't in Cromer Station. No one was, except for those already on the train.

His next port of call had to be the taxi company. The landlady had told him it was on Church Street?

Just as Philip was checking his phone for a street map of the town, a taxi pulled up.

A female tumbled out and tottered inside; leopard-print coat and matching bag flapping, Cuban heels clipping on the concrete.

Before the taxi could drive away, Philip knocked on the driver's window and bent to it.

The man buzzed down his window, slowly. "Where you want go?" the driver asked in Punjabi, pidgin English.

"It's not so much that, really," Philip replied. "I just need to ask you if you or any of your cabs have taken a fare over to Strand-next-the-Sea late this afternoon or earlier this evening. More accurately to The Reach; the guesthouse on the front?"

The taxi driver looked back at him as though Philip had just demanded his wallet. His turban was grey; his glasses thick like the bottoms of a milk bottle, and his expression so blank Philip wondered for a moment whether the man might be some new strain of taxi android.

Without taking his eyes from Philip, he plucked his microphone from the dashboard and muttered into it. A speaker somewhere in the car squeaked, squealed and hissed, and the man replaced his microphone in its cradle: "No, sorry, not this evening. No one going Strand this evening." He continued to stare at Philip, expressionless. "No one going Strand this evening. Just heard, road to Strand closed: Accident." He must have seen the alarm in Philip's face, because he immediately added, "Petrol tanker. Big problem. You want go somewheres?"

From behind him, Philip heard the whistle of the train conductor. "What about another taxi company? To Strand, I mean."

"No, I know other taxis; no one going Strand since before lunchtime."

"Fine, okay. Can you drop me down in town?"

"Little walk," he said.

Philip stood upright and ran his hands through his hair in frustration. "Mmm," he murmured, "I know." He paused; the taxi driver seemed to be in no hurry to leave. "Look, I appreciate you're a driver, but do you know if there is a walk over the hill to Strand; a path that follows the coast?"

The driver cocked his head slightly to one side and thinned his lips, "You must take path over the hill, near road. If you go by the beach there is no way round."

"Do you know how long it takes, I mean, generally?"

The driver ran his pudgy hand over his tied-back moustache. "Maybe one hour. In the dark, maybe longer. The path... in the dark... You have torch?"

"Is that the police station?" he asked, pointing over the road.

"Old one."

"Is there a new one?"

"Yes."

Philip decided he didn't have the time to pull teeth, "Look, drop me at the police station, please? Don't bother with the meter; I'll give you a fiver."

"As you wish," the driver mumbled.

65

Phoebe

The opportunity to run was too good to pass up. Phoebe slipped out through the hall and into her room. She felt a little dizzy and weightless; a kind of post-operative elation fizzing through her body.

The idea of going home came to her; of going home and throwing her arms around her father, hugging him tight and telling him she was sorry she'd doubted him and that she would never doubt him again. She would take Billy to the cinema and tell him she was so glad he was her brother, and that if she had to choose a brother she would, no matter how many choices she was given, always choose him. And she would tell her mother that she loved her and that whatever the future held and however long it lasted, it would be their future to share together in exactly the way a mother and daughter ought to share their future.

But first, she had to write a note to her other mother; to the lady across the way; to her birth mother. Though what she was to say, she wasn't sure. She just hoped upon hope that the right words would come to her.

66

Stella

Of course the girl had gone by the time she got back to the breakfast room. She knew she would be. But, at least she'd had the good manners to take her tissues with her. Mind you, the girl would only have taken them to her room for Stella to bring them back when she cleaned up the room in the morning.

The phone call was from Betty Laws. Evidently the Strand bush telegraph had been working overtime. One who preferred to remain nameless had told Betty that Will had not been at the Canaries game that afternoon, which was most unusual as he rarely missed one. Had Stella seen him?

Her mind screamed, but, summoning a tone she normally reserved for her Canasta evenings, she'd said, "No, dear, I haven't."

She set about clearing away the tea things from the table; the girl Phoebe had made a sizeable hole in her supply of Bourbons.

Funny kid, though. She was certain she'd met her before until the girl mentioned she was reading Law at Cambridge University. That definitely put the dampners on the likelihood of them ever having met. The only person Stella could remember with that many brains was poor Vernon, and he hadn't lasted very long in her company!

The girl was interesting, and interesting meant she didn't have to worry about her Will.

But something she'd said during their conversation left Stella with the feeling that there should have been more... but more of what she couldn't quite grasp.

As she loaded the dishwasher, counting the cups and saucers so that she was sure she'd have enough for breakfast service without putting the machine on, Stella wondered what the rest of her colourful assortment of residents were up to.

Mr Scott was no doubt out and about on the trail of the errant Mrs Scott. His wife was probably sozzled in some bar in Cromer; that was what usually happened. Still, she hoped he'd find her.

That Mr Hacker, that Cornelius... Stella smiled. He wasn't such a bad sort. Not what some would term good-looking, not like Mr Scott, but he was attractive in that remarkable way, rugged features rather than plain. He was an ex-footballer, that's what he'd told her after they'd drunk all that gin, and his muscles were well toned and he had a stomach as flat as a washboard.

Cornelius; that was his first name. Strange name for an English footballer: Name more suited to one of those Brazilians, like Ronaldinho or Socrates. Mind you, that clever girl, Phoebe, hadn't meant that particular Socrates when she'd mentioned the name earlier. She wondered where he was, Cornelius; probably down the Tern with all the other lame-brains watching football!

And then, as she wiped the table, she was reminded of her Will not being at the Canaries game and she shuddered.

The older lady, Mrs Poulter, was in her room. Stella had heard her moving about. Seemed like a nice lady; bit of a sparrow, but at least she smiled nicely when she said thank you.

67

Audrey

She knew Ms Anworthy was in; she'd heard her talking to the girl — the one she'd seen on the train and passed on her walk.

The landlady was in the hall, "Mrs Poulter? Is everything alright?"

"Yes, thank you, Ms Anworthy. Fine!"

"Mrs Poulter, I think it's about time we dispensed with formalities. Please, call me Stella."

"Yes, of course, Stella. How kind. I'm Audrey, how do you do?"

"I've had better days, thank you, Audrey. But then, I always say beggars can't be choosers. What can I do for you, Audrey?"

"Oh, small thing really," she held the card out towards the woman, "it's this. Oh, and I need to pay you for it. I took it off the stand this afternoon. I wondered if you would be kind enough to post it for me."

"Of course, I'd be happy to. Nice spot that, the Norfolk Flyer!"

"Oh yes! Couldn't agree more! Lovely! Good food, too. Changed a bit from the last time I was here."

"You know it then?"

"Mm," Audrey agreed. "I was here some years ago; too many years, to be honest. I'd forgotten what a lovely part of the world this is up here."

"Well, mixed blessings, you might say," Stella replied. "You stayed here, did you? Room 3 by any chance?"

"Yes, Room 3. Only for the two days. It was before I was married; a long time ago."

"Nice to have such memories," Stella said, reading her mind.

"Yes," Audrey replied, encouraging her eyes to focus. "Oh, and I need a stamp for the card. Do you by any chance have one? I mean, one I can buy? I have some change."

"Of course, Audrey dear. First or second? Where's it for?" Stella turned the card over to read the address.

"God, yes! Sorry, how stupid of me!" She glanced up at the ceiling, "You must think me daft. I mean, I need one of those stamps for the EU, for the Continent; France, actually."

Ms Anworthy stood and read the address on the card. "No, I don't think that..." she hesitated, "at..." she hesitated again, "...all. One moment?"

The woman seemed to be reading her card.

"I..." Stella began, but nothing further came. "I..." she began again.

Audrey stood and waited. "What's the matter, Stella? Are you feeling quite alright? You've gone as white as a sheet."

"I don't mean to be rude," she said, "but I couldn't help but notice you've addressed your card to a Monsieur Margetz. You... you know him then?"

"Yes, I... Yes, Laurent and I stayed here years ago," Audrey heard herself say. "It was the last time I was here at The Reach. Actually, it was the only time. Why, do you know Laurent?"

The silence amplified until it became deafening and Audrey knew all there was to know about silence; it was both her best friend and her worst enemy. She felt cold and then hot and then cold again, as though she was passing through a succession of rooms — one a sauna, the next a butcher's cold store. And Audrey felt dizzy, not falling-down giddy or faint, just light-headed as though she'd stood up too quickly.

"I think it's late enough," Stella was saying. "Would you like a drink, Audrey?"

68

Stella

They sat in her kitchen and Stella poured them two generous measures of Chivas Regal; no water, no ice, straight up. Stella didn't want to take Audrey into her living room in case the ghost of Laurent Margetz materialised from the walls and acted out his sordid tale.

Stella knocked back a good slug of the whisky and tried to choose her words as carefully as her nervous state would allow, "But I thought Margetz was a German name!" she said.

"French," Audrey said, "Most definitely French. Not German: From the Alsace. His family have a vineyard there. Mind you, over the years the area has been French one minute and German the next. But, Laurent's loyalties lie very definitely on the Gallic side of the Rhine; absolutely on the Gallic side."

"Uh-huh, of course. Just as you say,"

"He's been here before?" Audrey prompted.

"Yes," Stella replied, "He comes here every late autumn, usually for a week. Ever since I've been here he's been coming. But then, last year he came for longer; walked up to Cromer some days, went off to Norwich on others, and visited National Trust Houses, local museums; kept himself occupied. But, in December, he disappeared off to London for a few days. Said he was going to look for an old friend and that he would be coming back but didn't say when."

Audrey blanched and her mouth twisted in pain, as though she'd chewed on a bitter herb or bitten her tongue.

"Then he reappeared out of the blue a couple of days before Christmas. Bought some extraordinary brandy he said I might like. It was… I mean, it was like fire water."

Stella studied Audrey for any sign of a reaction to her tale, but, apart from not smiling quite so much and a slight loss of colour, she showed none. She just sat and listened and sipped at her whisky the way a bird dips into a still fountain.

But soon enough the glass was empty, so Stella refilled it. She poured and waited for Audrey to say when, but no such instruction came, so she stopped about halfway up the tumbler.

Audrey nodded her thanks.

"Anyway," Stella continued, fiddling with the postcard and then placing it between them in the centre of the table, "I was staring down the barrel of Christmas on my own and he didn't seem to have any particular place to go, so we had Christmas Eve dinner here and then…" Stella found she couldn't come out with it, not just like that. It didn't seem right, didn't seem respectful to either him or Audrey.

"I don't mean to be rude, Audrey," she said, "but did you know Margetz well? Had you known him long?"

Audrey glazed over, as if gazing at a colourful array of temptations through a confectioner's window. "Long?" she said and then repeated the word, more softly, "Long."

"I don't mean to pry," Stella said.

"No, that's quite alright. We met over thirty years ago, very briefly, in France. We spent only the one weekend at The Reach." Audrey quieted and gazed into the distance for a moment; the look lent her an air of regret. "Not much to tell, really. On another day, another month or year, things might have been different; it might have worked out. But, they weren't and they didn't. And I'm not one to waste any more time on how things might have been. They are the way they are, or were; no point in dwelling on it. Anyway, I married someone else and he passed away a while back, so now I'm on my own. That's all there is to it." She sighed, a long slow exhalation that spoke volumes of misplaced optimism. "I suppose you could say I've known Laurent all my life really. But, that wouldn't strictly be true." She shook her head and in doing so her hair, previously tucked back, fell forwards around her face.

Stella caught her breath. She was the woman in the photograph, the one the police had not taken when they'd cleared out Margetz' things. Audrey was the young woman sitting on the breakwater; the young woman with auburn hair whose smile fairly leapt out of the photograph.

Stella had found it when cleaning the room after the undertakers and police had gone, and had taken it downstairs and put it on her mantelpiece. It was still there; the picture had stood there ever since.

"So? What about Laurent?" Audrey asked, "You said he spent Christmas here, with you."

"Excuse me one minute, Audrey. Don't go away," she ordered, rising and going into her living room.

She did not look at the photograph as she took it from the mantelpiece. She was ashamed to, knowing what she'd done with Margetz and now knowing what he meant to the woman sitting in her kitchen.

When she got back, Audrey was bent over the table, examining her postcard.

"Here," Stella said, offering her the photograph and taking the postcard back in return, "he left this behind last time he stayed. I don't know why I kept it. I probably shouldn't have. But you look so happy. I suppose I must've envied you."

Audrey reached out and took the photograph. She studied it for a few seconds, a smile dancing across her lips. Then she said, "Oh, yes, Stella, you're so right to. There was never, ever anyone so happy as I was that day."

And before Stella had the chance to speak again, Audrey said, "Oh, you will be good enough to post the card, won't you Stella?" and she stood, let herself out into the hall, and padded off up the stairs.

69

Philip

The taxi dropped him in a car park beside what looked like a rather modern garden shed made noticeable by a squashed white turret on the corner. To his amazement the place was open and a policeman manned the desk.

"Yes, sir? What can I do for you?" he asked, somewhat quicker and more enthusiastically than Philip expected him to.

"Yes, officer, I er... I guess the best way to put this is, I've had a bit of a row with my wife and I can't find her."

"Sorry to hear that, sir. Where exactly and at what time did you have this row?" The policeman, a sergeant, Philip noticed, leant forwards across his desk.

"In the pub overlooking the pier, at about two-thirty, I suppose it might have been three at the latest."

The police sergeant glanced at the digital clock on the wall opposite. "Roughly five hours ago, sir. Is that about right?"

"Yes, 'bout that."

"And at what time did you notice your wife had gone missing, sir?"

Philip didn't catch the hint of sarcasm in the policeman's tone, "At about four."

"And where, if I might ask, have you looked, sir?"

"Pretty much all the pubs, bistros and coffee shops in town. And I've been all the way up to Runton, and checked at the station here in Cromer. I've asked the taxi company too. They say they've taken no one over to Strand."

The sergeant's desk phone rang.

"Excuse me, sir," he offered politely. He turned away and had a brief and very serious conversation. When he turned back, he said, "Sorry about that, sir, busy night and most likely will get busier; a bad accident on the Norwich Road." He paused for a couple of seconds. "Now then, where were we? Oh yes... your wife. May I ask where you are staying, sir? Please don't take this the wrong way, but you're obviously not from round here."

"No, sergeant," Philip replied, allowing the snake's tongue of impatience to flick into his tone. "We're from London and we're staying at The Reach in Strand-next-the-Sea. And," he countered swiftly, "I have checked in with the landlady, and my wife is not there."

"I see," said the sergeant. "May I ask you, respectfully, if there is any reason why you think your wife might be in any kind of trouble, sir?"

"No, there isn't. We had a bit of what you might call a domestic, nothing more."

"Might your wife be in any real danger that you know of, sir?"

"Well, yes, if she's decided to walk back over the coastal path to Strand and she's had some kind of problem on the way."

"Problem, sir?" The sergeant leaned further forwards, "What kind of problem?"

"Christ, I don't know, officer; tripped, fallen over or something, anything."

"May I ask you, sir, exactly where and when you last saw your wife? Exactly?"

"Well, I thought I saw her down on the pier, but then I may have been mistaken; it may have been another woman."

"Another woman?"

"No, sergeant! What I meant was the woman on the pier turned out not to be my wife; it was someone wearing a similarly coloured coat. From where I was sitting in the pub, I thought it might have been her, but when... Oh, never mind."

"Does your wife not have a mobile phone? I only ask, because it's unusual to meet a person who hasn't these days."

"No, she doesn't. For a reason too complicated to explain, her phone is in our room at The Reach. Oh, and before you ask, I've got mine too."

The desk sergeant frowned, "Do you have a car here, sir?"

"Yes, sergeant, I do. But-"

"Might I suggest that you check your car out? Where is it parked?"

"In the public car park and I have checked there."

The desk sergeant frowned again. "Might I also suggest that if you have been in the pub, you take a taxi for the rest of the evening? Your car will be alright where it is. We don't have many cars broken into down here in Cromer."

Philip briefly chewed the knuckle of his left hand in frustration. "Don't worry, Officer, there's not much chance of me driving anywhere. My wife has the fucking keys."

The police sergeant flinched, furrowed his brow and glowered, "Am I to take it then, you would like to report a missing person?"

"How long will that take?"

"Well, sir, for us to be able to open and conduct a proper investigation, I will need to make out a report. And, once I have the necessary basic information, I will need further details regarding friends and relatives, places your wife is known to frequent, any health and medical conditions, certain financial details, bank account, credit cards, store cards and the like, any benefits your wife may be receiving, some recent photographs..." he paused to draw breath, "And then we can get on to collecting a DNA sample... Would you like me to go on, sir?"

At that moment, the door behind Philip opened and a young man, looking considerably the worse for wear, stumbled in and up to the counter.

The police sergeant sucked his teeth loudly, glanced at Philip and said, "Would you mind hanging on for a minute, sir? I'll be right with you when I've finished with this all too well known sample of our very own home-grown DNA."

Philip turned, leaving the sergeant to his more demanding community, and left.

He trotted down the hill into town and looked in at the pubs on the way. But, as he expected, there was no sign of Fiona. She wasn't in the pub overlooking the pier either and neither had she been, or so the barman informed him.

"The walk over the hill to Strand?" Philip asked. "Tricky in the dark, is it?"

The barman turned to an older man bonded to a stool further up the bar, "Dougie, you live up over that way. The walk over to Strand, would you say it's tricky in the dark?"

Dougie, ruddy, weather-beaten complexion and squint lines around his eyes, examined his nicotine-stained fingernail. "I should say so," he replied and turned back to his newspaper. After reading a line or two, he turned back and offered, "Saw some woman walking over that way early on; thought it wasn't clever."

Philip bought Dougie a gin and the barman and himself a half. He shuffled down between the other drinkers to Dougie's end of the bar, "What time was that, if you don't mind me asking?"

Dougie's head was small and beady, like that of a cliff bird head to wind, "Must've been sometime after lunch, I suppose."

"After lunch? You're sure?"

"Sure as I can be."

"Can't remember the time exactly?"

Dougie glanced up at the barman. "What time did I leave 'ere?"

"After lunch," replied the barman.

"That'd be it then: After lunch."

"Do you remember what she looked like?"

The man set his glass unsteadily on the bar, then turned to fix Philip with a hard, but ultimately hollow stare. "Yes," he said loud enough for his cronies at the bar to hear.

Dougie's response garnered the intended sniggering and chortling from the audience.

Philip hadn't meant to imply the man might be stupid or that his adherence to the gin, as evidenced by his lacquered eyes and purple, pitted cheeks, had somehow rusted his recall. And when no further reply seemed likely, Philip drained his glass and turned from the bar.

"Pretty, dark coat; not the coat, I mean, the girl," the man threw after him.

"Thanks," he replied over his shoulder and made his way out of the bar.

So Philip hurried down the stairs to the esplanade and, with the wind at his back, set off along the front towards Strand.

Just before the Lifeboat Museum the road turned right, away from the sea. In front of him lay only the beach and darkness.

Philip could hear the waves breaking up the slipway and tried to imagine both what the terrain had looked like in daylight and which route Fiona was most likely to have taken. The road back to The Reach would've offered her little emotional warmth and, besides, the street map on his phone suggested the road turned inland at the top of the hill and did not lead directly over to Strand. He stood beneath a lamp and, after trawling through a list of sites, managed to locate an ordnance survey map of the area. The guide showed the footpath following the road up the hill and heading straight on over where the road turned inland. The greater problem was going to be seeing where he was going. The light on his phone would help, but it was not bright enough to see much other than what lay immediately in front of him.

The hill was steeper than it looked and the road running beside the path quieter than it had a right to be for a Saturday night. Still, he consoled himself as he marched resolutely up the slope, at least he was doing something about the wretched mess he was in rather than merely sitting in a bar, drowning the restless worm of his conscience in Old Habit.

70

Stella

Stella washed Audrey Poulter's tumbler and placed it carefully in the glass cabinet in the living room.

It had been a day to forget, and for all the wrong reasons. Everything she'd touched had turned to trash and she avoided the mirror on her dresser in case it reflected her dishonesty. There wasn't one person she could think of she hadn't upset, including herself.

She was a coward, not telling the Poulter woman about Margetz passing away; that was all there was to it. But, the shock of meeting the object of Margetz' lasting affections had completely thrown her. It wasn't so much that she'd slept with the man; it was more that the significance of Margetz' annual pilgrimage to worship at the altar of his memories in Room 3 weighed on her so brutally that Stella temporarily lost the ability to decide whether telling Audrey would be right. And, what with messing things up with Will, Stella was convinced that if she made a hasty decision, it would very probably be the wrong one. So, there was only one thing for it. She would sleep on it; in the morning she would know her own mind.

The amber lambency of the 12 Year Old Chivas Regal drew her like a moth to light. Stella poured herself another three fingers and prayed Mr Scott would return before the bottle grew too much older.

71

Hacker

The drive back out past the airport up the A140 was a slog. Saturday evening shoppers, a succession of road works and a serious accident all combined to draw out his journey.

Hacker listened to the sports reports, but all he could hear was Barney's uncomfortably accurate criticism. They may have discussed everything from the Champions League through to Borough's chances of avoiding relegation yet again, but Barney's words rang in his ears until he was punch drunk from the ringing and wished he'd never bumped into the old sod. Sure, he'd never known when to stop. Sure, his mother had said it when he was a boy, and every single one of his coaches at the academy. But, of course, he'd never listened; maybe it was about time he did. Maybe there were other games he should be playing.

It was past ten o'clock by the time he pulled off the main road at the sign for the town. The fish and chips in the Murderers had left him with indigestion.

72

Audrey

Audrey closed the door and sat down on the edge of the bed. She didn't turn the light on, but held the photograph against her heart and waited patiently for the memories to come to her. She wanted her recollections to come to her the way a gentle tide comes in, so that she would have time to notice and count each little lap of water as it crept up towards her: Laurent smiling, Audrey laughing, the wind playing at her hair, the warmth of his embrace, the pleasure in her touch and the tenderness of his kiss; the world a better place and her love better placed.

So, Laurent had come back to The Reach every autumn since their time together. Laurent had come back and slept in the same room, in the same bed in which all those years ago she had given herself up to him. "In this very same bed," she whispered.

If she was honest, Audrey saw her love for Laurent as more unrequited than unfulfilled. At least it had seemed that way. After all, it was Audrey who had deserted Laurent and, however unpalatable the truth, put plainly and crudely Audrey had, in her moment of doubt, abandoned him and in doing so had ensured that their love would remain incomplete. Her love had not deserted her. It was Audrey who had run away from love.

And yet it wasn't strictly true that her love for Laurent was unfulfilled, because, even though they had not enjoyed the physical proximity and therefore the physical comforts of love, Laurent had waited for her and in that there lay a form of fulfilment. His love for her had remained true; straight and honest and true. And what greater comfort could there be than to know one was deemed worthy of love; surely, that should be enough.

Audrey turned on the bedside light and got up. She could taste the whisky and smell its sweet odour on her breath.

While she brushed her teeth, she stared at the small envelope of Oramorph pills on the shelf below the mirror. The painkillers, prescribed for Richard, Audrey had kept for a rainy day — a day that would be of her choosing.

Now, as they glared back at her, Audrey wondered whether she really needed them. If Laurent still loved her, were they, would they ever be necessary?

She brushed her teeth vigorously; brushed them as though she was back in Braud leaning over a pail, cleaning them diligently, meticulously, readying her teeth, tongue and the pliant flesh of her cheeks as though preparing for her first kiss with Laurent.

Of course, he wouldn't look how he used to, but then neither did she. And they would have to make allowances for the ways in which they had both become set. She wondered about his body and understood that it too would not be the same, firm, young frame that she had laid beside and clutched and clawed and breathed against. He'd suffered a heart attack, that's what he'd put in his letter, and she wondered if that meant his love-making would be different in some way from before.

Audrey began to undress, but then, as she unbuttoned her blouse, she hesitated. Perhaps he would no longer find her attractive; she was, after all, no great admirer of her own form, not of late and not since having the boys and letting herself go a little. Would she be brave enough to undress in front of Laurent, never mind slip between his sheets, press herself against him and surrender to his form?

"You must be mad," she said to her reflection in the mirror, "Stark raving mad!"

And yet there was a vague excitement to the idea.

She re-buttoned her blouse, glanced once more at the envelope of Oramorph pills and lay down. Audrey turned out the light and clutched tight to her bosom the photograph Laurent had taken all those years ago.

PART 4

SATURDAY
NIGHT

73

Philip

Philip hoped above all that he would find Fiona safely tucked up in bed in their room at The Reach. He paused for a second and pulled at his socks, which had sunk down into his shoes and bunched into creases beneath his instep.

He had the sneaking feeling that running into that girl, Phoebe, had been the last straw. There was no way on god's earth he was ever going to persuade Fiona that he'd gone out of his way to help Phoebe rather than to bed her.

"Oh well," he murmured. "Every good deed deserves a punishment."

The wind still blew at his back and the wet pavement glistened as though recently varnished. The Reach came into view as a car, its radio booming conversation, passed him, pulled up and parked a few metres shy of The Reach.

Philip drew level with the car just as the driver's door opened. It knocked him against the wrought iron fence and he slipped and had to grab hold of the railing.

A man got out and helped him upright.

"Sorry, I didn't see you. Really sorry!" he said. The man was strong and agile, his hands large and sinewy.

For a long couple of seconds, they stood hanging onto each other like a couple of drunks battling to stay upright.

The fellow wouldn't let go of Philip's arm until he was confident Philip was steady on his feet.

"No harm done," Philip said. "Thanks."

The radio blared and the stench of stale tobacco wafted from the inside of the car.

"No, I apologise, I do. I didn't see you." He relaxed his grip on Philip's upper arm, but did not let go.

Philip was embarrassed at the sudden and rather too familiar contact.

The man eventually released Philip, shutting the door of his car gently behind him and they started to walk the last few yards to the front gate of The Reach. "You staying here too?" he asked. "Thought I recognised you from breakfast."

"Yes. Just here for the weekend," Philip replied. "Going off tomorrow."

"The same! Up here for a bit of business," the man added, turning and pointing his key at the car, and then waiting until the indicators flashed. "'Bit too chilly for me, this neck of the woods. That bloody wind seems to blow all the time. Think it'd drive me bonkers if I lived up here."

Passing beneath the wobbling, dull light of the streetlamp, the man extended his hand. "Hacker," he said.

"Scott, Philip Scott." They shook hands.

And as they turned to the gate, they both became aware of someone standing up the steps at the front door of The Reach.

The lantern, which hung in the eve of the portico and which usually flicked on when approached, was unlit. The figure was hunched against the door as though leaning against it, toying with a square shaped container which he appeared to be balancing against the door.

At first, Philip mistook the figure for a resident who was perhaps slightly drunk; a man who had probably enjoyed a better evening than Philip. But then he realised the man was going about his business rather too diligently and too urgently to be drunk. Most drunks, he recalled from his own experience, did their best to try to look sober and in doing so usually achieved exactly the opposite. This man, he realised, wasn't drunk at all.

Philip stepped forward to get a better look. The stranger was short and wiry, wore a bomber jacket; a straggle of curly, dark hair obscured his face.

Then Philip shivered as he wondered if perhaps the man was attempting to break in to The Reach. But as soon as the idea came to him, he realised the man was trying to jam something in through the letterbox of the front door.

"Excuse me?" Philip said. "Is there a problem?"

On hearing the voice behind him, the figure froze, then turned briefly to see who had interrupted him and turned back to hurry on with what he was doing.

Philip flinched and stood back. He smelt the heady, sour sweetness of petrol, which confused him as the cars were parked all along the front behind them. He exchanged a puzzled look with Hacker. The picture before them was somehow wrong. It was the middle of the night and the container in the man's hands smelt of petrol.

They both arrived at the same ghastly conclusion: The man was pouring the contents of the can in through the letterbox.

Philip stepped forward again. "Hey," he shouted at the figure, "what the bloody hell d'you think you're doing?"

Hacker, beside him, got hold of Philip's arm for a second time and pulled him back. "Steady on, you don't want that stuff all over you."

But then someone shouted "Hacker" from the road behind them and they both turned.

Whoever it was that was shouting was hidden behind the line of cars parked along the front.

When Philip turned back, the dark figure at the door also turned to see who was shouting. He looked down at Philip and Hacker and hurled the container at them.

Though they both leapt out of the way, the can caught Philip in the midriff, knocking the wind out of him and splashing his jacket with petrol. He staggered back and fell heavily.

As he tried to pick himself up, gasping for air and clutching at his stomach, Philip saw a yellow glow appear at the door. The glow was small and oddly subdued to begin with, as though the man was trying to light a cigarette against the wind. And then it was growing in height and expanding in volume. And, like the subtle, dancing flame from an oil lamp when it is lit, the world before Philip gradually gained perspective and came to life. And as it came to life, the flame multiplied and magnified ferociously until the rest of the world disappeared, and the door erupted in one violent, blinding flash.

The force of the explosion blew the arsonist off the steps and he lay unmoving, the clothes about his middle burning.

Philip, still trying to catch his breath from the blow of the can, was bowled back over onto his side. A hundred neon bulbs burst before his eyes and for a couple of seconds he could see nothing but bright stars and rockets with great sparkling tails.

He shook his head.

He was right. Something was wrong; very wrong. The whole scene was too bizarre. One moment Hacker had been standing beside him; the next, Philip was lying staring at a burning body.

For what seemed like a minute, he lay and watched tongues of flame begin to lick back through the letterbox, around the door jamb and up the sides of the door into the eves of the portico.

He knew he had to do something, but wasn't sure what. He shook his head again and urged his body to react. Slowly, and with considerable effort, he forced himself to breathe and hauled himself up onto his hands and knees.

Philip crawled over to the man who had been blown off the porch, took off his own jacket and tried to smother the flames on the man's midriff. But, the petrol on his jacket caught fire and all he succeeded in doing was flaying the man with his own flapping firebrand. It was as though he was engaged in a mad jig around a bonfire and exhorting it to burn by fanning its flames.

"Hacker?" he screamed. "Where the bloody hell are you?"

74

Hacker

But Cornelius Hacker was dealing with a problem of a very different nature.

Brian Chisholm was standing in the middle of the road pointing a shotgun at him.

"Hacker!" he shouted. "You bastard! You're going to get what you came for."

But the blast from the front of the house had blown Hacker backwards towards the road and he now lay spread-eagled halfway out of the gate onto the pavement. Like Philip, a little concussed by the sudden explosion at the front door of The Reach, Hacker couldn't comprehend why he should one minute be making polite conversation with a fellow resident and the next find himself sprawled on the pavement.

He lay, vaguely useless, and watched Brian Chisholm march towards him.

When Chisholm stood directly over him, he lowered the shotgun until it was pointed directly at him. "You think just because you can't bully anyone on the soccer pitch anymore, you can come up here and try to blackmail me with some sordid photographs from a dim and dismal evening some way off in the dim and distant past," Chisholm sneered.

It took Hacker a few seconds to work out what was going on. "Brian, wait," Hacker demanded. But most of the authority in his tone was lost when he tried to draw breath: his chest hurt, he might even have cracked a rib as he bounced off the gate post. He raised his hand, palm upwards, commanding Chisholm not to come any closer.

"Don't be such a bloody idiot, Brian, hang on a minute." Hacker felt his ribs beneath his left arm: they were tender and pained him if he breathed too deeply. Without putting too much weight on his left arm, he hauled himself upright, hoping his height might lend him some advantage, "Look here, Brian, just hang on a minute."

Brian Chisholm took a couple of steps back, but did not lower his shotgun, "No, Cornelius, you listen to me. I've had just about enough of you. If you distribute those bloody photographs, you'll destroy my life completely. And if my life is over, then there's no reason I can see why you should be allowed to carry on with yours." Chisholm's tone was low and gravelled, as though he'd had to dredge every league of his soul in order to locate just the right grotesque pitch.

"You're scum, Cornelius," he went on. "I may be guilty as sin of making a bloody fool of myself, drunk as a coot in some dingy, bear-pit of a nightclub, but that doesn't give you the right to come up here and threaten me and mine. Do I make myself clear?"

"Hang on, Brian, please?" Hacker pleaded, clutching his chest with one hand and reaching out in petition with the other. "Just hang on a minute; let's think about this, I-"

"Think about it, Cornelius? I've done nothing but think about it for the last twenty-four hours." He paused, "I'm done thinking, you think about this." He raised the shotgun and aimed it straight at the middle of Hacker's chest.

Hacker wasn't sure what alarmed him most: the crazed lunatic readying to shoot him or the fire whose roaring flames he could hear from over his shoulder. And yet, in all the confusion, common sense and logic stumbled across each other and combined to lend him one tiny grain of hope.

"Come off it, Brian," Hacker coughed, "You shoot me and you go to prison. Where's the profit in that?"

"I've thought about that too, Cornelius," Chisholm replied, but, if anything, his tone softened, "It seems I'm sunk whichever course I choose."

Hacker didn't want to break his gaze from Chisholm in case the slightest movement spurred him to some instinctive reaction, but he noticed the man lift his attention and glance over at the front door of The Reach.

When Hacker twisted slowly to follow Chisholm's gaze, he was faced with a vision of hell.

Philip Scott, the man to whom he had introduced himself not a minute before, was bent over, beating the unconscious arsonist with a flaming jacket.

The front face of The Reach was now licked by tongues of flame, the fire rolling and curling out from the eves of the portico and flaring up the wall.

Hacker found himself curiously torn between wanting to help Scott and needing to deal with Chisholm.

75

Philip

Philip looked up from the smouldering figure lying prone before him. The front of The Reach was now bathed in a glow he had only witnessed when standing before a bonfire on Guy Fawkes Night; the heat and the harsh and repugnant fumes given off by the fire were growing with every second. He coughed against the smoke. He'd extinguished the flames from the body beside him, but the bloke's jacket was still smoking.

He wasn't sure what to do next, but then remembered it was very possible that Fiona was upstairs in their room.

"Hacker?" he shouted. "Call the fire service. We've got to get whoever's inside out of the house."

He stood up and stepped back. The body at his feet was too close to the fire to be safe, so he bent down, grabbed the man by his collar and dragged him along the short path and out through the gate onto the pavement.

"Don't just stand there, man, call the bloody fire service," he repeated.

"It's not as simple as that," Hacker replied in a flat, hapless tone. "If I get my phone out, this idiot is likely to shoot me."

"Idiot, you say?" Chisholm shouted back. "Idiot? I'm the one holding the gun, Cornelius. Who's the idiot now?"

427

Philip looked beyond Hacker and saw a second man standing in the road brandishing a shotgun.

"Here," Philip growled through gritted teeth, "while you're standing there sorting out whatever problems you've got with this bloke, take my phone and call the bloody fire service." He thrust his phone at Hacker, "But do it now. I'll go round the back to see if I can get in."

Hacker turned back, "Brian, I appreciate you want to sort this out, but there's more important things to do than stand out here trading insults. Now's not the time."

But whatever Brian was being offered, it wasn't enough. He raised the gun until it was aimed at Hacker's face and spoke loud above the crackle of the flames, "You think you can come up here threatening to burn my house down if I can't resurrect Marchman's order, Hacker? So, tell me, why the bloody hell should I lift a finger to help you prevent someone else's house from going up in flames?" He stepped forward.

"Brian?" Hacker pleaded, "Put that bloody thing down before you hurt someone."

"Hurt someone? What the hell do you think you were going to achieve with those pictures?"

Hacker, for the moment, was lost for words.

But, Philip had to make a decision: Watch how it played out between Hacker and the man, Brian, pointing the shotgun at him, or do something about the fire. He dare not pull Hacker away in case that prompted the man to shoot, but the fire behind him was growing in intensity: He was running out of time.

So he ignored the man with the gun and turned back to face Hacker: "You deal with this; I've got more important things to do." He braced himself against the percussion of the shotgun and walked smartly away round the side of the house.

Once there he stumbled into absolute pitch black. The contrast between the front of the house, now lit by the flames, and the darkness down the side of the house couldn't have been more stark. The gap between The Reach and the neighbouring property was ten or twelve feet at most, and apart from a vague reflection off the next door windows, Philip was lent no light as he felt his way along the sidewall. But for a couple of plastic downpipes, the smooth, rendered wall of the house was bare straight up to the windows on the first floor.

He ran his hands along the wall until he came to the kitchen door.

The greatest obstacle was, though, that the ground floor of the building stood some two feet higher than the ground around it outside, so, as with the front, a couple of sizeable steps led up to the back door. The side door was plastic and double-glazed and, he realised after working the handle furiously a couple of times, locked.

He banged on the glass with his fist and shouted as loud as he could without sounding panicked, "Ms Anworthy. Ms Anworthy. Come to the door. Come to the door, now!"

Philip stood back, but no lights came on. No one stirred.

The landlady had told him to phone if he got back after ten and he'd given his phone to the fellow, Hacker.

The fire at the front of the house was now so fierce that finding his way back was no longer so difficult; the reflection of the flames projecting onto the flank of the adjacent house cast an eerie, flickering mural of Dante's Inferno.

When he got there he found an even more surreal scene: Hacker and the man with the shotgun stood, still arguing, while the house continued to burn before them.

Ignoring the shotgun once more, he shouted, "Have you called the fire service yet?"

"Yes," answered Hacker, not turning his face from the armed man before him. "They asked me if there were any persons reported in the house. I said it was very likely, but they won't be here for at least half an hour; something about the appliances from Mundesley and North Walsham being out on separate calls. And it appears the Cromer boys are dealing with a woman who's been reported missing off the pier."

Philip went cold. "Off the pier?"

"Apparently so," Hacker replied.

For a man staring down the barrels of a shotgun, Philip thought Hacker remarkably cool. But, immediately on the heels of his admiration followed the thought that whether Fiona was in the house or not, they needed to get whoever else was indoors out, and get them out before the fire took too great a hold.

He stepped in front of Hacker and spoke to the man wielding the shotgun in a hurried, but firm and clear voice, "Listen, my friend, I don't know what your beef is with this man here," he thumbed at Hacker, "but you'd be better off putting that away and helping us get the people out of this house, before..."

"Before what?" Chisholm jerked the gun at Philip.

Philip lowered his head and glared at the man, "Before the police pitch up and haul you off to the nick. Or worse, shoot you! With any luck they'll be here before the fire brigade. Now get a grip, man."

Chisholm baulked at the onslaught, but then his face twitched and crumpled, and his eyes surrendered their malice. Slowly, but ever so slowly, he lowered the gun.

Philip turned back to Hacker, "Come on. We need to work out a way of getting in. The back door's locked and I can't seem to raise the landlady."

"What about breaking a window?" Hacker asked.

Philip shook his head, "Double-glazed safety glass. It won't be easy."

"I'll get the wheel brace from my car." Hacker ran off.

When Philip turned round, the man Hacker had called Brian was standing behind him, wearing a forlorn expression like that of a puppy recently scolded. The shotgun had, miraculously, vanished.

"I can't understand why the noise of the petrol igniting didn't wake anyone up?" he said to the man.

The flames now spread from the top of the steps right up the front of the building, almost to the roof; the roaring noise growing ever louder.

"Perhaps no one's in," offered Brian.

Philip shook his head, "No, I know the landlady's in, but there could be at least one more, maybe as many as three. Christ, you'd think the neighbours would've noticed by now."

Hacker returned, armed with a wheel brace. It looked too small to be of much use.

"Which room are you in?" Philip asked.

"Number two, on the right, up there." He pointed to the window.

"I'm in number four, on the right, first floor, at the back. That leaves one and three and the landlady." Philip tried to think logically. "Her room's on the left at the back. That leaves the other lady, who I think is in Room 3, that one, up there on the left, and Room 1, which is on the ground floor at the back. I don't know if that's occupied."

"It is," Hacker said. "Some young kid, Phoebe."

"Phoebe?" Philip repeated, stunned. "Bright red, kind of pop-art, henna red hair, black jacket?"

"Sure, that's the one. Why?"

"Never mind."

But Hacker was intrigued, "What about the woman you're with?"

"With? My wife! She could be in our room, but might not be; long story." He paused. "Look, give me my phone. I'll try the landlady's line. Hope it wakes her."

Hacker handed it over and Philip worked the face of it until the number of The Reach came up, pressed the call button and waited. "Come on," he muttered.

Eventually, he heard the ringing tone.

He fidgeted on his feet, "Come on, woman. Come on."

431

But the phone just rang and rang and rang. "No good."

"What about your wife? Hasn't she got a phone?" Hacker asked.

Philip tried the number, but, as with the last effort, the phone just rang on. "Phone's in our room, which suggests she isn't, but I can't be too sure. We're not on speaking terms; she may be ignoring it. Come on, we'll try round the side; see if we can break in through a window."

"Hang on," said Hacker. "What about the bloke who did this?"

They stepped back to the gate and saw the man still flat-out, unconscious though no longer smoking, on the concrete pathway.

"Leave him," Philip suggested. "The police'll deal with him later. Let's go."

It was not now so dark round the side of the house. Chisholm lagged a pace behind them.

"Here," Philip pointed, "have a go at the window in the door."

Hacker eased Philip out of the way and stepped up to the level of the door to deliver the glass a testing blow.

The pane split with several small cracks, but didn't shatter.

"Try concentrating the blows in one place, in the corner," Philip suggested.

Hacker did as he was told, but his blows had little effect other than to split the pane into bullet-sized stars.

"Toughened glass," Philip suggested. "Try it again."

Hacker hit the window once more with as much force as he could wield.

Again the glass smashed, several small shards splintering and breaking over them, but again it didn't shatter or break right through.

"I'm going to be here all night at this rate," Hacker moaned. "Isn't there a shed with some tools; something we can use to break in with."

They looked round. A plot, the same width as the property, stretched out the back into the darkness. They could just make out a potting shed down the garden in the murk.

"You try down there," Philip said to Hacker, who immediately bolted off into the black. He then turned to the shorter man, "Brian, if I've got the name right, why don't you wake the neighbours up and ask them if they've got any spare keys to the back door? It happens sometimes. And ask them if they've got a ladder we can use to get up to the first floor."

Brian bridled. Clearly he wasn't supposed to be at The Reach and even more clearly he didn't want to be explaining away his presence sometime later, particularly when he may have been seen brandishing a shotgun.

After his day with Fiona and his fruitless search for her along the coastline in the darkness, Philip's reserves of patience were all but depleted. And yet, he knew there was no point in shouting at a man; he needed his help.

"Look, whatever it is between you and him, you can sort out some other time. As far as I am concerned, you just happened to be passing by and stopped to help. Let's forget I ever saw the shotgun, eh? Go on, give the neighbours a shout; there's a good chap."

Chisholm's face broke into a grateful-but-sorry smile and he scuttled away back towards the front of the house.

The noise from the fire at the front was considerable: roaring, crackling, splitting.

"Christ," he muttered, "it's bright enough here, it must be like daylight out on the promenade.

He hammered on the back door with his fist, then waited and listened. As far as he could make out, there was not the slightest movement from inside the kitchen.

He picked up the wheel brace from where Hacker had left it on the step and moved round to the windows at the rear.

Although he stood six foot two in his socks, Philip still had to jump up to bang on the windows. If the landlady and the girl Phoebe were in their rooms, surely there was no way they would be able to sleep through the noise he was making.

He slammed the heavy socket end against the windows several times in succession. He decided it made no difference if he cracked the window panes; if the fire brigade didn't arrive soon, the whole house would likely as not burn right through.

"Come on," he shouted in frustration, but again no light came on and no one came to the window.

Hacker appeared at his shoulder, carrying a planting spade. "Let's try the back door with this."

"I suppose a burglar's jimmy or a crow bar was too much to ask?" said Philip as they rushed back to the side door.

Chisholm reappeared. "No keys," he pronounced simply, "and the neighbours don't have a proper ladder. They're on their way round with a step ladder, though."

Philip and Hacker, balancing on the steps, tried to force the edge of the spade between the door and the jamb. For a second, it looked as though their tool might do the job. But then the plastic door creaked in protest and a large splinter cracked off the vertical stile, and, as the spade released, they both staggered backwards and tumbled down the steps.

"It'll do it. It'll work," shouted Hacker, scrambling back up. "I'll place it and then we'll both put our weight against it."

Hacker slipped the bottom edge of spade into the gap left by the splinter and once in place, with Hacker nearest the door and Philip right behind him, they pushed against the shaft of the spade for all they were worth.

Gradually, they forced more of the blade in through the gap.

"Bit more," grunted Hacker. "Just... a... bit... more. Now, push it towards the wall.

The door squeaked, creaked and squealed and began to bend their way.

"Careful, it's going to give any second," Brian Chisholm shouted.

But neither Philip nor Hacker relaxed their grip and, with a loud screech, the door split at the lock and burst open towards them.

This time they fell, with Chisholm trying in vain to catch them, in a tangled mess of arms and legs back down onto the concrete apron around the door.

Philip had skinned his elbows and clattered his knees, but, with Chisholm's help, he got back up and they grabbed Hacker.

"Good job," Chisholm remarked, as though they'd just put up a level shelf.

"Thanks," replied Hacker, rubbing at his head. "Now for the tricky bit."

The door hung open at a peculiar angle and looked as though it might fall from its hinges at any moment, but through the doorway there poured a steady stream of noxious smoke. Even in the darkness, they could see it; grey-white, ghostlike, billowing and puffing out like the kitchen housed some vast steam engine.

"Where are we going first?" Hacker asked.

"Landlady?" Philip replied. "Her room must be off the kitchen to the left."

"Then…?"

"Upstairs?"

"Lead on," Hacker said. "Try and find a light switch."

Philip crept up the steps and entered the kitchen on his hands and knees. He made to stand to look for a light switch, but above waist height he could see very little; there was too much oily, acrid smoke. But he found that if he crouched low enough below the smoke, where the air lay heavier than the smoke, he was able to breathe.

He came to a door and, without having to kneel up, reached out to grab the handle. "For god's sake, don't breathe in the smoke," he shouted over his shoulder. "A couple of breaths'll kill you."

The door opened towards him. He pulled it wide open. The

smoke was heavier and hung lower to the floor in the next room; it was carpeted, like a bedroom or perhaps a living room. He felt up the wall for a light switch. He flicked it and the room was immediately shrouded in an eerie, luminous fog.

He continued to crawl and came to a low table. He knew Hacker was behind him, because the man kept bumping into him every time he slowed. The roaring, crackling noise continued and was growing louder. He hated to think how hot the hall and reception area would be.

Philip first made out a bottle and glass on a coffee table and then realised there was a body lying prone on the sofa beyond it.

When he got to it, he saw it was Ms Anworthy; she appeared to be unconscious.

Still on all fours, he turned to Hacker, "Booze or smoke, I don't know, but we have to get her out."

Between them, Hacker at her shoulders and Philip at her ankles, they dragged, slid and manhandled her out of the living room and across the floor of the kitchen to the side door.

Chisholm was still standing outside and did his level best to make the landlady's transition out of the house as comfortable as possible, but her feet banged on every step down and her head lolled unpleasantly.

The three of them carried her round the front of the house. She stirred as the fresh air found its way into her lungs and she began to struggle against them.

A crowd of a dozen or so had gathered on the road; some in pyjamas and overcoats, and others dressed as though ready for church. Two elderly gentlemen had even brought fire extinguishers.

"Where's the bloke who started all this?" Philip asked Brian Chisholm.

He shrugged, "Dunno. Must have leg'd it."

They laid Ms Anworthy down as gently as they could.

The two of them gulped in the sharp, clean air. Philip's eyes stung and the rim of his nostrils and lips smarted from the smoke.

A policeman, a community support officer judging by the light blue band on his hat, rushed up to them, "Great work, gentlemen. Firemen should be here in fifteen minutes. They're on their way."

Philip glanced at Hacker and said, "There'll be nothing left of the place by then."

"Anyone still inside?" the policeman asked.

"We think two, maybe three," Philip replied, "We'll have to go back."

The whole of the front of the house was aflame now. Like one enormous, yellow bonfire, the heat of it pressing the onlookers back across the road.

"I can't let you do that, sir," the policeman declared, pulling himself up to his full height.

Philip stood a good foot taller than the copper and Hacker the same, "My wife might be in there, officer. I'll be going back in whether you want to let me or not."

"I-," the officer started.

Hacker cut him off, "I'll be going with you. But let's make it sooner than later."

They left the policeman to ponder and hurried back round the side of The Reach. As they got there Chisholm arrived with two fire extinguishers and passed them over.

The smoke issuing through the door was much thicker now.

Hacker studied the fire extinguishers in his hands. They were about a foot long and weighed about the same as a couple bricks. He handed one to Philip, "After you," he said, grinning and standing aside.

"Thanks," Philip replied, not holding back on the sarcasm, "You take the far room; the one the kid's in. I'll take upstairs."

Hacker nodded, no longer any sign of his previous, wry amusement.

They each took a fire extinguisher in with them, and crawled on their bellies through the kitchen and into the living room. The danger, they both knew, would be in opening the door to the reception room.

To get to the first floor, Philip had to make it across the hall and through the fire door at the bottom of the stairs. To get to the other ground-floor room meant Hacker would have to make it across the hall, too. Letting the oxygen from the living room into the reception room, where the fire was probably at its worst, would be their one biggest danger. Opening the door would feed the fire.

By the time they'd reached the living room door through to the hall, they were both coughing uncontrollably and their vision was blurred by their tears.

Philip paused, but only to count to three. "Ready with your extinguisher?"

Hacker slapped him on the back and held up his canister.

The door handle scorched Philip's hand, so he reached awkwardly into his pocket and pulled out his handkerchief. He tried the handle again. The door gave a little and then seemed to be sucked shut. Holding the extinguisher in one hand, he pulled harder and, as though the room beyond was part of some great vacuum, found he had to use all his strength to get the door open.

For a moment he had to heave against the pressure holding the door in place, and then with a loud bang and a rush of air, the door blew back against him, knocking him onto his side. He was fortunate to get in the way of the door because as it was blown back, it was followed immediately behind by a great tongue of orange flame that flicked into the room and up to the ceiling.

They played their extinguishers against the flame until both canisters were spent, but the flame continued to flick and lick at the ceiling as if it was being sprayed from a flame thrower.

Philip paused briefly and then crawled into the hall. The whole of the right-hand side of the hall around the front door was ablaze;

the heat unbearable. For a split second he considered getting the room keys from behind the counter, but then he felt the hairs on his head start to fry. He didn't wait to find out if Hacker was following him or even try to retrieve the room keys from behind the counter; he just staggered to the fire door at the entrance to the stairs and, still holding his handkerchief, pulled it towards him. Again, it did not want to budge and, again, he had to lean all of his weight away from it to pull it open. The pressure in the hall all but blew him up the stairs.

Even though the fire doors had succeeded in preventing the fire from spreading, the stairwell was thick with smoke.

By the time Philip had crawled like an infant up the stairs, he was coughing and spluttering so violently he was certain he'd never breathe properly again. The bitter smoke filled and seared his lungs, and he felt criminally dizzy.

He found a light switch, flicked it and was grateful that the electrics were still working. The landing at the top of the stairs sat in a small well; the rooms off it, up a couple of steps. The door to his room lay on his right.

"Fiona?" he shouted as loud as his smoke-filled lungs would permit. He staggered up the step to the door and hammered on it, "Fiona?"

He stood as far back to the left as he had room to and launched himself across the well of the landing at the door.

He bounced off it, but it gave just enough to encourage him that it might give completely if he put his shoulder to it once more.

Philip bent double and coughed as hard as he could, then he breathed as shallow and long a draught of the air close to the floor as he could, stood up and put his shoulder to the door twice more.

At the second time of asking, the door splintered and shattered on its hinges, and Philip tumbled through it and onto the bed.

76

Hacker

Hacker made it into the hall behind Philip Scott and crouched, mesmerised by the flaming walls about him. He'd never witnessed such a fire at firsthand and was both in awe of its beauty and petrified by its power. It seemed to be a living organism; it had form and substance, and danced upwards and along the ceiling like yellow water defying gravity.

He tried to breathe, but found he couldn't, and realised very quickly that he didn't possess enough oxygen in his lungs for what he was about to try. There was no point in asking his muscles to provide for him if they didn't have the juice. He crawled backwards into the living room and out to the back door.

"Did you get into the room?" asked Chisholm.

Hacker coughed, hawked and spat at the ground, "Not yet... Not good in there... I ran out of puff. Just need... to breathe... a bit."

Then he gulped in as much of the night air as his lungs would permit and bent down and crawled back into the kitchen.

Even though the heat burnt his forehead and singed his ears, he forced himself to crawl as far as the door through to the hall. Without pausing, Hacker pulled his jacket tight over his head, got up off the floor and charged at the door he knew to be across the way.

Fortunately, he hit it squarely in the centre and crashed through it as though it was made of balsa wood.

The blaze pursued him into the room and he could feel the flames at his back.

He could see from the light of the fire behind him that the room was empty; he knew it and was sure of it. The bed was neat and tidy, and the chair at the side table empty. And, besides, it would have made no sense to find someone there; no one, except perhaps Stella Anworthy's drinking companion – if she had one. Hacker slid the accordion door to the bathroom back and pulled on the light cord. The bathroom light flickered for a split second and then went out. But it was enough time for him to see that there was no one in there.

He turned back to face the fire in the hall.

Scott had gone directly up the stairs, and Hacker was about to do the same when a sixth sense whispered he was extremely lucky to have made it into the room; taking the stairs might be a couple of yards too far. He desperately wanted to get after the man Scott and help him find his wife, but he knew deep down in the pit of his stomach that he could not. He wasn't sure there would be another way down from upstairs and he'd said he would check the room for the kid, Phoebe, and he'd done that. It wasn't a question of being afraid, although he was very definitely that, and in some good measure; it was more a case of knowing when he was beaten; a case of knowing when to stop.

Hacker blinked and rubbed at his eyes. He needed to breathe, but knew that the smoke he would take in with his breath was only likely to render him incapable.

He dropped to the floor and risked a short, sharp half-lungful of air. It was scalding and scorched the inside of his throat like acid. He turned to the windows, but found them locked and could not in his haste find a key. There was no way out except back the way he'd come.

So Cornelius Hacker didn't wait; he rushed at the wall of fire separating him from the hall and leapt at full-stretch through it and towards the burning doorway into the living room.

77

Phoebe

The last train out of Strand-next-the-Sea rattled through the night. Phoebe hoped it would get into Norwich on time as there would only be five minutes before her mainline connection left for London.

She liked the train; the carriage was warm and clean, and her seat comfortable. She snuggled down in it, burying her head in her scarf, ignoring those passengers who stared at her. Sure, maybe her hair was a shade too red! Sure, she looked pale and in need of a good meal and a good night's kip in her own bed. But, hey, she knew where she was going, and that was the best thing anyone could do; do something as opposed to do nothing.

She gazed out the window at the stations and villages as they rushed by and wondered what her birth mother, Stella Anworthy, was doing right now; wondered whether she was sitting dispensing green tea, Bourbons and words of wisdom to some other ugly duckling.

Phoebe's letter, explaining why she'd skipped off without either paying or saying goodbye, she had left propped against the stem of the lamp on the bedside table. And, even though she knew the sheets would be laundered and pressed before the next guests occupied her room, she made the bed, paying particular attention to folding the corners as neatly as she knew how.

Phoebe had understood that she would have enormous difficulty

443

writing the letter, but knew without any doubt that she had to write it. She couldn't just up and leave; it was no longer her way.

When she reread her first attempt, she decided it was muddled. It meandered, a little like the path she'd trodden the past few months, so she ripped it up and began again.

In the second letter, Phoebe simply apologised for doing a bunk and hoped Stella would forgive her. But, she omitted any reference to the real reason for her visit and she enclosed her address and suggested that if Stella felt so inclined, she could write her at the college and that Phoebe promised she would send the money she owed as soon as her finances permitted.

But in this response Phoebe felt she was not being completely honest, so she ripped that letter up too and started a third.

In her final attempt, Phoebe wrote the plain and simple truth; that she'd traced her birth mother through an agency and that she'd come to the conclusion, after thinking long and hard, that she wanted to meet her. She wanted Stella to know that she bore her no resentment for giving her up for adoption, and wrote that if Stella wanted to get to know her daughter, she should write to her at the college and, perhaps, one day they might get together again. But, Phoebe added that she would try to understand if Stella did not want to. She had now met her birth mother and she would treasure their short time together; and that, and that alone, was the reason why Phoebe had come to Strand-next-the-Sea. She signed the letter with love, and added one single kiss beneath her name.

After reading the letter through twice more, she sealed it and placed it carefully on the table so that it could not be missed.

However and in the meantime, there were other, more urgent matters that required Phoebe's attention. She was going to go home; a course decreed by the woman who, for the moment, assumed the authority to decide her course. And going home was now no longer a journey Phoebe felt driven to put off. On the contrary, now, she very positively looked forward to it.

And yet, before crossing the threshold of her home and atoning for the doubts she'd harboured against her parents, Phoebe needed to return briefly to her college. She needed to explain and apologise for her own callous rejection of those who had attempted so valiantly and patiently to rescue her from the wilderness of her self-imposed exile.

One in particular of those veritable souls she needed to see more than any other. For Phoebe wanted Dame Clarissa to know that she had learned what those older and wiser already knew — namely, that it is true, there are some roads better left untraveled.

78

Philip

Much to his relief, Fiona wasn't in the room.

He rolled off the bed and turned the ceiling light on. It flashed and went out, leaving him crouching beneath the smoke which had pursued him up the stairs.

Philip crawled into the bathroom and felt around it until he was sure Fiona was not in there either. He wanted to shout out, but knew he had to preserve the air in his lungs. There was nowhere else for her to hide and, he didn't know why, but the idea amused him that she might be hiding somewhere in the room, waiting for him to find her.

So, it was time to leave. She wasn't in the room, that much he knew was the better result. Although, conversely, that meant he didn't have the first clue where she was.

Hacker's mention of a woman missing off the pier in Cromer played through his head.

Philip lurched out of the room and stumbled across the small, dark landing. The room on his right, at the back of the house, was a storeroom or cleaning room, and the door to Room 3, the one occupied by the older lady, stood to his left.

His assault on the door proved a shade easier because he did not have to negotiate the well of the landing as he threw himself at it. The first time he bounced off it, but the second time he broke through it and a wall of smoke followed him into the room, blinding him.

He dropped to the floor, hacking so savagely he was sure the lining of his lungs would appear with each cough. Quickly, he crawled to the side of the bed and felt around.

The woman lay fully clothed. She was limp, like a fresh corpse in a funeral parlour, but not cold. The bedclothes were neat and tidy and smooth beneath her, and Philip feared for a moment that all his efforts were in vain and that she was already dead. But, he didn't have the time to check for a pulse; the heat coming up the stairs was building and there was now no other way down from the first floor except out the window.

Kneeling down between the bed, he dragged her towards him and yanked her limp torso upright. She lolled against his chest, a slip of paper falling from her hands; her arms dropping limp, doll-like at her sides.

Philip thought he heard her moan, but he couldn't be sure; the fire roared and crackled below them.

He found, when he sat up, that the smoke was far too thick for him to move about in. He couldn't see for the tears in his eyes and he couldn't function without any oxygen to feed his lungs. Philip pulled the woman down onto the floor and lay down beside her.

A ghastly, foreboding glow lit the room from the stairwell. He imagined the hold of the blaze in the hall and hoped that Hacker had managed to get in and out in one piece.

Philip rolled onto his side, gasping short, sharp, shallow breaths. He saw the girl Phoebe as she had been in the bar in Covent Garden on Thursday evening and still found it hard to believe the coincidence of bumping into her in such an out of the way place. He hoped she wasn't anywhere near The Reach and hoped wherever she was that she... There was something about her he liked.

His mind was beginning to float; he recognised the pattern, like dreaming when it's more preferable to waking. The fumes given off by the burning paint were slowly asphyxiating him and he realised he couldn't stay where he was; he had to try to get out of the room.

Philip crawled round the bed to the window. There were two panes of glass with a handle in the middle about halfway up the divide. He reached up and pulled the handle down.

It didn't budge.

He yanked and hung all of his weight on it, but still it wouldn't budge.

It was a two-way tilt window, same as the one in his room; he was sure of it. He pushed the handle upwards. But, still, it wouldn't move.

"It's locked, you idiot," he shouted, "It's bloody locked."

Philip searched the sill and up the side of the frame, but as his eager fingers worked their way over the adjacent surfaces, he found no key.

He crawled across the room until he felt the chair by the bed. He picked it up and swung it against the window. It bounced back at him as though made of rubber. He smashed it against the window again, but it broke up and left him holding two legs no longer connected to a seat.

Philip understood he was in a bad place: He couldn't get the window open and the heat coming from the stairwell told him that there was no longer any chance of making it back down through the hall.

He crawled over to the door and pushed what was left of it back in place. It swung open, half off the upper hinge, so he crawled back to the other side of the room and worked the huge, old wardrobe over towards the door. It was heavy and cumbersome, but with a combination of pulling, pushing, dragging and sliding, he managed to set it against the door, and for a moment the blast of smoke from the stairs reduced.

Next, Philip crawled over to the small shower room and felt

around in the darkness for a bath towel. He pulled it off the rail and thrust it over his head into the sink. Hanging his head as low as possible, he reached up into the basin and turned on the tap.

When the towel was sufficiently drenched, he left the tap running and pulled the towel out of the sink and draped it over his head. He hoped he might buy him and the woman some time.

Philip felt his way back towards the bed, pulled the woman to him and dragged her close beneath the window. He coughed, gagged and was sick; his saliva bitter, acidic and unctuous in his throat. He pulled the inert body of the woman close and spread the wet towel over their heads. They lay still, together, side by side, faces inches apart; two adults sheltering from the voracious appetite of the fire like two children swapping secrets in a homespun wigwam.

The blaze thundered in Philip's ears and echoed in his head and he wondered again whether the ragdoll of a woman, the woman whose face was no more than a hand's width from his, was still breathing. He couldn't feel her breath, but then he couldn't feel much except a creeping numbness in his arms and legs. The floor beneath his aching body was now superheated like desert sand in the midday sun, and the air beneath the towel was no longer humid and misty; it was thin and dry.

He was glad that he hadn't found Fiona in their room; as long as she was neither trapped in the cloying heat of The Reach nor clinging to a stanchion of Cromer Pier in the freezing waters of the North Sea, he didn't care.

And he understood that he loved her more than he thought possible. Perhaps, he loved her more than that. And he knew his love for her was complex in its construction and, strangely, he understood its complexity: For, after all, it was he, Philip, who had been the one to construct it. He was the one who had built his love around her and his love was made up of many compounds and many mixtures, and of many great heights and corresponding depths. It didn't, as Fiona saw it, exist in one simple form; his love for her did not follow one universal instruction; there was no template for it. For if there was, love would be easy and quick to assemble, like flat-pack furniture, and on completion it would only be flimsy and brittle, and would not last because it had not been designed to. It would, inevitably, have no substance.

And he knew, in his heart of hearts, that his love for Fiona was not yet complete, that there were many layers he had yet to apply and that there were many levels he had yet to construct. His love was not finished, it was simply evolving; a work in progress.

Oh, he had been a fool! He knew that too and knew that for his foolishness he had no defence.

Philip closed his eyes and felt the trickle of cool tears run down across his face.

His love, his love for Fiona, was of many different kinds, and it was but one of those kinds of love that had driven him back into this fiery hell. For Fiona, he had returned to a burning building. He so hoped it would be enough.

79

Hacker

Cornelius Hacker was now back outside the house, standing beside the many other spectators while a paramedic gently cleaned the burns on his hands and his forehead. Brian Chisholm was holding a black-sleeved, oxygen bottle up to Hacker's face; a face blackened beneath hair singed in odd places down to his scalp.

Chisholm had been waiting for his return like one of the faithful gun dogs of his keeping and he now stood patiently beside Hacker as the pair of them watched The Reach burn.

Hacker began to shiver. His muscles, previously bunched and taught, surrendered their density. They gave up their obedience, and he began to shake as though standing naked before a glacier. But worse than that, if he breathed too deeply, he exploded in a fit of coughing that sounded like a sick dog barking a muddled, jarring staccato.

The paramedic, whilst doing his best to cool them, fought to hold Hacker's hands still. He said, "You need to go to hospital, chum. You need to keep these burns clean. If they become infected, you'll be in a whole lot of trouble."

Hacker shook his head at Chisholm. He'd had enough oxygen for the moment, and the mask grated against his grubby cheeks and ground the ash and soot into the skin around his mouth.

"Where's that bloody fire engine?" he asked no one in particular,

"That copper said fifteen minutes. It must be all of that. And where's that bloke Scott. He must still be upstairs. There's no way he'll get back through the hall now."

Chisholm glanced up at his nemesis, his eyes wide, "That was bloody brave, Hacker. Bravest and most reckless thing I've ever seen a man do. You must be off your trolley."

One of the neighbours from down the front had pitched up with a proper roofing ladder and a couple or three were trying to break in through the side window to what was Room 3, upstairs at the front. But, like Scott and Hacker had found only minutes earlier, the glass of the window was too tough to break.

Then, they heard the wail of the fire engine siren away along the promenade.

"'Bout time," Hacker mumbled and spat at his feet.

And soon enough the small crowd parted to allow the fire appliance, another police car and an ambulance through.

The fire engine lurched to a halt and two firemen in beige protective equipment and yellow helmets jumped down from the cab; they were already wearing their breathing apparatus. Another fireman wearing a high-viz vest stood a whiteboard up against the rear wheel of the appliance and supervised the first two as they removed their yellow tallies and inserted them in the board. A high-pitched alarm tweeted and both firemen jiggled and twitched as though they'd trapped a swarm of wasps in their clothing. The alarm quieted.

The community support officer ushered a fireman over to Hacker.

"Anyone still in there?" the crew manager asked, tipping back his black-banded, yellow helmet.

"Definitely one, possibly two," Hacker replied in between coughs.

"Are you certain?" the crew manager asked, "Because if I'm going to commit a BA crew to the building without the back-up of a second appliance, I need to be absolutely certain the situation calls for it. Do you know which floor they're likely to be on?"

"First floor," Hacker replied.

"You sure?"

"As I can be."

"What about the ground floor?" the crew manager asked.

"No one. I'm positive."

"How certain?"

Hacker coughed and lifted up his hands for the fireman to get a proper look at his burns. "I know," he growled, "I've just come from there."

The two firemen in breathing apparatus standing at the kitchen door waited, jiggling every now and then. The lead man sported a long, thin black hose with what looked like a shower head on the lead end.

"You'll need more than a garden hose in there, mate," Hacker observed dryly, dropping his hands back towards the paramedic. "The hall's a regular sea of flame."

"I can't send the lads in with a bigger gauge hose; the water creates too much steam and the steam's more dangerous than the smoke. Besides, the heavy gauge doesn't do tight corners when the pressure's up."

Hacker dragged his hands away from the paramedic again, "Look, I know you've got all that protective gear on, but I'm telling you, you'll never get through the hall and up the stairs; it's too ugly in there." Raising a blackened hand, he pointed to the upstairs window on the left wall of The Reach. "You should try that window first; on the side there, where those people are trying to get in. He's either there or in the back right on the first floor." He paused and breathed deep, "He's been in there way too long, though. It's the glass. I hope you've got something that'll get through it."

"We have." The senior fireman turned to one of his crew, "Let's have the 135 up against that window." He pointed up at the same window as had Hacker, "That one, now," and trotted away, issuing more orders.

Hacker offered his hands back to the paramedic for further treatment.

The crew manager and three other firemen unloaded a tiered ladder from the back of the appliance. They hauled it down the narrow gap between the two buildings and, in one seemingly fluid movement, stood the heavy ladder up against the side of The Reach and extended it.

As it hit the window, the top of the ladder smashed clean through it.

Smoke immediately billowed from the aperture.

One of the firemen with breathing apparatus climbed the ladder. The second passed him up a metal bar about the length of an axe with a fork on one end and a spike on the other. Using the halligan, he cleared away the broken shards of glass and then clambered awkwardly in through the window.

Hacker and Chisholm heard him report in a squeaky, piped tone, "Two casualties: both unconscious."

They watched as the firemen brought first Philip Scott and then a woman out the window and down the ladder with a minimum of fuss.

"As I said…" Chisholm began.

But as he spoke, he was interrupted by a woman pushing her way through the crowd.

"Excuse me?" she said, taking in Hacker and the paramedic, and assuming therefore that they must be involved in what was going on. "Excuse me?"

Hacker turned towards her. She had light brown hair and wore a dark jacket and a worried frown. She was attractive, perhaps more attractive because of the frown lines above her eyes.

"Excuse me?" she asked again. "You're staying at The Reach, aren't you?"

Hacker recognised her from breakfast, even though she'd been wearing sunglasses at the time, "I was, Mrs Scott."

"Yes, I saw you this morning. What the hell's going on? Well," she hesitated, "what I mean is, I can see the house is on fire. But, you haven't by any chance seen my husband, Philip, have you? Only I was hoping he might be here somewhere."

Chisholm glanced nervously up at Hacker and whatever he tried to conceal in his look, concern, anxiety, perhaps even a dose of distress, he didn't conceal enough of it from the young woman.

"Philip?" she asked, louder. "Have you seen Philip? Is he here? Where is he?"

Cornelius again wrested his hands from the paramedic, who, curiously, was trying to cover them in clingfilm. He moved towards Fiona as though to hug her. But his hands were blackened and red and raw and he frightened her, so she shrank from him.

"He was in there," Hacker said calmly. "The firemen have just brought him out."

Fiona moved back further away from him as his words finally sank in. "Oh God!" she moaned and then pointed at the burning pyre that was The Reach and asked, "You mean he's been in there? But the whole house is on fire."

For a moment he thought she was going to scream, but instead, gathering herself once more, she asked in a tone he imagined she reserved strictly for her children's schoolteachers, "What the bloody hell was he doing in there?"

Hacker glanced down at his burned hands, briefly at Chisholm and the paramedic, and then turned his attention back to Fiona Scott. He said, as slowly and as evenly as his wrath would allow, "Looking for you, Mrs Scott. Your husband was in there looking for you."

80

Stella

Stella Anworthy was dazed and confused and dizzy. She didn't have much of a clue about what was going on or why she seemed to hurt so much, and a very good-looking paramedic insisted on replacing a mask on her face every time she brushed it away.

She sat up when she came to properly, but the young man immediately encouraged her to lie down again. When she did so, her world began to spin.

But then Stella started to cough again, and once she'd started there seemed no way her body would let her stop until she wretched and then vomited all over the nice young man's green trousers.

The vile odours of whisky and charred carpet drove the onlookers away.

Stella was exhausted. "At least the witches down the front will have something to whisper about over their morning cauldron," she said to the paramedic as he wiped himself down.

"Is everyone out?" she asked him. "I mean, from inside? Are they all out?"

"We think so, dear. Just you lie back and calm down, please."

But even though she didn't know the exact fate of her residents, Stella hoped that, perhaps and with a bit of luck, things would turn out for the better. She could rebuild The Reach with the money her insurers would pay out or she could pack up what little the fire had seen fit not to consume, sell the smoking pile and move on. She'd done it once, in a manner of speaking; she would do it again. And there was some comfort in knowing the woman Doyle wouldn't bother her any longer; Stella no longer had anything much worth bothering over.

She wondered where that nice girl had got to. That nice, educated, well-spoken, young Phoebe with the funny red hair; the one who ate all her Bourbons and who knew Stella had given birth to a girl without telling her. It didn't make sense to Stella that the girl had known that tiny detail. But, then again, nothing really ever made sense to Stella, so she didn't let it bother her. Life just wasn't meant to make sense to some people.

She began to cough again. The paramedic backed away sharply.

81

Hacker

Naturally, when the firemen and paramedics allowed her access to her husband, Fiona Scott lost what little composure she was holding in reserve and had to be restrained by two policemen while the paramedics from the second, newly arrived, ambulance worked on him.

The woman, who they brought out after Scott, the charming older woman Hacker had seen at breakfast, looked to him to be completely lifeless; a frail puppet with slack strings. It wasn't that he was an expert in such matters, but, even though the firemen had handled her with considerable care, she looked to him like someone whose life had left her.

Scott, though, was a different matter. The paramedics busied over him like seagulls round a fishing boat. But, he didn't look good. He was unconscious to the clamour of the medics attending to him, and Hacker knew all too well that when paramedics hurried about their business like that, it was not a good sign.

Cornelius Hacker wasn't sure what to do next. He'd provided the police with a statement concerning what he could remember about the sinister arsonist he and Philip Scott had interrupted. The paramedic was done with him and again pressed him to accompany the landlady to the hospital in Norwich for more treatment. But, he didn't fancy being cooped up in the back of an ambulance with Stella Anworthy. He and Scott may have rescued her from the fire, but something told him that if he got too close to her he might spend the rest of his life rescuing her.

Yet his hands hurt enough to deter him from driving, so going anywhere under his own steam was out of the question. And to add to his dilemma, he had only the clothes he stood up in and they reeked of smoke and looked as though they'd been dragged along the floor of a steelworks. If that string of disappointments wasn't long enough, his head hurt and his ribs —

"So what are you going to do, Cornelius?" Chisholm butted in on the inventory of his aches and pains.

Hacker had completely forgotten Brian Chisholm was stood next to him.

"Buggered if I know, Brian," he replied. "Find another hotel, I suppose."

Chisholm twitched and examined his hands as though they were in danger of strangling someone without his permission, "No, Cornelius, I don't mean about where you hang your bloody hat tonight, I mean about those photos."

"Oh!" Hacker sighed, coming to his senses. What with all the excitement, he'd clean forgotten why he was staying at The Reach.

All he knew was that he wasn't going to do anything that might risk causing any pain to Chisholm's family. If he'd learnt one thing while he'd been standing there wondering whether he'd make it through the sea of flame in the hall, it was that Jean, Kaitlyn and Kayla had done nothing to deserve ending up as little more than cannon fodder on his battlefield.

"Yes, Hacker," Chisholm asked again. "What are you going to do with those photographs?"

Hacker fixed him with as hard and uncompromising a stare as he could muster, "Hadn't given it much thought, Brian."

There was a sudden, drawn-out, tearing, creaking noise from behind them and they turned to watch the roof of The Reach collapse inwards in a vast explosion of sparks and cinders.

And it was then that it dawned on Hacker that the only evidence of Brian Chisholm's misdemeanour was, in all likelihood, already deleted from his laptop; for his laptop was, right at that moment, little more than a slab of melted plastic, lost somewhere beneath the mountain of rubble that was The Reach.

They watched in silence for a while as the vast bonfire roared and hissed.

"Let's look at it this way, Brian," he said, turning to face him. "Why don't we put things on ice for the next few months? See if these foreign Johnnies are as good as their word; if not, if it doesn't work out, give me call and I'll see if I can't resurrect your order with Marchman."

Chisholm studied him hard, waiting for something more. When nothing further came, he said, "Sounds good to me, but what about the photographs, Cornelius? The photographs?"

Hacker chuckled, "Oh, I don't know, Brian. Perhaps I'll hang onto them for the time being. Perhaps my having them will encourage you to keep to the straight and narrow, so to speak. Wouldn't want Jean to find out you'd ever strayed, now would we?"

But, Brian Chisholm was after some more tangible reassurance. "If you think-"

"No, Brian, I don't think. I don't think at all. But, I intend to start. Believe you me, Brian, I intend to start."

Cornelius Hacker turned and walked away from the shorter man. He wasn't sure where he was going or what he was going to do. He didn't really and truly give a toss. But while his legs still possessed the strength to carry him away from Brian Chisholm and Norfolk Electrical, and heated phone calls from his ex-wife, and cold tea in rainy lay-bys and stodgy sandwiches in motorway service stations, and boarding house rooms and spider solitaire, and fumbles and embraces with alcoholic landladies, and old men who used to dress up as bears, and the bloody equal rights of the bloody unequal European Union, he simply didn't care. Just as long as his legs were good for it, he didn't care. After all, they'd got up and down enough football pitches in their time and, just when he'd needed them most, they'd got him across that flaming hell of a hall. His legs had a good few miles in them yet; they'd need to have if he was going to walk away and leave it all behind.

Epilogue

Hacker

Cornelius Hacker did walk away.

And he did his level best to leave it all behind and stay away. But news of his courage in tackling the fire at The Reach soon caught up with him. The following weekend the local paper loudly acclaimed his act of selfless heroism with a front page banner headline:

Ex-Borough hard man proves he still has what it takes

Cornelius Hacker, once the scourge of First Division forwards, showed his true mettle during last Saturday night's fire at The Reach B&B on the promenade at Strand-next-the-Sea. With little thought to his own safety, Mr Hacker not only returned to the burning building to make certain there were no other residents trapped inside, but he was also instrumental in the rescue of two guests from an upstairs bedroom. Crew Manager Bernard Holgate told us: "Whilst we cannot either condone or sanction a member of the public entering a building that is well ablaze, Mr Hacker's actions were extraordinarily brave. Clearly without his assistance this fire might have claimed more lives."

Sadly, a woman thought to be in her sixties died later from the effects of smoke. The cause of the fire is as yet unknown, but investigators believe it may have been started deliberately.

The news soon found its way back to the Borough ground.

Hacker, after a haircut and the application of a little make-up to disguise the unsightly injuries lent him by the fire, was feted by the home crowd. His appearance, though, was conditional: Barney the Borough Bear had to be present and a car was sent to Norwich to collect him. Lunch in the director's suite was enjoyable in spite of Hacker's awkwardness in the face of so many compliments. Eating and drinking were tricky, what with his hands being bandaged, but the upside was that he couldn't shake any hands.

Beasely collared him after lunch and questioned him as to what his future might hold?

"Dunno," he replied, "Must be loads of ex-pros queuing up at the Job Centre these days."

Marchman Engineering were surprised to receive his letter of resignation, though they did reluctantly accept it. He was good PR, they told him. They rued missing out on the opportunity of bathing in the reflected glow of their star salesman's glory. But, had they known the unsavoury lengths to which Hacker had gone to try to get the Norfolk Electrical order reinstated...

And the incriminating photographs of Brian Chisholm?

Well, Hacker grinned. He never really had many others apart from the one he'd shown Chisholm in the pub; the same one that was melted to destruction on his laptop. And as for Sherri, he chuckled as he erased the offending image from his phone; he hadn't seen her since that dreadful night with Chisholm, her birthday party had been but one part of his invention.

Later, while he sat in the back of a taxi and gazed out at a deserted pit head, he realised that there must be several thousand like him wondering how they would earn a living off the back of a football career cut short by either injury or slender ability.

He wondered if they, like him, felt as though life had simply chewed them up and spat them out, just like the gum that decorated the

Borough pavements. He wondered what, if any, support there existed for his kind: twenty premiership clubs, twenty-four Championship clubs, and a similar number in both the first and the second Divisions meant that a fair percentage of over two thousand professional footballers were cast upon the slag heap of redundancy every year.

So, with the help of a couple of new generation Borough fans who knew all there was to know about the internet, Cornelius Hacker and Associates was born: a newsy jobsite which soon evolved into an employment agency for retired ex-pros; a company formed with the altruistic intention of getting those who knew only boots and ball back into work.

The idea had come to Cornelius as he'd stood staring at the flames, wondering if Philip Scott was going to get out of the burning building alive. He'd come to realise that somehow, he had to be of greater worth; that there had to be something more to life than what he'd put up with over the recent years.

And later, when interviewed by the Borough club fanzine and the wider press about his actions during the fire, he described his experience simply as a moment of truth. He didn't necessarily think of himself as Saul on the road to Damascus, or Archimedes in the bath, or even de Brito watching Pele play for the first time at the Bauru Atlético Club in Brazil. But, it had come to Cornelius that he needed to help get the others out of The Reach in the same way that, had he been trapped by the fire, he hoped someone else might look to help him. If he hadn't, perhaps things would have turned out differently for that other fella, Scott.

Philip

Philip was taken by ambulance to Norfolk and Norwich University Hospital, where he was informed he would require a Bronchoscopy

464

to assess the damage to and remove any debris from his lungs. But just the idea of having a video camera inserted into his airways encouraged his respiratory system to recover sufficiently and swiftly enough to negate the need for such an unpleasant procedure. He was, though, kept on oxygen in the Medical Assessment Unit for a couple of days.

A week later, he was released. Though hoarse for a month and coughing for a further six, Philip was left with no lasting effects from the fire.

The same, however, could not be said of Fiona. She'd suffered a far more permanent injury, the pain of which she proceeded to tranquillise with a diet of opiates and alcohol.

The acid remorse, caused by her belief that she alone had been responsible for Philip's near death in the burning Reach, and the corrosive guilt from her perceived inadequacies in their relationship, combined to swell Fiona's already fathomless well of low esteem; a well, so profound and treacherous, that from its dark waters not even Philip's love and devotion could rescue her.

At a party one her friends remarked, unkindly and behind her back, that Fiona had very knowingly dug and filled her own private well of self-pity, and that she continued to wallow in it purely and simply to test her husband's love. More than a few were seen to nod in agreement; some agreed coldly that it had always been her way.

But, after innumerable sessions with countless psychotherapists, psychiatrists, homeopaths, faith healers and assorted witchdoctors, Fiona finally deserted Philip for what she supposed would be the greener pastures of Alcoholics Anonymous. Inevitably, and having pretty much exhausted the seemingly limitless reservoirs of familial patience, she found further and continued reassurance amongst the fresh, listening ears of a wider fellowship.

Archie Davy drew ever closer to her son-in-law, knowing that her daughter, like her husband, she could not save.

Philip reckoned her a little harsh in her treatment of Fiona, but he understood that Archie needed to protect herself from her daughter in much the same way she'd needed to protect herself from her husband. In truth, Philip had reached pretty much the same conclusion in leaving Fiona to go her own way.

The two of them, Archie and Philip, were wandering the marshy margins of the Thames estuary at Heybridge. The whipped, carillon calls of curlews heralded the last light of the day and the two children gambolled on ahead in pursuit of the Labrador puppy their grandmother had bought.

Archie touched his arm.

Philip turned to her and saw she was crying, quietly. He was embarrassed that he had not noticed.

"There comes a time," she said, softly, "when a single woman of a certain age has to know her own mind or she is lost."

Audrey

Audrey did not regain consciousness after the fire. Her lungs, not being as young as those of her would-be rescuer, gave up the ghost.

And yet it was the ghost of Laurent who had come to her in her final moments and eased the manner of her passing. In her last brief glimpse of life, he stood before her, smiling, offering her his hand. So Audrey reached out and took it; two lovers reunited to revisit the brighter pastures of their young love.

And yet, her final infidelity was not committed with Laurent or against Richard. In her final act of infidelity, Audrey had cast off the faith which had, for all her life, held her hostage. She no longer cared how God saw her.

Of course she could not know it, but at her inquest, the coroner recorded a verdict of accidental death, not suicide. Audrey had not, the coroner decided, died by her own hand, even though the autopsy noted the presence of morphine and alcohol in her system. And, though the fire was very obviously instrumental in her demise, it was not considered the absolute cause either. Her heart, the evidence suggested, had simply stopped beating.

If there was any profit for her to take from the manner of her passing, it was that in death she had achieved that which she had never managed in life, namely that Audrey was at the very last happy with her lot. And no one, neither man nor woman nor God was going to cheat her out of her slender slice of happiness.

Stella

Stella, on the other hand, grew more morose with each day the insurance company failed to pay her out.

The Crew Manager of the fire appliance from the local Retained Duty System station had, after he'd ascertained there were no more persons reported inside The Reach, proceeded to tackle the fire in defensive – as opposed to aggressive – mode. Initially, he took the decision that the fire could not be controlled by his team, what with their hand-held hoses and limited numbers, and he deemed the building too unstable and therefore too unsafe to allow his men access. So, finally, he turned his attention to stabilising the fire and preserving the adjacent buildings. In real terms, though, his change of tactics sounded the death knell for The Reach.

The small yet significant advantage of his change of attitude meant that by the time the fire had burned itself out, there was little or nothing left of the place; little or nothing more than a burned out shell and no evidence of her Will's shoddy workmanship. Stella's books were with the revenue, but her insurers didn't need to know that.

And what of her Will? He'd just upped and left like he'd always said he might. It was, as he'd told her more than once, how he liked to be; unattached and unfettered by relationships, and far too light on his feet for the police.

The insurance company asked for certificates proving the maintenance at The Reach was up to scratch, but these could not be provided; they had all been consumed by the inferno; every scrap of paper, including the letter from Phoebe.

Stella often wondered about that nice, strange, young girl who seemed to know so much more than she let on. In fact, Stella wondered more than once whether...

But, no, she decided again. She was only being silly.

Phoebe

Phoebe took the train back to London and managed to get a room in the hostel in the Marylebone Road. She hardly slept. Instead, she lay, insensitive to the nocturnal largesse of those who shared her room, and projected random images of recent events against the bottom of the bunk above her. She passed the night trying to marshal her thoughts into some semblance of order, some logical timeline.

The following day, she trained back to Cambridge and loitered outside Dame Clarissa's door until her Director of Studies returned from Sunday Service.

Dame Clarissa was unsurprised to find her waiting and straightaway made her a cup of coffee.

"I am heartened to see you," the Dame began, and once they were seated beside the unlit grate, she continued, "Talking of hearts, Phoebe, would I be correct in assuming you have passed the last couple of days looking into yours?" She paused and smiled warmly, "And, if so, what have you seen? Feel free to paint me as garish a canvas as you can manage. You will make it so much easier for us both if you do."

But, even though she'd spent the night doing exactly that, Phoebe wasn't sure of which brush to pick up or which medium to employ.

"Come now, Phoebe," Dame Clarissa urged gently. "Perhaps it would be easier if I asked you how you are feeling? Not about any one thing in particular or what has gone before, but about how you are in yourself? How does Phoebe Wallace feel just now?"

And, like the partner of a terminally ill patient who has devoted every waking moment to caring for another, the most elementary enquiry after Phoebe's own health broke her resistance and forced her to admit that she was, right at that moment, desperately in need of some similar care.

As Phoebe poured out her tale of woe, she was prompted to realise that her view of the world was unacceptably narrow and that, perhaps, she'd fashioned the landscape around her in order to match the limits of her own convenient perspective. Perhaps it was that she'd sculpted a domain which pandered to her strengths and disavowed her weaknesses.

For as the river of her tears coursed freely down her cheeks, she saw that the world was not simply divided between Phoebe and the Muselmänner. And, in order to survive whatever life threw at her, Phoebe needed to do more than merely dance around the idea of her own Fate whenever it reared its ugly head. Perhaps, she needed to embrace it and accept the possibility of it, rather than continually deny its very existence.

When she'd settled down and stopped sobbing, Dame Clarissa moved to put her arm around her young charge. This casual, yet surprising act from an individual who was, it was whispered from the cloisters of the glittering spires, possessed of a great intellect but a gelid heart, only served to cause Phoebe greater upset.

Later, Phoebe understood that that had been the Grande Dame's purpose; her very personal act had been carefully designed to tear down the gargoyles still lurking above Phoebe's psyche and to catch and collect the rubble of her disintegration, so that she could clean it and grade it and, later, use it for Phoebe's reconstruction. For the wisdom of Dame Clarissa's years had taught her that undergraduates like Phoebe stood a better chance of abandoning the dark halls of their adolescent insularity if they could be convinced there lay a brighter future outside, beyond the gates. After all, the wise old woman knew, teaching someone how to love was the most valuable tutorial of all.

Phoebe returned to her college in the Lent Term and resumed her studies. When she did not hear from Stella, she decided, reasonably, that it was because her birth mother did not want to hear from her. The realisation of this bare, plain and simple fact was not easy to come to terms with at first. But once the pain of rejection had been permitted time to dull, she decided that, just possibly, things had turned out for the best.

After all, it was Fate, the hunter, who had predetermined her course, not Phoebe Wallace.

Phoebe would never know that the letter she'd left behind for her mother was, by then, only so much feathered ash, blown and dispersed by the constant winds that blew in from the sea over the ruins of The Reach.

About the Author

Peter Crawley was born in Chiswick in 1956. He was educated at Cranleigh School in England and at the Goethe Institut Freiburg-im-Breisgau in Germany. He spent much of his youth in Germany, Austria, France and Corsica. Upon leaving full-time education, and after a short period with the army in Germany, he worked in Stuttgart, as a translator, and on luxury motor-yachts in and around the Mediterranean and the West Indies. After further travels he started his own business dealing in Mercedes-Benz in London's West End. He has now returned to writing full-time and his first novel, Mazzeri, a novel of Corsica, was published by Matador in July 2013. Peter Crawley is a former transatlantic yachtsman and historic motor racing driver. His interests include his family, his research and writing, and skiing. He lives in Chertsey, Surrey, with his wife, Carol. They have three daughters.

Mazzeri

Love and Death in Light and Shadow
A novel of Corsica

It is the last summer of the twentieth century in Calvi, Northern Corsica, and an old man sits watching the kites fly. The festival of the wind is a lively and colourful celebration, but the old man's heart is heavy, he has heard the Mazzeri whisper his name. He accepts that people prefer to believe the dream hunters belong to the past and yet he knows only too well that at night they still roam the maquis in search of the faces of those whose time has come.

Ten years later in the high citadel of Bonifacio, in the southern tip of the island, Richard Ross, armed with only the faded photograph of a Legionnaire standing beneath a stone gateway, finds the locals curiously unwilling to help him uncover his family's roots. He rents a villa on the coast and meets the singularly beautiful Manou Pietri, who enchants him with tales of the megalithic isle, its folklore and the Mazzeri – the dream hunters.

For a while Ric's life beneath the Corsican sun is as close to perfect as he could wish. Then a chance encounter with a feral boy turns Ric's life upside down, and he is drawn deep into a tangled web of lies and deceit. On an island where truth and legend meet, where murder is commonplace and most crimes go unsolved, only the Mazzeri know who will live...

Nominated for the American Library in Paris Book of the Year Award 2014.

Published by Matador June 2013
ISBN 9781780885384 (pb)
ISBN 9781780885814 (eBook)